An author of more than ninety books for children and adults with more than seventy-five for Mills & Boon, **Janice Kay Johnson** writes about love and family, and pens books of gripping romantic suspense. A *USA TODAY* bestselling author and an eight-time finalist for the Romance Writers of America RITA® Award, she won a RITA® Award in 2008. A former librarian, Janice raised two daughters in a small town north of Seattle, Washington.

New York Times and *USA TODAY* bestselling author **Cindy Dees** is the author of more than fifty novels. She draws upon her experience as a US Air Force pilot to write romantic suspense. She's a two-time winner of the prestigious RITA® Award for romance fiction, a two-time winner of the RT Reviewers' Choice Best Book Award for Romantic Suspense and an RT Book Reviews Career Achievement Award nominee. She loves to hear from readers at www.cindydees.com

Also by Janice Kay Johnson

Hide the Child
Trusting the Sheriff
Within Range
Brace for Impact
The Hunting Season

Also by Cindy Dees

Navy SEAL's Deadly Secret
Special Forces: The Recruit
Special Forces: The Spy
Special Forces: The Operator
Colton Under Fire
Undercover with a SEAL
Her Secret Spy
Her Mission with a SEAL
Navy SEAL Cop

Discover more at millsandboon.co.uk

THE LAST RESORT

JANICE KAY JOHNSON

COLTON IN THE
LINE OF FIRE

CINDY DEES

MILLS & BOON

First Published in Great Britain 2020
by Mills & Boon, an imprint of HarperCollins*Publishers*
1 London Bridge Street, London, SE1 9GF

The Last Resort © 2020 Janice Kay Johnson
Colton in the Line of Fire © 2020 Harlequin Books S.A.

Special thanks and acknowledgement are given to Cindy Dees for her contribution to *The Coltons of Kansas* series.

ISBN: 978-0-263-28060-9

1220

FSC™
www.fsc.org

MIX
Paper from
responsible sources
FSC™ C007454

Printed and bound in Spain
by CPI, Barcelona

THE LAST RESORT

JANICE KAY JOHNSON

For Barb, a great editor and even better friend,
and for her faithful sidekick, Panda.

Chapter One

Leah Keaton eased up on the gas pedal too late to prevent her right front tire from dropping into an epic pothole with a distinct *clunk*. She winced.

Along with a gradual rise in elevation, the road was getting narrower, the dense northwest forest reclaiming it. The roots from vast Douglas fir, spruce and cedar trees created a corrugated effect as they crumbled the pavement. Long, feathery limbs occasionally brushed the sides of her modest sedan. Pale lichen draped from branches. Thick clumps of ferns and wiry branches of what might be berries overhung the edges of the pavement.

Her mother could have been right, that this was a wasted and even unwise journey.

All of which was assuming, Leah thought ruefully, that she hadn't taken a wrong turn. In her distant memory, a carved and painted wood sign had marked the turnoff to her great-uncle's rustic resort in the north Cascade Mountains, not that far from the Canadian border. She reminded herself this was rain forest, which by definition meant wood rotted quickly. Once the sign fell, moss and forest undergrowth would have hidden it in a matter of weeks.

Forcing herself to loosen her grip on the steering

wheel, Leah caught a glimpse of Mount Baker above the treetops. At not quite eleven thousand feet in elevation, Baker wasn't the largest of the string of volcanoes that stretched from California to the Canadian border, but it was plenty imposing anyway with year-round snow and ice cloaking the mountain flanks. Leah remembered from when she was a kid seeing puffs of steam escaping vents at the summit, a reminder that Mount Baker still had the potential to erupt.

Weirdly, the memory relaxed her. This road felt familiar. If she was right, it would soon climb more sharply yet above a river carrying seasonal snowmelt that ultimately joined the larger North Fork Nooksack River. As a child, she'd hated the drive home from the resort because the edge was so close to the road, the drop-off so precipitous. She hadn't trusted the rusting guardrail at all.

What if a tumultuous spring had undercut the cliff and the road no longer went all the way to the resort?

The tires of her car crunched onto gravel as the pavement ended. She had to go slower yet, because potholes and ruts made the way even more perilous.

Although he'd closed the resort something like fifteen years ago, Uncle Edward had continued living here until his death last fall. Had he really not minded navigating this road when he had to stock up on groceries? According to Leah's mother, he'd declared flatly, "This is home," and remained undaunted by the perils of living in such an isolated location as an old man.

"Stubborn as that old coot Harry Truman, who wouldn't evacuate when Mount St. Helens blew," Mom had grumbled, mentioning the name of a rugged individual who'd refused to leave the mountainside before the volcano erupted in 1980. "He'll end the same way. You just wait and see."

Leah's dad had gently pointed out that, despite being in his nineties, Uncle Edward hadn't displayed even a hint of dementia and therefore was fully capable of making his own decisions. Dad had shaken his head. "He's lived up there most of his life. Imagine what it would be like for him to move to a senior apartment with busybody neighbors all around and traffic going by night and day."

"But we could find him a nice—" Mom had broken off, knowing she'd lost the argument. She just didn't understand her uncle, who'd spent his entire life in the north Cascade Mountains.

She did understand why he'd left the resort to Leah, the only one of his nieces and nephews who had genuinely loved vacations spent at the remote resort. Leah would have been happy to spend every summer there— at least until teenage hormones struck and hanging out with friends at home became a priority—but her mother refused to let her stay beyond their annual two-week family vacations spent in one of the lakeside cabins.

The road started to seriously climb, blue sky ahead. A minute later she saw the small river to the left, water tumbling over boulders and pausing in deep pools. This was July, the height of the melt-off on the mountain above. By fall, the water level would lower until barely a creek ran between rocky banks.

She stayed close to the steep bank on the right. After sneaking a few peeks at the guardrail in places it had crumpled or even disappeared, she decided she just might do the same thing coming down. It wasn't as if she was likely to meet any oncoming traffic, for heaven's sake. She could drive on whatever side of the road she wanted. And, while she'd brought a suitcase, sleeping bag and enough food to hold her for a night or two, she knew the old resort buildings might be so decrepit she'd have no choice but to turn right around and head back down the mountain. Uncle Edward had been ninety-three when he died. He wasn't likely to have done any significant maintenance in many years.

Still…the location was great, the view of Mount Baker across a shallow lake and an alpine meadow spectacular. There'd even been a glimpse of the more distant Mount Shuksan, too. Backed by national forest, the land alone had to be worth something, didn't it? She hoped Uncle Edward hadn't envisioned her building up the resort again and running it; despite good memories of the stays here, she'd grown up in Portland, Oregon, gone to college in southern California. Wilderness girl, she wasn't.

Learning about the inheritance had given her hope. She'd been dreaming of going back to school to become a veterinarian. The cost was one factor in her hesitation. Animal doctors didn't make the kind of income people doctors did, but finished four years of graduate school with the same load of debt.

Never having dreamed Uncle Edward would leave the resort to her, she couldn't help feeling as if he'd somehow known what it would mean to her.

To her relief, the road curved away from the river and plunged back into the forest. Leah's anticipation rose as she peered ahead through the tunnel formed by the enormous old evergreen trees.

It was another ten minutes before her car popped out into the grassy meadow, spangled with wildflowers, and there was the resort.

Except…there were already people here. Her foot went to the brake. Half a dozen—no, more than that—SUVs were parked in front of the lodge and cabins. Not a single car, she noted in a corner of her mind. These all looked like the kind of vehicles designed to drive on icy pavement and even off-road.

This was weird, but…she'd come this far. Surely, there was a legitimate reason for people to be here.

After a moment she continued forward, coasting to a stop in front of the lodge. Head turning, she saw that some of the cabins had been repaired in the recent past. Several new roofs and the raw wood of new porches and window frames were unmistakable.

A woman on one of those porches looked startled at the sight of her and slipped back inside the cabin, maybe to tell someone else about the arrival of a stranger.

Two men appeared around the corner of the lodge, probably having heard her car engine.

Who *were* these people? Had Mom been wrong, and Uncle Edward had kept the resort open? But still, he'd died eight months ago. Could he have sold it, with no one knowing?

She'd braked and put the gear in Park, but unease stilled her hand before she turned the key.

What if—? But she'd hesitated too long. The men had reached her car, their expressions merely inquiring. There had to be a reasonable explanation. She should be glad the resort buildings hadn't begun to tumble down.

In the sudden silence after she shut off the engine, the car keys bit into her hand. Taking a deep breath, Leah unbuckled her seat belt, opened the door and got out.

One of the men, gray-haired but as fit as a younger man, smiled. "You must be lost."

The muscular guy behind him had full-sleeve tattoos bared below a muscle-hugging tan T-shirt. And…could that be a holstered pistol at his waist?

Dear God, yes.

Say yes. Claim you were heading anywhere else. Let them give you directions and then drive away.

She could go to the nearest small town—Glacier, population 211—and ask about the group staying here. There was only one highway in and out of this area. These people had driven here. They'd have been noticed.

But the older of the two men looked friendly, not hostile at all. There'd be a logical explanation.

"No, actually," she said. "Um… I own this resort."

His smile fell away. "You're the *owner*?"

"That's right. I inherited the place from my great-uncle, Edward Preston."

Outwardly, the man relaxed. "Oh, we've been wondering what was going to happen to the place. The old man let us mostly take over the resort these past few summers in exchange for working on it. We had no idea he'd died until we got here in late June and found it empty."

"Didn't you ask in Glacier or Maple Falls? Surely, people there knew he'd died."

"Some bed-and-breakfast owner I talked to said she hadn't heard anything." He nodded toward the lodge. "Why don't you come on in and we can talk? I don't know about you, but I could use a cup of coffee."

Conscious of the other man's eyes boring into her, she hesitated again, but what else could she do but say, "Sure. Thanks. I'd forgotten what a long drive it is to get up here."

The pair flanked her as they started toward the lodge, which sounded deceptively grand. The old log building only had six guest rooms, all upstairs, a large kitchen and living space and the owner's small apartment at the back. Mostly, Uncle Edward had rented out the ten cabins. What guests he'd allowed to stay in the lodge understood they had to bring their own food and cook for themselves. "Not like I'm going to wait on them hand and foot," he'd snorted.

Leah became nervously aware that several other men had stepped out of cabins, their gazes on her. Most wore camo cargo pants, as did the so-far silent man walking to her right. None of them called out. Their appraisal felt…cold.

She was imagining things. They were curious, that was all.

Only…why weren't there other women? Children?

The porch steps were solid, having obviously been replaced. The older man opened the front door and they ushered her in. *Herded me in*, that uneasy voice inside her head whispered.

She did smell coffee. In fact, a couple of empty cups sat on the long plank table where guests had eaten or sat around in the evening to play board games or poker.

"Let me get that coffee," the gray-haired man said. "You want sugar? I have milk but no cream."

"Milk's fine. Just a dash, and a teaspoon of sugar."

"Coming right up. Have a seat." He nodded toward the benches to each side of the table.

Knowing she'd feel trapped once she was sitting with her feet under the table, she strolled instead toward the enormous river-rock fireplace where she had once upon a time roasted marshmallows for s'mores.

None of the men she'd seen thus far looked as if they'd do anything that frivolous. Chew sixteen-gauge steel nails, maybe. Graham crackers, gooey charred marsh-mallows and melted chocolate? Hard to picture.

The silent guy remained standing, a shoulder against the log wall right beside the door out to the porch. He watched her steadily.

Maybe he'd be friendly if she was. But before she

could think of anything to say that wasn't too inane, the older man returned from the kitchen with a cup of coffee in each hand.

He glanced toward the second man but didn't offer to fetch him a cup, too.

Leah didn't feel as if she had any choice but to go back to the table and sit down.

He took a sip before asking, "Mind telling me your plans?"

"Um… I wanted to see what condition the buildings were in. And, well, probably I'll sell the place."

"Sell it, huh? You have a price in mind?"

"I have no idea what land is worth up here." If it was worth anything. She had to be honest with herself. "Are you interested?"

"Could be. We'd hate having to relocate."

Feeling and sounding timid, she asked, "Do you mind telling me what you're doing up here? I'm assuming you're not all vacationing here three months a year."

The flicker of amusement in his eyes wasn't at all reassuring. He thought she was funny. Naive.

"No," he said thoughtfully. "No, this is a business."

More unnerved by the minute, she gripped the handle of the mug. She could buy herself time by throwing hot coffee in one of the men's faces if she had to run for it.

Just then, the front door opened and two more men walked in. Cool gazes assessed her. One of them raised dark eyebrows as he looked at the man acting as host. Leah had no trouble hearing the unspoken question.

Who the hell is she and what does she want?

One of the newcomers was short and stocky with sandy hair. Sort of Dennis the Menace, with the emphasis on *menace*.

The other was formidable enough to scare her more.

Eyes a crystalline gray could have been chips of ice. Tanned and dark-haired, he had the kind of shoulders that suggested he did some serious weight lifting.

And, dear God, both men wore holstered handguns at their waists.

Paramilitary was the word that came to mind. What had she walked into?

Be up front, she decided.

"I'm starting to feel a little uncomfortable," she said, focusing on the older man who almost had to be the leader of this bunch. "Why don't I head back to Glacier and find a room for the night? I'll talk to a real estate agent, and if you'd like you can come down tomorrow, meet me for lunch, maybe. We can talk."

Still appearing relaxed, he said slowly, "That might work. Ah…in answer to your earlier question, what we do is run paintball camps. It's mostly men who come up here. They immerse themselves in the wilderness and harmless war games, have a hell of a good time. We've built up a serious seasonal business. Like I said, finding another location anywhere near as perfect as this one would be next to impossible."

Because this land was so remote. Leah had to wonder whether it was true Uncle Edward had let them use his place for several summers in a row, or whether they'd somehow heard he had died and moved in under the assumption no one would be interested enough in a falling-down resort in the middle of nowhere to bother checking on it.

She stole another look at the three men on their feet, now ranged around the room. "Those…look like real guns."

Boss Man across from her shrugged. "Sure, we have a shooting range set up. A bunch of us have been out there all morning. Gotta keep sharp, even if we're mostly using paintball guns."

Nobody else's expression changed.

"Well," she said, starting to push herself up.

The sound of the back door opening was as loud as a shot. Bounced off the wall, she diagnosed, in a small, calm part of her mind surrounded by near hysteria.

All of the men turned their heads.

Grinning, a man emerged from the kitchen. Over his shoulder, he carried a *huge* gun, painted army green. Even as he said, "Hot damn!" before seeing her, Leah's blood chilled.

She'd seen pictures, taken in places like the Ukraine and Afghanistan. That wasn't a gun—it was a rocket launcher.

Son of a bitch.

Spencer Wyatt restrained himself from so much as twitching a muscle only from long practice. His mind worked furiously, though. Could this juxtaposition be any more disastrous? An unsuspecting woman wandering in here like a dumb cow to slaughter, coupled with that cocky, careless jackass Joe Osenbrock striding in with an effing *rocket launcher* over his shoulder? *Yee haw.*

Especially a young, pretty woman. Did she have any idea what trouble she was in?

Flicking a glance at her, he thought, yeah, she had a suspicion.

In fact, she said, in a voice that sounded a little too cheerful to be real, "Is that one of the paintball guns? I've never seen one before."

Good try.

Ed Higgs didn't buy it. "You know better than that. Damn. I wish I could let you go, but I can't."

She flung her full coffee cup at his face, leaped off the bench and tore for the front door, still standing ajar. Smart move, trying to get out of here. She actually brushed Spencer. He managed to look surprised and stagger back to give her a chance. No surprise, the little creep Larson was on her before she so much as touched the door.

She screamed and struggled. Her nails raked down Larson's cheek. Teeth set, he slammed her against the wall, flattening his body on hers. Spencer wanted to rip the little pissant off and throw *him* into the wall. Went without saying that he stayed right where he was. There was no way for him to help now that wouldn't derail his mission.

He had more lives than hers to consider.

Ed snapped, "Get her car keys. Wyatt, go over the car. When you're done, bring in her purse and whatever else she brought with her. Make sure you don't miss anything. Hear me?"

"Sure thing." He knew that once he had the keys, he'd have to hand them over to Higgs, who kept all the vehicle keys hidden away. No one had access to an SUV without Higgs knowing.

Arne Larson burrowed a hand into the woman's jeans pocket. When he groped with exaggerated pleasure, his captive struck quick as a snake, sinking her teeth into his shoulder. Arne yanked out the set of keys and backhanded her across the face. Her head snapped back, hitting the log wall with an audible *thunk*.

Spencer jerked but once again pulled hard on the leash. If she would only cooperate, she might have a chance to get out of this alive.

Arne tossed the keys at him and Spencer caught them. Without a word, he walked out, taking with him a last glimpse of her face, fine-boned and very pale except for the furious red staining her right jaw and cheek where the blow had fallen.

She hadn't locked the car, which didn't appear to be a rental. He used the keys to unlock the trunk and pull out a small wheeled suitcase, sized to be an airline carry-on, as well as a rolled-up sleeping bag and a cardboard box filled with basic food. Then he searched the trunk, removing the jack and spare tire, going through a bag of tools and an inadequate first-aid kit.

He couldn't believe even Higgs, with his paranoid worldview, would think the woman in there was an undercover FBI or ATF agent.

She hadn't packed like one, he discovered, after opening the suitcase on the trunk lid once he closed it. Toiletries—she liked handmade soap, this bar smelling like citrus and some spice—jeans, T-shirts, socks and sandals. Two books, one a romance, one nonfiction about the Lipizzaner horses during World War II. He fanned the pages. Nothing fell out. A hooded sweatshirt. Lingerie, practical but pretty, too, lacking lace but skimpy enough to heat a man's blood and in brighter colors than he'd have expected from her.

Not liking the direction his thoughts had taken him, he dropped the mint-green bra back on top of the mess he'd made of the suitcase's contents.

There was nothing but food in the carton, including basics like boxes of macaroni and cheese, a jar of instant coffee, a loaf of whole-grain bread and packets of oatmeal with raisins. The sleeping bag, unrolled, unzipped and shaken, hid no secrets.

A small ice chest sat on the floor in front. No surprises there, either, only milk, several bars of dark chocolate, a tub of margarine and several cans of soda.

He took her purse from the passenger seat and dumped

the contents out on the hood of the car. A couple of items rolled off. Plastic bottle of ibuprofen and a lip gloss. Otherwise, she carried an electronic reader, phone, a wallet, hairbrush, checkbook, wad of paper napkins, two tampons and some crumpled receipts for gas and meals. Her purse was a lot neater than most he'd seen.

Opening the wallet, he took out her driver's license first. Issued by the state of Oregon, it said her name was Leah E. Keaton. She was described as blond, which he'd dispute, but he didn't suppose strawberry blond would fit on the license. Weight, one hundred and twenty pounds, height, five feet six inches. Eyes, hazel. Age, thirty-one. Birthday, September 23.

She'd smiled for the photo. For a moment Spencer's eyes lingered. DMV photos were uniformly bad, no better than mug shots, but he saw hope and dignity in that smile. She reminded him of a time when his purpose wasn't so dark.

Did Leah E. Keaton know it wasn't looking good for her to make it to that next birthday, no matter what he did?

Chapter Two

Leah watched out the small window in an upstairs guest room with fury and fear as one of those brutes dug through her purse. He'd already searched her suitcase; it still lay open on the trunk of the car, the scant amount of clothing she'd brought left in a disheveled heap.

Everything that had been in her purse sat atop the hood. She felt stripped bare, increasing her shock. They would now know her name, her weight, that she used tampons. Her credit cards and checkbook were in their possession, along with her keys and phone.

That wasn't all. They had her, too.

Wyatt, if that was really his name, stood for a moment with his head bent, staring at the stuff he'd dumped out of her bag, before he began scooping it up and dropping it unceremoniously back in. Then he systematically examined the car interior, under the seats, the glove compartment, the cubbies designed to hold CDs, maps or drinks.

Following orders, of course.

Still gripped by fear, she saw him lie down on his back and push himself beneath the undercarriage. Looking for a bomb? Or a tracking device? Leah had no idea.

Her heart cramped when he shifted toward the rear of the car. How could he miss seeing the magnetic box holding a spare key?

From this angle, there was no way to tell if he pocketed it.

Eventually, if her parents didn't hear from her, they'd sound the alarm and a county deputy might drive up here looking for her, but that wouldn't happen for days. Maybe as much as a week. She'd been vague about how long she intended to stay, and they knew she was unlikely to have phone service once she reached the rugged country tucked in the Cascade Mountain foothills.

Would these men kill a lone deputy who walked into the same trap she had?

When the man below climbed to his feet and closed her suitcase, she took a step back from the small-paned window. He didn't so much as glance upward as he carried the suitcase and her purse toward the lodge, disappearing beneath the porch roof. The groceries, ice chest and sleeping bag sat abandoned beside her car.

A rocket launcher. Or was it even a missile launcher? Was there a difference? The image flashed into her mind again. Leah tried to absorb the horror. Her knees gave out and she sagged to sit on the bed, fixing her unseeing gaze on the log walls with crumbled chinking. She wasn't naive enough not to be aware that, with enough money and the right connections, anybody could acquire military-grade and banned weapons. But…what did these people intend to *do* with this one? And what other weapons did they have?

Her cheekbone throbbed. When she lifted her hand to it, she winced. The swelling was obvious at even a light touch. By tomorrow, a dark bruise would discolor half her face and probably crawl under her eye, too. Her head ached.

Leah wished she could hold on to hope that, whatever the group's political objective, the men might follow some standards of honor where women were concerned. After the stocky blond guy who'd slammed her against the wall had leered and tried to grope her while his hand was in her pocket, that was a no-go. Not one of the other men present had shown the slightest reaction.

But she was sure she'd seen a woman on the porch of one of the cabins. If women belonged to the group, would they shrug at seeing another woman raped? Somehow, she had trouble picturing this particular group of men seeing any woman as an equal, though. Armed to the teeth, buff, tattooed and cold-eyed, they made her think of some of the far-right militia who appeared occasionally on the news. Every gathering she'd ever seen of white supremacists seemed to be all male. If they had women here, they might be no more willing than she was.

But maybe…this group had a completely different objective. Could they be police or, well, members of some kind of super-secret military unit?

That thought didn't seem to offer an awful lot of hope.

Nausea welling, Leah pressed a hand to her stomach and moaned. She'd driven right into their midst, offering herself up like…like a virgin sacrifice. Except for not being a virgin. Somehow, she didn't think they'd care about that part, not if their leader decided to let them have her.

No one would be coming for her. She had to escape. Would they leave her in this room, the exit guarded? Feed her? Talk to her? Give her back any of her things?

Not her keys, that was for sure. She'd have to take the chance that Wyatt had missed the spare key. If not, she'd rather be lost and alone in the dense northwest rain forest miles from any other habitation than captive here. It would get cold at night, but this was July. She wouldn't freeze to death. At least she had sturdy athletic shoes on her feet instead of the sandals she'd also brought. Thank goodness she'd thrown on a sweatshirt over her tee.

The idea of driving at breakneck speed down the steep gravel road running high above the river scared her almost as much as those men did, but given a chance, she'd do it. If she got any kind of head start, she might be able to reach the paved stretch. Along there, she could look for a place to pull the car off the road and hide.

The hand still flattened on her stomach trembled. Great plan. If, if, if. Starting with, *if* she could get out of this room. *If* she could escape the lodge. *If*...

No, at least she knew she could escape the room. For what good that would do, given that she'd still have to pop out in the hall where a guard would presumably be stationed.

Footsteps followed by voices came from right outside her door. Her head shot up.

AT WAR WITH HIMSELF, Spencer sat at the long table with a cup of coffee. Other men came and went, buzzing with excitement. They liked the idea of a captive, particularly a female. They were eager to see her. Only four of the guys had brought women with them, and they weren't sharing. Wasn't like the single guys could go into town one evening and pick up a woman at a bar. For one thing, Spencer hadn't noticed any bars or taverns any closer than Bellingham. The only exception, in Maple Falls, had obviously gone out of business. Higgs didn't let them leave the "base" anyway.

Their great leader had gone upstairs a minute ago. If he didn't reappear soon, Spencer would follow him. He thought Higgs intended to bring Leah Keaton downstairs. Let her have a bite to eat, try to soothe her into staying passive. The way she'd sunk her teeth into Larson's flesh, Spencer wasn't optimistic that passive was in her nature, but maybe she'd be smart enough to pretend. He was screwed if she didn't—unless he kept his eye on the goal and accepted that there were frequently collateral losses—and this time, she'd be one of them. Except, he wasn't sure he could accept that.

Footsteps.

He took a long swallow of coffee and looked as if idly toward the woman Higgs led into the big open space.

She'd come along under her own power, without Higgs having to drag or shove her. If she had any brains, she was scared to death, but her face didn't show that. Instead, it was set, pale…and viciously bruised.

Spencer's temper stirred, but he stamped down on it.

"Have a seat." Higgs sounded almost genial.

Leah Keaton's gaze latched longingly on to her purse, sitting at one end of the table. Wouldn't make a difference for her to grab it; Higgs had taken the keys and probably her phone, which wouldn't do her any good anyway, not here.

"Dinner close to ready?" Higgs asked.

The wives and girlfriends were required to do the cooking and KP. Spencer had heard a couple of them come in the back door a while ago. Soon after, good smells had reached him.

Tim Fuller leaned against the wall right outside the kitchen to keep an eye on his wife, who was the best cook of the lot. Now he wordlessly stepped into the kitchen and came out to say, "Ten minutes. Spaghetti tonight."

Higgs smiled. "Sounds good. That'll give us all a chance to settle down, talk this over."

Leah sat with her back straight, her head bent so she could gaze down at her hands, clasped in front of her on the plank tabletop. Her expression didn't change an iota. Higgs's eyes lingered on her face, but he didn't comment.

Spencer continued to sip his coffee and hold his silence.

Eventually, Shelley Galt, thirty-two though she looked a decade older, brought out silverware and plates, then pitchers of beer and glasses. She kept her gaze down and her shoulders hunched as though she expected a blow at any moment. Spencer wanted to tell Shelley to steal her husband's car keys and run for it the next chance she had, but he knew better than to waste his breath even if that wouldn't have been stepping unacceptably out of his role. Shelley had married TJ Galt when she was seventeen. She probably didn't know any different or better.

Spencer had read and memorized her background, just as he had that of every single person expected to join them up here. He wasn't a trusting man.

The food came out on big platters, some carried by Jennifer Fuller, and the remaining members of the group filtered in, the men almost without exception eyeing Leah lasciviously. The four women were careful not to make eye contact with her.

Leah shook her head at the beer but took a can of soda—one, he suspected, from her own ice chest—and allowed Ed Higgs to dish up for her.

You can lead a horse to water, Spencer thought… but this one was smart enough to drink. And eat. She understood that starving herself wouldn't accomplish a damn thing.

Higgs tried to start a few conversations, earning him startled looks from his crew. He didn't do any better with Leah, who didn't react to any comments directed her way. What did he think she'd say to gems like, "Spectacular country here. Your uncle was smart to hold on to the land."

She blinked at that one but didn't look up.

Only when they were done and he said, "I need to talk to Ms. Keaton," did Spencer see her shoulders get even stiffer. "Wyatt," Higgs said, "you stay. You, too, Metz."

Rick Metz was an automaton, following orders without question, whatever they were. He carried the anger they all shared, but kept a lid on it. He rarely reacted even to jibes from the other guys. Spencer didn't see him raping a woman just because he could, which allowed him to relax infinitesimally.

Grumbles carried to Spencer, but none were made until the men stepped out onto the porch. If Higgs heard them, he offered no indication. Among this bunch, rebellion brewed constantly. Metz might be the only one who wanted to be given orders to carry out. The others accepted them, maybe seeing dimly that Ed Higgs, a former US Air Force colonel, was smarter than they were, his leadership essential to their accomplishing their hair-raising intentions. He reminded them constantly of his military service, happiest when the men called him Colonel. Compliance didn't mean they didn't seethe at the necessity and bitterly resent the inner knowledge that they were lesser in some way than Higgs. Spencer took advantage of that ever-brewing resentment when he could, giving a nudge here and there, inciting outbursts that had helped him climb to second-or third-in-command.

Once the other men were gone, Higgs said into the silence, "No reason for you to be afraid."

Leah did raise her head at that, not hiding her disbelief.

"We only need a couple more months. You'll have to

stay with us that long. Once we're ready to move, you can go on your way."

A couple more months? Did Higgs really think he'd have this bunch whipped into shape that soon? Although maybe it didn't matter to him; he wanted to make a statement, truly believing that somehow an ugly display of domestic terrorism and some serious bloodshed would inspire a revolution. The men who shared his exclusionary, racist, misogynistic views were supposed to join the fight to restore America to some imaginary time when white men ruled, women bowed to their lords and masters, and people of color—if there were any left—served their betters. How a man of his education had come by his beliefs, Spencer hadn't figured out.

"What is it you intend?" she asked, voice clear and strong. She hadn't yet so much as glanced at Spencer or Metz, who stood to one side like soldiers at attention on the parade ground. Pretending they weren't there at all?

"For you?" Higgs asked.

"I mean, your plans. Once you *move*."

If there was irony in her voice, Higgs either didn't acknowledge it or didn't hear it at all.

He launched with enthusiasm into what Spencer hoped would be a short version of his rabid passion.

"What made this country great has been lost since we started paying too much attention to the elites, who believe in opening the floodgates to immigration—and it doesn't matter to them if plenty of those immigrants are the scum of society, criminals who sneaked into the US. What happened to the days when people whose ancestors built this great country decided what direction it would go? Now we have people running for office with such thick accents you can hardly understand them! People that don't look American."

Leah blinked a few times, parted her lips…and then firmly closed them. Definitely not dumb. Then she spoke after all. "That doesn't explain what you plan to do to get attention."

He smiled at her as if she was an acolyte crawling before him. Not that he'd accept her into the fold, her being a member of the weaker sex and all.

"You don't need to worry about the details. Just know it's going to be big. We're going to shake this whole, misguided country and raise an army while we're at it." More prosaically, he added, "You can see why we need to keep our plans quiet until we're ready to launch our op. I'm asking for your cooperation. I don't think I'm being unreasonable. After all, this isn't the worst place to spend the rest of the summer." His sweeping gesture was presumably meant to take in the vast forests, mountains, lakes and wildflowers. "Got to be one of the most beautiful places in the world."

"I don't suppose you're going to let me go hiking or fishing like I did when I was a kid up here."

"Once you've settled in, why not?" Higgs said expansively. "I think you might learn something while you're here, come around to my way of thinking." He paused, a few lines forming on his brow. A thought had clearly struck him. "What do you do for a living, young lady?"

Please, God, don't let her be an attorney or an activist working with migrant workers or… Spencer sweated, running through the multitude of dangerous possibilities.

"I'm a veterinary technician."

When Higgs looked blank, she elaborated, "I treat injured or sick animals under the direction of a veterinarian. I assist him in surgery, give vaccinations, talk to pet owners."

His eyes narrowed. "So you have some medical knowledge."

"I know quite a bit about health issues affecting dogs and cats, and even horses. Not people."

"Never stitched up a wound?"

She hesitated.

"You might be able to help us. In the meantime—" the colonel pushed back from the table, the bench scraping on the worn wood floor "—I'll have one of these fellows carry your suitcase upstairs for you, and wait while you use the bathroom." He nodded at Spencer.

Was he to guard her overnight? If so, could he let her club him over the head and flee into the night? He'd have to make it look good.

For the first time since she'd come downstairs, Leah looked at him. Her dignity might be intact, but the raw fear in her eyes told him she knew what she faced. He hated knowing she was afraid of *him*.

Earlier, her eyes had been so dilated he hadn't been sure of the color. Had he ever seen eyes of such a clear green? And, damn—the courage she'd shown hit him like a two-by-four. With her fine bones and the redhead's skin that wouldn't stand up to any serious exposure to the sun, not to mention the purple bruising on her puffy cheekbone and beneath her eye, Leah Keaton couldn't hide her vulnerability. It moved and enraged him at the same time.

She was a complication he couldn't afford, but knew he couldn't shrug off, either. Spencer couldn't pretend to understand men like Arne Larson and Ed Higgs who didn't feel even a fraction of the same powerful wave of protectiveness that he did at the sight of her, damaged but using her head and holding herself straight and tall.

He picked up her suitcase and nodded toward the staircase. She rose stiffly and stalked ahead of him as if he was less than nothing to her. He admired her stubborn spirit, but knew it would backfire big time if she tried it on some of the other men. He still couldn't risk offering her a word of advice.

If he had to step forward to save her, it would be only as a last resort.

EVERY NERVE IN Leah's body prickled as she climbed the stairs ahead of Wyatt. She'd felt his gaze resting on her throughout dinner and also while the apparent leader spoke to her afterward, yet his thoughts had remained hidden. It was all she'd been able to do not to shudder when some of the men looked at her. This one almost scared her more because he didn't seem to have a single giveaway. All she knew was that he might be the sexiest man she'd ever seen—and that he had the coldest eyes. Her skin crawled at the idea that he was sizing up her body from his current vantage point. Or was he wishing he didn't have to waste time on the woman who'd stumbled on their training grounds and in doing so became a potentially dangerous problem? One *he* might be assigned to solve?

At the top of the stairs, she hesitated, hoping he'd forget how well she knew the resort.

He said only, "Isn't your room at the end of the hall?"

Her room. Sure.

"We can put the suitcase down and you can get out your toothbrush and toothpaste."

Without looking at him again, she continued down the short hall and went back into the very rustic room that had been designated her cell.

He followed, setting down the small suitcase on the

bed, unzipping it and then stepping back. Of course, the contents were in a mess. Thanks to *him*.

Resisting the urge to hide the bra that lay on top, she poked through the tangle of clothing, feeling for her toiletry bag and evaluating what was missing. Unfortunately, the closest thing to a weapon she'd packed was her fingernail clippers. Useless, but if they were still in the toiletry bag, she'd pocket them.

"Your name is Wyatt?" Appalled, she couldn't believe she'd blurted that out.

His hesitation lasted long enough to suggest he was deciding whether even that much information would be dangerous in her hands. "Spencer Wyatt." His voice was deep, expressionless and tinged with a hint of the South.

Finding the toiletry bag, she asked, "Are you supposed to go into the bathroom with me?"

Something passed through his icy eyes so fast, she couldn't identify it. "I'll wait in the hall."

He let her pass him leaving the room, clearly assuming she knew where the bathroom was. She took pleasure in closing that door in his face.

Honestly, there was enough space in here, he could have come in, too. There were two wood-framed toilet stalls, two shower stalls and two sinks. This bathroom had served for all six guest rooms. It was lucky they'd rarely if ever all been in use at the same time.

The fingernail clippers were there. She hurriedly stuck them in her jeans pocket, brushed her teeth, then used the toilet. Not exactly eager to face him again, Leah thought about dawdling, but couldn't see what that would gain her. Presumably, once he'd escorted her to the bedroom, she'd be left alone anyway. So she walked back out to find Spencer Wyatt lounging against the wall across from the bathroom door.

He looked her over, his icy eyes noting the bag still in her hand, and jerked his head toward the bedroom.

Head high, she obeyed the wordless command, walked into her room and shut the door. Her fingers hovered over the lock, which could probably be picked, and she made the decision not to turn it. Why annoy them?

They'd be annoyed enough in the morning when they discovered she wasn't where they'd left her.

Chapter Three

Lying on the bed in the dark, Leah waited for hours, even though eventually she had to struggle not to fall asleep. Twice she heard men's voices outside her room. The first time Spencer Wyatt's was one of them, the other unfamiliar. She tensed when one of the two walked away. Which man remained? Whoever he was, he didn't even look in.

Sometime later a muffled sound of voices had her hurrying to the door and pressing her ear to the crack in hopes of hearing what they were saying.

"…saving her for himself," growled one man.

The second man said something about orders.

She jumped when a thump came, followed by a scraping sound. Had they brought a chair upstairs so they could guard her comfortably? This had to be a change of shift, she decided.

Damn, she'd counted on one man being stuck on guard all night. He'd get sleepy, nod off, sure he'd wake up if her door opened. But if he stayed alert…

Or, oh, God, was the new guard the one complaining that someone was saving her for themselves? Who was he talking about? The gray-haired leader? Or Spencer Wyatt? What if grumbled defiance led to this latest guard deciding he could walk right into her room, and who was awake to stop him?

Rigid, she wished she'd locked the door after all. At least that would have slowed him down.

Receding footsteps were followed by silence out in the hall.

She needed to get out of here. In one way it might be smarter to pretend to be docile for a few days, until they lowered their guard. But the blatant sexual appraisal from so many of the men scared her more than any thought of being killed. Would she really be safe from rape if she played dumb and stayed?

Leah didn't believe it. At the very least, she could hide temporarily. She wished desperately that she knew what time it was. In her fear, she might have exaggerated the passing of time, until only a couple of hours felt like half the night. She had to go with her instincts.

After slipping out of bed, she put on her athletic shoes and tied the laces while straining to hear the slightest sound. Then she used most of the clothes in her suitcase to create a mound beneath the covers that might fool someone who glanced in to be sure she was really there. Finally, she tiptoed to the closet.

Earlier, she'd pulled the folding doors open. If Wyatt checked on her, she reasoned, he'd assume she was exploring, looking hopelessly for some out. Now, once inside the closet, she gently pulled first one door and then the other closed behind her. Kneeling on the floor facing the right side of the closet, she felt for the crack that betrayed the presence of a removable panel.

Uncle Edward had showed her and her brother the spaces between closets upstairs. She'd have been sunk if they'd locked her in either of the first bedrooms at the top of the stairs. But rooms two and three on each side of the hall had closets with removable panels that *connected* one closet to another. He guessed the builder had intended the few feet to be storage. Guests staying all summer could stow a suitcase away, for example. By the time Uncle Edward bought the resort, though, either the spaces—the passages—had been forgotten, or nobody had thought to tell him about them.

Apparently, all of the interior walls were what he called board and batten, which in the old lodge meant horizontal boards had been nailed up in rows. In the rooms and hall, they'd been covered by either plaster or wallpaper. Nobody had bothered in the closets. If you looked closely, you could see into cracks between the old boards, which might have shrunk over time. The whole subject had come up because her brother Jerry had cackled at the idea of spying on guests in the next room.

After issuing a stern warning against trying any such thing, Uncle Edward had smiled down at his great-niece and great-nephew. "Took me a few years here to notice the outline." He'd looked at the dark, dusty opening with satisfaction. "If we were down South, I'd think these were built to hide runaway slaves. 'Course, this place wasn't built until just over a hundred years ago, long after abolition."

He'd had to explain what abolition was for Jerry's sake. Leah remembered from school.

Now she held her breath, lifted the panel away and leaned it where she'd be able to reach it once she was inside. There hadn't been so much as a creak. If the next bedroom was occupied…she'd have to retreat.

Hesitating, she wished she'd brought a flashlight, instead of intending to rely on her phone. Although, that, too, would have been confiscated. Well, the spooky dark wasn't nearly as frightening as the men holding her captive. And yes, as she started to crawl through the opening and cobwebs brushed her face, she shuddered but kept moving. She could do this. She could deal with a few spiders.

Awkwardly turning around, she closed her fingers around the crude panel and tried to pull it into place. A quiet *clunk* had her freezing in place, but it wasn't followed by anyone swinging open the bedroom door and turning on the overhead light.

Dizzy, probably because her pulse raced, Leah used the short file from her fingernail clippers to pull the panel back toward her until it slotted into place—at least, as well as she could. Sliding her fingers over the edges, she thought it was snug. Her next challenge was to open the panel on the other side while preventing it from falling to the floor. *That* would make enough noise to bring the guard to investigate.

She scooted forward until her head brushed the rough wood that was the back of the panel leading into the next room.

Somehow, this wasn't nearly as fun as it had been when, as children, she and Jerry used these passages to perplex their parents.

She lifted her hand, feeling for the crack at the top… and something crawled over her hand. Suppressing a shriek she shook off the bug—a spider?—and made herself start again. Finally, she applied a little pressure, then more—and when the panel gave way, she grabbed the top of it.

And then she froze. She reminded herself that one of the men might be *sleeping* in this room. Surely, the group was using at least some of these upstairs guest rooms.

Breathing as slowly and steadily as she could, she told herself she'd made the assumption about empty rooms for a good reason. She hadn't seen anyone go up or come down the staircase, unless it was with her. When the leader had dismissed the group, nobody had headed for the stairs.

Which was reassuring, but hardly conclusive since it had still been early evening when she was escorted to bed.

Would she have heard someone come upstairs, a door opening and closing? Surely, her guard and another man would have exchanged a few words.

Her pulse continued to race and her teeth wanted to chatter. Could she have chosen worse timing for a panic attack? She took a deep breath. She wouldn't hesitate now.

Gradually, a surface level of calm and resolve suppressed the fear.

If she was quiet enough, she could grope around the closet and find out if someone was using it. She could peek into the room without waking a sleeper. If there was one, well, then she'd have a decision to make.

She eased the panel out and leaned it against the back of the closet. Creeping forward, she patted her way along, cursing the complete darkness. She waved her hands over her head, not feeling any hanging clothes.

Would men like this bother hanging up a shirt, or would they just stuff clean laundry into a duffel bag? No shoes, either. But feeling confident the closet was empty didn't mean the room wasn't occupied. Somehow, she suspected these guys hadn't packed big wardrobes for their training session.

If someone really was sleeping in this room, he'd probably set his handgun aside. If she was quiet enough, she could take it. She might actually have a chance then.

If, if, if.

AFTER METZ TOOK his place outside Leah Keaton's door, Spencer had made a point of hanging around downstairs for a while. Higgs wanted to talk through the problem she presented. He rambled, Spencer mostly keeping his mouth shut.

"Would have been better if you'd been able to let her go in the first place," he couldn't resist saying.

The colonel grunted. "That idiot Osenbrock."

Knowing the variety of weapons of mass destruction the group had acquired, Spencer's blood still ran cold. Spencer refrained from saying the whole damn bunch were idiots, including and especially Air Force Colonel Edward Higgs, retired. Spencer could almost wish to be present to see Higgs's face when he learned that he had a snake in his cozy hideaway.

Yeah, not really, Spencer thought, even as he nodded and made supportive noises.

Eventually, he'd had no choice but to announce he was heading for bed. He'd rinsed out his cup and set it on the dish drainer, gone out the front door after a last good-night and headed straight for his cabin. He had no doubt there were eyes on him. At least three of this crowd resented him bitterly. So far, they hadn't risked laying it on the table and thereby earning Higgs's displeasure. Sooner or later, someone would find a good enough excuse to throw down the gauntlet. The longer he could put that challenge off, the more likely he'd get out of here alive.

Although the likelihood of that had plummeted with the arrival of a gutsy woman who didn't deserve to become a victim.

Grimacing, he clumped up on the small front porch of the cabin he'd claimed, unobtrusively drew his weapon and went in for the usual search before he could relax at all.

And before he slipped out again, this time staying unseen, to maintain a long-distance watch over Leah.

THE ROOM PROVED to be vacant, and likely had been for a decade or more. A broken bed frame left the mattress tipping. A front on one of the dresser drawers had split in half.

Light from the hall showed beneath the door.

When Leah tiptoed over to the sash window, she felt a draft. Standing to one side, she felt the cold glass until she found the corner that had broken out.

Taking a chance, she stood right in front of the window, turned the window latch and tried to heave the lower sash upward. Absolutely nothing happened. The warped, painted-too-many-times frame didn't so much as groan. For an instant she thought she saw something—some-*one*—move out at the edge of the treeline, but then decided her eyes had tricked her.

She could break out the rest of the glass—but that would alert the guard. If she could swing out, dangle and drop, she might make it to the ground uninjured… but they'd be on her right away. And what if she sprained or broke an ankle? She might not be able to drive, even if the hideout key was still there, and she sure as heck couldn't run away.

If only she knew what time it was. If the door to the hall would crack open without a squeak of rusting hinges.

She stopped herself from creating a list of dire consequences for every decision she made. She'd come this far. She had to peek into the hall and see if there was the slightest chance at all of making it unseen to the stairs. Maybe even whether there were any lights on downstairs, or whether she'd be able to descend into blessed darkness.

No floorboards creaked underfoot as she crossed the room. Prayed the door and frame had been as solidly built. Holding her breath, she very gently turned the knob, then drew the door toward herself a fraction of an inch at a time. It was quiet, so quiet.

Until she heard a muffled sound. A curse?

She had the door open wide enough to allow her to poke her head out into the hall. When she did, she saw a tattooed, muscular guy who hadn't stood out to her if she'd seen him at all. Chair pushed aside, he sat on the floor, leaning back against the door to her original room, legs stretched out. His head sagged to one side, and another snort came from him.

He was snoring. Asleep.

If she'd opened that door, he'd have awakened instantly. As it was…she slipped out into the hall and tiptoed toward the stairs. There was a light on down there somewhere—the kitchen?—but not in the main room.

First step, second, third. She hesitated. One of the stairs had squeaked on her way up. The next—she thought. Gripping the handrail, she stretched to reach the step below, then kept going. Once she was far enough down, she turned her head, searching for movement. For a second guard. For a Rottweiler. For anything, but all remained still.

Within moments she was at the front door.

SPENCER KEPT STARING at the window into the middle bedroom upstairs in the lodge. He'd seen someone; he'd swear he had. Durand, who was currently on guard? Maybe he'd heard something outside, was doing some rounds? But he was an exceptionally big guy, and the figure Spencer had seen had been slight. But how in hell could that woman have gotten past Durand and into a different guest room? He shook his head. Maybe it had been a damn ghost.

He waited. Waited.

Something happened in the deep shadows of the front porch. A person, moving tentatively, emerged into the moonlight and started down the half dozen steps.

Careful, Spencer urged silently. She reached the ground, apparently unheard and unseen except by him, and ran for her car. She went straight for the back fender, crouched out of sight and then stood and rushed around to the driver's side.

A light came on in one of the cabins. For an instant, the woman froze, looking in the same direction.

It was probably just somebody out of bed to take a leak, but you never knew. Spencer had crossed paths with some other night owls from time to time. Paranoia had that effect on a man.

She opened the car door, still unlocked, and jumped in. She was smart enough not to turn on headlights, but seconds later the engine purred to life. Given the silence out here in the forest, it sounded more like a roar.

Lights in other cabins came on.

The car didn't move.

Goddamn. Somebody must have taken the precaution of screwing with her car. Disabled the transmission, maybe, or the CV joint.

Why hadn't Higgs mentioned that to him? Spencer wondered.

Men were running toward her. She flung open her door, fell out and scrambled back to her feet, then took off for the trees.

He couldn't intervene. Even feeling a crack tear open in his iron control, Spencer knew there was too much to lose, and she wasn't going to make it anyway.

It killed him to stay back in the darkness and watch her be tackled by the fastest pursuer. Even down, she screamed and fought furiously. Finally breaking, he started toward them, but too late.

A second guy reached her, and the two of them wrenched her to her feet, still struggling but in an uncoordinated way, as if her limbs no longer worked right.

It was TJ Galt who'd reached her first. Curt Baldwin second. They'd pay for the unnecessary brutality, Spencer swore.

By the time they dragged her to the foot of the lodge steps and dropped her on the ground, the porch light had come on and lights shone in all the cabins. They'd all been awakened and closed in on her. Spencer circled until he could join them in a way that would appear natural.

"What the hell happened ?" Spencer asked, just as Higgs pushed his way to the center of the group.

The colonel swore viciously before turning his head. "Where's Durand?"

"Here."

Everyone else drew back from the man who'd failed at his appointed task. Higgs didn't accept failure.

"How did she get by you?"

"She couldn't have." Seeming dazed, Don Durand gazed down at the woman lying in the dirt at his feet. "That bedroom door never opened. Maybe…the window."

All but Spencer looked up at the obviously closed windows.

Was she conscious? It was a minute before he could reassure himself that at least she was breathing. He should have run to her first, pretended to smack her around to avoid this. He gritted his teeth, wishing she'd made it into the woods.

"Get her up!" Higgs snapped.

Galt pulled her up in one vicious motion. One of her

eyes was swollen completely shut. The other was open, but dazed. How aware was she?

"Who has a gun?" Higgs demanded.

After a heartbeat, Durand handed over his. Higgs grabbed a handful of her hair and yanked hard while grinding the barrel into her temple.

"How'd you get out?"

It was a long time before she spoke. Then her voice was a mere thread, so faint Spencer found himself leaning forward to hear.

"Way to get from one bedroom closet to another."

Spencer stirred. When he was a kid, his still-intact family had vacationed at a rustic resort on one of Georgia's barrier islands. He remembered discovering that a panel could be removed in the back of the closet to expose an additional space.

Higgs swore some more. "Why shouldn't I kill you?"

Half the men clustered around her wore avid expressions Spencer had seen too often before, the kind you'd see on faces in the audience at an MMA fight when blood spattered, or in the crowd at a car race after a collision that might leave fatalities. These men were excited, wanted the shock of seeing blood and a young woman go down right in front of them. If Higgs's finger tightened even a fraction…

Spencer pushed forward. "That'd be an awful waste."

"What?" Higgs's head jerked around.

"You heard me." Spencer smiled slightly and leaned on his Southern accent. "She's a real pretty woman."

A chorus of agreement broke out. "Hell, yeah. We can keep her too busy to get in trouble."

Spencer looked into Higgs's eyes. "Give her to me, and I'll guarantee no more trouble from her."

The two men stared at each other; Higgs's eyes narrowed. Spencer didn't dare relax enough even to see how she had reacted, or if she had. Arguments broke out around them. They wanted to share her, or a few of the men thought they were entitled to have her, sure as hell more than that Southern bastard who'd joined the group late. This was a gamble that Higgs would acknowledge him as second in charge by giving him what he wanted.

Higgs's hand holding the gun dropped away, and he used his grip on her hair to twist her toward Spencer. Then he gave her a hard shove, sending her flying into Spencer, who pulled her tight against him.

"She's all yours," Higgs said in a hard voice. "You screw up, on your head be it."

Spencer nodded at their fair leader, then half carried Leah through the crowd, ignoring the chorus of protests and the glares. Every hair on the back of his neck stood up as he broke free and steered her toward the refuge of his cabin.

How the hell *was* he going to control her?

Chapter Four

Supporting most of Leah's weight, Spencer propelled her up the steps to his porch and into his cabin. He laid her down on the futon that would have once served a dual purpose when a family rented this cabin. The damn thing was uncomfortable, but he didn't suppose she'd notice right now. Aware that they'd been watched all the way, he was glad to be able to close and lock the door.

The damage to her face was severe enough this time; he wondered whether her cheekbone might be broken. He worried even more that her brain had been traumatized. Knowing there wasn't a thing he could do if that was so, Spencer gritted his teeth and went to the corner of the room that served as a kitchen. She hadn't moved when he returned with an ice pack and a T-shirt he'd left lying over the back of a chair.

He sat beside her on the futon, wrapped the ice pack in the thin cotton T-shirt and gently laid it over her cheekbone, eye and brow.

She jerked and flailed.

"Hey," he said quietly. "I know this doesn't feel good, but it's only ice. You've got some major swelling going on."

Her eye—the one that wasn't swollen shut—opened, looking glassy and uncomprehending.

"That SOB clobbered you," Spencer continued, working to keep his voice reassuring instead of enraged. "I'll give you something for the pain once the ice has had a chance to help." And once she demonstrated some coherence. If she didn't...well, that was a bridge he'd cross when he had no other choice.

Her eye closed and a small sigh escaped her.

His hand was cold, but he didn't move it, just kept looking down at her, taking in every detail of her face, from the old and new damage to her lashes and eyebrows, both auburn instead of brown. Just long enough to tuck behind her ears, her hair was ruffled but obviously straight. A high forehead gave her some of that look of innocence and youth he'd first noticed. She had a pretty mouth, now that it wasn't pressed into a tight line.

With a grimace, he corrected himself. What he'd really meant was, *Now that it was lax because she was semiconscious.*

"Leah?"

His anxiety ratcheted up a notch when she didn't respond.

He tried again. "Can you hear me? I need to know how you're doing."

Her lashes fluttered and the single eyelid rose. She tried to focus a still-dazed eye on him. "Why—" she licked her lips "—would you care?"

He'd bent his head closer to hear a question that was more a prolonged breath than words. There were any number of possible responses, but he went with, "You didn't deserve this."

"Tried...run away."

"I know."

"You...missed car key."

Okay, she was with him, if still feeling like crap. He smiled. "I didn't miss the key. I left it for you."

"Car wouldn't drive."

"I didn't do that. Didn't know anyone else had, either."

Tiny lines formed on her forehead above the ice pack. "Why would you want me to get away?"

The side of him that was utterly focused on his mission hadn't. A police response would have majorly screwed up this operation. He'd invested too much in it to want it ended prematurely. But he hadn't been able to stand back and watch her be raped or killed, either.

"I don't hurt women," he finally said.

Was that a snort? He wasn't sure, and she'd closed her eye again.

"If you can hold this in place—" he lifted her hand and laid it over the ice pack "—I'll get you some painkillers."

"'Kay," she murmured.

He kept a sharp eye on her for the short time it took him to dig in his leather duffel bag in the bedroom and return to the main room with a bottle of over-the-counter meds. He had some better stuff tucked away, too, but he'd hold off on that for now.

Bringing a glass of water, too, he helped her half sit up and swallow the pills, then gently laid her back again.

"Have you gotten any sleep tonight?" he asked.

Her nose wrinkled. "Maybe...hour or two?"

That was what he'd thought. "Once the pain lets up a little, I'm hoping you'll be able to get a few hours."

She didn't comment. Spencer had to wonder if her busy little brain wasn't already plotting how to escape. As in, waiting until he had fallen asleep. And, damn it, he did need some sleep. He didn't like his best option here, and she'd like it even less, but he didn't see a workable alternative. Now that he had her safe, he wouldn't let her

risk herself unnecessarily…and he was back to focusing
first on what he needed to do.

She paid enough attention to him to lift her arms when
he asked, and tell him where else she hurt. He manipu-
lated her right shoulder and decided it, too, was inflamed
and deeply bruised from when she hit the ground with
TJ's weight atop her.

He cracked open another ice pack and applied it to
her shoulder. When she started shivering, he grabbed
his fleece jacket and spread it over her.

Leah peered suspiciously at him from her one good
eye.

Finally, he said, "Okay, tell you what. I'm going to
move you to the bed so you can really get some sleep.
We'll ice any swelling in the morning." Which wasn't
very far away.

She didn't move. Spencer took away the ice packs and
tossed them in the small sink. Returning to her, he slid
an arm behind her back and said, "Upsy daisy."

"I want to stay here."

"Not happening," he said flatly.

"Why not?"

"You didn't get away. There won't be a second chance."
She twisted out of his grip. "I won't!"

"I didn't ask you." This time he lifted her using both
arms.

Her pliancy vanished. She fought like a featherweight
champ, landing blows with her small fists. He averted
his face and endured as he walked to the bedroom, but
when she managed to clip his jaw, he snapped, "That's
it," and dropped her on the bed.

Of course she rolled for the other side and thudded off
onto her knees, then scrambled to her feet. "If you think
I'm getting in that bed with you—"

"I'm not giving you a choice," he said grimly, and pulled a set of handcuffs from his back pocket.

ALREADY SCARED, LEAH completely lost it then. Gripped by a suffocating terror, she knew only that once he clicked those cuffs on her, she'd be utterly helpless.

He was already shifting toward the foot of the bed, expecting her to come around. She threw herself across the bed instead, her shoulder hitting his hard belly when he moved to intercept her. Fighting mindlessly, Leah used every weapon she had, including her teeth and nails. He let out a stream of invectives when she raked her fingernails over his cheek and sank her teeth into his biceps. Sobbing for breath, she kept fighting even as he subdued her with insulting ease, throwing her again onto the bed and, this time, coming down on top of her.

Even that didn't stop her. She bucked and kicked and screamed until he covered her mouth and half her face with a big hand, somehow managing to capture both her wrists with his other hand and plant them above her head.

Now she couldn't breathe at all. With that powerful body, he was crushing her. She wrenched her head side to side until she was able to bite the fleshy part of his hand below his thumb.

"Enough!" he snarled, and before she knew it he'd pushed her to her side and clicked the handcuffs around one wrist. Her face was wet with tears and probably snot as she continued to fight uselessly against his greater strength.

He snapped the other side of the cuffs onto the old iron bedstead and rolled off both her and the bed to land on his feet where he glared down at her, his teeth bared, his hands half curled into fists.

Leah went still, hurting everywhere, terrified in an

all new way. She had no doubt at all that he intended to rape her.

I don't hurt women.

Sure. Right. Her shoulder screamed and her head throbbed. One hip hurt, too, and she tasted blood. Her gaze flicked to his powerful biceps where she saw the bite mark. It was *his* blood in her mouth.

"Damn," he said suddenly, and scrubbed one of his hands over his face. When he looked back at her, his expression had changed. Instead of triumph, she thought she saw regret. No, probably pity. But even that was good news, wasn't it? If he felt sorry for her, would a man still rape a woman?

"Let me get a wet cloth to wipe your face," he said unexpectedly, and left the bedroom.

She tugged at the cuffs, just to be sure they really had clicked shut. The metal bit into her wrist. Leah turned her face away from the door.

A moment later she heard his footfall.

"If I sit down, will you attack me again?" he asked in that deep voice tinged with a softening accent.

Did he wear a pistol? She couldn't remember noticing. If she could get her hand on it…

She had to roll her head to see.

No gun.

He held a wet washcloth.

"No," she whispered.

Watching her, those oddly pale eyes unblinking, he sat beside her, much as he had out on the ancient couch. When he'd tried to take care of her, Leah couldn't help remembering.

That didn't mean she was safe from him, though. Why would he have claimed her if he didn't want sex from her?

But she only closed her own eyes when he laid the

warm washcloth over her face and very carefully wiped away her tears and probably some blood and, yes, snot. The heat and rough texture felt so good, she heard herself make a tiny sound that might have been a whimper.

"Better?" he asked quietly.

She bobbed her head. Pain stabbed both shoulders, now that her arm on the uninjured side was stretched above her head, but everything was relative.

"Then we need to talk." He paused. "I want you to look at me."

Leah rolled her head enough to be able to see him out of her right eye. The other one had to be swollen completely shut despite the ice this man had applied to it. Why would he have bothered unless...

"You're not going to escape at this point," Spencer said, his gaze steady, his tone rock hard. "You're alive, and not in the hands of one of those animals, because I took responsibility for you. Everyone here will respect that unless they see me as failing. Say, if you make any kind of serious attempt at taking off. It'll be a free-for-all then, and you could end up in anyone's cabin. Or shared between them. Do you understand that?"

After a moment she nodded. She did see that; she just didn't know what kind of threat *he* represented.

"You have to cooperate. For both our sakes, I wish you could stay holed up in this cabin, but that's not an option. I have to participate in training exercises and planning sessions. That would leave you alone. What you need to do is join the other women and imitate them." He paused. "You saw them at dinner."

This time her nod was uncertain. She hadn't paid that much attention. Mostly, she'd hoped for...she didn't know, maybe a signal from one of them? Any hint that one or all of the women would help if they could?

"They're abused women." His expression was grim. "They each try not to meet the eyes of any man but their own husband or boyfriend, and that rarely. They tend to keep their heads down, shoulders hunched. They scuttle across open ground."

Could she act that well? Leah thought so. Fear was a great motivator.

He continued relentlessly. "The women are expected to do all the cooking and cleaning. They don't complain, because they know their role in life. They talk among themselves only when they're working together in the kitchen, and then it's quietly, and about their work. One of the men—the husbands and boyfriends—always keeps an eye on them while they're together. The message is that they can't be trusted."

Feeling growing horror, she whispered, "You'll do that, too?"

"Damn straight I will, as often as I can."

He startled her by planting a hand on each side of her torso and leaning over her. Dominating her, so she couldn't look away from him if she tried. The triple scratches she'd inflicted showed vividly on his angular cheek above dark stubble. A small bump on the bridge of his nose wasn't her fault.

"*I* am your only protection," he continued relentlessly. "You can't forget that. Right now they're all afraid to cross me."

"Even the boss?"

"Colonel Higgs?"

The irony in his voice had her blinking. "That's what he's called?"

"He is a retired US Air Force colonel. He doesn't let anyone forget it."

"That's scary."

His eyebrows twitched. Leah couldn't tell if he agreed or was pleased to have a leader with a legitimate military background.

"I wouldn't say he's afraid of me," Spencer continued. "Wary, maybe. Preferring to keep my loyalty. Apparently, he has no interest in taking you on himself."

She shuddered.

"You might have been safer with him," the big man with the icy eyes told her. "Nobody would have thought to argue with him. I'm…not popular with a few of the men. We may run into trouble if someone works up the guts to challenge me."

We? This bizarre conversation had her bewildered. *Us against them.* Did he imagine she'd be *happy* to be one of those stoop-shouldered, timid, obedient women?

Or… Leah replayed everything he'd said. His expressions, subtle though they were. His actions, if it was true he'd left the hideout key to the car deliberately to give her a chance to get away. His care with her injuries, the flickers of rage she'd seen. Even when she fought, when she hurt him, he'd still been careful not to hurt *her.*

Very slowly, she said, "You're not one of them, are you?"

SPENCER QUIT BREATHING as he stared at her. Only long practice allowed him to keep his face impassive despite his shock. After a moment he said, "That's not a smart thing to suggest. Not to me, and especially not to anyone else."

Her eyes searched his. The impulse to confide in her took him by surprise. Part of it, he understood. Seeing her so terrified of him that she'd fought with crazed ferocity had hit him hard. If she hadn't calmed down, he might have had no choice. As it was…he shouldn't even *think* about trusting her to that extent. One careless word, a reaction that seemed off to one of the men, and he and she both would be dead. She *had* to be seen to be scared of him, unwillingly bowing to necessity, or somebody might get curious. No cover was good enough if someone was willing to dig deep.

No.

Bending even more closely over her, he said softly, "Do you hear me?"

She shrank from him. "Yes."

"Good." He straightened so that he was no longer caging her body with his.

"You can't tell me—" she began.

Spencer almost groaned. She was either very, very perceptive, or just naturally rebellious. Neither quality served them well right now.

"I've got to get some sleep," he said abruptly, bending to pull off his boots and socks. "I don't think you have a concussion—your eyes seem pretty focused to me—but I'll keep a watch for any problems. You can try to sleep."

Her eyes widened.

Ignoring her, he pulled his belt from the loops, then unbuttoned and unzipped his cargo pants.

Wearing only the T-shirt and knit boxers, he went out to the living room to check locks again, pick up his Sig Sauer and turn off lights. Returning to the bedroom, he briefly thought about switching the cuff from the bed frame to his wrist but decided against it. She couldn't go anywhere, and if she attacked him again, he'd wake up in the blink of an eye and deal with her. He might have slept on the futon so that she could relax a little—but he couldn't afford for someone to look in the uncurtained window above the sink and see that he was pandering to Leah. Besides—even rocky ground would be an improvement over the futon.

He adjusted the bedroom curtains to block anyone trying to steal a look, turned off the light and tugged the covers out from beneath her so that he could pull them over both of them. Then he claimed one of the two nearly flat pillows, doubled it over and stretched out beside her.

Leah lay rigid, as close to the far edge of the bed as she could. Given that the bed was only a full size—his feet hung over at the bottom—that wasn't very far away. Besides…the mattress was as old as the futon and the stained kitchen sink. Once she nodded off, she'd roll to meet him in the middle.

A rueful smile tugged at his mouth as he pictured how happy she'd be waking up plastered against his body.

Chapter Five

She dreamed about being stretched on a medieval rack.
At the same time she was weirdly comfortable, the cozy
warmth feeling as if it came from a heated blanket, but
more…solid. Comforting.

Leah surfaced slowly, realizing that she lay on her side
with her head resting on her upper arm. That arm was
stretched above her, and ached fiercely. Not stretched,
she thought on a sudden memory; pulled.

And somebody spooned her, his hips pressed to her
butt, thighs to the backs of hers. A heavy arm lay over
her, his hand tucked—Leah quit breathing. If his hand
wasn't so relaxed, it would have enclosed her breast.

His chest felt like a wall. Was it possible she could feel
his slow, steady heartbeats?

He. Spencer. The man who'd claimed her and now
expected complete obedience as payback. How had she
let him wrap her in such an all-encompassing embrace?

When he climbed into bed with her as if that was routine, she'd resolved to stay awake. Obviously, that hadn't
gone so well, and no wonder, considering how desperately tired she'd been by then. Not just from lack of sleep.
Shock and pain and fear had taken a toll.

Lying completely still, as if she could fend off the reality that she shared the bed with a very large, muscular

man who might well have squeezed her breast in his hand while she slept, Leah understood how poorly prepared she'd been for any of this. She'd grown up in a middle-class home with loving parents, had a good relationship with her sometimes irritating little brother, enjoyed college and even her job, although she did want more. Her only major stumble had been being so blind where Stuart was concerned, and compared to her current predicament, that was…normal. Her letting love, or some facsimile thereof, blind her. And to think of the agonies she'd suffered over that jerk. If only she'd known.

Now she had to face the fact that there was a really good chance she'd be gang-raped or—no, make that *and*—killed in the next few days. It would seem her only chance at survival was to obey the stranger who shared this bed.

His pelvis wasn't all that was pressing into her butt, she became gradually aware. That hard bar hadn't been there when she first woke up. His breathing had changed, too.

"I have to use the bathroom," she said loudly.

His chuckle ruffled the tiny hairs on the back of her neck. "Gotcha."

He gently squeezed her breast, gave a regretful sigh, and he rolled away from her. The mattress rebounded without his weight.

"Now, what did I do with that key?" he said.

She growled; he laughed.

A moment later he'd unfastened the cuff on the bed frame. Leah scrambled to get out of bed. She hadn't thought about her bladder until she'd told him that, but now she *really* needed to go.

Amusement on his face, Spencer stepped out of her

way. She rushed for the small bathroom. The warped door didn't quite latch, but stayed closed. Relief.

The mirror was spotted, but she inspected her face. It wasn't pretty. She could see out of both eyes, although the one side was still really puffy, the discoloration gaining new glory. The last time she'd had a black eye, a scared Labrador mix had head-butted her in an attempt to escape. This one would be way more spectacular before it was done.

She surveyed the bathroom before she went back out, but didn't see anything useful. A good, old-fashioned straight razor, or even a disposable kind of razor, might have come in handy. But no; a rechargeable shaver lay on the pedestal sink.

Arming herself might be stupid at this point anyway. A razor blade would look wimpy to men all carrying semiautomatic pistols. And really, given her inexperience, even a gun in her hands might get her in more trouble than it would solve.

Whatever else she could say about the man who'd stepped forward on her behalf—an optimistic way of phrasing it—he exuded danger. So much so, none of the other men had been prepared to challenge him, as he put it. That made him the best weapon she could have acquired…assuming he didn't have an end game that had nothing to do with her welfare.

She ran through a plus list. A) he hadn't raped her when he could easily have done so; B) he had done his best not to add to her injuries, even when she was attacking him; and C) he had actually seemed to care that she was hurt and had tried to make sure she was comfortable.

Plenty of negatives came to mind readily, too, starting with the fact that he was a member of a frighteningly well-armed white supremacist militia with big, scary plans. Moving on to B, if she tried something, he could handle her without breaking a sweat; and C, she had no idea how much of what she'd seen was facade and how much real.

She didn't know him, and one of the greatest threats right now was an unreasoning belief that he wasn't a member of the group at all, that he despised them and was really an honorable, good man. Oh, yeah—and she would have been sexually attracted to him in any other circumstances at all.

Maybe even *these* circumstances, which meant…she didn't know. Was this a primitive response to the fact that he claimed to be standing between her and the world?

Not happening, she told herself firmly. She'd do as he asked, for now. What choice did she have? But she'd watch for an opportunity to escape, and she couldn't afford to soften toward Spencer Wyatt—or to entirely trust him.

SPENCER FELT ANTSY from the minute he left Leah in the large kitchen at the lodge and headed out to the shooting range with the others. The women were washing up from breakfast, Lisa Dempsey planning lunch while Jennifer Fuller handed out cleaning assignments. Spencer wasn't sure he could have made himself walk away if TJ Galt had been the one "supervising," but Dirk Ritchie was staying behind this morning. He'd brought the fourth woman along, Helen Slocum.

Helen didn't seem so much terrorized as mentally slow, Spencer had come to think. Dirk could be unexpectedly patient with her, even showing flashes of genuine caring. In fact, he seemed like a decent guy in many ways, which left him the low man on the totem pole in this crowd. Decency registered as weakness here. Spen-

cer made a point of supporting the guy. Dirk's background suggested a reading disability, a lousy school
district and a father who was disappointed in his only
son's spinelessness. As with Shelley, Spencer wanted to
quietly tell Dirk to take Helen and drive away—and not
go home to daddy.

He'd as soon not feel sorry for any of this crowd, but
couldn't entirely shut down that side of himself.

Obviously, or he'd be able to keep his mind on business. As it was, he should have taken this shot two minutes ago.

He lay prone in the dirt looking through a scope at a
target that he'd calculated was five hundred and seventy-
five yards out, give or take a little. It was crystal clear. He
breathed in, out, in, out…and gently pulled the trigger.

Higgs squatted beside him, peering through military-
grade binoculars. "Hell of a shot."

As had been every one he'd taken today.

Higgs was in love with the Barrett M82 rifle, not because of accuracy, although it was fine. What he liked—
and why he'd acquired several of these rifles—was that
they fired the exact same .50 BMG cartridge used in
the heavy machine gun. The heavy-duty round excelled
at destroying just about everything up to armored vehicles. Higgs wasn't interested in subtlety. He wanted
a big boom.

One of the downsides of this particular rifle was the
lack of accuracy for truly long-range shots. In fact, anything over nine hundred yards. Personally, Spencer had
preferred the M40A5, one of many descendants of the
Remington 700 rifle commonly owned by hunters. He
had comfortably made shots at twelve hundred yards
and farther, although there were military snipers who
could make longer ones. So far, Higgs hadn't asked for

anything remotely difficult for a man with Spencer's experience, which meant a simple assassination wasn't on Higgs's agenda.

Now Spencer peeled off his ear protection and rose to his knees still cradling the rifle. "That's it for me. You know I had sniper training at Fort Bennett. I've spent enough time on a range to stay sharp. Let's focus on some of the guys who need the work."

Happy with what he'd seen, Higgs stood, too, letting the binoculars fall to his chest. "I agree. We'll be lucky if any of the men become reliable at even a hundred yards out. We could use another real sharpshooter, but unless you have a former army buddy you can recruit, we'll have to get by with what we have."

Temptation flickered at the opportunity to bring in another agent, but Spencer was inclined to think the risk was too great. Aside from backup, how much could a newcomer achieve anyway? He was well enough established to be in a good position to be included the next time Colonel Higgs met with his arms dealer. Nailing down who was stealing and selling contraband US Army weaponry to the group was one of his highest priorities, along with finding out the final details of the spectacular attack that Higgs was so convinced would not only deal a major blow to the government, but also fire-start a civil war.

The crack of shots interspersed their few words. Spencer didn't need binoculars to see how badly Tim Fuller, stationed closest to him, was shooting.

Another week or two, he told himself, but he'd thought the same before. Ed Higgs was being cagey even with Spencer, who wanted some serious time alone with Higgs's laptop. As it was, he had to hold out for that upcoming exchange of cash for arms.

He'd had better luck tracing the source of the funding, and managed to share that much with his superior the last time he'd been part of a supply run to Bellingham and had had a minute to get away to make a call. Some names weren't all, though. A lot of the money was coming from someone who remained cloaked in shadows. Even the one chance to share what he'd learned had been a few weeks ago, but now instead of hoping he'd have the chance again, his gut told him bad things would happen if he left Leah for an entire day.

In fact, when he looked around he didn't see Joe Osenbrock.

"Where's Joe?" he asked sharply.

The older man's gray head turned. "Don't know. Taking a leak?"

The AK-47 Osenbrock had been using lay in the dirt where he'd apparently left it. Spencer had spent time drilling these idiots in how important it was to treat their weapons with care, but nothing he said had sunk in. They thought they were ready, their impatience building almost as fast as their confidence, until they had begun looking at their great leader with doubt. What use was more target shooting? Hand-to-hand combat? Why did they need any of this, when they had the weaponry to shoot planes out of the sky? Spencer had heard the whispers.

Just the other night, for example. Thinking he was alone with Shawn Wycoff walking at the edge of the trees, TJ had said, "I'm starting to think he's all talk." Hidden in the darkness, Spencer hadn't been ten feet away. He didn't miss so much as a mumble. It never occurred to them anybody could be near, far less breathing down their necks.

That arrogance was good. It would bring these fools down.

Unfortunately, it also explained Higgs's continuing hesitation as well as his unwillingness to trust anyone.

Speaking of trust, Spencer said, "I need to go check on Leah. Make sure she's behaving herself and that Joe hasn't forgotten who she belongs to."

Leah's face had looked better this morning, but that wasn't saying much. He still feared she'd suffered a concussion. He'd checked on her a few times in the night and not seen anything too worrisome, but he wanted to be vigilant.

Higgs's eyebrows rose, but he nodded. "I don't need you out here. Let's talk after lunch, though."

Yes. Why don't we talk about who's footing the bills, he thought. *Better yet, some details about your endgame.*

But Spencer only nodded and, carrying his rifle, walked toward the lodge. He was careful to keep his pace unhurried until he was out of sight of the range set up in what had been a beautiful high alpine meadow. They'd undoubtedly destroyed much of the fragile ecosystem.

Then he broke into a run.

LEAH WAS ON her hands and knees scrubbing the floor in the downstairs bathroom when she heard someone stop in the hall. She stiffened, sneaking a look. Without lifting her head, all she knew was that a man stood there, and he wasn't Spencer or Dirk.

Feet in heavy black boots were planted apart, meaning he filled the doorway. Camo cargo pants didn't hide powerful legs.

"May I help you?" she asked timidly.

"You sure can," he said.

Oh, God. She'd heard his name at breakfast. Joe Osenbrock. He hadn't been one of the two who'd tackled her during her escape attempt, but his perpetual sneer didn't make him likeable. Plus, she'd seen hunger in his eyes when he looked at her. Almost as tall as Spencer, he was broad and strong.

Swallowing, she stayed on her knees and kept her head bent.

"See, Wyatt's got no reason to keep you to himself. What he don't know won't hurt him, now, will it?"

She bit her lip so hard she tasted blood. Where was Dirk Ritchie? Had he seen Osenbrock come in?

"You think he won't know?" she asked, still diffident.

"If he finds out, so what? Not like I'd be spoiling the goods." His voice changed, hardened. "On your feet, woman."

Her mind scrambled for any way to get away from this would-be rapist. She couldn't just let this happen. Finally, she straightened her back, lifted her head and met his eyes, holding his gaze. "If you touch me, he'll kill you."

"Nothin' to say I won't kill him, you know."

A dark shape materialized behind him. "*I* say you won't," Spencer said, voice as cold as his eyes.

Joe whirled to face the threat he hadn't anticipated. "What're you talking about?"

Spencer spoke softly, but with a sharp edge. "I'll also tell you right now that if you bother her again, if you lay a finger on her, she's right. I *will* kill you."

"I was just teasing her a little. That's all. Ain't that so, Leah?"

She kept her mouth closed, even though agreeing might lessen the tension that made the air hard to breathe.

Spencer leaned toward the other man until he was right in his face. "Do you hear me?"

"I hear you!" Joe yelled, and stormed forward. His shoulder bashed Spencer's, but he kept going. A slam seconds later was the front door of the lodge.

Spencer took Joe's place in the doorway. "Where's Dirk?"

"I don't know." She used the hem of her T-shirt to wipe her forehead. "He might still be in the kitchen. Why?"

"I expect him to watch out for you when I can't be here."

"I thought he's here to make sure none of us make a run for it."

The grim set of Spencer's mouth didn't ease. "Well, that, too."

"Will you expect TJ Galt to watch out for me? Or Jennifer's husband? Or… Is Lisa married?"

"Not married. She lives with Del Schmidt. And no, I wouldn't ask any of the other men to protect you. Which leaves me with a problem."

How reassuring. "Leaves *you* with a problem? That sounds like *my* problem."

He shot a glance over his shoulder. "Keep your voice down."

Leah opened her mouth again but had the sense to close it. She hadn't sounded meek or deferential at all, which would set any of the others wondering about him, too.

"I'm sorry," she whispered.

As usual, his expression remained unemotional, even as his gaze never left her face. "Did you have a choice of jobs?" he asked after a minute.

Leah shook her head. "I wouldn't expect to when I'm the newcomer. They don't know me."

"No." He rubbed a hand over his face in what she'd decided was the closest to betraying frustration or indecision that he came. "Finish up here. I'll decide what we're going to do after lunch."

She nodded, hesitated…and went back on her hands and knees to resume scrubbing. Not that this ancient linoleum would ever look clean again.

"I'll take over here this afternoon," Spencer said during a break in conversations around the table while they ate.

Heads turned, the silence prolonged. When Higgs said, "I'll stick around, too," the atmosphere changed.

Many of them had the same interpretation: their leader intended to discuss plans with Spencer, the chosen, while everyone else, the mere grunts, continued physical training.

And yeah, Spencer thought with some irony, he'd been guilty of plenty of apple polishing to achieve just this outcome. What he earned today were some hateful glances directed his way only when the colonel wouldn't see them.

Only Rick Metz kept chewing with no visible reaction. It wouldn't have crossed his mind that he could have a planning role. The question was why Dirk looked relieved. The same man was never allowed to hang around the lodge all day. Spencer wondered if Dirk knew the other women weren't safe from TJ or Tim Fuller.

By God, maybe he should slip Leah a knife so she could protect herself.

Nice thought, but even if she could bring herself to stick it into her attacker, the ultimate outcome wouldn't be good.

Fear of him was her only real protection. He had to say a few quiet words to men besides Joe Osenbrock.

As he and Higgs waited while the other men left the lodge and the women cleared the long table, Spencer tried hard to focus on what might be an important step in closing this damn investigation, instead of on the woman who had become his Achilles' heel.

LEAH WISHED SHE could hear what the two men were talking about at the table, but she couldn't make out a word. She had a feeling it was important, but she couldn't think of an excuse to sidle close enough to eavesdrop. Jennifer Fuller was in the pantry making sure she had everything for tonight's dinner, which was to be lasagna. Leah had noticed that she poked her head out pretty regularly to survey her worker bees. As intimidated as she was around the men, she seemed to relish lording it over the other women.

Helen was well aware of when they were alone. Now, as she handed over a rinsed pot for Leah to dry, she whispered, "Spencer said something to Dirk that shook him up real bad. Do you know what happened?"

Just as quietly, Leah said, "Joe Osenbrock got me alone when I was cleaning the bathroom and threatened to…you know."

Helen blushed and ducked her head.

"Spencer heard him and was really mad. I guess he thought Dirk should have kept Joe away from me."

"Dirk didn't know nothing about Joe being back here in the lodge. He wouldn't have let anyone hurt you if he'd known!"

Leah hadn't known a whisper could sound indignant. She smiled at the small, anxious woman. "I believe you. He seems nice."

She didn't actually know any such thing, but at least he didn't look at her the way most of the other men did, and she hadn't been able to help noticing that Helen didn't seem afraid of Dirk.

"Spencer was mostly mad at Joe," she confided.

"I bet." Elbow deep in sudsy water, Helen wielded a scrubbing pad with vigor on the pot that had held the baked beans that were part of the lunch menu. They'd been really good, considering the limited resources anyone cooking had to draw on. Plus, the commercial stove and oven had been installed at least thirty years ago. The miracle was that they mostly still worked.

Possibly that was because Uncle Edward had hardly ever used them himself. Most of the time, he'd insisted the hot plate in his apartment was all he needed. Why make baked beans from scratch when you could open a can? Leah remembered her mother's rolled eyes. Mom had bought him a microwave their last summer here, which had intrigued him. It was safe to say that, as her great-uncle got older and crankier, he would have been even less likely to be inclined to bake a cake or cook anything from scratch.

Too bad he hadn't lingered as a ghost. If he could know, he'd be horrified by the consequences of his gift to her. If he'd actually rented the resort to this group in previous summers—and she increasingly doubted that story—he couldn't have known what those men believed, and especially not what they intended. He'd been courtly, old-fashioned in some ways, but also accepting of people's vagaries. Not for a minute would he have condoned hate-mongering or a threat to the country he loved. Having served as a paratrooper in World War II, Uncle Edward had spent time in a Nazi prisoner-of-war camp. Maybe those experiences explained why, upon returning, he'd chosen a solitary life in the midst of one of American's wildest places.

Handing Leah the next pan, Helen whispered again. "Dirk says you *own* this place."

"My great-uncle left it to me in his—"

Helen jabbed her hard in the side. "Sshh!"

"What…?" Oh. Spencer had settled himself in the doorway between the main room and the kitchen, his posture relaxed, his gaze shifting between the two women. Leah almost whispered that Helen didn't need to worry about Spencer—but if his reputation as the baddest man here was to survive, she needed to keep her mouth shut. If Helen told Dirk what she'd said, he could tell anyone.

She was supposed to be afraid of him, and she needed to act the part. In fact, she immediately imitated Helen's fearful posture. But her forehead crinkled as her hand stopped in the act of wiping out the pot. *Wait*, she thought in alarm. *I am afraid of him*.

Wasn't she?

Chapter Six

"How would you feel about going for a walk?" Spencer asked once they left the lodge, post Leah's KP duty after dinner. He felt restless, but didn't dare take a run and leave her behind. The sky was still bright, with night not falling at this time of year until close to ten o'clock. Then he took another look at her. She moved without any noticeable pain, but she'd been brought down to the ground hard yesterday. "Scratch that. You're probably beat."

Flashing him a surprised look, Leah said, "Beat? Why…oh. The cleaning. You do know I don't sit behind a desk all day back home, don't you?"

He hadn't thought about it, but of course she wouldn't.

"I'm on my feet all day long. I see patients, package bloodwork to send out or run screens myself. Medicate and give fluids. Assist in surgery. Like just about everyone else, I help clean kennels and runs. And I subdue everything from snarling Dobermans to raging bulls while one of the vets does an exam or procedure. Oh, and then there's the wildlife. We do the care for a local refuge, which means holding down an eagle with a broken wing or a cougar dented by a car bumper. A little house cleaning is nothing."

Spencer would have laughed if he hadn't felt sure they

were being watched. He appreciated this woman. Leah's bravado was welcome in place of self-pity.

"Of course," she continued, her tone musing, "on the job I wouldn't be worrying whenever a man walked into the room whether he had in mind raping or murdering me. That does take a toll."

"Yeah," he said, a little hoarsely. "It would do that."

"A walk sounds good. After all," she added wryly, "as Colonel Higgs said, I couldn't be held captive in a more beautiful place on earth."

Spencer turned his head, for a rare moment letting himself take in the extraordinary panorama. It had been many years since he'd spent time in the Pacific Northwest, a fact he suddenly regretted.

White-capped Mount Baker dominated the sky to the southeast, while more jagged, and farther distant, Shuksan would have been impressive enough. Other mountains were visible almost everywhere he looked. This was rugged country, and yet not far from the Puget Sound and Strait of Georgia to the west. They were surrounded by forests that had never been logged, an arc of vivid blue above, thin grasses and a dazzling array of flowers. Once they passed the last cabin, he found himself picking his way more carefully than usual because of the wildflowers.

"This is one of the prettiest times of the year here, with so much in bloom," Leah remarked.

Grimly focused on his task, he'd hardly noticed the flowers until five minutes ago. After a moment he said, "I know a few of these. Who hasn't seen a foxglove or a tiger lily?"

For some reason the idea of him gardening in some distant future crossed his mind. Not like he wanted to spend another decade living this way. Once this was over…what if he bought an actual house? Even thought about a wife, having children. What would it be like, coming home at five most days?

His picture of that kind of life was vague, not quite in focus, but he discovered it did include a bed of flowers and a lawn. He hadn't mowed a lawn since he was a boy.

As if she'd followed his thoughts, Leah looked around almost in bemusement. "My mother is a gardener. I always figured someday I'd have a house and yard, too." She went quiet for a minute, likely reflecting on the very distinct possibility she'd never have that chance. But she forged on. "I remember Uncle Edward telling me about the wildflowers. There." She pointed. "That's an easy one, a red columbine. And yarrow, and bleeding heart, and monkshood."

"Isn't monkshood poisonous?"

"I think so. I don't remember if it's the leaves or the flowers or what." She looked pensive, then shook her head. "Oh, and that's goat's beard and…"

He let the recitation roll over him. He wouldn't remember which flower was which, but he liked that she knew and was willing to talk to him.

"When's the last time you were up here?" he asked at one point.

"I think I was twelve, so it's been forever." A pained expression crossed her face. "I'm thirty-one. I don't know why I never thought to get up here to see Uncle Edward. I loved our visits when I was a kid."

"We tend not to look back." He was ashamed to realize how many friends he'd let go over the years. He couldn't even claim to have a close relationship with his own brother or parents anymore. Disappearing for months at a time wasn't conducive to maintaining ties with other people.

Leah stopped walking feet away from the bank of the lake that filled a bowl probably scoured by a long-ago glacier. That was not where she was looking, though. Instead, she turned a gaze on him that was so penetrating, it was all he could do not to twitch.

Instead, he raised an eyebrow. "See anything interesting?"

"Yes. Is there a single other man up here even remotely interested in the names of wildflowers?"

"It's not the kind of thing we talk about," he admitted, although he knew the answer. No. "Anyway, who said I am?"

She frowned. "Do you have any hobbies?"

He ought to shut her down right now, but she'd taken him by surprise, as she often did.

"I target shoot. That's relaxing." More reluctantly, he said, "When I can, I play in a basketball league." Baseball, too.

"All militant white supremacists?"

"Ah...we don't talk politics." For good reason.

"Why didn't you assault me last night?"

Spencer was offended enough, he was afraid it showed.

"I told you, I don't hurt women," he said shortly. "It doesn't turn me on at all." Except that she had to have felt his morning erection, so she knew that she did turn him on. For all she knew, though, he woke up with one every morning.

She nodded slowly, the green of her eyes enriched by the many shades of green surrounding them. His fingers curled into his palms as he resisted the desire to cup her good cheek, trace her lips with his thumb.

Damn, his heartbeat had picked up.

But she wasn't thinking about him kissing her, because what she said was, "I don't believe you'd blow up innocent people to make a point."

This time he felt more than alarm. "Who says we intend to kill anyone who's innocent?"

"How can you not?" she said simply. "Unless you plan to blow up Congress…"

That idea was enough to make him break out in a cold sweat. He was beginning to fear that Higgs's plans really were that grandiose.

But she shook her head. "I refuse to believe there aren't good politicians."

Having met some decent men and women who had run for office because they believed in service, he conceded her point. "What are you saying?"

"I think you're an undercover federal agent."

He should laugh. Jeer, tell her to take the rose-colored glasses off. He should slap her, which would fit with the role he played.

Instead, he growled, "I told you how dangerous it is to suggest that."

"We're all by ourselves."

She'd made mistakes today. Carried herself with too much pride, looked people in the eye when she shouldn't. Would she be more careful, or less, if she knew the truth?

"If I tell you why I'm here, you have to become an Oscar-worthy actress," he said harshly. "I can't afford for you to get mouthy with anyone, or say something to me when we can be overheard. Do you understand?"

Her expression altered. "Yes. That little episode today with Joe was a good reminder that not only am I in danger every minute, but you are, too."

"I would be either way." He shrugged. "Me demanding an exclusive on you came on top of what some of the men see as Higgs's favoritism. I wasn't popular anyway. Now it's fair to say jealousy and dislike have become hate."

"Isn't hate their reason for existence?" Leah pointed out.

"For the men." Whether the women took the same world view, he had no idea. And it wasn't all of the men. He wished he could figure out how to get Dirk out of the hole he'd dug, but nothing had come to him. There were a couple of others he'd wondered about, but it wasn't his job to separate the deadly fanatics from the ones who were willing to go along. As Leah put it, to blow up innocents.

She didn't say anything else, just waited.

While undercover, Spencer had never, not once, told anyone his true identity or purpose. He'd also never let himself get tangled up with a nice woman who depended on him for her very survival, and who was handling a terrifying experience with dignity and determination.

He sighed, half turning away from her. "You're right. I'm FBI. I've been under with this group for five months now, although we only moved up here for intensive training four weeks ago. Higgs has been on our radar for a long time. Even before he retired, he'd expressed some really marginal ideas. In fact, his obvious contempt for his boss at the time, a two-star general who happened to be black, led to a behind-the-scenes push to early retirement. Unfortunately, it appears that enraged him, helping motivate him to turn militant."

Out of the corner of his eye, he saw that she hadn't done much but blink during this recitation. She'd seen right through him, all right, which made him question how convincing *his* act was.

"I have plenty of evidence to bring down everyone here. We can't let them get to the point of launching their attack. But there's more I need to know. Like when that main event is scheduled for, and what the target is."

"Does that matter if, well, you prevent it from ever happening?"

"Yeah. What if there's another cell training for the same attack? I've seen no indication Higgs is working with anyone else, but we don't have phone service up here. A few times he's made a trip down to Bellingham. Nobody knows what he does while they're shopping for supplies. He could be meeting someone. If he's emailing, it could be from a computer at the library." Frustration added extra grit to his voice. "He has added new posts to a couple of extremist sites, but they're so cryptic we suspect they might really be messages." He gave his head a shake. "We need to keep walking."

"Oh!" She cast a nervous glance back toward the lodge. "Yes, of course."

Circling the lake, he walked fast enough she had to ask him to slow down. He kept talking, telling her his larger goals: making sure they knew who was backing the group, and who was supplying the arms. Moneyed, powerful men were his real target.

"That really is a…a rocket launcher?"

His jaw tightened. "US Military issue. We have two of 'em."

Leah breathed what was probably really a prayer. He agreed with the sentiment wholeheartedly.

Well before they neared the tree line, he said, "I shouldn't have told you this much, but I don't see that it matters. Just remember, even the smallest hint of any of it is a death sentence for me."

She wasn't looking at him. "And me."

"Unless you get the idea you can bargain with Higgs."

Her shoulders stiffened and her chin came up. "I wouldn't!"

"No." He let his tone soften. "I don't think you would."

She sniffed indignantly.

The color of the sky was deepening, the purple tint making it harder for the eye to see outlines.

"This is the end of our discussion," he told her. "I can't be a hundred percent sure the cabin isn't bugged. From here on out, your job is to avoid notice as much as you can."

"What if...if I was able to get a look at Colonel Higgs's room when I'm cleaning?"

"Don't even think about it," he said flatly. "You are not a federal agent. You're a vet tech."

"My life depends on you learning what you have to so we can leave, you know. I'm not going to sit and wait if I can help."

"If you found names or numbers, you wouldn't recognize their meaning. I would. I repeat. The answer is no."

Her chin went back up but she didn't argue again. Spencer wasn't entirely reassured. This was why he shouldn't have told her so much. That said, people talked within earshot of the women as if they were pieces of furniture, much as servants might have been treated in a big house in eighteenth-century England. They could get lucky—but he didn't mention that possibility, because she was too gutsy for her own good. If she got caught where she shouldn't be, *trying* to eavesdrop—she was dead.

They were dead, since he couldn't stand back and let her die, whatever his priorities ought to be.

As they approached the line of cabins, she whispered, "Is Spencer your real name? Or Wyatt?"

Damn her insatiable curiosity.

"It doesn't matter," he snapped.

A faint squeak came to his ears. In response to his irritation, Leah's step hitched and she hunched a little, probably not realizing that she was looking cowed. As little as he liked having that effect on her, her timing was impeccable. That little creep Arne Larson had just stepped out on the porch of his cabin, the one at the end.

"Got her trained, I see," Arne remarked.

Spencer gave her an indifferent glance. "She's smarter than Osenbrock. She knows what's good for her."

Arne laughed, acid in the sound. "Yeah, I heard you told Joe what's what. He didn't like it, you know."

Spencer shrugged. "He's not thinking about what counts. I watched you shooting today and saw a big improvement."

Arne might not like him, but he preened. Spencer's sniper creds inspired some awe among this bunch.

Then he and Leah were past Arne's cabin and the one beyond it, finally reaching his. She trailed him up the porch steps like the obedient little woman she wasn't. She stayed right inside next to the door, too, while he did his usual walk-through with his Sig Sauer in his hand.

THE SHOWER AFFORDED only a tepid stream of water, but it was adequate for Leah to wash her hair. The shampoo dripping down her face stung, though, and had her mumbling, "Ow, ow, ow."

Somebody had absconded with her hair dryer before Spencer grabbed her suitcase. He had even reclaimed her purse, minus everything important.

"I have your wallet," he told her, not offering to return it. "Phone and keys are in our great leader's possession."

She'd heard him use that phrase before, equally laden with sarcasm. Never in anyone else's hearing, of course. She couldn't wrap her mind around everything he'd

told her. He'd confirmed her suspicion and more, but…
could he have lied to ensure her cooperation? Of course
he could have—but she didn't believe he had. The very
fact that he'd gone out on such a limb in the first place
for her sake was a strong argument for his honesty and,
yes, possession of what some people would call the old-
fashioned quality of honor. Personally, Leah was big on
honor right now. Where would she be without it?

She towel-dried her hair as well as she could, brushed
it and left the bathroom.

Spencer looked up from where he lounged on what
she'd realized was a futon in the living area. Every time
she saw him, she was hit afresh with awareness of how
sexy he was. Partly it was a matter of bone structure and
the contrast between icy, pale eyes and deeply tanned
skin, but that wasn't all. He had a brooding quality that
got to her. And he'd tried to protect her.

He hadn't even taken off his boots, and his gun lay
within easy reach. He was prepared for anything at a
moment's notice. The tension really wore on her, but he
seemed to take it for granted.

"What are you reading?" She nodded at the book.

"Huh?" He seemed to turn his eyes from her. "Oh. It's
Calvin Coolidge's autobiography."

"Really? Is he that interesting?"

"You might say he's become relevant again." If there
was dryness in his tone, Leah doubted anyone else would
have noticed it. "Coolidge endorsed a law in 1924 that
cut immigration by half, with national origin quotas. He
considered southern and eastern Europeans to be geneti-
cally inferior. The law led to something like forty years
of reduced immigration. Higgs thought I'd like to read
this. I'm not sure he paid any attention to Coolidge's
other policies."

"Is it interesting?"

"His prose isn't riveting." With a grimace, Spencer stuck a torn strip of paper between pages as a bookmark. "You ready for bed?"

"I guess."

He ushered her into the bedroom, then returned to the main room to make his rounds of the windows and check locks. For what good they'd do, she couldn't help thinking. There were new, shiny dead bolts on the front and back doors, but two of the windows had cracked panes, and the frames would splinter under one blow. Of course, that would alert him instantly, and she'd already seen how fast he could move.

When he returned, she still stood beside the bed.

He raised his eyebrows.

"You aren't going to put handcuffs on me again, are you?"

"That depends. Can I trust you not to try anything?"

Somebody could be listening, she reminded herself. "I won't." She went for very, very humble. "I know you'll take care of me."

He cracked a smile that made her mouth go dry, so drastically did it alter his face. Not soften it, exactly, but a hint of warmth along with wicked sensuality shifted her perception of him. Sexy when somber, angry or expressionless, he might be irresistible if he just kept smiling at her.

Of course he didn't. Dear Lord, he wouldn't dare get in the habit! Imagine what the others would think if they saw him.

His eyes burned into hers. Had he read her mind? Well, thinking he was sexy, and okay, feeling a yearning ache deep inside didn't mean she was having sex with him.

She managed a glare that resulted in the corners of his mouth curving again, but once she climbed into bed, he did turn off the light before he stripped and slid in beside her.

Even his whisper held a little grit coming out of the darkness. "I'd complain about the mattress, but I like knowing what'll happen the minute you fall asleep."

The trouble was, so did she.

Chapter Seven

Leah had zero chance to get anywhere near her great-uncle's apartment, appropriated by Colonel Higgs. Jennifer Fuller had the privilege of cleaning it, although only when he was there. Otherwise, another of those shiny new dead bolts kept the nosy out.

However tempting an opportunity would be, Leah wouldn't have seized it. Spencer was right; she'd have no idea what she should be looking for. Anyway, she had no desire to find herself in another spot like she had when Joe Osenbrock cornered her. If Spencer hadn't shown up, she wanted to think she could have fought back effectively or that Dirk would have intervened, but she wasn't stupid enough to buy into comforting lies. Joe was muscular, mean and lacking in a conscience. Dirk had an athletic body, but his muscles didn't bulge quite as much, and he struck her as a little quieter and less aggressive than most of the others. Even if he'd tried to step in to protect her—albeit for Spencer's sake, not hers—he'd have had the shit beaten out of him. Then Joe would have been mad.

Today, in between breakfast and lunch, Leah volunteered hastily for cleaning jobs that would keep her in the main spaces and working with at least one of the other women. There were four of them here, instead of five; TJ said Shelley wasn't feeling well.

Lifting benches around the table while Lisa Dempsey swept under them, Leah tried to start a conversation. If she made friends, she might learn something, right? Well, it wouldn't be with Lisa, who completely ignored her, responding only when Leah said something relevant, like, "I see something under there you missed."

She never looked Leah in the eye, either, which was a good reminder to her that she was supposed to imitate the other women, not befriend them.

Jennifer cracked briefly when Leah said, "That lasagna you made was amazing. You must have worked in a restaurant."

"Thank you," she said grudgingly. "I learned from my mother, that's all."

"Oh, well, I hope you have a daughter who'll learn from you."

Jennifer turned her back and walked away.

A few minutes later Helen whispered, "You shouldn't've said that to her. She's had miscarriages. I think—"

A footstep presaging the appearance of Del Schmidt silenced her.

Chagrined, Leah scraped frost out of the old chest freezer. Could Jennifer's body just not hold on to a fetus? One of the veterinarians Leah worked with had had two miscarriages. She and her husband had been devastated.

In this case, though, Leah couldn't help wondering whether abuse from her husband had ended each pregnancy. Maybe that was unjust, but she didn't like the way Tim talked to his wife, or how he'd shoved her hard up against a wall when he thought she was giving him some lip. It was all Leah could do to pretend she hadn't seen what happened.

Spencer was one of the last to show up for lunch, shredded beef tacos and Spanish rice today. He glanced at Leah when she was the last to sidle up to the table and take a seat, but he was immediately distracted by something the man beside him was saying. Shawn somebody. Or was that Brian… Thompson? Townsend? These guys looked an awful lot alike, all Caucasian although tanned, hair shaved or cut very short, big muscles, tattoos on their arms or peeking above their collars. Arne Larson's looked a lot like one arm of a Nazi swastika, which she thought was more than a little ironic, given how the Scandinavian countries had resisted the Nazi invasion. Obviously, he identified with the invaders and maybe even their genocide.

Leah had a sickening thought. What if her mother had married a black or Latino man? Things would have been different if she, a woman with dark skin, had driven up to announce that she owned the resort. Would Spencer have had any chance at all to save her?

No. How could he have? Higgs wouldn't have bothered giving her his impassioned speech about inciting a civil war to restore this great country to the *true* Americans, because she wouldn't have been one in his eyes.

Her appetite scant, she picked at her food and kept her head down by inclination as well as orders, not even looking toward Spencer.

Toward the end of the meal, though, she heard Tim Fuller say into a lull, "We're running low on food. Jennifer made a list."

Higgs mulled that over for a minute before saying, "Wyatt, you take Lisa tomorrow." He scanned the men around the table. "Schmidt, you go, too."

Leah didn't dare look at Spencer to see if he'd betrayed any emotion at all. She hoped she'd succeeded in hiding how she felt, but she was quite sure she wouldn't be able to take another bite, not when she couldn't swallow it. Fear squeezed her throat as if a powerful hand had closed around it.

HIGGS TURNED A cold stare on Spencer, who had stopped in front of him with crossed arms. The two men were on their way toward the obstacle course built their first week up here, taking in part of the meadow and forest. "I don't want to hear it."

Spencer said what he was thinking anyway. "You didn't like me taking Leah out of your control."

Frosting over, the colonel said, "*Nobody* here is out of my control. Did you forget that?"

He had, misjudging how Ed Higgs would see him stepping in to remove Leah from the chessboard. Damn, Spencer thought incredulously, he was going to have to take her and run, tonight while they still had a chance.

"Are you planning to have her yourself?" he asked.

Higgs's eyes narrowed. "I don't rape women."

"You just encourage your followers to do it."

"Is that what you think?"

Jaw jutting out, Spencer couldn't back down. "I think that's what you're threatening. Take me out of the picture, show me how I rate."

"I've developed a lot of respect for you. I thought I could trust you. Since you set eyes on her, I'm having to wonder."

What was it he'd said to Leah? *You have to become an Oscar-worthy actor.* That was it.

He scoffed, "You seriously think I'd let a sexy piece of tail divert me from our plans? I took her because I don't like doing without, and I figured I was entitled. If you want her—" *I'll have to kill you. Nope, shrug as if she's nothing to you.*

Higg's relaxation was subtle. "I don't."

"Then what's the problem?"

"The problem is you getting in my face because I chose you to run an errand and you don't want to do it because you're afraid someone will put a move on her in your absence."

"No," Spencer said coolly. "I'm afraid someone will think they can get away with taking what's mine, and then I'll have to kill him. You don't want to lose a soldier in our war, do you?"

"You said yourself, she doesn't matter worth shit," the colonel said impatiently. "What's your problem?"

"My problem is that I laid my reputation on the line. *That* matters to me. If you expect me to exert any authority over this bunch, it should matter to you, too. If someone hurts her and smirks at me when I get back tomorrow, what's it going to look like if I back down from what I promised?" He let that settle for a minute before shaking his head and raising an eyebrow. "I'm not willing to do that. I'll do your errands tomorrow, but if I find out anyone touched a hair on her head, there'll be violence. I'm just telling you, that's all. Don't be surprised."

Higgs muttered an obscenity. "Fine. I get it. I'll reinforce your message tomorrow. If that'll satisfy you, General?"

Spencer snapped a salute. "It's Captain, as you know quite well."

"I never could verify your service." This was an old complaint.

"The army can be secretive, even with an air force

lieutenant colonel. More so when it comes to the records of spec-ops soldiers."

"Especially snipers," Higgs grumbled. "I got nothing out of them at Fort Bennett."

"Well, it's not as if that's something I could fake," Spencer pointed out. "You want to get me a different rifle, I can make a kill shot from over a thousand feet out."

"Why not the rifle you're using?"

Spencer had said this before, but he didn't mind repeating himself. "The M82 loses accuracy over nine hundred yards. It's a mallet, not a stiletto."

"A mallet's what we want, and you're right. You've proved your abilities and more. I'd take one of you over ten of the rest of these grunts."

"They have their uses."

Higgs smiled. "Indeed they do."

Repelled by that smile, Spencer stifled his need to hear Higgs promise that they had a deal. Demanding any such thing would undo all the good he'd just accomplished.

If he had to kill someone tomorrow, he was prepared, but that would do shit for Leah.

His self-control was rarely strained, but as he held back a growl, he was freshly reminded that she'd put more than a few cracks in it.

SCUTTLING ALONG AT Spencer's shoulder in the morning, Leah asked, "Won't Higgs be outside most of the day, like usual?" Spencer hadn't wanted to talk about it last night. In fact, his mood had been foul.

"Probably." His long stride ate up the ground. "He promised to reinforce my message where you're concerned. He knows what will happen if anyone bothers you."

"Well, that's reassuring," she mumbled. Nothing like

knowing he'd take revenge for her, even if by then she was a bloody, bruised piece of pulp.

"Stick with the other women and you should be all right," he ordered before they reached the lodge and there was no more chance to talk.

Should was not the most reassuring word in this context.

Since she'd been designated cook for the first time this morning, she had to shove her worries to the back of her mind. With only a little advice on the quantities needed to feed nineteen men and five—no, four—women, she competently turned out pancakes and two platters piled with nice crisp bacon. Nobody said, "Hey, good job," but as they served the food she felt part of the quartet in a way she hadn't before.

Of course they'd pretend not to see if someone like Joe Osenbrock assaulted her in the middle of the kitchen.

During the meal Spencer ate mechanically, never so much as glancing at her. The table was barely cleared when he, Lisa and Del Schmidt went out the door. Feeling hollow, Leah pretended not to notice.

While the other men headed out for whatever training scheduled for today, Tim Fuller took up a position in the kitchen, his irritation plain.

Did he hate this detail? His wife seemed more self-effacing than usual, which made Leah suspect either he'd been posted out of rotation or was missing something especially fun—say, they were going to find out today what happened when they fired a rocket into a big pile of boulders.

Had they tried out their rocket launchers yet? They surely wouldn't dare shoot one upward. Wouldn't that be picked up on air force or civilian airport radars?

As she was setting the table for lunch, two men walked

in. Joe Osenbrock and Carson somebody, another look-alike. Joe's expression turned ugly as he looked at her.

"Coffee," he snapped.

She set down the pile of silverware on napkins and wordlessly returned to the kitchen.

"Joe and Carson want coffee," she said.

"I'll pour it," Helen offered.

Leah smiled weakly. "Thanks."

A minute later she set the mugs down in front of the two men, careful to follow Spencer's instructions. Head bowed, shoulders rounded, avoid meeting their eyes. She hoped they couldn't tell that her pulse was racing so fast she felt light-headed.

Neither thanked her, of course. Joe flicked a glance past her, as if checking to see whether anyone was watching.

Knowing she had no choice, she continued setting the table. She finished and headed for the kitchen just as she heard the front door open again, followed by a burst of voices. She hadn't realized Tim had come out to the dining room until she almost bumped into him.

He stopped her with one hand on her arm. "You're a lucky bitch," he murmured. "Don't count on that lasting."

Leah shuddered. The minute he released her, she hurried into the kitchen. Had he been assigned to watch out for her? Was that why he'd followed her from the kitchen...and why Joe had kept his distance?

Maybe...but she knew a threat when she heard one.

GETTING AWAY FROM Schmidt long enough to make a phone call wasn't easy, but Spencer managed. He'd ordered Schmidt to stay with Lisa while he used the john. Then he helped himself to a phone he had spotted at a momentarily empty cashier's station and took it down the hall

toward the public restrooms, an office and what appeared
to be an employee break room. It was likely password
protected, of course, and he had a phone he could use, but
he couldn't be a hundred percent sure that it was still secure. Even if it had been found, he doubted anyone in the
group was sophisticated enough to know how to record
his conversation or trace numbers he called, but better
safe than sorry. If he could get away with borrowing—

Yes. He'd gotten lucky.

Thank God Ron answered. "Special Agent Ron
Abram."

"This is Wyatt." No, that wasn't his name, but he didn't
use his own name even in theoretically safe moments.
He had to *think* of himself as Spencer Wyatt. "I've only
got a minute."

"I'm glad you called. I've been worrying."

A woman emerged from the restroom, head bent over
her own phone as she passed.

"I have problems," Spencer said. He summarized the
events of the past few days, from Leah Keaton's arrival to
the "deal" he'd made with Ed Higgs to ensure her safety.
"Even though I don't want to quit until I have all the info
we need, part of me wants to throw her in my SUV and
take off. Trouble is, I'm not even betting we'd get away
with that. Del Schmidt drove today. I'm wondering if I
won't find the starter or alternator have kicked the bucket.
Or worse, it runs for five minutes and then dies. As it is,
Higgs keeps the keys when we're not using the vehicles."

"You're not driving today?"

"No. I wasn't given the option, which is one reason I
suspect sabotage. By standing up for Leah, I awakened
suspicion. Higgs has called me on it. I think I talked him
around, but I can't be sure."

"If you have to cut and run, we'd have no choice but to raid the resort and pull the plug on the operation."

"Exactly." He watched two teenage boys laughing and bumping shoulders as they headed for the men's room. "Leah's smart. I think she can play her part for a few days. Higgs wants me with him for a meeting Saturday." The day after tomorrow. "I think it'll be a meet to acquire some new arms."

"That's worth holding out for," Abram said.

"I hate keeping a civilian in the mix," Spencer said.

Abram was quiet for a minute. "Damn. I wish you had a panic button."

"You and me both. I can't promise when I'll be able to call again." He saw a woman wearing a checker's nameplate at the cashier station where he'd swiped the phone. "Gotta go."

He quickly deleted a record of his call, shoved the phone in a pocket and strolled that way. Just as he reached it, he said, "Hey! Somebody lost a phone," and bent over, rising with it in his hand.

"Oh, thank goodness!" she exclaimed. "You'd think I'd have heard it drop."

"It's not damaged, is it?"

"Well, there's no crack anyway." She beamed. "Thank you."

"No problem."

When he rejoined Lisa and Del, now heaping packages of meat into one of the two carts, he asked, "We get any desserts? My sweet tooth has been aching."

Lisa almost forgot herself so much as to smile. "I'm supposed to pick up some flats of strawberries and blueberries for pies, and rhubarb for a cake."

"What about some apple pies? Let's get plenty of ice cream."

Nodding in agreement, Del said, "We need to load up on chips, too."

"I'm supposed to keep to a budget," she said nervously.

"If it looks like we're going to run over, I'll pick up the extra," Spencer said. "Remember, we're feeding another mouth, too." Even if Leah hadn't eaten enough to keep a bird alive, as far as he could see. He'd have to get on her about that.

"Thanks," Lisa said shyly. "I don't want to make anyone mad."

"I'll be mad if I don't get an apple pie," Spencer joked.

The mood stayed good as they shopped and then packed huge quantities of food in the rear and on one backseat of the big SUV. Spencer made sure neither of the others saw even a trace of his growing tension as they made the drive heading northeast on increasingly poor roads.

If he found Leah hurt, he wasn't sure he wouldn't grab the closest fully automatic weapon and start spraying bullets.

When at last they pulled up in front of the lodge, he hopped out, waited for the rear hatch to rise and grabbed bags of potatoes and a couple of flats of canned goods, then took the steps to the porch. He had to shift the load a little to reach the knob, shouldered the door open and walked in. The first person he saw was Joe Osenbrock, sitting beside Tim Fuller at the long table. Spencer clenched his teeth until his back molars hurt.

He passed the two without a word, without pausing long enough to read expressions, and went into the kitchen.

One of the other women was off to his right. He didn't even know which one. All he saw was Leah, turning from the sink, her hands encased in plastic gloves, a scrub brush held in one of them. The relief and something more that suffused her face did a number on him.

"Leah," he said hoarsely.

Can't drop my load and take her into my arms.

He couldn't even ask if she was all right. He hated that.

Her eyes widened at whatever she saw on his face. What she did was flush, draw a deep breath and say, "Oh, good. I was hoping potatoes were on the list. I'm not sure we have enough…" She bit her lip and ducked her head. "I'm sorry."

Sorry for? But he knew. Some men here would have backhanded her for that artless chatter, especially given the implication that he might have screwed up by not buying everything that was needed.

He tore his eyes from her, saw Jennifer watching them. "Where do you want this stuff?" he asked.

"Oh, in the pantry." Maybe reading his expression, she added hastily, "Or…anywhere is good. We can put everything away."

Footsteps behind him heralded Del's arrival with more food. On his heels, Lisa carried more than she should have to.

"Wherever is best," he said shortly, and went to the pantry.

As he made three more trips back and forth from the SUV, he couldn't help wondering what Jennifer thought she'd seen, and whether she talked to her husband. Or whether he listened to her if she did.

After depositing the last load, he said, "I hope dinner isn't far off. I'm starved."

It was Jennifer who answered, the tiniest edge in her voice. "No, not if Leah gets on with that potato salad."

"I'm hurrying," Leah said, sounding chastened.

Turning to stalk out of the kitchen, Spencer knew he'd
be happy never to hear her sounding so diminished again.

But if they were going to hold out long enough for
him to make this mission a success, that was one wish
he wouldn't get.

Chapter Eight

They didn't talk during the walk back to the cabin. With the sun still high in the sky, it might have been midafternoon. Days were noticeably longer here than even in Portland, Oregon, she'd noticed.

Inside, Spencer did his usual walk-through, then said, "Waste of a goddamn day."

"We…we really were running out of food."

He made a rough sound. "Higgs should have sent Ritchie or Jack Jones."

Leah only vaguely knew who the second man was. Would Spencer dare talk like this if there was any chance at all of a listening device?

Maybe. This barely muted contempt went with the arrogance he projected so well. Deliberately, she thought. Higgs would expect it from him.

"I want apple pie tomorrow," he said. "See to it there is some."

Seeing her bristle, he winked.

In her best "I'm nobody important" tone, Leah said, "Jennifer makes up the menu. She doesn't like it when any of the rest of us make a suggestion."

"Tell her it's from me." He flat-out grinned now. "Lisa knows what I want."

Leah rolled her eyes.

Smile gone, he growled, "Did any of the men bother you today?"

"I... No."

His gaze bored into hers. "You're mine. If anyone so much as laid a hand on you..."

"No. I think they're all scared of you."

"They should be."

Neither of them had sat down. It was too early to go to bed. Leah felt restless and could tell he did, too, but they couldn't go for a walk every evening.

Eyes heavy lidded, he took a step toward her, his fingers flexing. The hunger on his face ignited her own. Leah swallowed. Sex was something they could do. In fact, if the cabin was being bugged, they definitely *should* be having sex. And if that wasn't an excuse, she'd never heard one before.

But he seemed to pull down a shutter, turning away from her and saying gruffly, "You have some books in your suitcase. Why don't you get one? I want to read before we go to bed."

Would anybody buy that? But she knew; he didn't really believe there was a bug, he was just being cautious. She should be grateful he wasn't the kind of man who would use "we need to convince any listener" as an excuse to get her naked.

So she only nodded, went to the bedroom and grabbed one of the books at random. She didn't want to read; she wanted to hear whether he'd had a chance to call his office today and, if so, what he'd learned. She wanted to tell him about the threat issued by Tim, and about the inimical way he and Joe Osenbrock had stared at her. She wanted to know what his lips would feel like on hers.

And she wanted desperately to know when he thought

they could leave—if there was any way they could without getting killed.

But he'd finally lowered himself to one side of the futon, stacked his booted feet on the scarred coffee table and opened his book. He appeared to immediately immerse himself.

Leah sat at the other end of the futon, which really meant she could have stretched out an arm and touched him, and opened her own book. She read a few pages, realized she hadn't taken in a thing, and turned back to start over. She thought the one side of his mouth she could see curled up. So he wasn't any deeper in the biography than she was in the romance she'd picked up.

The next hour dragged. She read, reread and finally plunked the book down without bothering to save her place. She was going crazy here, and Spencer continued to read as if unaware of her. She felt quite sure that wasn't true.

Her mind wandered.

He hadn't answered her question about his name. She *liked* the name Spencer Wyatt. What if his real name was something like…she entertained herself by coming up with a list of not-so-sexy possibilities. Elmer. Homer. Barney. Cornelius. Wilbur.

All names, she realized, that would have been her grandparents' or even great-grandparents' generation. If she'd been born then and *her* name was Dolly or Kitty or…or Winnie, she'd probably have been fine with Barney.

The name Barney wouldn't reduce the man beside her in any way, she admitted to herself in dismay. She couldn't think of much that would.

I can't fall in love with him, she thought in shock. What a ridiculous idea. This gooey mess of emotions in her were completely natural, considering he'd dedicated himself to saving her life and virtue. And *that* was a silly way to think of a vicious crime like rape.

She sighed. She couldn't exactly whine that she was bored.

Only, she didn't want to know when they'd get there; she wanted to know when they could *leave.*

"Why don't you go take a shower?" he said irritably.

"Fine." Leaving her book where it lay, Leah stomped into the bedroom, grabbed clean clothes and went straight to the bathroom without so much as looking in his direction.

The fixtures were all chipped and stained, but they worked. At least she'd be bored *and* clean.

Or scared for her life and clean.

She was sitting on the toilet to take off her shoes and socks and tug her shirt over her head when the bathroom door opened again, almost bumping her knees in the tight space. Startled, she looked up at Spencer.

He crowded her even more to allow him to shut the door behind himself. Then he squeezed past her and turned on the shower.

"What…?" she whispered.

He crouched in front of her. For a second she fixated on the power of his forearms before being distracted by the long muscles in his thighs outlined with the camouflage fabric pulled tight. Then she lifted her gaze to meet his eyes.

"I thought we should talk," he said in a low voice. "I worried about you all day."

"I really am fine. There was only one weird moment." She told him about Joe and Carson coming in, the glance Joe exchanged with Tim and then what Tim had said.

"That son of a bitch threatened you."

"It wasn't that overt. I mean, he didn't say, 'I'll hurt you.' It was more like, 'Next time I won't stop Joe.'"

"I still want to shove his teeth down his throat." Spencer rolled his shoulders. "Damn. Saturday I'll be gone part of the day again."

A greasy ball lodged in her stomach. "Why?"

"Don't know for sure. Higgs asked me to accompany him for a 'meet.'"

"To buy weapons?"

"That's what I think."

The pale silver of his eyes was almost like glass, except not so transparent. Quartz crystal. Shimmering, clear, but still hiding the secrets inside.

"That was one of your goals, wasn't it?"

"Yeah." He cleared his throat. "But I'm asking a lot of you."

What if she said, *Too much?* Could she persuade him to take her and leave? Leah didn't know for sure, but thought he might choose her if she begged.

It took her only a moment to steady herself. "What you're doing is important. If all goes well, you'll prevent a cataclysmic attack on this country." If her voice shook a little, well, who could blame her? "It's my country, too. What's more, anybody stealing weapons bought with my and every other American's tax dollars needs to be locked up for good."

She'd swear that was pride in his eyes. He lifted a hand to her face, gently cupped the injured cheek and said, "You're an amazing woman, Leah Keaton."

Her tremulous smile probably didn't enhance the kick-butt speech, but it *was* a smile. "And don't I know it."

Now he grinned openly. "Pretty bra, too."

"What?" She looked down at herself and felt her face

heat. The vivid green satin probably made her skin look pasty, but she liked the color.

If she wasn't mistaken, his gaze lingered on the swell of her breasts above the fabric, not the bra. He was so close, his hand still holding her jaw, his face nearly level with hers. If she scooted forward...

His pale eyes speared hers. "I won't do that to you." Low, his voice was even grittier than usual.

"Even if I want you to?"

"Even if. You know the balance of power thing. It's swinging heavily in my favor right now."

Leah couldn't deny that was true. But... "I know what I want."

He rose to his feet, letting her see his arousal, but his gaze never left hers. "I want, too," he said quietly. "But we can wait."

She managed a nod, and he left the bathroom.

Did they *have* enough future to allow for some distant, ideal day? she asked herself. But...he was right. Of course he was. What if they triumphed and made it out of here and then she realized she didn't really like him that well? Mightn't she question whether she'd used her body as bribery so he'd keep her at the top of his priority list?

And no, she didn't think he was that man, or she was that woman.

Maybe what she needed to do was believe in him and herself. Believe they'd make it.

She could do that...but she was more aroused than she could ever remember being just from a touch, an exchange of looks.

Now that Spencer knew Leah was willing, he didn't know if he could survive many more nights with full-body contact but him blocked from being able to make a single move. He seriously considered sleeping on the futon, but that would be as torturous in a different way. He still had the original issues, too: he didn't want to be seen sleeping separately from her, and he didn't like the idea of her alone, a room away from him.

Her cheeks were pink when they met in the bedroom, but she wore a long T-shirt over panties that did a number on his libido, slipped into bed and turned her back on him without saying anything.

Spencer swore silently, set his gun within easy reach and stripped down to his own boxers and T-shirt. He turned his back on her, too.

It was not a good night. Far as he could tell, Leah slept better than he did. He couldn't get comfortable, couldn't control his body's reaction to having hers pressed against him, and when he wasn't brooding about why he hadn't taken her up on her offer, he worried about Saturday.

If Tim's suggestion to her meant what Spencer thought it might, she could be in big trouble. Individually, they were all afraid of him, and rightly so. But what if, when he returned, he wouldn't be facing a single man, but several? Would Higgs intervene, or let them tear him up? If he did step in, would the simmer of resentment boil over?

Did Higgs know a couple of the guys were cocky enough to think they could take his place?

Spencer knew he had allies, guys that were glad he could hold the vicious ones in check. Joe Osenbrock, Tim Fuller, TJ Galt and Arne Larson weren't popular with the rank and file. The question was, how many of the others would have the will and guts to stand up with him?

Who should he talk to before he left Saturday with Higgs? Or was there someplace he could stash her before he left? She probably knew this mountainside better than any of them did. She might have an idea.

But then, could he afford the fallout from her temporary disappearance?

Spencer groaned and rolled over again.

One day, a lot of decisions to make—and another night tucked into bed beside Leah.

THE FOLLOWING EVENING, as they left the lodge after dinner, he said curtly, "We're taking a walk." Well aware several men were within earshot, Spencer ignored them. Beside him, Leah ducked her head and nodded.

He strolled down the line of cabins, Leah keeping up. A single sidelong glance let him see her bewilderment.

"What will they think about us doing this?"

He used an obscenity to tell her how little he cared. He *should* care; he and Leah had been so careful to fly under the radar. Somehow, today, he'd met his breaking point.

Leah looked alarmed but was smart enough to say nothing.

When they reached the meadow of wildflowers, he pointed at one with deep pink, almost bell-shaped flowers. "You know that one?"

"Um…a penstemon, I think. There are clumps of hybrid penstemons in my mother's garden."

Last time they were here, he hadn't noticed the faint trace of a path. Left from the days when the resort would have been filled with guests? He followed it toward the lake.

"What did you want to tell me?" Leah asked.

He appreciated her directness.

"I want to talk about tomorrow, but I needed to get away," he admitted.

"Oh. Me, too."

"Everything okay today?"

"Sure. It was a relief having Dirk there again."

"You're getting Del tomorrow. I don't think he'll bother you."

She didn't say anything, but Spencer knew what she was thinking. Would Del stand up to any of the dangerous men on her behalf? Why would he?

Spencer asked himself again if he was doing the right thing. He didn't know any of the potential victims of the planned attack. He knew, liked, admired, wanted Leah. She was the first woman in years who'd gotten to him like this, and he'd only known her for a matter of days. Maybe it was her spirit, relentless in the face of adversity. Or her courage, facing up to dangerous men while suppressing her fears. She'd sure as hell complicated his life. If they had the chance, he could see being happy to have her go right on doing just that.

"Once you sell this place, what'll you do with the money?" he asked, going for the positive. The question was out of the blue, but he was hungry for a few minutes of normalcy. At least, what he vaguely remembered as normalcy.

Obviously surprised, Leah stayed quiet for a minute. Then she said, "I want to go back to school to become a veterinarian. I'd have done that instead of training as a vet tech, except the idea of graduating with such a massive load of debt is really daunting. I'm pretty sure I have the grades and now the experience to be accepted. The money…would make a difference."

"Your parents can't help?"

"I don't want to ask. Mom's a teacher and Dad works for our local utility district. They make a decent living, but they're not rich. They put me through college, and now they should be saving for retirement."

"You intend to specialize as a veterinarian?"

"I don't know. Surgery fascinates me, and I think I'd

get bored if I had to do spays and neuters all day, even if they're important." She shrugged. "One step at a time."

Unfortunately, her next step wouldn't be talking to a real estate agent or filling out graduate school applications.

He said gruffly, "I never asked whether you have a boyfriend."

Leah shook her head. "It's been a while. What about you? I suppose it's hard, given your job."

He fixed his gaze on the mountain, gleaming white, somehow pure. "Next to impossible."

"I don't believe that," she said stoutly. When he didn't say more, she asked, "Was becoming an FBI agent always your dream?"

Dream? Spencer wasn't sure he'd ever had one, the way she meant. Given his lousy mood, that struck him as sad.

He didn't love talking about himself, but he owed her. No, he corrected himself immediately; if he had any thought of pursuing these unexpected feelings for her, he had to open up, at least partway.

"My goal was to get away from home." He hoped she couldn't hear the sadness. "My father and I butted heads for as long as I can remember. I think he loved me—loves me—but his way of showing it was by being a harsh disciplinarian. I joined the army two days after my high school graduation. Barely looked back."

They'd reached the lake now, the surface of the water utterly still, mirroring the rich blue of the sky. Some plants that probably thrived in wetter conditions grew on the shores, but he didn't ask about them.

"I spent ten years in the army." Too much of it killing people. "Got my college degree along the way. A friend who'd left earlier suggested I apply to the FBI, too. I was feeling less sure that the US military was accomplishing anything. I thought I might do more coming at problems from a different direction."

"Isn't one of their biggest divisions counterterrorism?"

"Yeah, I'm in domestic counterterrorism. Unfortunately, we never have the chance to get bored."

"You said you've done this before."

"Gone undercover? Oh, yeah. I'm good at it." His struggles this time all had to do with her.

"I can't imagine living under that kind of stress."

"Right now you are," he pointed out.

She made a face. "That's why I know I wouldn't like it long-term."

"This may be my last time," he heard himself say. "I've almost forgotten who I am."

Ignoring her role, Leah reached for his hand and squeezed.

He turned his body to block anybody watching through binoculars from seeing the physical contact. When she started to withdraw her hand, he held on.

Her cheeks turned pink, but she didn't look away from him. "To me, you're a hero. That's a good place to start."

Spencer shook his head. "Undercover, you get your hands dirty. It's too easy to forget the moral standards you began with. That's one reason—" He broke off. "If I'm ever going to have a life outside the bureau, I figure I ought to get on with it. I'm thirty-seven."

They had reached the edge of the forest on the far side of the lake. His gaze strayed to shadowy coves between tall fir and cedar trees. It wouldn't be such a sin to draw her out of sight and kiss her, would it? If things went south tomorrow… But he refused to think like that. No reason to believe anyone would be stupid enough to attack Leah. He'd made himself clear enough. And what he'd told her last night would hold true until they got free of this bunch. What if she kissed him back mostly because right now she needed him desperately?

Shoring up the walls of his reserve, he released her hand but moved to face her. "Let's talk about tomorrow," he said. "I'd rather you follow your usual routine, but do you know anyplace you could hide if necessary?"

"Now I wish I hadn't given away the hidey-holes between the closets."

He wished she hadn't, either. "No other secret passages in the lodge?"

Leah shook her head. "If I could get as far as the tree line…"

"That would work only if you had a serious head start. Otherwise, they'd be on you like a pack of wolves."

Seeing her already creamy white skin blanch, he was sorry he'd been so blunt, but she needed to know what she faced.

He'd ruled out giving her his backup gun. It would be a disaster if anyone noticed her carrying. He'd also had to consider whether, in a struggle, she could bring herself to pull the trigger quick enough, or at all. However courageous, Leah was at heart a gentle woman, if he was reading her right. Even if she did manage to shoot and kill or at least disable her assailant, then what would happen? He didn't have a suppressor fitted to either of his handguns. The sound of a shot in the vicinity of the lodge versus at the range would bring everyone running.

"Chances are good I'll only be gone for a few hours. Nobody has said anything, so I don't think the rest know Higgs and I are going anywhere tomorrow. I'd try to get you the key to my SUV, but I can't think how to check it out for sabotage without drawing notice."

She was shaking her head even as he spoke. "Even if

I could take off…what would happen to you when you get back?"

"That doesn't matter."

Her expression turned mutinous. "I'm not going to just run away and desert you."

"Leah." Unable to help himself, he took her hand again. "If you ever see an opportunity—a good one— take it. Let me worry about myself. You got that?"

She searched his eyes in that way she did, undoubtedly seeing more than he wanted her to. Finally, she said, "I'll think about it."

Always stubborn.

"You do that," he murmured, and turned away to resume their walk.

Chapter Nine

"Turn in here." Higgs leaned forward, the action pulling against his seat belt. "Go around behind the building."

The long, ramshackle log structure along the old highway might once have been a restaurant or tavern. "What's this place?" Spencer asked as he braked and turned into a weedy gravel lot.

"Somebody told me it was a visitor's center back in the fifties or sixties. Then a restaurant and gift shop." The older man shrugged. "Not sure what else. Not a lot of traffic up this way anymore."

The reason this meeting had been set for here.

Given how little traffic he'd seen in miles, he was surprised the highway was maintained this well. About all he'd seen in ten miles or more was beautiful forest, a waterfall plunging off a cliff only feet from the road and moss and ferns everywhere. Pale, lacy lichen draped like tinsel over branches. When they first set off, mist had clung in dips of the road, blurring the outlines of the evergreens. Half an hour ago they'd risen above it.

Spencer tensed as he drove around the building and saw a pickup already here, parked facing out. It was a dually built for especially heavy loads; black plastic tarps crisscrossed with cord hid whatever was being hauled in the full bed.

"Park so we can load easily," the colonel suggested.

As he backed in, two men climbed out of the pickup, slamming their doors. Even before he saw faces, he noted both men were armed. Of course Spencer was, too, and he felt sure Higgs was, as well.

Turning off the engine and setting the emergency brake, he was slower getting out than Higgs was. He and the older of the two men were already shaking hands when Spencer walked forward.

He knew that face. It set off alarms in him, even if a name to go with it didn't come to him immediately. He just needed to figure out the context where he'd seen the guy before—or his photograph.

Photograph, he decided. In his line of work, he studied thousands. Soon, he'd have a name to go with that face.

The high and tight haircut on the younger man looked military. His scrutiny suggested he, too, was trying to fit Spencer's face into a context. The older guy's was more buzz-cut, graying like Higgs's hair. Same generation, sure as hell their paths had crossed during their military careers. Both, maybe, getting more and more dissatisfied with the direction their country was going as gay marriage became approved, a black man was elected president of the United States and now women wearing hijabs had been elected to congress.

They'd believe passionately that the violent mission they'd chosen was patriotic. Spencer didn't see any hint of deference between them. They saw themselves as equals, he decided. The younger guy was just muscle. Hey, maybe that was all Higgs considered Spencer to be, too.

Spencer exchanged nods with both. The closest to an introduction came when Higgs said, "My second-in-command." Two pairs of eyes raked him appraisingly. He lifted his eyebrows but didn't otherwise react.

"Let's get this done," Higgs's buddy said.

Spencer unlocked and opened the rear doors on the Suburban. Evaluating the load, he thought it would fit. Then he joined the younger guy in pulling the cord off so the tarps could be removed.

This was just like Christmas Day, he thought sardonically. What would be inside the wrapping?

THAT MORNING LEAH and the other women hadn't even started clearing the table before Colonel Higgs swung his legs over the bench and said, "I'll be running an errand."

Everyone around the table looked startled, except for Spencer, of course. He nodded. "Shall I drive?"

Higgs took a set of keys from his pocket and tossed them to Spencer. "We'll take my Suburban. It has more hauling capacity."

Spencer gave a clipped nod, took a last swallow of coffee and rose to leave with Higgs. His gaze passed over Leah without pausing on her, but she made a determined effort to hold on to this last sight of his face as if she'd taken a snapshot.

None of the men moved until they heard the engine start outside. Tim Fuller looked at her.

"Where are they going?"

"I don't know," she said softly. "He doesn't tell me anything."

Every man in the room was staring at her. The effect was unnerving, making it easier to act scared. She stood up and began gathering dirty dishes.

"We're running low on some of the ammunition," one of the men she didn't really know commented.

"He's been promising a new rifle the army is supposed

to be testing. I wouldn't mind getting my hands on that."
Brian Townsend.

They threw out wilder and wilder ideas. But when somebody said "bomb," a deafening silence ensued. Apparently, there were some things they weren't supposed to talk about in front of the women.

Leah had been pushing through the swinging kitchen door and hoped they all thought she'd already gone back into the kitchen. Carrying a teetering load of dirty plates, Helen was right on her heels. Leah set down her pile, then took some of Helen's.

Jennifer clapped her hands. "Let's hurry! Along with lunch, we should do some baking."

By all means. Bake goodies while the men planned to build bombs.

Not waiting to be assigned a task, Leah filled the sink with hot, soapy water and began washing while the others brought in the remaining dirty dishes and Lisa carried a coffeepot out to top off mugs.

Leah let most of the talk about the menu go over her head, but when the women turned to discussing what to bake, she decided to volunteer. Staying in the kitchen, in company with other women, would be smart today.

"I make a really good apple-raisin cake." She suggested they think about picking huckleberries, too, currently ripe. "They're as good or better than blueberries, and they'd stretch our supplies."

Picking huckleberries would give her a reason to be well away from the lodge, too. She might be able to give herself a significant—no *serious*—head start. Wasn't that how Spencer had put it? She couldn't help remembering the rest of what he'd said, too.

If you ever see an opportunity—a good one—take it.

Let me worry about myself. The ache in her chest told her it wouldn't be that easy.

"I'll ask Tim," Jennifer said briskly.

Leah only nodded. She wasn't sure she'd ever been truly timid a day in her life, and she could only hope all this deference didn't get to be a habit.

Finished with the dishes, she joined the other women in the baking, putting together a double recipe of her apple-raisin cake while they worked on blueberry pies.

After lunch Jennifer reported that Tim said they could maybe pick berries tomorrow, but not today.

Damn.

She assigned Leah to mop the floor in the main room. She was to do beneath the table by hand, Jennifer said firmly.

The scarred fir planks really needed a new finish. After this many years, the original varnish had been almost entirely worn away. Soap and water weren't really good for the wood, she couldn't help thinking, in one of those absurd moments. Because, gee, did it really matter if the floor rotted and collapsed? As things stood—no.

At least the task shouldn't leave her isolated. Helen had to clean the downstairs bathroom today, Lisa to sweep the front and back porches and clean the mudroom. Jennifer intended to reorganize the pantry and continue baking.

The benches pulled out, Leah was underneath the table on her hands and knees when she saw Del go into the kitchen and let the door swing shut behind him. On a sudden chill, she stopped scrubbing. From here, she couldn't hear voices in the kitchen. He'd probably gone out the back to check on Lisa, she realized. He might stay there for a few minutes talking to her. Helen, here in the lodge, wasn't that far away, but more sweet than a lioness at heart.

Leah made herself get back to work. Any minute Del would return as part of his appointed rounds. Anyway, the men were all too scared of Spencer to mess with him. She'd *seen* Joe back down. Still, she listened hard for any sound at all.

Like the sound of the lodge door opening. She froze. Del might have circled around. That would make sense—

Booted footsteps approached. From her low vantage point, Leah peered out. This wasn't Del, who wore the ubiquitous desert camo today with desert tan boots. This man had on black boots with heavy cleats and forest-green camouflage cargo pants.

Joe Osenbrock.

Staying as utterly still as a mouse that had seen a hawk's shadow nearing, she even held her breath. Did he see her beneath the table?

Who was she kidding? How could he miss her bucket filled with soapy water and probably her lower legs? In fact, he walked right to her.

"Alone at last," he gloated.

Go with ignorance. "Who's there?" She dropped the sponge in the bucket and turned to sit on her butt facing the threat. "Joe? Do you want a cup of coffee?"

"You know what I want."

Maybe she ought to hold to her timid—now terrified—persona, but she couldn't make herself. Still unable to see his face, she said, "Have you forgotten what Spencer said?"

"He's not going to mess with our team. What we're planning is more important than any piece of ass," he scoffed. "He told Higgs that himself." He crouched to look straight at her. "Don't kid yourself that he gives a damn about you."

"I don't." Scared as she was, Leah knew her chin jutted out at a defiant angle. "But I know he *does* care about his reputation. You'd be a fool to challenge him."

Seeing the fury on his face, she knew she'd just made a big mistake. *She'd* issued a challenge. To save face, now he almost had to rape her and face down Spencer. What she'd forgotten was that Spencer wasn't the only one to value his tough-as-nails reputation.

Lightning quick, Joe grabbed her ankles and wrenched her toward him. Leah screamed and grabbed for purchase, not finding anything. Her butt slid on the wood floor. No, there was the bucket. Even as he was still dragging her forward, she snatched it up and flung the water, followed by the bucket, too, in his face.

Joe bellowed and momentarily let her go. Maybe the soap stung his eyes. Leah seized the chance to scramble backward, desperate to come out the other side of the table within reach of the kitchen.

Water dripping from his hair and face, he ducked to grab her again. His head clunked against the edge of the table. By now he was yelling a string of invectives.

At that moment the swinging door slapped open and she heard the thud of running footsteps. Whimpering, Leah crawled out from the shelter of the heavy table right beside Del.

He didn't even look at her. His hand rested on the butt of his pistol, though. Beyond him, Jennifer hovered in the doorway, watching.

Joe snarled as he rose to his feet. "Get out of here."

Leah hardly dared take her eyes off Joe, but she turned her head anyway to see Del. What if he shrugged and walked back into the kitchen?

But his hard gaze stayed on Joe and he said, "No. She's Spencer's girl. You got no right."

"He had no right to snatch her away right out from under our noses."

Del's expression didn't change. "You could have done something then. You didn't."

Joe's eyes narrowed to mean slits. "You calling me a coward?" And—oh, God—his hand slid toward the butt of *his* gun.

"That's not what I said."

Preparing to drop to the floor at any sudden movement, Leah hoped Jennifer was smart enough to fade back into the kitchen. Couldn't they feel the tension?

As the two men held a staring contest, she prayed for Spencer to appear. He hadn't expected to be gone long, and it had already been at least four hours.

Joe said in a low growl, "Butt out of this, Schmidt. She's not your business."

"My job today is to watch out for the women. All I'm saying is, you need to take this up with Spencer, not sneak behind his back."

"You and who else will stop me?"

That should have sounded childish, but didn't. The threat of violence had a weight; it raised prickles on the back of her neck. These men wouldn't take a few swings at each other. They'd pull semiautomatic weapons and start shooting. Killing.

Over her.

Would either of them notice if she eased back until she could dart for the kitchen? And would that do any good if Del lost this confrontation?

A man's voice came from the kitchen. Then heavy footsteps. Two men walked in. Jennifer was no longer visible.

Shawn Wycoff, tall, lean and blond, was accompanied by another of the men who'd so far remained anonymous to Leah. He didn't say much around the table, and like too many of the others, was distinguished by a shaved head, a powerful build and full-sleeve tattoos.

When the men took up positions to each side of Del, Leah did edge backward.

The guy she didn't know was the one to say, "What's this about?"

"None of your goddamn business!" Joe snapped. "Get lost."

"He wants Leah," Del said, not taking his eyes off Joe. "I told him to take it up with Spencer, face-to-face, not stab him in the back."

"What's he done to you anyway?" Shawn asked.

"He's suddenly giving us orders? Where was he six months ago? Where'd he come from? Does anybody even *know*?" Joe asked.

No-name said with surprising calm, "I'm betting Colonel Higgs does, or he wouldn't be here. And the only orders he's given are during training. The guy can shoot like no one else I've ever seen, and I had two deployments. I hear while he served he was spec ops. You don't think you can learn from him?"

Joe made a disgusted noise. "He's so sold on himself, I wouldn't be surprised if he didn't make up that shit."

"You think the army would keep a guy who can make his shot from a thousand yards plus as a regular grunt?"

Joe let them know, obscenely, that none of that mattered. Spencer had overstepped himself when he claimed exclusive rights over the only decent-looking woman any of them had seen in six weeks or more.

"Del doesn't have to do without." He was trying for persuasive, which scared Leah enough to have her inching back again.

Should have gone sooner. Should have run for it.

"What say the three of us have a good time? I mean, come on. What's Spencer going to do? Take us all on?" He grinned. "I've seen you looking, Wycoff. You can't tell me you haven't." He tipped his chin at the other man. "You, too, Zeigler."

Zeigler shook his head. "Not me."

"Looking ain't the same thing as taking," Shawn Wycoff told him. His lip curled. "*I* can get women without raping them."

By goading such an unstable man and appearing to enjoy doing so, Shawn might as well have lit the fuse on a stick of dynamite.

Joe's face turned ugly again with a snarl. "You saying I can't?"

"I'm not saying nothing, 'cept Del's right. Take it up with Wyatt. We're teammates. We gotta trust each other. That's the right thing to do."

Hear, hear! Except the idea of Joe Osenbrock "taking it up" with Spencer scared her. He hated Spencer and would kill him in a second, if he could.

Before, he hadn't had the guts to face off with him. After this standoff, with not one but three of the other men looking at him with doubt, he'd think he had no choice.

And, oh, dear God, did she hear a vehicle outside?

FOLLOWING ORDERS, SPENCER drove around behind the lodge to the sturdy outbuilding that served as their armory. It was a natural. Constructed of logs, too, it appeared to have been added some years after the lodge and cabins had been built, which meant it was solid. Even the shake roof was in good shape. Mostly empty when they first opened it up, it had held only a few chainsaws, a heavy-duty weed whacker, assorted hand tools and an old Jeep with a custom-mounted snowplow. A quiet guy named Jason Shedd had given the Jeep a lube job and oil change, replaced a few belts and gotten the thing running. It was too small to be of much use, but Spencer figured you never knew. He'd been thinking a lot about that Jeep in recent days. The key hung on a string from a nail just inside the rusting steel garage-style door.

The trick was that a heavy hasp and padlock on the door ensured it could only be opened by Higgs, a fact that pissed off some of the men. The ones who'd begun to question his leadership.

Spencer really wanted to get his hands on that key.

Now he backed the Suburban up to the outbuilding door, set the emergency brake and turned off the ignition.

"I'll look inside and see if anyone's there to help us unload," he said, careful to betray none of the edginess he felt.

"Do that." Higgs reached for the door handle.

Spencer crossed the twenty-five yards to the back door into the lodge with long strides. His nerves had been buzzing since they left this morning. Pretending he was unconcerned had taken everything he had. There wouldn't be any relief for him until he saw Leah unhurt, safe.

The unlocked door opened into a mudroom and then the kitchen. Lisa and Jennifer hovered just outside the entry into the pantry, their anxiety palpable.

His heart lurched. Ignoring them, he walked quietly to the swinging door that stood open.

Before he reached it, voices came to him.

"I'll wait." Joe Osenbrock. His voice turned vicious. "But sweetheart, I'll win. I know better than him how to treat a woman."

"Gee, that might be why you're so desperate," Leah said flippantly.

Spencer hoped no one else heard the slight tremor in her voice.

One part of his tension abated. She was still on her feet swinging, which meant she had to be all right.

The ugly epithet from Joe sent Spencer into another state of being, one all too familiar. He felt…very little. Combat ready, he walked into the dining room just as something big crashed.

On the far side of the table, Joe must have just picked up and thrown one of the long benches. He stood above it with his teeth showing, breathing hard, face flushed with rage.

Only a few feet from Spencer, her back to him, Leah faced Joe…as did three men, all in battle stance, hands hovering over their guns.

Voice arctic, Spencer announced his presence. "Seems I missed some excitement."

Chapter Ten

Leah and two of the three men spun to face him. Del Schmidt had the presence of mind to keep his attention on the armed idiot throwing a temper tantrum.

Both gladness and fear shone from Leah. He wanted her to fly into his arms, but at the same time he hoped she'd know better than to do that. They needed to maintain their cover—and he needed to keep his mind on what was coming.

The two men looked relieved at the sight of him. From the sweat and dirt coating them, it appeared Garrett Zeigler and Shawn Wycoff had just come from running the obstacle course.

Harder to tell with Joe. He was either sweat-soaked or had dunked his head under running water.

Spencer nodded at the two backing up Del. He didn't like owing any of this bunch, but this was different. "Thank you."

Garrett Zeigler's lip curled as he glanced over his shoulder. "He thinks he can take you," he said quietly enough not to be heard by Joe.

"He can try." Would he really have to kill Osenbrock? Yeah. Probably. "Higgs and I need help unloading."

Quick as a rattlesnake striking, Joe started to pull his weapon. In the blink of an eye, Spencer had his own in his hand. "I wouldn't mind blowing your head off, and you know I don't miss."

Joe's face went slack with momentary fear, but he blustered, "Hand to hand. Winner takes Leah." His eyes slid to Leah, who looked strong in spirit but physically fragile as she stood with head high and expression defiant.

Not seeing a way out, Spencer inclined his head, even as he held his Sig Sauer in a two-handed stance aimed at Joe Osenbrock's heart. "Tomorrow morning. In the meantime, put that gun down. You've shown us all you're not trustworthy." Seeing such hate in another man's eyes disturbed Spencer, even as he stayed cold inside.

When Joe didn't move, Spencer said, "Del?"

The other man walked around the table. "He's right, Joe. Give it to me. You can have it back later."

That burning stare turned briefly to Del. "I won't forget this."

"Let me have it."

Spencer took a step closer, making sure even Osenbrock couldn't miss his deadly intent.

With a jerky, furious motion, Joe yanked the handgun the rest of the way from the holster and slapped it on Del's outstretched hand. Then he wheeled around and stormed out of the lodge.

There was immediately relaxation in his wake, although Spencer didn't share it. Joe probably had half a dozen more weapons stockpiled in his cabin. Whether he'd go get one and commit cold-blooded murder in front of his fellow "soldiers" was another matter. This was all about ego, and if he really wanted respect, he had to make the fight seem aboveboard.

Spencer straightened and reholstered his own gun. "Higgs must be wondering where I am. Let's go unload," he said as if nothing had happened.

Leah stood ten feet away, her face parchment-pale, her eyes dilated. Her hands were clenched in small fists. He wanted to know everything that had happened, how it was that not only Del had stepped in, but the other two men, as well. But that had to wait. Right now appearances were everything.

"Don't you have a job to do?" he asked.

Some emotion flew across her face, too fast to read, which was just as well considering they weren't alone. She nodded, but also stole a look toward the front door.

"Del," Spencer said. "Can you stay?"

"That's the plan."

"I need to refill the bucket," she said tightly.

"Throwing it at him was smart," Del said unexpectedly, addressing Spencer rather than her. Still, he'd gained some respect for her, which might or might not be good.

So the bucket hadn't spilled because someone tripped over it. A pail full of soapy water explained Joe's dripping wet hair, and some of his temper, too.

Ignoring all the men, Leah circled around the table and picked up the bucket, then trailed Spencer, Zeigler and Wycoff into the kitchen. As she went to the sink, the other two women stared at the men.

Walking out the back door and across the bare yard to the Suburban with Zeigler and Wycoff, Spencer asked, "How'd you two get mixed up in that?"

"Del sent Lisa to get help. We were, ah, heading up to the lodge to take a break."

Shawn grinned. "What he means is, the women did some baking this morning. Blueberry pie and an apple-raisin cake. Decided we needed seconds."

"I'll look forward to dessert tonight."

Higgs had the garage door lifted and the back of the Suburban open. "What took so long?" he grumbled.

"Osenbrock was up to the same crap," Spencer said as if unconcerned. "These guys and Schmidt told him he had to take it up with me."

Higgs's attention sharpened. "He attacked Leah?"

"Appears so. She fought back. Del came running. He sent Lisa to get these two."

The colonel flicked a glance at the other two men, then leveled a steady look at Spencer. "Can you handle him?"

"We agreed to hand to hand in the morning." He nodded at the packed rear of the SUV. "Let's get this done. Be careful. Some of the boxes are heavier than they look."

He wasn't sure what was in all the boxes, except the one crate he'd watched Higgs inspect. It held at least a dozen rifles. Markings on some of the boxes indicated they were the property of the US Government. A lot of those contained ammunition to replace what they'd used. Then there was the something mysterious that had had Higgs and his confederate talking quietly for quite a while.

Given half a chance, Spencer intended to find out what other weapon had just been handed to a bunch of alt-right nutjobs.

The men worked in silence, Higgs directing where he wanted each box put.

"Getting crowded in here," Wycoff remarked at one point.

Higgs frowned at the Jeep. "We can move it out of here if we have to."

Spencer liked the idea but didn't want to go on record saying so. Even if the key stayed on the nail inside the armory, he was confident he could hot-wire a vehicle as old as this one. The Jeep was a standard CJ-5, probably dating to the sixties or seventies.

Five minutes later Spencer turned with deliberate incaution and bumped into Zeigler, who bashed a hip into a sharp corner of the old Jeep. Cursing, he barely held on to the box he carried.

"Oh, hell," Spencer said. "I'm sorry."

"Let's get the damn thing out of there." Higgs took care of moving it himself, parking it to one side of the armory. "We can throw a tarp over it if it looks like rain."

"I wonder if you could sell it to some classic car buff?" Wycoff suggested.

Spencer laughed. "I doubt you could give it away. You know how common these were?"

"Yeah." Wycoff studied the rusting metal and tattered remnants of a canvas cover that had snapped on. "It's no beauty, I'll give you that."

They continued to work. Once the Suburban was empty, Spencer moved it to its usual parking spot out front of the lodge and handed the keys to Higgs.

The two men were now alone.

"Osenbrock is becoming a problem," Higgs remarked.

"Becoming? He's an arrogant hothead."

The boss grunted. "I'd boot his ass out, except that would mean turning him loose. Resentment and a big mouth make for a dangerous mix."

"He's a fighter," Spencer said more mildly than he felt. "He believes in our goals."

Higgs's brows climbed. "You plan to leave him alive?"

"Depends how it goes."

"Whatever you have to do." Higgs nodded and walked away.

Spencer followed him only as far as the dining area, where Leah seemed to be finishing up. Sweaty and disheveled, she looked worse than the men who'd come to her rescue—but she was still on her feet, doing what she had to do.

She was also beautiful, even now. In the intervening days, the discoloration and swelling on her face had diminished significantly, making more obvious the delicacy of her features. The pale, strawberry blond hair was sleek enough to fall back in place whatever she put it through.

"Can I get some coffee?" he asked.

He especially liked the glare that should have incinerated him.

She grabbed the bucket and rose to her feet. "Anything else?"

He barely refrained from grinning. "How about a piece of that cake?"

Leah stomped into the kitchen.

It was Helen who delivered the cup of coffee and a generous square of a rich, dark cake. He could see the apples and raisins in it.

"Leah made this," Helen said softly.

"Did she?"

She backed away. "If you need anything else..."

"I'll be fine." He nodded, watching as she hurried away and out of sight. It was unlikely any of the women would go to prison, but he wondered what would happen to her without Dirk.

Shaking the worry off, he took a bite of the cake. The taste lit up all his synapses, as rich as it looked. Sweet, but with enough spice to offer complexity. Damn, Leah could cook, too.

She appeared ten minutes later, hesitating when she saw him but then advancing. "Do you want a refill?" She nodded at his cup.

"Sure. That's fabulous cake. Helen says you made it."

"My grandmother taught me. It's my go-to recipe when I have to contribute to potlucks."

He nodded and lowered his voice. "You're really all right?"

"Yes. He…was dragging me out from beneath the table when Del came running. He tried to talk Shawn and—"

At her hesitation, Spencer supplied the name. "Garrett."

"Garrett into having some fun with him. He suggested you wouldn't take on all three of them."

Enraged, Spencer ground his molars. "They didn't consider going for it?" If they had…

But she shook her head. "Joe said he'd seen Shawn looking. I had the feeling Shawn doesn't like him."

She was right. With very few exceptions, these were aggressive men, angry at the world. Small as the group was, it had broken into cliques, the alliances shifting.

Leah continued, "He sort of sneered and said *he* could get women without raping them. It was like he wanted Joe to blow."

"Joe's got friends here, but not those three." His voice still sounded guttural. If Joe had had Arne and Chris Binder and TJ Galt backing him, Leah would have been gang-raped. TJ wouldn't have let a marriage certificate stop him.

Slammed by how he'd have felt if he'd gotten back to find Leah huddled in a small, battered ball, forever damaged by that kind of assault, all the violence in his nature rose in outrage. That was a mistake none of them would have survived to regret.

"Are you all right?" Leah still hesitated several feet away.

"Yeah." It was all he could do to clear his throat. "Coffee?"

She took his cup, reappearing a minute later. As she carefully set it down, she asked, "Is anyone else here?"

"No, I think we're alone except for the women."

"Are you really going to have to fight him?"

"Yes."

"He wants to kill you. Did you see the way he looked at you?" She shivered.

"I saw." He reached out and squeezed her hand quickly before releasing it. "He can't take me down."

"You won't underestimate him?"

"No." Hearing the front door open followed by voices, he said, "You'd better get back to work."

Without another word, she fled. Thinking about his last glimpse of her face, Spencer had a bad feeling he'd failed to reassure her. And the truth was, he'd spent most of his time in the military belly down, with an eye to a scope and his finger resting gently on the trigger of a rifle. He'd wrestled and boxed, sure, but had never tried out any martial arts.

He didn't picture Joe Osenbrock embracing martial arts, either, though. They required discipline he lacked. He was a brute force kind of guy. Joe lost it when he got angry enough or things weren't going his way.

Spencer had to count on cold determination defeating blind fury.

LEAH KEPT SNEAKING peeks down the table during dinner. Spencer acted as if nothing at all was wrong. He ignored Joe, but not so obviously that he was doing it as an insult. More as if… Joe just didn't impinge on his awareness at all.

Joe ate, but she doubted he knew what he was putting in his mouth. He barely took his burning stare from Spencer. Everyone else noticed, which made for awkward conversation and uncomfortable silences.

Shelley Galt had reappeared for the first time in days

to help with dinner and join them at the table. Leah could see immediately that she hadn't been sick at all. She'd been beaten. She still moved stiffly, her left wrist was wrapped in an ACE bandage, and while the long-sleeve tee probably hid bruises, the foundation she'd plastered on her face wasn't thick enough to disguise the purple, yellow and black that enveloped her cheek, temple and part of her forehead, wrapping around an eye that wasn't yet quite all the way open.

Leah knew exactly how that felt. Just looking at the other woman made her shake with fury. Once she saw Spencer's gaze rest on Shelley's face. His expression never changed, but she knew what he thought behind the mask.

After dinner the group broke up more slowly than some times. As usual the women took turns refilling coffee cups or bringing second servings of one of the desserts. Helen was the first to be able to leave. Dirk took her hand and led her out the back door. That he didn't mind people seeing him touch Helen, or his tenderness toward her, said a lot about him. Too bad he was part of a group planning some kind of major attack meant to shake the foundations of Americans' faith in their government.

Shelley left alone. TJ had told her to go, she said. No kindness there. Twenty minutes later most of the rest departed en masse, leaving Leah by herself in the kitchen. She peeked out to see Spencer and Colonel Higgs sitting across from each other at the table, engaged in a conversation that even an outsider could see was intense. What were they talking about? The morning fight? Or the attack that was to be the climax of all this planning and training?

She sat on a stool in the kitchen and tried to think about something, anything, except Joe and Spencer slamming their fists into each other, twisting and tangling in combat. Would the other men surround them and cheer on their favorite, like middle-school boys excited by a fight? She shuddered, imagining the rise of bloodlust, and wondered if Joe's death—or Spencer's—would satisfy the audience.

She knew, *knew*, that Spencer would never concede, not with her life at stake. As terrified as she was of being left to Joe Osenbrock's mercy, that wouldn't be the worst part. How could she ever accept Spencer's death?

She couldn't. Wouldn't.

As a woman who cried when an animal hit by a car didn't make it onto the vet's operating table, she wasn't used to wanting to hurt anyone. But there was no doubt in her mind.

If Joe somehow won, she'd make him pay. No matter what it took.

THEY WERE BARELY inside the door of the cabin when Spencer groaned and snatched Leah into his arms. Leaning back against the closed door, he held her tightly, his cheek pressed to the top of her head. This had been one of the most hellish days he could remember.

He should have taken her and fled already, to hell with his job. Yeah, he'd had two breakthroughs today, but the price was too high. He'd been so cocky, too sure he could protect Leah. He still believed he'd come out the winner tomorrow...but what if he didn't? Or what if he won but was injured badly enough that he was unable to keep protecting her? Joe wasn't the only threat.

She burrowed against him. His resistance to making love with her had hit a low. He needed that closeness, that relief, and thought she did, too.

"Leah," he muttered.

She lifted her head from his shoulder, letting him see the tears in her eyes. "I don't want you to do this."

Desperately, he said, "Let's forget it all, just for a while. Can we do that?"

Even with her eyes shimmering wet, he'd swear she saw deep inside him. He made himself wait until she whispered, "Yes. Oh, yes, please."

He tried to start off gently. They'd never kissed before. His good intentions lasted maybe thirty seconds before one of his hands was on her ass, the other gripping her nape. His tongue was in her mouth, her arms locked around his neck, and she seemed to be trying to climb him. He ached to have her cradle his erection. Her taste, her softness, her acceptance and eagerness, her vulnerability and strength, combined to blast his good intentions to smithereens. He wanted to strip her, lift her up against the door and take her without any finesse. He actually started to turn her and gripped the hem of her T-shirt to strip her when he remembered that damn uncovered window.

He couldn't do it like this. A monumental shudder racked his body. The effort of persuading his fingers to release her shirt tore another groan from his chest. Wrenching his mouth from hers, he said rawly, "Bedroom."

Her green eyes were so dazed, he doubted she understood.

Too frantic for her to wait, he bent to slide an arm beneath her knees and swing her off the floor. Since he started kissing her again, he blundered more than walked across the small living room.

As he turned to fit her through the opening into the bedroom, some part of her body thudded into the door frame and she cried, "Ouch." The next second she pressed her lips back to his and the kiss became deep and hungry again.

Once he laid her on the bed and came down on top of her, they slid into the dip at the middle of the mattress. Spencer didn't care. All he could think about was getting her clothes off. As he tugged her shirt over her head and groped for the fastening for her bra, he wished he'd thought to turn on the light so he could see her. Much as he wanted that, he couldn't make himself leave her.

He had to rise to his knees to untie her athletic shoes and peel her jeans and panties down her legs. While he was there, he took care of his own clothes. He barely had the sanity to remove a condom from his wallet. She was trying to touch him but wouldn't have been able to see well enough to put the damn thing on. He felt clumsy, and realized the dark wasn't responsible. His hands were shaking.

Too much tumult, fierce need and the knowledge that they could fall any minute off the knife-edge that constituted their only safety, all combined to rob him of any patience. The incoherent, needy sounds she was making—moans, whimpers, he didn't know—told him she was as ready as he was.

Sliding inside her was one of the best feelings of his life. Tight, slick, she welcomed him by planting her feet on the mattress and pushing her hips up to meet every thrust. He set an urgent, hard pace that couldn't last. Her spasms, the way she cried out his name, pulled him with her. His throbbing release seemed to last forever. He collapsed, unable to find the immediate strength to roll off her slender body.

For all the joy and satisfaction he felt, Spencer hated that she hadn't cried out his real name. That she didn't even know it. She'd just made love to a man playing a role, not him.

Whoever I am, came the bleak thought.

Chapter Eleven

Leah woke up to find herself alone in bed. She didn't hear a sound. Not the shower or a whistling teakettle or the creak of a floorboard. Where was Spencer?

They'd made love a second time, slower and more tenderly, his voice deep and almost velvety in the darkness, the Southern accent strong as he told her how beautiful she was, how soft. He called her strong, defiant, smart. He hadn't said how he felt about her, but that would have been expecting too much. Really, how could either of them know so quickly?

Just for a minute she pushed back at the sense of dread that would swallow her if she let it, and instead remembered the feel of Spencer's callused fingers, the raw hunger in his kisses, the way he filled her until she felt complete. She wished…she wished so much, but her chest suddenly felt as if a band squeezed, tightening until she couldn't draw a breath.

He wouldn't have left her behind when he went to meet with Joe, would he?

Horrified, she threw back the covers, struggled out of bed and only grabbed a dirty T-shirt of Spencer's to throw on before she rushed out of the bedroom.

Spencer sat on the futon, feet on the coffee table, appearing his usual composed self. He held a coffee cup in one hand and gazed at her in mild surprise.

She lurched to a stop, her heart hammering. "I thought…"

"I might be gone?" His voice was low and tender despite his impenetrable expression. "I wouldn't do that to you."

"What…what time is it?"

He glanced at the steel watch he wore. "We have twenty minutes."

"I didn't know you'd set a time."

"Higgs did. He wants us to get the fight out of the way before breakfast."

"Oh, God." Her sense of impending disaster wasn't alleviated. "I need to take a shower."

She should have done laundry yesterday at the lodge, she thought in that part of her mind still capable of mundane thoughts. Rooting through her suitcase, she found a pair of jeans that she'd only worn one day and a clean T-shirt. Her last pair of clean panties.

Right now she couldn't care less if she was filthy. Even the shower was only a way to put off facing what was coming.

Clutching the small pile of clothes, she went to the bathroom without looking again at Spencer.

What if…? But she couldn't let herself think that.

She stayed under the thin stream of water only long enough to get clean before drying herself with the pitiful towel and hurrying to dress. She combed her wet hair, then looked down at herself. Her battle armor didn't seem adequate.

Taking a deep breath, she went back out, set on not letting Spencer see how scared she was. What he needed from her was trust and confidence. She should have felt both wholeheartedly, but the dread remained.

As soon as she appeared, his gaze landed on her. "I've been in fights before," he said calmly.

Some of her fears had to be leaking out, like too-bright light between the slats of blinds. "Don't hold back," she begged him. "He'll do anything to win."

He still looked unfazed. "Cheat, you mean?"

"Yes!"

"Let's go out on the porch."

He rose effortlessly to his feet. Bemused, she followed him. He closed the door behind them and leaned against the porch railing. Leah desperately wanted the chance to soak in the comfort of his strong arms around her, but they could be seen.

Not heard, though, she realized, at least not from a bug inside the cabin.

Confirming her guess, he spoke very quietly. "There's something you need to know. You're imagining that I always take the high road. I don't. I've long since lost count of the number of men I've killed. I told you I was military, but not that I was a sniper. I saw those dying men's faces." Gravel roughened his voice even as he kept it low. "Some of them will haunt me for the rest of my life, but I kept doing what I thought I had to do. If I have to kill Joe Osenbrock today, I won't hesitate. Do you understand?"

"Yes," she whispered. "Maybe I shouldn't be glad, but I am. It's not just for my sake that you need to win, you know."

The bones in his face seemed more prominent than she remembered. "I do know."

She nodded.

"We need to get going."

He touched the back of her hand lightly as they descended the steps. She studied him, bothered by that seemingly unbreakable calm. Today he wore black cargo pants and a gray T-shirt that showed his powerful pecs and biceps, as well as flexible black boots that would allow him to move fast. He wouldn't be able to kick or stomp the way Joe would, but speed was surely more important. At Spencer's belt, he wore his usual black leather holster holding a steel-gray and black handgun. The men here seemed to go armed all the time as a matter of course. Maybe as a law-enforcement officer, Spencer always did. Leah hoped not, that he could sometimes set that part of his nature aside.

The minute they started down the porch steps, she saw the crowd gathered in front of the lodge. Were they excited about the entertainment? Or were some worried about the outcome?

"If you get out of here and I don't," he said in that same low voice, "the attack's set for November 11, Veterans Day. The president is set to speak, although the location hasn't yet been identified. And they have the components to make a dirty bomb. Remember that."

She opened her mouth in an instinctive protest but closed it. Nodded. "Will you tell me your real name?"

He cut a glance at her sidelong. His hesitation was infinitesimal but real, replaced by a flicker of amusement. "Alex Barr. Alex, most of the time. But stick to Spencer."

"Thank you."

That was the last thing she had a chance to say. They'd reached the crowd, now re-forming into a circle. She followed in his wake until she was close enough to the front to be able to see.

Joe Osenbrock already waited in the center. Not patiently; he was pacing, rolling his shoulders, acting like

Leah vaguely thought heavyweights did in the ring before the bell.

Spencer stopped to unclip his holster and hand it and
the gun to Garrett Zeigler. Then he walked into the clear
space within the ring of bodies and stopped, still seemingly relaxed. Despite appearances, he had to be poised
to explode into action.

The mood was more subdued than she'd expected.
Even low-voiced conversation stopped when the lodge
door opened and Colonel Higgs appeared. He walked
forward, took in the scene with one sweeping glance,
then asked, "Are they both disarmed?"

"Yes." Del Schmidt held up one weapon. Zeigler raised
Spencer's.

"Good. Let's not waste too much time with this." •
Higgs studied the two men in the ring, his thoughts hidden. Then he said, "Go."

It all happened so fast, Leah wasn't sure which
man moved first, only that within seconds they were
toe-to-toe, fists swinging. Grunts of exertion and pain
rang out. Blood splattered.

Spencer swiped blood from his face with his forearm,
then stepped back to let Joe charge past him. When their
bodies collided again, they fell hard to the ground. Spencer got a headlock on Joe, but only briefly. They rolled,
pummeling each other, grappling for any advantage, punishing each other brutally with fists and holds that con-
torted their bodies in ways that had her whimpering.

They fought their way back to their feet.

A few men called out. Occasionally a warning, sometimes a "Good one!" But mostly they were silent, so intent
on the battle in front of them, she could have plucked a
gun from one of their holsters and started spraying bullets.

Except…she couldn't tear her eyes from the savage fight, either.

Twice she had to step back along with the entire side of the circle when the two men flung themselves in that direction. Mostly, she knew she was begging, or even praying.

Please, please, please.

After a strike against his neck, Joe roared with rage and seemed to redouble his attacks. Spencer countered them, once tripping Joe, who crashed to the ground, somersaulted and came back up.

Spencer spat out some blood and jeered at his opponent. "Getting tired?"

With another roar, Joe charged forward like a three-hundred-and-fifty pound linebacker ready to drop the quarterback. But Spencer was not only fast, he was as big a man if not quite so muscle-bound. A quick side step and an elbow to the gut sent Joe to the ground again. He seemed slower to get up, pausing with one knee still down, even his head slightly bent. Was he done?

Spencer came at him with a kick that sent Joe sprawling again, but he latched on to Spencer's leg and brought him down, too. And suddenly, something metal flashed.

"Gun!" somebody yelled, but it wasn't. It was a knife, and he slashed at Spencer. Blood didn't just spatter, it spurted.

Ready to leap forward herself, she saw Spencer grab Joe's wrist and wrench his arm back. Spencer's teeth showed in a snarl; Joe fought that powerful grip in silent agony.

A couple of the men did surge forward, but before they reached the two combatants, Spencer flipped Joe, slammed his hand on the ground to force him to release the knife, and slugged him in the face so hard Joe's head bounced.

The next second he'd gone limp.

Spencer rolled off him and lay on his back, his chest heaving, his clothes blood-soaked.

Above the tumult of other voices, she heard Higgs's. He'd descended into the crowd and now raised his voice. "Wyatt's the winner. Tim, Brian, haul that cheating scum up to one of the bedrooms." He jerked his head to indicate the lodge behind him. "Shawn, Rick, you're responsible for getting Spencer back to his cabin." Higgs looked around, spotting her. "You've had practice sewing up wounds. Make yourself useful."

Oh, God, oh, God. Her teeth wanted to chatter. Somehow, she managed to say, "Do you have a first-aid kit?"

"Townsend, you know where it is."

It took three men to lift Joe and carry him up the porch steps and into the lodge. Leah only peripherally saw them go, Joe's arms flopping. On her knees beside Spencer, she snapped, "I need something to stop the bleeding."

Spencer watched her, one eyelid at half-mast. The socket holding his other eye was grotesquely swollen, purple. His teeth were clenched, and she'd swear what skin she could see was gray beneath the tan. Or maybe it only looked gray as an accent to the shockingly vivid color of the blood.

She bent her head close to his. "You'll be all right. You won."

One side of his mouth lifted as if he was trying to smile but couldn't quite make it work.

Two bare-chested men thrust cotton T-shirts at her. Neither looked very clean, but they were the best she had. She wadded one and pressed it hard against Spencer's thigh, looked around until she saw Del Schmidt and said, "Can you hold this?"

He dropped to his knees and complied. She pulled up Spencer's shirt, used the second T-shirt in her hand to wipe at the blood until she saw a narrow slit over his rib cage, and pressed it down. Panic scratched at her. If there were more wounds, they'd have to wait, but what if one she hadn't found was fatal? The slit frightened her the most. That one was a stab instead of a slice. She hadn't seen it happen. What organs lay beneath?

Out of the corner of her eye she saw someone pick up the huge knife lying in the dirt. Blood dripped from the double-edged blade.

A man ran up carrying a metal box big enough to look as if it held fishing tackle. "Do you want it here?"

"Take it to the cabin," she decided. Three men prepared to lift him, Leah ordering Del to keep the pressure on his thigh while she did the same on his muscular torso.

They moved slowly, awkwardly, with five of them bumping into each other, but finally made it up the two steps onto the porch.

"Not locked," Spencer growled.

The man with an arm under his shoulders—Rick Metz, built like a boulder—fumbled for the knob with one hand and got the door open. Once inside, she said, "Can we pull out the futon?"

Del did it while she used her free hand to maintain pressure on Spencer's thigh, too. The mattress looked grungy enough she wished desperately for a clean sheet to lay over it, but hadn't seen one. Pain tightened Spencer's face until it was all bones and skin stretched taut between them. He groaned when they laid him down.

To her distant surprise, the men continued to follow her orders. One put on water to boil on the single work-

ing burner here, while another ran for the lodge to boil
more. A third went for any clean bedding and towels he
could find.

Spencer never looked away from her.

HE COULDN'T DIE.

Through the pain, that was all Spencer could think.
Leah needed him. *Don't give in. Don't lose consciousness.*

A couple of times she whispered, "Stay with me,"
and once he even managed a nod. He didn't know if she
meant stay in the sense that he had to remain conscious,
or that he couldn't abandon her by dying. Either way,
he hung on. At least he was done with Joe, who was as
good as a dead man.

The guys around him seemed to be doing their best for
him. He wasn't even sure who *was* here. He'd have had to
look away from Leah to be sure, and he couldn't do that.

He managed to tell her he had pills in his duffel. At
least, he thought he'd told her.

Don't give in. God, that hurts. He wanted to curl up to
protect his belly, sensing that wound was the most dangerous. If the knife had sliced into his guts, all the resolve in the world wouldn't save him. Half-digested food
would be spilling into the abdominal cavity, introducing
bacteria where it didn't belong.

But Leah looked focused and determined in a way he
didn't remember seeing her before. She was fighting for
him, and he could do his part.

Don't give in. Trust her.

He floated in a sea of pain as she worked. There had
to be broken bones.

Paper ripped. Somehow, she'd come to have a wicked-
looking pair of scissors in her hand and was cutting most

of his clothes off him. Wet washcloths, hot enough to have him jerking involuntarily, ran over his legs.

"I'll need to stitch that one up," he heard her say to someone else.

All he felt was pressure on his thigh again.

Once, they rolled him. His back hurt like hell, but in a generalized way.

"Man, he's going to be one solid bruise," a familiar voice said. Del.

It went on like that. He hazily understood that they were searching his body for knife wounds.

"Think the blade hit a rib," Leah said. "If it went very deep…"

He lost the thread of what she was saying.

Eventually, something cold was sprayed on his thigh. Her face appeared above his. "This should numb you enough to help," she said.

Still gritting his teeth, he nodded.

He felt the needle pricking in and out of his flesh. Pricking, hell; stabbing. The spray hadn't numbed anything, but he fought to hold still.

Then on his torso, almost on his side. He couldn't stop a raw sound from escaping.

They produced ice and what he vaguely saw were bags of frozen vegetables to lay on his face and half a dozen other places on his body. The worst bruising? He didn't know, only that the cold burned.

Time passed. He wasn't always sure he *was* conscious. Leah was his anchor, distressing him when she moved out of his line of sight a few times. Dripping ice packs and frozen veggies were removed and replaced at least once.

Rick—yes, that was Rick Metz—was the first to leave and not reappear. Given his lack of emotional content, Rick was a strange one to tend him with care.

When Spencer was able to roll his head slightly, he saw Shawn Wycoff and Del Schmidt. They were more logical as nursemaids. He also became aware that when Leah asked for something, they jumped. Funny that Higgs had appointed her medical director early on. The first day? He didn't remember. Spencer hadn't guessed *he* would be the one to need whatever trauma-care expertise she possessed.

He had to get her to safety so that she could go to veterinary school, the way she deserved. Since the slightest move brought stabbing pains—yeah, that was a pun— he couldn't figure out how he'd protect her, but he'd do it. Somehow.

He surfaced to hear her thanking the two men, sounding almost tearful. Del shrugged. "Let us know what you need."

Say, *I need to go home. Help me get away.*

Of course she didn't. "I will."

The door closed quietly behind them. The mattress shifted enough that he knew Leah had sat down beside him. Her fingertips stroking his forehead was the first good thing he'd felt.

No, he could wriggle his toes with no pain. In fact, thanks to his boots, his feet seemed unscathed. That was good news. If they had to walk out of here, that was what they'd do, he decided.

"You with me?" she asked softly, her eyes so vividly green he would have been happy never to look away.

"Yah," he mumbled.

Her smile lit the room like the sun coming out from behind a cloud. She sobered faster than he liked.

"Thank heavens you didn't lose consciousness! Even so, I'd give a lot to be able to send you for X-rays, or even a CT scan. I think your left wrist might be broken, although I can't be sure. It's wrapped tight enough to immobilize it."

He arrowed in on his wrist. Yeah, that felt like a break. Ribs, too, he guessed, although those might be only cracks or even just bruising.

He could hope.

"It's really lucky you had that oxycodone. Aspirin wouldn't have helped much." She gave an exaggerated shudder.

He shared that gratitude. So he had told her. He hadn't quite realized what those pills he'd swallowed were.

"What will they do with Joe?" she asked, worry carving lines in her forehead. "Should I go volunteer to look at him?"

"No." That sounded almost normal. "Don't shink—" he tried harder "—*think* he'll survive."

"Why? Did you—" Comprehension changed her face. "You mean…"

He managed a tiny nod. Best not to say it out loud.

"Oh, dear God," Leah whispered.

He somehow lifted a hand enough to lay it on her arm. She looked down, then up to meet his eyes, and understood. *Careful.*

"Later I'll have Del and Shawn or somebody else move you to the bedroom. I know the futon must be horribly uncomfortable. But if we were going to ruin one or the other with blood, I decided it should be the futon."

He absolutely agreed. After last night, he'd developed fond feelings for that bed.

"*Could* somebody take you to an ER?"

She meant, would it be allowed. "No," he said. Steeled himself and added, "Okay."

That earned him a wrinkled nose. "You're a long way

from *okay*. But I suppose you must have been injured during your years in the military."

Another slight inclination of his head, although even that set off fireworks. He had to close his eyes momentarily.

Yes, he'd been hospitalized several times. Strange to think that he might have come closer to dying today than he had from bullet wounds or shrapnel from an IED. If that knife blade had plunged deeper, or struck higher or lower, it could easily have been curtains for him, given that the best medical care available was from a veterinary technician with access only to a basic first-aid kit. He'd been damned lucky, and he wouldn't waste that luck.

He really was done with undercover gigs. No hostage rescue for him, either. He'd transfer as soon as he could— once he'd taken down Colonel Higgs and his hatefully misguided army.

And Leah. If she wanted him, he'd do what he had to do to have her in his life, too. He could transfer to the Seattle office, or the office closest to wherever she would be attending grad school.

All good plans. Unfortunately, right this minute a soon-to-be-needed trip to the bathroom reared ahead like Kilimanjaro. Only positive was, he knew he was thinking more clearly.

These injuries would buy him a day or two off from a role that he hadn't been able to set down in months. That said, would Leah still be expected to cook and clean rather than care for him? That would leave her vulnerable…although he thought Higgs had been pissed off enough about Joe's behavior to lay down the law where she was concerned.

Maybe.

Spencer grunted. What he needed was to get back on

his feet as quickly as possible. For starters, he wouldn't
have a chance to pocket the key to start the Jeep unless
he rejoined activities, even if only as a spectator.

A good place to start was with that short journey to
the bathroom. The hell he was going to piss in a jar and
make Leah dump it out.

Despite the explosion of pain, he started to shift his
body toward the edge of the futon amid her cries of,
"What are you *doing*? Stop!"

Chapter Twelve

The stubborn man insisted she lay a sheet over the dirty, blood-stained futon mattress and bring him some pillows so he could spend the day out there. Leah would have argued more vehemently, except he was right that he could get up and down more easily from the futon than the sagging mattress in the bedroom that fought every attempt to escape it. She'd had to stick her head outside and ask the first person she saw—someone named Jack, she thought—to bring bedding and towels from the lodge. Actually, she said meekly, "Spencer wants some bedding for the futon, and, um, our towels are all bloody. I'm afraid to leave him yet. Do you think…?"

The guy complied.

Spencer refused to let her fetch help for him to go to the bathroom. Pain aged his face a decade or more as he pushed himself to his feet, leaning heavily on her. Two hours ago she'd never have considered that he could shuffle even this short distance on his own.

Needless to say, despite the fact that he was swaying in front of the toilet, he evicted her until he was done and flushed.

Around midday she did leave him alone long enough to walk to the lodge for food. She slipped in the back door, where all the women surrounded her and, whispering, demanded to know what had happened. Leah gave them the CliffsNotes version, then filled a bag with a few dishes, a saucepan and some silverware as well as sandwich makings, cans of soup and desserts. She didn't see a single one of the men as she hurried back to the cabin.

During her absence Spencer had gotten to a sitting position again on the edge of the futon. Stress on his face eased the minute he saw her.

"What took you so long?" he asked. With his lips grotesquely swollen, words were hard to make out, but Leah found she got the gist.

"I wasn't gone very long." She set down the two bags on the short stretch of counter next to the tiny sink. "Jennifer and everyone wanted to know about the fight. They were all ordered to stay in the kitchen and missed the whole thing."

"You get an update on Joe?" A note in his voice she didn't recognize had her turning to look at him.

"No. They served breakfast like usual, and when Lisa asked if she should take a plate up to Joe, Higgs snapped at her. Said he isn't in any shape to eat."

"He wouldn't be," Spencer agreed slowly.

Was he wondering if he *had* killed Joe? Or disturbed by the possibility of his death, however it came about? Yes, she decided, that was it. She wondered if, instead of becoming numb and inured to tragedy after all the death he'd seen, Spencer still had the capacity to grieve. There'd been nothing about Joe Osenbrock she could sympathize with, and yet… Who knew what his childhood had been like? What had made him so violently inclined and insecure enough to need so desperately to win?

And if Spencer's suspicion turned out to be true, she really hated the idea that one of those men she'd gotten to know was willing to steal upstairs in the lodge—per-

haps to the very room where she'd been held captive—to
break Joe's neck or slit his throat or… Leah didn't even
want to think.

It bothered her even more to picture one of the men
who'd protected her or helped Spencer today as the one
willing to commit cold-blooded murder. Del? Shawn or
Garrett? Chilled, Leah thought, *surely not Dirk Ritchie.*
And yet…all of them intended to commit mass murder
in the near future. Why balk at killing a single man?

"Will you eat something? I thought you might be able
to drink soup from a cup."

"Not hungry."

She turned in alarm. What if the knife had reached
his intestines or…maybe his liver or kidney? The pain
relievers could have masked the effect that was only now
catching up with him.

She evaluated him, deciding that his color was much
better than it had been when they first carried him to the
cabin. His eyes—well, eye—looked clear. If she made
him open his mouth so she could look at his gums the
way she would an injured dog's, would they be a healthy
color or worrisomely pale?

"Will you try?"

He grunted and very carefully rested against the extra
pillows Jack had included in the pile he brought from the
lodge earlier. Spencer lifted each leg individually, using
his good hand to guide it into place so he could stretch
out. Only then did he say, "Yah."

She warmed cream of tomato, thinking it would go
down easily and that milk would be good for him. When
she took him a mugful and sat beside him to help prop
him up, he did slowly drink it all.

Relieved, she had a bowlful herself.

She checked his watch, sitting on the old coffee table

that had been pushed aside. "It's almost time for another painkiller. You won't try to be a tough guy and do without, will you?"

On a face that had suffered that much damage, it was hard to be sure, but she *thought* his expression was sardonic.

"No. Not tough."

When she gave him the pill half an hour later, he swallowed it, and after a period of staring broodingly up at the wood-paneled ceiling, dozed off. Leah tried to read but couldn't concentrate. Fictional adventures—or the very real ones during World War II—couldn't keep her attention when her current situation was so perilous.

Spencer was fighting his infirmities with a willpower that awed her. If the damage had been limited to the punches and bruising, however massive, she thought he'd be up and around in only another day or two. As it was, he'd lost a lot of blood, and she couldn't help fearing what harm that knife blade thrust between ribs might have done.

Had Spencer been ready for them to attempt an escape? He'd obviously learned a lot of what he'd been sent to find out. Now...how could they get away?

Was it possible for someone to get to any of the car keys?

Helen was the only one of the women Leah could imagine being willing to try to help her, but she wouldn't betray Dirk by helping Leah steal his truck, even if that was possible.

She and Spencer couldn't possibly set out on foot. Certainly not for days.

Her worries went round and round, but even when he was awake, she didn't vocalize them. Didn't need to. He was surely running the same scenarios and coming up with the same dead ends.

We should be okay for a few days, she told herself, but didn't quite believe her own assurance.

SPENCER HAD A hell of a time sleeping. No position was comfortable. Once Leah dropped off, she couldn't prevent herself from rolling into his aching body, or her arm would flop across his torso, and it was all he could do to stifle a bellow. Her head on his shoulder awakened sharp pain.

He didn't think he'd ever been battered from head to... not toe, calves before.

Come morning Spencer woke feeling as if he'd just regained consciousness after being run over by a semi-truck with lots of huge tires. He tried not to move a muscle. Even breathing hurt. When he assessed his body, he found several places that felt like burning coals against the more generalized pain. Wrist, left cheekbone, the site of the stab wound, a searing strip down his thigh and his rib cage on the left.

All those could be managed, he convinced himself, and he knew from other times he'd taken a beating that the day after was the worst. Then the body would start healing itself.

Okay. One more day before he seriously considered an escape plan.

Leah stirred beside him and he had to grit his teeth. "Are you awake?" she whispered.

"Yah." His mouth was still swollen, making it difficult to shape words. But he got out the two that were most important. "Pain pills."

"What?"

He had to repeat himself before she said, "Oh, no! I

should have woken you up earlier to take those. I'll get them right now."

She had to separate herself from him, the mattress rocking as she clambered out of bed. Teeth clenched, he held back the groans.

She hurried back. Sitting up enough to swallow the pills was agonizing. He needed the bathroom, but his bladder had to wait.

He caught glimpses as she got dressed, but as much as he normally enjoyed being tantalized by the fleeting sight of her curves, he didn't dare lift or even roll his head.

Wait.

It was a full half hour before the rigidity in his body eased enough, he was able to get up, shuffle to the bathroom and then lie down on the futon. As uncomfortable as the thing was, he needed to be out here where he could keep an eye on Leah and any possible entrances. He was able to half sit against the pile of pillows, so if something happened he could easily reach for his handgun.

Leah poached eggs for him and poured him a glass of orange juice. He was swallowing it when there was a polite knock on the door.

He called, "Who is it?" before Leah could reach the door.

"Del."

Spencer nodded at her and she let Del and Dirk in.

Del's gaze flicked to the gun then back to Spencer. "I'd say you look better, except…"

Spencer might have grimaced if that wouldn't have hurt. "Colorful?" he got out.

"Pretty as a rainbow," the other man confirmed. "You on your feet yet?"

"Sure." Spencer gave what was probably a death's head grin. "Hurt like hell today, though."

"Yeah, ain't that the way."

Dirk looked at Leah. "Anything you need?"

She succeeded in looking shy and even submissive. "I think we're okay. I went over to the lodge yesterday for some food and dishes. You know."

"Helen said you'd been by."

Spencer couldn't help asking. "Joe?"

Del answered, voice expressionless. "Died during the night."

Leah pressed her fingers to her lips to stifle a gasp. Both men glanced at her before returning their gazes to him. Dirk wasn't hiding his perturbation as well as Del was. He didn't like knowing Higgs had ordered—or even committed—the murder.

"Whatever I said about killing him, I didn't mean him to die," Spencer managed to get out.

Del obviously made out what he'd said because he nodded. "Figured. Ah…the colonel says he'll stop by later."

"Good. It'll be tomorrow before I can walk as far as the lodge." And, damn, he wished that wasn't true.

Leah saw the two men out, closed the door and waited through the thud of them descending the few steps before she turned around, distress on her face. "You were right."

"About Joe?" He was careful to sound…indifferent. "He wasn't in good shape when they hauled him away yesterday."

"Neither were you," she said tartly.

He let himself smile, although it couldn't look good. "I had the services of the only medic on site."

She opened her mouth, no doubt to remind him that she'd volunteered to look at Joe, too, but was again smart enough to let that remain unsaid.

"You were restless last night. Why don't you try to get some sleep?" she suggested.

He might do that. She'd wake him up soon enough when Higgs came calling. "You'll be here?"

"Won't go anywhere." She sketched a cross over her heart.

That made his misshapen mouth twitch.

He drifted in and out of sleep for much of the afternoon, helped along by the pain meds. Leah made sure he ate a little for lunch, and did wake him up midafternoon when Higgs came knocking.

He didn't have a lot to say, probably thanks to Leah's presence. "Shame about Joe," he remarked, his tone holding not a smidgen of regret.

Spencer met his eyes. "Sure is."

"We picked out a place to bury him. Can't let authorities get involved."

No shit. Couldn't let the body stay in the lodge long enough to start decomposing, either, Spencer reflected.

He stiffened when Higgs looked at Leah. "We're missing you in the kitchen. I suppose Spencer needs you today, but he should be on the mend by tomorrow. I'm hoping you'll make that cake again."

Her eyes glittered with dislike. Her acting had some limitations, it appeared. But she said, "I'll be glad to make it again."

Spencer spoke up. "I liked it, too."

To Higgs, she said, "Did Jennifer talk to you about picking huckleberries? We could make some great cobblers and pies with them, and stretch supplies, too."

He looked surprised. "No. I noticed some ripe berries. Wasn't sure whether they were edible."

"They're delicious. The mainstay for birds and bears and probably some other animals."

"I'll set it up," he said, glanced at Spencer and added, "Hope there's a big improvement by tomorrow."

Was that an order? Irritated, Spencer didn't show how he felt. "You and me both. I'm not built to sit on the sidelines."

A monster cloaked in an average body and mild manner, Colonel Higgs left. Spencer ground his teeth a few times to keep from verbally venting his anger.

Leah didn't like it, but he started doing some stretches and getting up to walk for a few minutes every half hour or so. They could not afford for him to stay down.

THE NEXT MORNING they took the short walk to the lodge slowly. Leah stayed close to him, but Spencer didn't reach for her. His face was so blank, she knew he was intent on hiding how much pain he was still in. Somehow, he walked evenly, betraying no need to favor one side or the other. He had allowed her to rewrap his wrist, and of course his face was at its worst: still swollen and vividly colored. The black eye was barely slitted, his mouth distorted.

Something like halfway, he said out of the blue, "Know how to hot-wire a car?"

"Hot-wire…?" She sounded startled. "Unfortunately, no. To tell you the truth, I'm completely ignorant where cars are concerned. Beyond how to start and drive them, of course."

He grunted.

"What are you thinking?"

"The Jeep." He'd mentioned it. "Want to get my hands on the key, but if I can't…" He frowned. "I can hot-wire it myself. Old vehicles like that are easy. Plus, the Jeep is back behind the lodge. We'd have a chance of getting a real head-start. I was thinking just in case."

Just in case he was dead or captive and she had to run

by herself. Sick to her stomach, she said, "The Jeep is out if I'm on my own."

He nodded, almost matter-of-factly. "We'll make sure it doesn't come to that."

Oh, good. She was completely reassured. She didn't have a chance to comment, though, because Arne Larson emerged from his cabin and fell into step with them.

"Good fight," he said admiringly.

So much for what had appeared to be a friendship with Joe. This was a guy who wouldn't have felt at all squeamish watching one gladiator troop mop up the other in the Colosseum. Spencer put on a front of being unemotional about what he'd had to do in the army and now, with the FBI, but she didn't believe in it. He still had a human reaction to events and people. He must; she couldn't be falling for him if he didn't. He wouldn't be so ready to sacrifice himself for her.

As for Arne…she'd swear she saw a trace of envy and dislike in his eyes.

Spencer didn't comment, probably saving his energy for mounting the lodge steps.

HE FELT ON edge all day, starting with finding out that Leah had been sent with two of the other women—Shelley and Lisa—to pick huckleberries.

"Galt will make sure no bears get 'em," Higgs told him, smirking.

"What's he going to do if a bear charges them?" Spencer asked.

"Shoot it, what else? What are you worrying about? Black bears are supposed to be afraid of people."

"Not all. And they're big enough to be dangerous, you know. Bullets from a handgun wouldn't even slow one down. And then there are the grizzlies. No matter what, you wouldn't want to get between any bear and her cub."

"Grizzlies? What are you talking about?"

Spencer looked at this idiot. "Grizzlies were reintroduced to the north Cascade Mountains years ago. They're around. I've seen plenty of pictures of them browsing through thickets of berries."

Not sure his slurred speech had gotten through, he was satisfied to see Higgs alarmed and studying the tree line covertly. Spencer instead looked around at the empty range. "I thought the others would be here."

"I had them stop to pick up the new rifles and ammunition."

He'd have to find a way to involve himself in returning the weaponry to the armory at lunchtime.

"You're pulling my leg, aren't you?" Higgs said suddenly.

"Pulling your leg?" Ah. "Nope. We'd have seen any bears around if we'd been careless enough to leave out food."

Colonel Higgs scowled at him. "Why didn't you say something?"

Spencer pulled off surprised. He hoped, given the state of his face. "You'd already chosen this site. I assumed you'd done your research." He shrugged. "I've heard guys talking about bears. Anyone from the northwest would know."

"You're not from around here."

"No, but I've climbed mountains here and in Alaska." He let the silence draw out a little before adding, "You're right that bears are mostly shy. If you stumble on 'em, they can be a problem, but we make enough racket to warn them off."

But the women picking berries wouldn't be, unless

they maintained a conversation, something that was unlikely with TJ Galt standing over them with his sneer and his Beretta M9A3 semiautomatic, a shade of brown that went with his favorite desert camo T-shirts and cargo pants. Spencer found his sartorial taste especially ironic since TJ was one of the few men here who had never served in the military.

"You up to trying out the new rifle?" Higgs asked. "I'd like your take on it."

"Tomorrow," Spencer said. "I'm one solid bruise right now. Getting up and down is a chore, and any recoil wouldn't help me heal."

Higgs accepted his answer, which made Spencer grateful that some of his injuries were so visible.

He did take one of the rifles that were supposedly being tried out by army rangers. The balance was okay. The optics were as good as anything he'd used before, but not an improvement. He only said, "Interesting," staying noncommittal as he handed it back to Ken Vogel. Then he glanced around.

"Where's Fuller?" He frowned, realizing a couple of other men were missing, too.

"More supplies. Fuller took his wife along with Jones."

Damn it. What did they need so soon after the last shopping expedition? Only food? This group did eat like hungry locusts. Still... Spencer tried to remember what day he, Lisa and Del had gone down to Bellingham. They'd seriously stocked up. Wednesday, he decided after counting back. Only five days ago.

Mine is not to reason why, he thought flippantly, before remembering the rest of the quote. *Mine is but to do and die.*

That seemed to sum up his current situation all too neatly.

Chapter Thirteen

After giving the other women instructions on how to tell which berries were ripe, Leah kept a sharp eye out for bears while they picked. For what good advanced warning would do. Either a black or grizzly bear could outrun any human over a short distance, should it feel inclined.

She ignored TJ, even when he wandered by her.

Otherwise, as she plucked berries and dropped them into a plastic bowl, she pondered the others, starting with him and Shelley.

If he wasn't such an unpleasant man, TJ would have been attractive: tall, broad-shouldered, fit. He walked like an athlete, had medium brown hair and hazel eyes. His nose had clearly been broken at some point, which didn't detract from a handsome face…except she couldn't help thinking he'd probably deserved to be slugged. She was ashamed to find she actually hoped that was what had happened, rather than a collision on a soccer field or a baseball pitch delivered too high.

She had only enough abstract knowledge about the dynamics in abusive relationships to understand why Shelley stayed with him. Real understanding eluded her. The dullness in that poor woman's eyes, her body language, the way she cringed whenever TJ came close… Leah would be willing to bet Shelley had grown up abused as a child, too, or at least watching her mother being hit by her father, or even by a succession of men. If somehow she escaped TJ, the odds were good she'd find another abusive man.

Jennifer was deferential around Tim, but not scared in the same way. Helen lit up when she saw Dirk. Lisa Dempsey... Leah was less sure about her. She wouldn't think of challenging Del or any man, but Leah had heard Lisa talking comfortably to him a few times, and his low voice as he actually talked to her, too.

It felt weird to imagine them all under arrest, diminished by convict uniforms and handcuffs, the women seeing their men only through glass if they stuck by them at all.

Shelley would, Leah knew, and Helen, too. The others...she was less sure.

How on earth had all these men gotten sucked into an objective so horrifying? She wanted to be able to hate them all, but discovered it wasn't that simple. Colonel Ed Higgs, she could hate. *He'd* dreamed up this evil, a betrayal of the nation that he had supposedly served. *He'd* recruited all these guys, who were fearful of a changing America but not necessarily fanatical until then. *He* could coolly and with a secret smile say, *Shame about Joe*, when he had ordered him to be executed.

Rick Metz...lacked personality. Did he need to be told what to believe? Maybe he'd been at loose ends until Colonel Higgs gave him a clear objective and whatever nonsense justifications he used.

She sifted through the names of the men she knew best, finding it harder than it should be to label them evil, or even bad. Del Schmidt pretty much ignored her, and Lisa sometimes shrank from him. Beyond that, he mostly seemed decent. He'd been courageous defending her. Same for Garrett Zeigler and Shawn Wycoff.

Except…she wondered if any of the three had been thinking about *her*. Maybe all they'd been doing was currying favor with Spencer while Shawn at least could enjoy poking a stick at Joe.

Dirk Ritchie seemed downright nice.

Arne Larson wasn't nice; Leah remembered him slamming her against the wall and groping her while leering. And she hadn't forgotten how brutally TJ Galt had tackled her when she tried to escape, slugging her before hauling her back to face Higgs, their unlikely alpha wolf, without a semblance of gentleness.

Gee, could that be why she hoped someone had, once upon a time, slugged *him* hard enough to permanently dent his nose?

There were others she definitely didn't like, and a whole bunch who treated the women as if they were barely useful. Did they really feel that way? Or were they just blending in, the way school children were sometimes cruel because they didn't have the courage to stand up and say no?

Spencer must know them all a whole lot better than she did. Did he regret what would happen to some of these men? Or had he become inured from previous undercover investigations? Nobody was all bad or all good; she did believe that. Even though Spencer must use people he was investigating to achieve his objectives, he'd have to stay focused on the crime they'd been willing to commit—or *were* willing to commit, in this case.

"Leah!" A heavy hand gripped her shoulder and spun her around.

Wide-eyed, righting her bowl before the berries spilled, she realized it was TJ.

"What were you doing, spacing out?"

She knew what she had to do. Bow her head, hope her hair fell forward to partly veil her expression and grovel. "I'm sorry," she mumbled. "I... I was worrying about bears."

The other women stole surreptitious glances at their surroundings.

"Their bowls are full. Yours is, too," he said impatiently. "Time to get back. This is a waste of my time."

Except she knew perfectly well that all he'd do once they got back was lean against the wall in the kitchen and watch them with both contempt and suspicion.

She bobbed her head and hurried toward the lodge, Lisa and Shelley keeping pace with her, TJ silently following. So much for using a berry-picking expedition to make a run for it. That scheme had been downright delusional.

FROM PARTWAY DOWN the table during dinner, a low voice carried to Spencer.

"...get down where I can have internet access..."

He didn't turn his head, making himself depend on peripheral vision. For once Higgs hadn't taken a seat near him. Instead, he'd grabbed a place beside Tim Fuller, and they'd had their heads together ever since. Damn. Had Fuller and the others gone to Bellingham at all?

"Don't like losing you for two days..." Higgs's voice got drowned out. Surfaced again. "...think it's important enough."

Fuller's fervor made the hair rise on the back of Spencer's neck. Probably whatever nugget of information he so eagerly sought had nothing to do with Spencer or Leah—but there was a lesser chance that it did.

Higgs seemed unconcerned, though. Even talking quietly, his enthusiasm could be heard. "...more like the SAKO TRG 42...big jump forward from the..."

Spencer couldn't hear the rest, but didn't need to. The SAKO TRG 42 was a Finnish rifle, much admired among the sniper community. He knew guys who'd sworn by it. Except for the unusual stock design, which did indeed remind him of the SAKO, he couldn't say anything special had jumped out at him about this latest weapon sent to army spec ops for experimentation. Arms makers did that often. Most of those rifles didn't prove themselves any better than what snipers were currently using or regular infantry carried.

When Higgs called down the table, "You handled that baby, Spencer. Tell Fuller what you thought."

Spencer dredged up a few admiring comments that got all the men excited, even though most of them lacked the skills to take advantage of a cutting-edge weapon.

What worried him more was the disappearance this afternoon of two of the men along with Higgs. Spencer had seen them coming out of the makeshift armory, expressions satisfied. He knew from background checks that Ken Vogel had spent a decade on a police bomb squad, while Steve Baldwin had been expelled from Stanford's physics program for reasons no one had wanted to talk about. Another Ph.D candidate had hinted that he'd been caught walking out with materials too dangerous to let out of the secure labs.

Spencer knew how most of these men had hooked up with Higgs: the internet. As fast as one fringe site that urged violence and revolution was shut down, another popped up. Like recognized like. He'd also done enough research to know that quite a few members of the group had been at a crossroads in their lives when they saw an opportunity that gave them a sense of purpose.

Baldwin was one example. No other grad program would take him. He must already have been working out what he could do with his knowledge, education and possibly some stashed-away dangerous material. Vogel had just gone through a divorce during which his wife claimed he abused her and the children. His visitation with those kids was to be supervised. He'd have seen that as an unforgivable insult; not only an attempt to humiliate him but also to steal *his* children.

Higgs, of course, had been forced out of the military for his views. Likewise, Arne Larson, given a dishonorable discharge that would limit his job opportunities.

And so it went. TJ Galt had had an unapologetic, vile presence on alt-right websites for several years.

Spencer had to make guesses about a few of them. Leaving the military to find themselves qualified only for poorly paid, low-end jobs, maybe. Don Durand's wife had left him, too. Dirk Ritchie's father had disowned his "embarrassment" of a son.

Yeah, most of these guys had been desperate to latch on to something that would salvage their self-esteem, make them feel important. Not hard to understand.

They wouldn't like prison, he thought grimly.

Even if he was knocked out of the equation, the investigation had been going on long enough, and these men, the pawns, would go down. It would be a shame to see them taking the fall for the scum financing Higgs's great dream, or stealing munitions from the United States.

Dinner was ending, people drifting away as the women cleared the table. Spencer took his time finishing a sizeable piece of Leah's cake and his third cup of coffee. When Higgs, bringing his own coffee cup, slid down the bench to join him, Spencer said, "Did you see Durand today at the target range? He's showing a real knack." Which was, unfortunately, true. "I may try him out at two hundred yards tomorrow. Get him working on positional shooting. It's never safe to assume you can settle in prone and not have to move. Plus bullet trajectory, zeroing in and understanding his range finder." He paused. "Is there any reason to focus on night observation devices?"

"Shouldn't think so." Higgs mulled that over. "If we have time, it probably wouldn't hurt."

Apparently, the plans were still in flux. Or else Higgs knew his small army might find themselves pinned down into the night.

Spencer nodded.

Looking frustrated, Higgs asked, "Is Durand the only one with sniper potential?"

Spencer waggled a hand. "Jason Shedd is getting there. He wasn't a hunter and didn't have comparable experience to the others with a rifle coming in, but he does have patience, an understanding of things like bullet trajectory, and a soft touch. He just had further to go."

"Given his experience as a mechanic, some of that makes sense."

"You don't mind me cutting the two of them out of the herd for more intensive training?"

"No, I'm lucky to have you. Originally, I thought I had two other former snipers on board, but one of them…" He shook his head. "Art Scholler. He was too glib. I got a bad feeling."

"You think he wanted in undercover?"

"Yeah."

Art Scholler *was* FBI, although of course that wasn't

his real name. Spencer had been brought in when Art got cut off cold.

"The other guy?"

"Didn't think he'd take orders. The guy had serious issues."

Spencer grunted. "After enough deployments, a lot of men bring home a cargo plane full of issues."

The colonel grimaced. "True enough. The anger is useful. The rest of it gets in the way."

From a man who'd been a member of the "Chair Force," Higgs's know-it-all attitude rubbed Spencer the wrong way. He knew plenty of airmen who'd been in war zones, but Higgs didn't impress him as one who'd gotten his hands, let alone his boots, dirty. As usual, he stayed agreeable and emphasized how invested he was as they discussed problems concerning a couple of other men on the team, including TJ Galt.

"He makes me think of a pit bull trained for fighting. Keeping him on a leash takes some effort," Higgs observed.

The guy did have a gift for reading people, which wasn't uncommon in predators. Talk about useful skills. In this case… Galt made no effort to hide his anger. If he had PTSD, it likely dated to his childhood. Spencer hadn't uncovered any adult trauma that would explain it.

They parted amicably, which didn't entirely settle the uneasiness Spencer felt, awakened by the half heard conversation. All he could do was pack it away with all his other worries. The weight of them, he thought, was like the kind of hundred-pound pack he'd once thought nothing of hefting. The cargo plane…well, he had other issues, too.

THE NEXT DAY passed in what Leah thought of as deceptive peace. Tim Fuller took off on some errand of his own, which surprised her. This was the first time since she'd been here that any of the men had left alone. Had he been sent to make phone calls for Higgs? Or might he have something personal he had to take care of? She had the uncharitable thought that he could have a meeting with his parole officer.

Along with the other women, she baked, cooked, cleaned and waited on the men. Her real life had come to be out of focus enough to seem hazy. She told herself she was better off that way. She was surprised when she counted back to realize she'd been here nine days. It seemed longer. Well, she couldn't afford to dwell on resentment or have an outbreak of rebellion.

Spencer couldn't afford for her to blow it, either. She suspected he was hurting a lot more than he let on, especially once he joined the other men. His eyes met hers briefly before a large group left for the shooting range. She read reassurance in that instant, but who knew?

In a few minutes the quiet would be shattered by the nonstop barrage. Were these guys really getting a lot more accurate, or were they just wasting ammunition and scaring wildlife for a mile or so around? It spoke to the isolation of the resort that nobody at all had heard the gunfire and reported it to the county sheriff's department or a ranger.

At lunchtime the men inhaled cheeseburgers, baked beans and apple pie *à la mode*. During the afternoon they seemed to break up into smaller groups for—who knew?—hand-to-hand combat training, lessons on stealth?

Or were some of them building a bomb?

That made her shiver.

Dinner was Jennifer's lasagna, loaves and loaves of garlic bread, and a grated carrot and raisin salad Leah made. It was sweet and substantial enough to appeal to men who wouldn't touch a green salad or plain broccoli, but still mostly qualified as a vegetable.

As if she cared about their nutritional intake. But everything she could do to blend in, to make herself valued, was good.

She was first setting out serving bowls when Tim Fuller walked in. Higgs didn't notice at first; Tim ended up sitting at the far end close to the women. The colonel glanced that way but didn't comment.

In her intense dislike, Leah thought, too bad the mythical parole officer hadn't found cause to lock up Tim and throw away the key. She must have smiled, because she discovered he was looking at her with an ugly expression. He and TJ Galt were two of a kind. With Joe Osenbrock, they'd made a vicious triumvirate.

With dinner over, Spencer stayed at the table with his usual refill of coffee, tonight talking to two men she hadn't had much to do with. Jason something and… She couldn't remember the other man's name at all.

The swelling in Spencer's face was going down, she noted, but the bruises had turned a multitude of colors. As she poured coffee from the carafe into Jason's cup, Spencer was saying something about wind, his speech much clearer than it had been even that morning.

The three of them weren't alone; a bunch of the men lingered, happy to hang out with friends, she gathered. During her last trip around the table to refill coffee cups, she shivered at the way several of the men watched her. She wasn't *afraid* of them, exactly—certainly not with Spencer present—but she could tell what they were thinking, and it gave her the creeps.

If there was another demand for more coffee, one of the other women could handle it. Clearly, Spencer wouldn't be ready to go for a while yet, so once she put leftovers away in the commercial refrigerator, she borrowed a sweatshirt hanging on a hook and slipped outside. She'd stay close to the door so she could hear Spencer calling for her. She knew eventually someone would notice she was out here. Sometimes, the other women took breaks like this, only to be chased inside when one of the men came to check on them.

The crisp evening air felt good, and when she tipped her head back, she saw the first stars appearing against a deep purple sky.

It had to be a lot later than usual, to be already getting dark. Fine by her; her new domestic tasks didn't exhaust her, but she'd barely sat down today except for perching on the bench to gobble each meal. Besides…she'd seen a glint in Spencer's eyes when his gaze strayed her way while she was wiping down the table. If he was feeling better enough…

Uncle Edward had built a couple of crude benches back here, wide boards laid over cut-off tree stumps. She chose one and sat, knowing she was almost hidden in the shadow of a cedar that would soon have to be cut down if the lodge was to survive. The roots probably already burrowed beneath the foundation.

Male voices drifted to her, abruptly becoming louder. Leah stiffened, ready to hustle back in the kitchen door if they came any closer.

One of them was Ed Higgs's, she realized.

"You're *sure*?" It was a demand; he didn't want to believe whatever he'd been told.

"Positive. It took some serious searching, but I found a picture. He was coming out of a courthouse, wearing the typical FBI getup."

She quit breathing. *Oh no, oh no.*

Tim Fuller was ebullient, really glad to be able to bring down a man he'd deeply resented. "You know," he continued, "black suit, white shirt, shiny black wingtips, blue tie. He was identified as Special Agent Alex Barr. Chicago office then. Now, I don't know."

"God damn." Anger threaded Higgs's weariness. "I can't believe it."

"Believe it," Tim said. "I printed the picture. Left it in my cabin."

Leah rose to her feet and began feeling her way toward the two steps up to the kitchen door. She stopped just short. No—the minute she opened it, light would spill out. Slip all the way around the lodge, she decided. Spencer might have only minutes.

The last few words she heard before going around the corner of the old log building were "no choice."

Chapter Fourteen

Spencer had stood to go looking for Leah when the front door opened. He turned automatically to see who'd come in. It was her, and the flat-out terror he saw on her face had even the hair on his arms rising. An instant later she'd mostly blanked that out, and he hoped the two men with him hadn't seen her naked emotion.

"I'm ready to head back to the cabin," he said easily. "See you two in the morning. We'll do some more work on setting up shots from different vantage points."

Both appeared eager. Neither had let ego get in the way of learning all they could from him. Amidst the "goodnights," he walked toward Leah.

"Ready to go?"

"Yes." The tremor in her voice would have had him on full alert even if he hadn't already shot straight to maximum readiness. He took her arm as they went out the door and descended the stairs. Then, seeing no one, he bent his head and asked softly, "What's wrong?"

"They know." It tumbled out of her. "Even your real name. Tim told Higgs he'd found a photo of you coming out of a courthouse somewhere."

"Where were they?"

"Out back."

The wheels in his head spun. "We don't dare go back to the cabin." He started hustling her in the opposite direction, to the nearest tree line. Thinking aloud, he said, "The Jeep."

"But…it's dark. And don't you need some tools to hot-wire it?"

"Got the key today," he said, more grateful than he could remember being for anything, except maybe seeing an unconscious Joe Osenbrock being carried away. He still didn't like their only option. The minute anyone heard the sound of the engine being fired up in back, the hunt would be on.

Their best hope, he concluded, was that neither Higgs nor Fuller had had a chance to spread the word. The other guys would wonder, maybe think someone was using the Jeep to drive out to the range to collect something that had been forgotten earlier.

The longer the hesitation, the more chance he and Leah would have to make a clean getaway.

The bigger, more powerful vehicles wouldn't have much, if any, advantage over the Jeep during the first mile or two. The rutted, winding gravel road on the edge of that steep plunge to the river had to be taken with care no matter how hot the driver was to catch someone ahead of him. Unfortunately, he'd have to drive cautiously, too.

Once past that stretch, they'd be overtaken quickly unless they got a big enough head start.

A plan forming in his head, he said, "We have to go for the Jeep. Pray nobody noticed the missing key."

Leah didn't say anything, just jogged at his side. He was glad to see that she'd put on a sweatshirt over her T-shirt; borrowed, he thought. He didn't have any equivalent, which meant he'd be damn cold at night, but the temperature hadn't dropped below freezing anytime this past week, so they should be all right.

He didn't want to even think about how long it would take for them to walk out to the closest neighbor or tiny town where someone might have a working telephone. Shit, why hadn't he kept his own with him, even if it was useless up here? He might have had coverage before they got as far as Glacier or Maple Falls.

Or…what would happen if they headed north for the border? He tried to envision a map, but had a bad feeling that was even rougher country. And it wasn't as if they'd know when they reached the border, or that the entire thing was patrolled 24/7. No towns or highways within remotely easy reach of where they'd emerge, either.

At least heading for the Mount Baker highway, they'd be going downhill. Given his condition, that was a real positive if they had to eventually go on foot.

He stopped Leah as close to the armory as they could get without stepping out in the open. As they stood in silence, he searched the ground between them and the lodge. The only movement was the dart of bats. A faint "whoo" came to his ears from somewhere behind them.

"Okay," he murmured, "I want you to turn around and go back to the head of the road leading out of here." The moon had risen enough to let her see where he was pointing. "When I get there, I'll stop for you to jump in."

"Why don't I just get in the Jeep with you now?" she asked.

He shook his head and talked fast. "There's a chance they'll be waiting for me. If so, you need to take off on your own. You can't follow the road—they'll find you. Traveling in the dark is hard, but try to get a ways before you hide. Got that? I know you can do it. You know this area, wildlife. Better than they do."

"Do you really think we can outrun them?" she whispered.

"No, but I have a plan for that, too."

She pressed her lips together, but nodded instead of arguing as he felt sure she wanted to. Her resistance to the idea of abandoning him to save herself was a part of why he'd fallen for her so fast.

Right now all he did was give her a quick, hard kiss and a push. "Go."

She went, slipping away and disappearing more quickly in the thick darkness beneath the big trees than he'd expected.

He had no choice but to cross the thirty yards or so of open ground to reach the back of the armory. Hating to be so exposed, he did it at a trot. Reaching the back wall, he flattened himself against it, pulled his Sig Sauer and took a moment to slow his breathing.

Then he slid like a shadow around the side, instinct throwing him back to when he'd been a soldier, letting him place his feet soundlessly.

There were no voices. The only light came from lodge windows and, more diffused, the first cabins. The Jeep sat where it had been since Higgs moved it out of the building.

Spencer stepped from the cover of the building, just as another man appeared from where he'd hidden behind the low branches of one of the old cedars. Spencer froze, weapon trained on the man.

"Is what Fuller says true?" asked Dirk Ritchie.

Finger tightening on the trigger, Spencer sweated over

what to do. If he fired, men would pour out of the lodge. And, damn, he didn't want to kill Dirk.

"How did you know I'd be out here?"

"I saw you take the key," Dirk said simply. His hands remained at his sides, even though he was carrying, too.

"Did you?" Spencer said tensely. "You and Helen need to take off, too. Use the confusion after I'm gone."

Dirk stayed quiet.

Spencer pitched his voice low, yet filled it with intensity. "Do you really want to be party to slaughtering what might be hundreds of people who are just thinking about going to their kids' parent-teacher meetings, or the guy they just met, or a sick parent? Remember the Oklahoma City bombing that killed *fifteen* preschooler children?"

Somebody else would come out any minute. He had to *go*.

He took the last steps to the Jeep. "Stop me, or don't."

Only a few strides separated the two men now. Shooting Dirk would feel like murder, but if he didn't—

Dirk stepped back. "Get out of here."

"Thank you."

The other man turned and walked toward the lodge, not hurrying. Switching his attention to the Jeep, Spencer had a sickening thought. What if Dirk had told Higgs he'd seen Spencer pocket the key? What if the Jeep had already been disabled?

He couldn't hesitate. Didn't have time to think of a Plan B. What were the chances he'd make it to the tree line? Gripping the overhead bar above the seats, Spencer swung himself in behind the wheel, grimacing as the quick movement tugged at his stitches and ignited pain in his ribs. No need to open or close a door. He pulled the key from his pocket, inserted it, held his breath and turned it.

The engine roared to life.

The porchlight above the back door into the kitchen came on. A voice called out.

He put the Jeep in gear and slammed his foot down on the gas pedal.

LEAH HADN'T QUITE reached the meeting place when she heard the engine start. Spencer had gotten that far. Thank God. Thank God.

Running, she crossed the weedy gravel to reach the other side and turned to see the Jeep racing toward her. The headlights switched on just before he came even with her. He braked, she grabbed for the door handle and yanked. Metal squealed, but the door refused to give way.

"Jump in."

What she did was fall in, but it worked. The Jeep was rocketing forward long before she untangled herself enough to sit up. If there was a seat belt, her groping fingers didn't find it. Instead, she gripped the edge of the seat with one hand and flattened the other on the dashboard.

The feeble, yellow beams cast by the headlights didn't illuminate the road ahead more than ten or fifteen feet.

"I hope you know this road," she heard herself gasp.

"I do."

He'd been aware from the beginning that there was the possibility he'd have to run for it, she supposed, which meant being ultra-observant about little details like the only outlet from the resort. Spencer sounded awfully tense, though.

"Do you hear—?"

He didn't have to finish. Yes, deep-throated engines had been started. Aside from her own car, every vehicle she'd seen up here dwarfed this old Jeep. The giant SUVs and pickups could almost run right over the top of it.

She craned her neck to see behind her. Bright lights appeared.

Spencer mumbled a few obscenities.

"You have a plan." How did she sound even semi-calm? The cold wind whipped her hair and made her eyes water. Gravel crunched beneath the tires. She dreaded the moment when they reached the stretch above the river.

She ought to be thankful it was dark, and she wouldn't be able to see the valley floor.

"I'm going to take a few curves," he said tersely, "brake long enough for you to leap out and run for the woods, then try to set up a skid so that the Jeep goes over the edge and down into the river. They'll think we screwed up."

"What if you can't jump out?" she said numbly.

"I don't have time to try to find a heavy enough rock to brace the accelerator."

"There's something behind the seat." She'd caught a glimpse when she was facedown after her tumble into the Jeep. She didn't know what she'd seen, but now she got on her knees and felt down in the cavity. "I think it's a car battery. They're heavy, aren't they?"

"Yes. Damn. That should work. Can you pick it up?"

"I think so." Her position was completely unsafe, crouched instead of sitting while trying to heft a heavy object between the seat backs. If he started that skid too soon… Laughter almost bubbled up. Unsafe. *Right*.

She tugged and rocked it until she got her fingers beneath the rusty metal, and then twisted, plunked onto her butt and lowered the battery to her lap.

She sensed Spencer's quick glance.

"We're coming up on a good place to let you out. Just

beyond, there's a gap where the guardrail has rusted and broken. That's what I'll aim for."

Leah's head bobbed as if she was just fine with any of this. "You'll find me?"

"Yes." He braked, skidded enough to have him swearing again and stopped. She scrambled over the door, leaving the battery on the seat. He accelerated again before she started running.

THIS WOULD ALL be for nothing if the Jeep hung up on a stubbornly intact stretch of guardrail, but he had no time to waste to scout ahead to be sure he knew where the break was. All Spencer could do was judge distances from his memory.

Here.

He braked, cranked the wheel hard, then lifted the battery over the gearshift. Got out.

The sound of approaching engines was too loud. No time.

He slipped the gearshift into Neutral and shoved the battery down on the accelerator at almost the same moment. The Jeep leaped forward, the open door whacked him and he tumbled free.

Without looking to see if he'd succeeded, he ran full out for the bank on the uphill side of the road and scrambled up it. There, he paused only momentarily, turning. The Jeep had disappeared, the sound of its engine drowned out by approaching vehicles. Had the steering somehow corrected itself?

Then he heard metal tearing, screaming in agony... followed by an unholy explosion.

Just as the first set of headlights illuminated that stretch of road he faded back into the forest.

DEEP IN THE TREES, Spencer couldn't see any better than he would have in a cavern a mile below the ground. He should have set up some kind of plan for him and Leah to find each other when separated. If she didn't stick pretty close to the road, it would take sheer luck for them to stumble onto each other.

Swearing silently as the receding shouts faded behind him, he made his way uphill, trying to stay twenty feet or so from the road. If the sound of pursuit reached him, he wouldn't be able to keep doing that. At least he could be assured he *would* hear anyone chasing him on foot; it was impossible to pass through the tangle of vegetation without making some noise.

Something swiped him in the face. He shook his head and spun. A swag of lichen, pale even in the limited light, still swayed.

He had a memory of telling Leah *not* to follow the road if she had to take off on her own. Surely to God she'd use common sense and realize they didn't have a prayer of finding each other if she didn't.

He kept moving, pausing every ten feet or so to listen.

Uphill, he heard a muffled cry. Animal? Bird?

Some thrashing followed.

Moving as quietly as he could, he headed that direction. What if she'd hurt herself? he thought suddenly but pushed the fear aside.

Quiet closed around him. Maintaining any orientation took determination, and Spencer wouldn't swear he wasn't veering off a straight line toward a sound that could have been a porcupine waddling through the forest, or a bear crashing on its way.

Guessing himself to be close, he finally said, "Leah?" All he could do was hope he wasn't too close to the road—and that Higgs hadn't been smart enough to have men walking it, listening and watching for any indication that someone was in there and not dead on the rocky bank of the low-running river.

"Spencer?"

"Hold still."

She didn't answer. He stepped forward carefully. He felt renewed irritation at himself; if he'd had his phone, he'd have also had a flashlight—although he wouldn't have dared use it now.

He put out a foot and found only space, teetering before he drew back.

A woeful whisper came from the darkness. "I fell in."

Spencer crouched. His eyes had adjusted well enough for him to see fern fronds waving wildly. Presumably, they disguised a hollow. Maybe a giant tree stump had rotted into nothingness; who knew?

"I'm here," he murmured. "Are you hurt?"

"I don't think so."

"Okay." Relief flooded him. He held out a hand. "Can you see me?"

"Yes." More stirring among what he thought was mostly lush clumps of sword ferns. A slim hand seized his, and he exerted steady pressure until she scrambled out of the hollow and fell against him.

Her arms wrapped his torso even as he held her tight, ignoring the pain in his wrist.

Against his chest, she mumbled, "I was so scared! And afraid I couldn't find you, and—"

Exhilarated because they *had* found each other, he chuckled. Her hair stirred against his cheek.

"I was getting a little worried myself," he admitted.

Her head came up. "What *happened*?"

"The Jeep sailed over the cliff and exploded when it hit the rocks at the bottom. Last I knew, the SUVs coming up behind us stopped there. I heard voices. Whether they bought it entirely… I don't know. I'm betting they don't find a way to get to the Jeep until daylight, though. Whether they're taking into account the possibility we weren't in the Jeep, I don't know."

After a moment she nodded. "Now what?" she asked, sounding as if she was running through options in her head.

That was an excellent question. From where they stood, downhill would take them southeast. They'd almost have to hit the highway. Even so, he'd give a lot for a topographical map. And, hey, food, warmer clothes, possibly a sleeping bag, the flashlight and phone, the absence of which he'd already regretted, and probably a lot of other things that hadn't yet occurred to him but would as soon as he or Leah needed them.

He winced. Like the bottle of pain meds. Except, he'd stuck two of them in his pocket, meaning to take them with dinner but decided not to show his vulnerability so publicly. He'd hold out as long as he could before taking them one at a time.

Preferably after they came on at least a trickle of water. Right now…

"Two choices. Keep going, away from the road. Or hunker down for the night. If we're going to do that, you found us a great place to hide."

He kind of thought she made a face before saying, "I agree. What's your preference? You okay?" She glanced at his still-bandaged wrist.

Reluctantly, he said, "I'm fine. I think we move on. We're too close to the road here. By morning, if not sooner, they'll be looking for us. I haven't had the impression that any of them are real outdoorsmen. A few say they've hunted, so maybe I'm wrong. Still, most outdoor experience doesn't prepare you for a temperate rain forest."

"Have *you* ever spent any time in the north Cascades?"

"Yeah, did some climbing here years ago." Over the course of several leaves, a buddy, Aaron, and he had ascended seven mountains altogether, from the Rockies to the Teton Mountains and here in the Cascades. Spencer hadn't gone climbing since Aaron had been killed in a firefight.

"What about bears? I know what they can do, remember."

He decided not to remind her about porcupines, also nocturnal. "They're rarely aggressive with humans, as you know."

After a minute Leah straightened away from him. "I'm ready."

Conscious of his many aches and the sharp pain in his side and thigh and wrist, he'd have liked to sleep for a few hours. But he wouldn't feel any better tomorrow morning, the next day, or the next. Even a little distance covered tonight would give them a head start tomorrow.

He nodded and led the way, hoping like hell he was going approximately in the right direction—and that they wouldn't stumble out on the winding road where someone might be waiting for them.

The parable about the blind leading the blind crossed his mind. Aesop? Just as well he couldn't remember how that story ended.

Chapter Fifteen

Because of his recent wounds and undoubted pain, Leah insisted they take regular breaks to rest. He didn't argue, but gave away his tension by regularly pushing a button on his watch to check the time. She didn't bother asking how long they'd been on their way, and he didn't offer the information. The day's stresses had caught up with her ages ago—and if she found out that was really only half an hour ago, she might scream—but really she was grateful to be so tired; she couldn't do any concentrated worrying. She just followed in Spencer's wake, knowing at least that she wouldn't tumble into another hole unless he did first.

The ground was soft and uneven, though. Squishy in places, more from the depth of the moss and decomposing organic matter. They clambered over and walked around fallen trees, some that might have come down last winter, others already rotting and serving as nurse logs for saplings. In some of those places faint rays of moonlight found them, and she glimpsed tiny distant stars. Much of the time enormous trees reared above them, blocking out the sky. She had a vague memory of Uncle Edward talking about some true old-growth forest close by and wondered if that was what this was.

It might be, because at some point the walking became easier since they weren't having to fight the ferns and salmonberries and who-knew-what that scratched and tripped them. The darkness was almost absolute, the boles of standing trees enormous. Not that the ground didn't remain uneven, the extreme dark hiding obstacles that would cause Spencer to growl under his breath before he helped her around or over them.

She walked right into him when he stopped.

"I'm beat," he said. "I suggest we get on the other side of this log and try to sleep a little."

Since she was very close to sleepwalking, Leah thought she could do that. And she knew Spencer must be dead on his feet to actually admit to needing a rest.

They had to go around this time. Taking her hand, he guided her. The trunk must have been six or eight feet in diameter. Even decomposing, it reared above her head. On the back side, he advanced slowly before stopping, seeming to feel his way. "This looks as good as anyplace."

Looks? *She* couldn't see a thing, but she wasn't about to quibble, either.

Once she'd squatted and then plunked down, she tried very hard not to think about what insects inhabited a rotting log. Would there be snakes around? Not poisonous ones, she was pretty sure. Her hand bumped something that sort of…crumbled. Recoiling, she made out a lighter shape against the dark backdrop of loam and moss. Mushrooms. Now, *those* could be poisonous, but she didn't plan to eat one.

She heard a groan as Spencer carefully lowered himself beside her. Oh, heavens—she should have helped him. Given the possibly broken wrist, he wouldn't lean any weight on that arm, and the gash in his thigh had to hinder him.

Too late.

"God, this feels good," he said after a minute.

"Uh-huh." Except she felt herself listing sideways until she came up against his big, solid body. "Can we lie down?" She was slurring.

"We can."

They shifted, she squirmed, he wrapped her in his arms and they ended up prone. He spooned her body from behind. His arm made a perfect pillow. Her eyelids sank closed, she mumbled something that was supposed to be "good night" and fell asleep.

CRADLING THIS WOMAN he suspected he loved, Spencer wasn't as quick to drop off to sleep.

When things went to shit, it happened fast.

If not for the damn fight, he'd be in a lot better physical shape and thus more confident that he and Leah would make it safely out of this densely wooded, uninhabited forest. If he'd had even ten or fifteen minutes' warning, he could have filled a pack with food, first-aid supplies, flashlight and more. As it was, they were screwed if either of them so much as developed blisters on their feet. His boots protected his ankles, while Leah's athletic shoes were fine for walking, but wouldn't keep her from turning an ankle.

They just about had to move during the daytime rather than at night even though they might be spotted. Especially given their physical condition, they had to be able to see where they were stepping. In fact, they were lucky no disaster had already occurred with them blundering around in the dark.

He cast his mind back to that brief encounter with Dirk. Spencer had had no idea he'd been seen pocketing the key. If it had been anybody but Dirk…if Dirk had told

Higgs, or when he saw Spencer at the Jeep had opened his mouth and yelled… No point in going there now.

He hoped Dirk *had* kept his mouth shut and did find a way to take off.

His thoughts jumped again.

How the hell had that idiot Fuller stumbled on the photo?

He actively tried not to be photographed. With the press sticking their noses in everywhere, he'd been unable to completely evade them given that he had to testify in court. Most outlets were good about not publishing those pictures, but he knew of a couple that had made it into newspapers or TV news stories. There were undoubtedly more online. In fact, the one Tim Fuller had described in Leah's hearing had to be one of those.

His ascendancy in Higgs's estimation had rubbed Tim, in particular, wrong for months. But had he made mistakes that gave away his law-enforcement background? Spencer shook his head slightly. He had no idea, and at this point that was irrelevant. Permanently irrelevant, if he declined to go undercover again.

Tim had to have sensed/heard/seen something to make him do that kind of online prowling. Or, hell, had he contacted a friend who was more of a computer wizard? Maybe, Spencer concluded.

For all that things had gone to shit, he and Leah had made their getaway and, right now, were fine. They wouldn't starve to death in the next two or three days.

The tricky moment would be when they had to approach a road.

He nuzzled Leah's silky hair and let sleep claim him.

HIS BODY'S DEMAND awakened him before Leah had so much as moved. In fact, it didn't appear either of them had made any of the restless shifts in position normal to sleepers. Her head still rested on his biceps; he still spooned her.

He'd have enjoyed the moment if he didn't need to empty his bladder, and if his body wasn't reporting multiple other complaints. His shoulder ached, his arm was stiff, his wrist felt broken, his thigh throbbed and his whole left side was on fire. In a general way, he felt like crap. What if he was coming down with a cold or the flu?

Stuffing a groan back down where it came from, he gently shook Leah. "Time to rise and shine."

She whimpered, stirred and whimpered again. "I'm stiff. Although I don't know why I'm whining. You're the one who is injured."

He didn't say so, but he dreaded getting up.

Leah did get to her hands and knees, then to her feet. She suddenly said, "I need—" and bolted for a nearby tree.

Since he'd rather she not see him dealing with his infirmities, he got up, too, in slow increments. Water or no water, he was taking one of those damn pills. Just as she reappeared around the tree, he shuffled toward a different one.

There, he used the facilities, then did some stretches before returning to Leah.

"Turns out GrubHub can't find us to deliver that Denny's breakfast," he said. "Guess we'll have to do without."

Her smile rewarded him. "There are berries ripe, if we can find a clearing."

"Stumble on one, you mean."

"At least we can *see*."

That was an improvement, he'd concede.

He started out. He got the pill down, but was left with a foul taste in his mouth. Walking loosened muscles, and the pill did some good, too, but he felt as if someone was stabbing his thigh with a red-hot poker. All he could do was block out what he couldn't change and go on.

By the time sunlight made it to the forest floor, it was diffuse, soft, even tinted green-gold. He still had to watch carefully for the best places to set down his feet, which made for slow going. Common sense did battle with a sense of urgency; what if finding out they were being dogged by the FBI inspired Higgs to launch an early attack?

Helplessness didn't sit well with Spencer, but practically, there wasn't a damn thing he could do to prevent any immediate action Higgs took. He doubted a bomb had actually been built, but the debacle during the Boston Marathon had demonstrated how much damage could be done by really primitive bombs. He was afraid Ken Vogel, with his bomb squad experience, could put together any number of lethal explosive devices even without input from a budding physicist with an interest in nuclear fission.

Until he got his hands on a phone, he had no way to alert his office that the operation had blown up on him.

Then focus on the moment. Except for my aching body. Best not to think about that.

Deciding it was time for a short break, he spotted a moss-covered rock more or less the right height to let them sit.

Once they did so, Leah looked at him with worry in her eyes. "What do you think they're doing?"

"Right now?" He checked his watch. "Struggling up-river to the wreck. That'll take them at least a couple of hours from the best place to leave vehicles."

"And then?"

Trust her to echo his concerns.

"I think there are two logical options for Higgs. One is to pack up and leave, probably have the others disperse until he can line up an alternate place for them to train. The other is to go for an immediate attack."

"Immediate?"

"Once he realizes we're on foot, he may decide to have the men hunt us for a day or two. Catching us would solve their problem with timing." He didn't have to say, *executing us.* "Otherwise, he could pull together a plan for an attack that might not be quite as spectacular as he intended, but those rocket launchers alone give him the firepower to threaten a gathering of politicians or even the president himself."

"You know him. Which is more likely?"

He didn't hesitate. "Dispersing. He likes the pieces to fit together. He'll want the big bang, so to speak. To accomplish that, the attack was to take place on a lot of levels. Bomb or bombs, rocket launchers, snipers picking off counterattackers or survivors trying to get away. Maybe even sending in a squad of men who don't have the range to be snipers to mow people down."

Leah looked more horrified by the minute. "That's why he wanted you."

"He needed a sniper to train others. That's what I was doing."

The urgency tapped on his shoulder, and he rose to his feet. "I'll stiffen up if we stop for long. Let's get going."

They continued in silence, Spencer straining to hear any sounds unnatural for the forest. Every now and again, a bird would flit by, most unidentifiable, a few common enough he recognized them, like the crow and later a jay, although that had unfamiliar coloration. They weren't plagued by a lot in the way of insects. Mosquitoes and even flies would prefer moist areas, butterflies open meadows with flowers. The rotting logs were no doubt rife with crawly things, centipedes, sow bugs and the like. Nothing that stung, as far as he knew.

And, on a glass half-full note, it wasn't raining. He knew from experience that rain wasn't uncommon here even in July and August. Some water to drink would be welcome; in fact, thirst was increasingly making itself known. But getting wet and having to keep going, pants chafing their legs, even socks soaked, that could be miserable.

"I hear something," she whispered.

He stopped and cocked his head. Speak of the devil. That had to be running water.

He turned, held a finger to his lips and progressed with even greater care. The small stream they found took enough of a tumble over rocks to have caused the delicate rippling sound. A deer that had been drinking saw them and bounded away.

"Oh, my."

"This water will likely make us sick," he told her, dredging through his memory. "Giardia is the problem, as I recall. If we could boil it…"

She wrinkled her nose. "No stove handy."

"Nope. I don't think symptoms will catch up with us for at least a week or two." He hoped that recollection was accurate. "We'll need to ask for treatment once we have a chance to see a doctor."

If she doubted that time would come, she didn't comment.

Spencer splashed his face to cool it, and wished for a water bottle, too.

If wishes were horses…

His head had begun to throb. He debated taking the

last pill now versus waiting, deciding on the latter. He might need it more come morning.

LEAH'S STOMACH GROWLED. She pressed a hand to it, hoping Spencer hadn't heard. He had enough to worry about, and given the toll his injuries took, he needed fuel for his body even more than she did.

He'd gotten quieter as the day went on, too. Pain tightened his face whenever he didn't remember to hide it. The flush she saw on his lean cheeks above dark stubble made her more uneasy. Even with all the willpower in the world, pushing himself to get back on his feet as soon as he did couldn't have been good for his recovery. She'd known all along that his risk of infection was high. She'd been able to don sterile latex gloves, and the gauze, scissors, needle and suturing material were sterile, too. Unfortunately, the blade of that black-handled knife Joe had used on him wasn't. Then there were the dirty shirts used to stem the bleeding. This was an awful time for the infection to appear. Dumb thing to think—was there a time that would have been *good*? If only there'd been antibiotics in that first-aid kit, or Spencer had stocked them along with the pain meds.

He was capable of going on with a fever, at least for now, Leah convinced herself. But what if they hadn't found their way out of the wilderness two days from now? Three?

He did go on, and on, hours upon hours, until her thighs burned and she'd quit thinking about anything but the next step. She'd thought of taking the lead but decided against it. With Spencer in front, he was more likely to stop when he needed it, while she might misjudge his stamina.

Just then Spencer stopped, Leah stumbling to a halt

just before she walked into him. Blinking, she realized the light had changed without her noticing, deepening into purple.

"We risk getting injured if we continue in the dark," Spencer said, his voice rough. "I'm sorry we didn't come across any berries."

She took the hand he held out. "Going without for a day or two isn't that big a deal. Isn't fasting supposed to be good for you?"

"I've read that. I'm not convinced."

"Me, either." Studying him anxiously, she said, "I should look at your wounds while there's still some light."

"Why?" He let her go and lowered himself to another mossy piece of ground with a few pained grunts he apparently couldn't hold back.

"Why? Because—" She didn't finish.

"I'm not sure we even dare wash the wounds out in a stream," he said wearily. "What if that introduces different microorganisms into my body? And, in turn, I'd be introducing bacteria into the stream that might be deadly to fish or mammals downstream that drink out of it. What's more—" he continued inexorably "—we have no supplies to rewrap my wounds and especially my ribs."

The ribs might be hurting him more than anything, she realized. The binding did offer some support. Yes, she could tear her T-shirt into strips, say, but the knit fabric would be too stretchy to provide the same kind of support.

"I'm sorry." She sank down beside him. "I wish I could do something."

"I'll be okay. I just wish—" He shook his head as if regretting having said that much.

"Wish?" Leah prodded.

"I was sure I'm not leading us astray."

"Short of your watch converting into a compass, I don't see how you can know. You're not Superman, Spencer." Then she stopped again and frowned. "Why am I still calling you that?"

"You don't have to." With a sigh, he rolled his head. "But I might not answer to Alex."

"Really?"

He managed a smile. "No, I'm kidding, but I've even been thinking of myself as Spencer. It's like... Do you speak a foreign language?"

"I'm pretty fluent in Spanish."

"You think in it when you're speaking it, right?"

"Yes."

"When I go undercover, I immerse myself to that extent. I'm not Special Agent Alex Barr. I *am* Spencer Wyatt. I can't slip."

"I can see that," she said slowly, even as she wondered how he could possibly do that. He'd said something once about not being sure who he was anymore, and how he'd done things, bad things, he didn't name. Not raped women, she felt certain. If he'd beaten men to death, or shot them, she believed he'd had adequate provocation.

Apparently losing interest in the subject, he said, "I think I'd like to lie down."

He let her help him, which said a lot about his condition. He encouraged her to join him, and soon they were curled up together. As the temperature dropped with nightfall, he had to be cold on top of everything else—unless he was burning up, of course. Leah rubbed his bare arms and lifted his hands to her skin beneath her sweatshirt. That he didn't protest told her how lousy he felt.

She kept thinking about a man who'd spent—she didn't know—much of the past several years, at least, undercover with violent fanatics who wanted to remake the country into their twisted ideals. She hadn't heard any slurs from him, as she had from some of the other men, but he must know all the right things to say to allow him to blend in.

How jarring it must be to return to his real life, whatever that was. An apartment? How homey was that, when it stayed empty for months on end? He presumably had no pets, he'd said he wasn't close to family and she didn't believe he had a girlfriend or fiancée waiting patiently for him. Spencer Wyatt—no, Alex Barr —wasn't the kind of man to make promises to one woman and have sex with another.

Feeling him relax into sleep, she thought, *I do know him. Of course I do.*

He'd been willing to give his life for her. That said enough about him to erase even fleeting doubts.

Hunger pushed off sleep for another while, but she was exhausted enough to drop off eventually.

Waking suddenly, the darkness unabated, she lay very still. What had disturbed her…? The answer came immediately. A wave of convulsive shivering seized Spencer. His back arched and his teeth chattered before he could clamp them shut.

Terrified, she realized there wasn't a single thing she could do except hold him, and keep holding him.

Chapter Sixteen

A murky haze that made Leah think of smog had settled over the usually crystal-clear silver-gray of Spencer's eyes. Or maybe it was more like a film. All she knew was that he couldn't possibly be seeing as well as usual. He couldn't hide that he was still shivering, too.

She watched as he staggered out of her sight to pee, returning a minute later. His usual grace had deserted him. How could they keep going? If they'd been on a smooth path or the road, maybe, but as it was...

How can we not *keep going?* Leah asked herself bleakly. It wasn't as if he had a twenty-four-hour flu bug. He wouldn't get better until he was on powerful antibiotics. If they didn't reach a hospital, he might die.

Even if they'd both been healthy, each day would be more grueling than the last, considering that they were able to drink only occasionally, and had nothing whatsoever to eat. It surely couldn't be that far before they reached the highway.

"You ready?" he asked gruffly.

Leah nodded. "Let me go first today."

He stared at her for long enough, she wasn't sure whether he was really slow in processing what she'd said, or resisting the idea. But finally, he nodded. Good.

She had to look around before deciding which way

they'd come from, and therefore which way she needed to go. Some feature of ancient geology had formed a shallow dip here, and the forest was dense enough, she couldn't see very far ahead. As they started walking, her thighs let her know when the land tilted downward again.

Once, she said, "Oh, did you see that?" and turned, for a minute not seeing Spencer at all. Her heart took a huge, painful leap.

He plodded around the trunk of one of the forest giants. He hadn't heard her, and the small mammal she'd seen had long since dashed out of sight. His teeth were clenched, his eyes glazed, but he was able to keep moving.

No choice.

From then on she made sure to look over her shoulder regularly to be sure he was still with her.

The pace seemed awfully slow, but she felt sure that raw determination was all that kept Spencer moving.

A distant sound caught her attention. She grabbed Spencer's arm to stop him and listened, momentarily confused. That could be a river, but if it was the Nooksack, that meant they'd also reached the highway that followed it. Of course there were tributaries, like the one that flowed from the side of Mount Baker, running past the resort to meet the larger Nooksack, but the water didn't rush like—

It was a car engine. It had to be.

Traffic on the highway? Or had they unintentionally come close to the resort road?

Leah wished she could be sure where the sound came *from*, but her best guess at direction wasn't even close to precise. It wouldn't be so bad if they spotted the resort road, would it? At least they'd know where they were.

She glanced at Spencer, and fear gripped her. He looked bad. Really bad.

Maybe she should take the gun from him, start carrying it herself. If one of the men suddenly appeared in front of them, was Spencer capable of reacting quickly enough?

Could I? she asked herself, and was afraid she knew the answer. There was a reason cops and soldiers were supposed to spend so much time at gun ranges. *She'd* never fired a weapon in her life. To aim it at a person, one she knew, and pull the trigger—and that was assuming the gun didn't have a safety, which she had no idea how to identify.

Keep going. She had a very bad feeling that, if they took a break and sat down, she might have a hard time getting Spencer up again. She wouldn't be doing it with sheer muscle, since he had to outweigh her by eighty pounds, at least. There had to be a way…but he was still walking.

The light began to seem brighter ahead. They emerged from the trees between one step and the next. Stumps and the kind of mess left by logging told her this land had been clear-cut, probably a couple of years ago. Some scruffy small trees grew, alder and maple, she thought. And a wealth of huckleberry bushes, many growing out of rotting stumps.

"Berries!" she cried.

Spencer bumped into her. For the first time in several hours, comprehension showed on his face. She steered him to a bush covered with purple-blue, ripe berries. Once she saw that he was able to pick them himself and stuff them into his mouth, she started doing the same.

They shouldn't eat very many; the last thing they

needed was to end up sick, but oh, they tasted good, the flavor bursting on her tongue. And she was so hungry!

Within minutes her fingers were stained purple, as were Spencer's. But who cared?

Bushes a short distance away shook. Hand outstretched for more berries, Leah stared. It kept shaking, and that was an odd sound. Sort of…snuffling. Or grunting.

"Spencer," she whispered.

His head turned, his eyes sharp. He had to have heard the alarm in her voice.

He stared at the trembling leaves, and in a move so fast it blurred, had his gun in his hand.

"We need to back away," she murmured.

He nodded agreement.

"Probably won't pay any attention to us," she said, just as quietly.

A stick cracked under her foot. She'd have frozen in place if his hand hadn't gripped her upper arm and kept her moving.

Craning her neck, she saw brown fur. An enormous head pushed between bushes. Supposedly, bears didn't have very good vision, but it was staring right at them. And, oh, dear God, it kept pushing through the growth, canes snapping.

"Not too fast."

The bear wasn't charging, but Leah would have sworn it grew to fill her field of vision. Seeing the hump between the shoulders had her already racing pulse leaping.

"Spencer!" she whispered loudly.

"I see."

Another step, another. The head swung back and forth. Leah would swear the small eyes looked angry.

Suddenly, Spencer cursed, and she, too, heard a deep-throated engine cut off. Car doors slam.

"I see them!" yelled a voice she recognized and detested.

TJ Galt.

The racket off to the right made the bear even more agitated. It took a few steps toward them. Ignoring the two voices Leah now heard, Spencer held her to a slow, steady retreat.

Until the scrubby growth toward what had to be the resort road began to shake and snap as the men trampled through it. One of them yodeled, "Got you now, traitor!"

The grizzly lowered its head and charged.

"Run!" Spencer ordered. She didn't hesitate, racing as fast as she could back the way they'd come. It was a minute before she realized he'd split away, probably intending to draw the bear's attention.

But a gun barked. Again and again. TJ and Arne intended to shoot them down.

She heard a crashing behind her and dared a look back. The bear had stopped and swung toward the two men who were yelling gleefully. One took a shot at her that stung her arm. Spencer... She saw him trip, recover his footing and keep running.

The grizzly charged the men. One of them bellowed, "Bear!"

As if she'd stepped into a noose, Leah pitched forward. She didn't land gently, but didn't even acknowledge pain. Pushing herself to her hands and knees, she twisted to see what was happening.

Gunshots exploded but didn't slow the bear. Screaming, one of the men went down. The other stumbled backward. Even from this distance, she saw his horror.

"Keep going!" Spencer roared.

She used her position like a sprinter on a starting block to run, gasping, hurting, horrified by the snarls and terrible screams she heard behind her.

Leah hadn't gotten far into the woods when she slammed against a hard body. Even as she fought, she couldn't stop herself from looking back.

"Leah! It's me. It's just me."

She was whimpering as she took in his face. If she'd thought he looked bad before, it was nothing to now. He was as sickened as she was by what was happening behind them.

"Come on." He all but dragged her forward. She jogged to keep up with his long strides. Then she realized which hand he gripped her with.

"Your wrist."

"To hell with my wrist." He still held his gun in his right hand. "Let's circle around. If they both went down, we might have transportation."

The words were barely out of his mouth when the engine roared to life. Tires skidded on gravel as the driver floored it.

There was one more strangled scream.

SPENCER'S LUNGS HEAVED like old-fashioned bellows, and his heart was trying to pound its way out of his chest.

He and Leah had slid down an unexpected drop-off and collapsed at the bottom, their backs to a big tree.

She breathed as fast as he did, her eyes dilated, each exhalation sounding like a sob although she wasn't crying. "TJ," she gasped. "That was TJ."

"Yeah," he managed. "And Arne."

"He took off and left him." She sounded disbelieving.

He and she had taken off and left TJ to a terrible death, too, Spencer couldn't help thinking. They'd had more motivation to run even than Arne had, but Spencer also thought sticking around to try to rescue the grizzly's victim would have been useless and possibly a death sentence.

Shaking from reaction or the damn fever or both, he got out, "You okay?"

"I...don't know."

He wasn't a hundred percent sure he hadn't been shot. In fact, he bent his head to search for blood. He saw some, but on Leah, not him.

With an exclamation, he laid down his Sig Sauer and reached for her arm. "Does this hurt?"

She tipped her head to peer dubiously at the bloodstain on her upper arm. "Something stung me."

Yeah, there was a rip, all right. He parted it enough to see that the bullet had barely skimmed her flesh. Its passage might leave a scar, but the blood flow wasn't worrisome. Her face was decorated with some new scratches strung with beads of scarlet like polished rubies crossing her cheek and forehead.

He lifted a hand to smooth her hair, tangled with leaves and twigs. "Damn," he whispered. "I thought that was it."

"Me, too." She blinked against some moisture in her eyes. "TJ sneered at me when I said I was watching for bears. You know, when we were picking berries..."

"We'd better not stick around," Spencer said after a minute. As shitty as he felt, he wanted to kiss her, and maybe more. Nothing like a shot of adrenaline to fire up a man's blood and clear his head. Unfortunately, adrenaline didn't hang around long, and he'd crash when it dissipated. "That bear has to have taken a bullet or two. It'll be mad."

"It won't die?"

"I don't know. Not immediately, I'm guessing. Probably it just thinks it got stung by some yellow jackets."

Gutsy as always, Leah nodded sturdily. She got to her feet faster than he did and picked up his gun for him. Holstering it, he said, "I guess we found the road."

"Yes, and I'm pretty sure we're close to the turnoff."

"We still have to be careful, you know."

Her head bobbed. He had the feeling she was checking to see how *he* was, even as he did the same for her.

She looked like she'd been in a cat fight. Scratches, new and old, on her face and hands. Hair a mess. Her clothes, ripped and dirty, hung on her as if she'd already lost weight. Horror darkened her beautiful eyes.

He hadn't taken very good care of her.

They were alive, he reminded himself. Unlike TJ Galt.

An hour later they had circled around the clear-cut land and saw the resort road. It was paved here, which encouraged him. Not that far to go.

They hiked on, trying to move parallel to it, just near enough they could see it occasionally. Twice they saw a black SUV driving slowly along the road, once heading out, then coming back up.

"They still think they can cut us off," he said.

"What if the driver let off a couple guys who are on foot out here with us?"

The possibility was real, but there was nothing he could do that he wasn't already. He fought to stay in the moment while fighting a blinding headache, chills and a tendency to find himself in other times and places.

A kid, hiding in the woods near his house after his father had used his belt on him. Rage and fear and shame filled him. Sunlight in his eyes, and he was baking in the heat of a street between mud-colored buildings in a village in Afghanistan, feeling eyes on him from every direction. Skin crawling.

Turning his head to see Leah anchored him, so he kept doing it. She needed him. He couldn't let her down.

"I think I see someone," she whispered.

He stared hard in the direction she was looking. Yeah, that desert camo didn't quite work in the green northwest forest.

He nudged Leah, and they very, very quietly retreated, then turned east to parallel the highway, heading toward Mount Baker. Should have known they couldn't pop out right here. Had Higgs sent out his minions to drive up and down the highway, too? Should they hunker down and wait out the day, not try to flag anyone down until morning?

Might be safer...but Spencer bet that by morning, Higgs and the others would have decamped. He would very much like to round them up here and now. Brooding, he thought, yeah, but what were the odds of getting a team here in time?

Even if the sheriff's department had a SWAT unit, could they stand up to the kind of weaponry Higgs's group had? An image formed in his head of the flare of rocket fire followed by a helicopter exploding.

He grimaced.

And, damn, as disreputable as he and Leah looked, how long would it take for police to be able to verify that he was who he said he was, and take action?

What if his head was in Afghanistan or Iraq when they reached a police station? Hard to take a crazy man seriously.

They trudged on, Leah in the lead again.

Her head turned. "I hear a car."

Pulled from the worries that had circled around and

around, he listened, too. That was definitely a car, not an SUV or pickup. Which would have been good news if they'd been close enough to the highway to stick out a thumb. Also, if they could convince some backpacker on his way back down to civilization to hide them on backseat and floorboards so they weren't seen as they passed the resort road.

He realized he'd said that out loud when Leah said, "What if we *cross* the highway and follow it until we're past the resort road?"

It was lucky one of them had a working brain.

HER IDEA HAD sounded practical, but preparing to run across the empty highway, she was almost as scared as she'd been with a grizzly charging after her and bullets flying, too.

She and Spencer would be completely exposed for the length of time it took to slide into a ditch, climb up onto pavement, race across the highway and get across another ditch and into the woods on the far side. SUVs and pickup trucks with powerful engines could approach fast. Yes, but they could be heard from a distance, she reminded herself, even out of sight around a curve.

She stole an anxious look at Spencer. "Ready?"

"Yeah," he said hoarsely. "You say go."

"Okay." She took a few steadying breaths, tensed and said, "Go!"

Side by side, they slid on loamy soil into the ditch, used their hands to scrabble their way up to the road and ran.

Not until they plunged on the other side through dangling ropes of lichen and the stiff lower branches of evergreen trees did she take another breath. They stumbled to a stop, momentarily out of sight from the highway, and Spencer grinned at her.

Her heart gave a squeeze. That smile was delighted and sexy at the same time, and it didn't matter how awful he looked otherwise. When he held out his arms, she tumbled into them, wrapping her own around his lean torso.

She might have stayed longer if he didn't radiate worrisome heat.

"We're not safe yet," she mumbled into his shoulder.

"No, but we're one step closer."

Stupidly teary-eyed, she was smiling, too. Swiping her cheeks on his grungy T-shirt, she made herself lower her arms and back away.

"I don't know about you, but I'm starved. I vote we get going."

The jubilant grin had become an astonishingly tender smile. "I'll second that."

Chapter Seventeen

Two hours later they passed the turn-off to the resort without seeing a single vehicle or any camouflage-clad, armed men hiding in wait. They'd heard a fair amount of passing traffic, but chose not to attempt to stop anyone yet.

Their pace grew slower and slower. The trees weren't as large here, resulting in dense undergrowth. Leah's body had become more and more reluctant. Her legs didn't want to take the next step. She quit diverting to avoid getting slapped by branches. Stumbling, she'd barely catch herself before she did another face-plant. She had never in her life been so tired—and she didn't have a raging fever. She kept checking on him, sometimes slyly so he wouldn't notice. Despite a sheen of sweat on his face and glazed eyes, he plodded on.

Neither of them spoke. What was there to say?

Spencer glanced at his watch. She went on without bothering to ask what time it was. Occasional glimpses of the sun showed it still high enough to give them a few hours before nightfall. If she was wrong…they'd stop. Curl up together and sleep.

"Hey."

Hearing his rough voice, Leah didn't make her foot move forward for that next step.

"Let's get in sight of the road. It's time to flag some-one down."

"Oh." How long had it been since she'd seen him check the time? She had no idea. "Okay." She turned right. Just the idea that they might catch a ride and not have to walk anymore inspired a small burst of energy.

It only took a few minutes—five?—to find themselves a spot to crouch barely off the highway, but probably not visible to passing motorists.

The first one they saw coming was traveling east to-ward Mount Baker. A red Dodge Caravan, it had a rack piled with luggage and kids in the backseat.

They let several more go.

"I'd be happiest with a sheriff's deputy or forest ser-vice," Spencer said.

Of course, they had to identify those quick enough to give them time to burst out onto the road, waving their arms and probably jumping up and down.

Vehicles passed. She began to wonder if Spencer was too sick to make a quick decision. Maybe she should make one.

But suddenly he said, "That's it," and launched him-self forward.

She stumbled behind, finally seeing what he had. It was a white 4X4 with a rack of lights on the roof. Spen-cer waved and so she did, too. A turn signal came on, and a siren gave a brief squawk. The vehicle rolled to a stop only a few feet from them. From here Leah could see green trim and the sheriff's department logo.

Spencer didn't wait for the deputy to get out. He jogged along the shoulder to the passenger side. So a passing motorist might miss seeing them, she realized.

The deputy climbed out and circled the front bum-per. Probably in his thirties, he looked alarmingly like the men they were fleeing: fit, clothed in a khaki uniform and armed. In fact, his hand rested lightly on the butt of his gun.

That changed in an instant when he saw the gun holstered at Spencer's waist. In barely an instant, the deputy pulled his gun and took up a stiff-armed stance, the barrel pointing at Spencer, who immediately lifted his hands above his head. "Set that gun on the pavement," the deputy snapped. "Do it *now*."

Moving very slowly, Spencer complied. With his foot, he nudged the handgun over the pavement toward the cop. The deputy never took his eyes from Spencer when he moved forward and used his foot to push the gun behind the tire of his SUV.

"You're not a hunter."

"No," Spencer said. "I'm not carrying identification, so I can't prove this, but I'm FBI Special Agent Alex Barr. I was undercover with a violent militia group training at an old lodge near here. Ms. Leah Keaton—" he nodded at her "—recently inherited the lodge from her great-uncle. She decided to check on the condition of the buildings, and surprised the men who'd taken it over. They took her captive."

The guy watched them suspiciously. "You took her and ran?"

"Eventually. One of them found a photo of me online leaving a Chicago courthouse. We were lucky because Leah overheard two men talking about it. We didn't dare even take the time to grab supplies or my phone, just ran. I urgently need to call my team leader. These guys have some serious weapons, including a couple of rocket launchers."

"What?"

Leah spoke up. "I saw one of them. That's when they decided they couldn't let me leave."

"Some of their weapons are US military, stolen by a like-minded active-duty army officer. The leader of this group is a retired air force lieutenant-colonel. We need the FBI to handle this, not local police."

The deputy studied him for a long time. "No way I can verify this story."

"I don't see how."

Leah said, "The resort was called Mount Baker Cabins and Lodge. My uncle's name was Edward Preston. If you're local, you might know about him. He died last fall. I'm his great-niece. I'm…a veterinary technician."

The deputy eyed her. "We drove up to check on Mr. Preston now and again. Annoyed him, but we kept doing it."

"That sounds like him," she admitted. "Mom tried to get him to move to somewhere less isolated, but he refused."

Looking marginally less aggressive, the deputy said, "Special Agent Barr, will you agree to be handcuffed before I give you and Ms. Keaton a lift?"

"Yes."

"He's wounded," she interjected desperately. "He has a knife wound in his thigh, and another between his ribs. I think the ribs are broken, and his wrist, too. He's fighting an infection."

The deputy's eyebrows rose and his gaze snagged on Spencer's wrapped wrist before moving to the blood soaking the upper arm of Leah's sweatshirt. "You appear to be hurt, too."

"Yes, I was shot, but it's just a graze. Spencer's wounds—I mean, Alex's wounds—are infected. He's running a high temperature. It's a miracle he made it this far. Please don't—"

"I'll be okay," Spencer said gently. "We need to get off this road."

He had to explain why she'd called him by two different names, and why it would be a bad thing if they were spotted by any of the men fleeing the lodge.

The deputy cast uneasy glances up and down the highway, patted them both down and made them sit in the back—in the cage, she thought was the right terminology—but didn't insist on the handcuffs. He took Spencer's gun with him when he got behind the wheel, and did an immediate U-turn to head west toward Bellingham and, presumably sheriff's department headquarters. Then he got on his radio.

LESS THAN TWO hours later Alex had set the ball to rolling. In his own imagery, he'd tapped a domino, which would knock down the next and the next, until the last fell.

He was rarely in on the grand finale, although his reasons this time were different. In the past, when he'd completed an undercover investigation, it was just as well not to show up days later as his alter ego, Special Agent Barr.

This wasn't the first time he'd had to jump ship, so to speak, but he'd never before had to help someone else make the swim to shore. It *was* the first time he'd been injured badly enough, he had to be hospitalized.

That partly explained his frustration. He did not like being stuck flat on his back in a hospital bed where he was allowed no voice in how the cleanup was run. He was pretty irked at Ron Abram, who'd delegated much of the response to someone at the Seattle office. Since Alex didn't have his phone, the only update offered to him came via the clunky phone on the bedside stand, and

that was from Abram, not the agents who'd joined with
the local police to raid the compound—yeah, that was
what they'd called it—only to find it deserted. According to Abram, they were packing his and Leah's stuff and
bringing it down, as well as having someone bring her
car once they figured out how to get it moving.

Alex couldn't help thinking that Jason Shedd could
have fixed the car in less time than it had probably taken
him to disable it.

The Tahoe Alex had borrowed for this operation from
the Seattle office had started, once they reconnected the
battery. No surprise it had been disabled. He doubted
they intended to return it to him. He guessed he'd have
to find his own way to the airport.

Truthfully, he still felt like crap, although the pain
meds had helped. He wouldn't be released until morning,
at the very soonest. He was on some kind of super-pow-
erful antibiotic being given by IV, along with the fluids
the doctor thought he needed. They wanted to see how
he responded to the antibiotics before they cut him loose.

What had him antsy was Leah's absence. He wanted
to rip the needle out and go looking for her. They'd been
taken to different cubicles in the ER and he hadn't seen
her since. There wasn't any chance she'd been admitted,
too, was there? He couldn't believe she'd leave without
finding him. Anyway, she'd need to wait for her purse and
phone, even if she was willing to abandon her car for now.

He'd tuned the TV to CNN, but had trouble caring
about the latest congressman embroiled in a sexual scandal or tension in some godforsaken part of the world.
With a little luck Higgs and company would be rounded
up, weaponry confiscated and their entire scheme would
become little more than a note on a list of terrorist op-

erations thwarted. No breathless reports on CNN or any other news outlet.

Recognizing the quick, light footsteps in the hall, he turned his head. Since hospital security had been asked to vet any visitors to his room, he wasn't surprised to hear a man's voice and then a woman's. A second later Leah pushed aside the curtain. Her hair was shiny clean and dry, shimmering under the fluorescent lights, and she wore scrubs.

"Spencer?" She sounded tentative, as if unsure he'd welcome her. Then she wrinkled her nose. "Alex."

"I'd really like to shed having multiple personalities," he told her.

She chuckled and visibly relaxed, coming to his side. When he held out his hand, she laid hers in it.

"Will you sit down?" he asked, tugging gently. The minute she'd perched on the edge of the bed, he said, "You saw a doctor. What did he say?"

She reported that, like him, she was being treated for potential *Giardia lamblia*, the microorganism commonly found in otherwise crystal-clear waters in the Cascade Mountains. A dressing covered the bullet graze on her arm, and she was also on an antibiotic for that. Otherwise, she'd been able to shower, a nurse had produced the scrubs for her and she'd been given a chit to pay for a meal in the cafeteria.

"I couldn't eat nearly as much as I wanted," she concluded ruefully.

With a smile lighting her face, she was different. Her eyes sparkled, her mouth was soft, her head high and carriage erect but also relaxed. Seeing her now was a reminder that he didn't know what she'd be like when she wasn't abused and shocked. She could have a silly sense of humor; she might be a party girl; she could habitually flit from one interest to another. Maybe she'd already dropped her determination to go to vet school and come up with another way she could spend any money earned from her great-uncle's legacy to her.

No, not that, he thought. That was unfair. He'd seen her unflagging determination. Her courage. Her strength and intellect.

Her smile had died, and she was searching his eyes gravely. "What about you? What did the doctor say?"

Was that the caring expression of a woman at least halfway in love with a man? Or caring only because the two of them had gone through a lot together?

"Nothing unexpected," he told her. "It was the gash on my thigh that was infected. Strangely enough, this one—" he started to move his free hand to touch his side before remembering that it was now casted "—appeared clean. One rib is broken, one cracked. My ulna is fractured close to the wrist." Rueful, he lifted the casted arm. "They expect a complete healing, but I may need physical therapy once this is off."

"I don't know how you kept going. You saved my life, over and over."

He shook his head. "You saved mine. Over and over."

She didn't seem convinced, and said, "Oh, you mean when I heard Higgs and Fuller talking."

"And when you treated my injures," he reminded her.

"Which you got because you were protecting *me*."

"You also knew enough to find berries to eat, to keep that bear from seeing us as dinner, and you led us to safety when I was too feverish to know which way we were going."

"I don't think any of those measure up to a knife to the—"

He smiled crookedly. "We'll call it even."

Leah laughed. "Not even close."

"Did anyone corner you with more questions?" he asked.

"Oh, yeah. A pair of FBI agents. Apparently, the doctor wouldn't let them go at you, so I got grilled instead."

He was the one to laugh this time. "Grilled?"

Her severe expression melted into a smile. "Okay, asked questions. Only…they wouldn't tell me anything. Do you know what's happening?"

The reminder renewed his irritation. "Not as much as I'd like. As we speculated, Higgs and his crew absconded with all the weapons, down to the last bullet." He told her the rest of what he'd learned, and she appeared relieved to know she'd get her possessions back soon.

"I was worrying about my car," she admitted. "I hated to have to call my insurance agent and say, 'Well, see, these domestic terrorists got mad at me, so they blew it up with a rocket launcher.'"

Laughing, Alex realized he hadn't felt this good since the last time he'd made love with Leah, and then the astonishing pleasure was transitory. They'd both been all too aware of the frightening reality awaiting them.

Before he could say anything else, he heard voices in the hall, followed by one that said, "Knock knock," even as a hand drew back the curtain.

The visitor was Matt Sanford, the deputy who had picked them up off the side of the highway. He had a black duffel bag slung over one shoulder and was pulling a small suitcase with the other hand. "I thought you might like to have your stuff," he said cheerfully.

Leah beamed at him. "Yes, please. Is my purse there somewhere? You do have my phone?"

He let her seize the suitcase handle from him. "I'm told your purse is in the suitcase. The phone, I don't know.

If anything is missing, I'll follow up on it." He looked at Alex. "And I take it this is yours."

"Well, the bag is."

"Do you want your phone?" Leah asked, starting to reach for the zipper.

"Eventually. Unfortunately, I don't dare use it until we know it's clean. Somebody was supposed to bring me—"

The deputy pulled a phone from a pocket. "I'm the somebody."

"Turned you into the pack mule, huh?"

"Beats my average day. You introduced some excitement into our lives."

Alex's eyes met Leah's. "More than I ever want to experience again."

"Amen," she murmured.

"Thank you," Alex added. "You don't know how glad to see you we were."

"That's what they all say," Deputy Sanford joked, but he also smiled. "I'm happy I came on you when I did. Oh, I forgot to say I have an update."

Both focused on him.

"I hear the FBI has caught up with four men. A guy with a Scandinavian name..."

"Arne Larson?"

"That's it. He was with a Robert Kirk."

Leah's hand tightened on Alex's. "I don't remember a Robert."

Alex wasn't surprised. Unremarkable in appearance, Rob had never seemed interested in pushing himself forward.

"The other two were Don Durand—his truck was loaded with rifles, they said—and Garrett Zeigler."

"Those two were together?"

"Not from what I heard."

"I'm glad someone is willing to tell us what's happening."

"Yeah, I figured." Sanford sounded sympathetic. "I put my number in that phone. Call if I can do anything."

They expressed more thanks. He left, leaving silence in his wake.

THIS SILENCE FELT awkward to Leah. She wouldn't try to leave until morning at the soonest, Saturday if it looked like she'd have her car by then, but...should she hang around and keep Alex company now? Or make this breezy but plan to stop by in the morning to say goodbye?

Would she hear from him someday?

"I almost hope Del and Dirk get away," she blurted.

He grimaced. "Me, too, but that won't happen with Del. He got himself in too deep. Dirk... I'll try to keep him from being charged if he followed my advice."

He'd told her about the confrontation with Dirk and what he'd suggested. "If he didn't, there's not much I can do for him."

"How will you know?"

He ran a hand over his rough jaw. "As long as he doesn't have any stolen weapons on him when he's stopped, I'll assume he's running from Higgs, not still taking his orders. Dirk saved us by keeping his mouth shut."

Leah nodded. "They didn't let you shave?"

"Wasn't high on their list of priorities, but, damn it, I itch."

His disgruntlement made her smile. It also, for some obscure reason, made her sad. *Just ask*, she told herself.

"You'll be going back to Chicago, won't you?"

An emotion she couldn't read passed through his light gray eyes. "For the short term," he agreed. "I'm in no shape to be useful here."

"No. Um, I'm expected back at work Monday. So…"

"Have you talked to your parents?" he asked.

She scrunched up her nose. "Yes. Mom was next thing to hysterical. I could hear Dad in the background reminding her that I'm okay."

Annoyingly, amusement curved Alex's very sexy mouth. "Did you mention getting shot?"

Feeling sort of teenaged, she said, "I figured that could wait."

He laughed, but there was something intense in the way he watched her. "Leah…"

"Yes?"

"I don't want to say goodbye."

"I don't want to, either," she whispered, praying he didn't mean that in a "We had quite an adventure, and I'll miss you" way.

"Are you still serious about applying to vet school?"

"Yes, except…there's still the money issue. I suppose I should talk to some real estate agents tomorrow. It might be a while before they can actually take a look at the resort, though, huh?"

"I'm guessing a week or so," he agreed. His gaze never left hers. "I want to keep seeing you."

Her heart did a somersault. "But… Chicago."

"I'm done with undercover work. I can apply for a transfer to be near you."

He meant it. Suddenly, tears rolled down her cheeks. "I was so afraid…"

"I've been afraid, too," he said huskily, tugging her toward him.

Leah surrendered, lifting her feet from the floor so she could snuggle on the bed beside him, her head resting on his shoulder, her hand somewhere in the vicinity of his heart. The familiar position felt *right*. She hated the idea of going to bed without him.

"I had the terrifying thought that you might like night-clubs," he murmured.

She actually giggled at that. "Not a chance. Please tell me you don't bag a deer every year."

This laugh rumbled in his chest. "Nope. Guess that wouldn't go over very well with an animal doc, would it?"

"No." Her cheeks might still be wet, but Leah was also smiling.

"Now that we have that covered, I guess we know everything we need to about each other," he said with an undertone of humor.

"I guess we do." No, he wouldn't be able to go home with her to meet her parents immediately; she could only imagine the kind of debriefing he'd face. "Is there a Portland office?"

"FBI? Yeah, a field office. That's what I'll aim for in the short term. If you want me to."

"I do." She was in love with this man who was willing to make big changes in his life to be with her. The sexiest man she'd ever met. A man who just never quit.

"Good," he said. A minute later his breathing changed as he relaxed into sleep. Apparently, she'd removed his last worry.

Not planning to go anywhere, she closed her eyes, too.

Epilogue

Ten days later Alex strode off the plane at Portland International Airport. Leah had promised to be waiting for him at baggage claim. In part because of the cast he still wore, he carried only his laptop case. He'd taken a two-week vacation, the best he could manage until a transfer came through. This was a "meet the family" trip. Even as alienated as he often felt from his own parents, he supposed he'd be taking Leah to meet them one of these days, too. They loved him, if not in a way he'd want to replicate with his own kids. For the first time he was seriously thinking he'd like to start a family.

Only two days ago he'd gotten word that Higgs had been captured trying to charter a boat in Florida. When the local FBI located the beach cabin where he'd been staying, they'd surprised two other men: Steve Baldwin and Ken Vogel. They'd also found two rocket launchers and a small amount of uranium as well as evidence that the men had been constructing a bomb.

Higgs wasn't talking, but under pressure, Baldwin admitted they'd intended to sail to a Caribbean island where they wouldn't be found until they were ready to make their strike.

Alex felt sick, imagining what might have happened

if the charter operator hadn't had an uneasy feeling he'd seen Higgs's face, and not in a context he liked.

Yeah, the FBI had ended up putting Lieutenant Colonel Edward Higgs on a watch list, and released his photo. This time it had paid off big.

They had also quietly arrested army Colonel Thomas Nash, the man Alex recognized when he and Higgs met the suppliers. Turned out Nash and Higgs had been friends for years.

Of course, the single arrest was the equivalent of peeling open the proverbial can of worms. Nash couldn't have stolen that quantity of weapons on his own. Even with help, procedures were designed to prevent things like this from happening. It was fair to say that army base would be crawling with investigators for months to come, making a lot of people's lives miserable.

Dirk had been picked up and released, at Alex's recommendation. They'd spoken last week, Dirk shaken at his weakness in letting his father push him into something so hateful. He and Helen were getting married and moving to Montana, where he'd found a job with a well-drilling company based in Billings. Alex intended to stay in touch. He and Leah might not have survived if Dirk hadn't listened to his conscience.

Suddenly, he didn't want to think about any of that. The baggage claim carousels were just ahead…and his gaze locked on a woman hurrying toward him, her face alight. Relief and something more powerful flooded him. He let the laptop case drop to the floor and held out his arms.

Leah flew into them, saying only his name. His real name.

* * * * *

COLTON IN THE
LINE OF FIRE

CINDY DEES

Chapter One

Bedroom eyes.

Detective Reese Carpenter had no-kidding bedroom eyes.

And he was flashing them at her right now, leaning his elbows on the high counter at the front of her crime lab. How was a woman supposed to get any work done with a guy so flat-out sexy hanging around? It was all she could do not to stop, stand and stare at him. And maybe drool a little.

"Have you got anything for me?" he asked.

His hair was dark, his eyes bright, movie-star blue, brimming with sultry charm, sophisticated intelligence, wry humor and a hint of mischief. Totally made her think of sex—great sex and lots of it.

"Earth to Yvette Colton. Come in."

She blinked rapidly, clearing the image of her sister's cop-partner naked and in her bed, taking her to the stars and back. Darn his bedroom eyes, anyway.

"What do you want, now?" she asked in an aggrieved tone. "Or are you finally going to give up telling me how to do my job and just take over the forensic lab yourself?"

As pretty as he might be, Reese Carpenter was also an almighty pain in the tuchus. A know-it-all who got all up in her business and was forever telling her how to do her job. This might be her first time running her own crime lab, but she'd trained with the best forensic scientists in the business, thank you very much.

"You gotta help me out, here," her unwanted visitor declared. "I need something concrete I can pin on Markus Dexter. Give me a smoking gun. I *know* he did it."

"It" being the double murder of a woman, Olivia Harrison, and a private investigator, Fenton Crane, twenty-six years ago. Their bodies had been hidden in the walls of the Crest View warehouse in Braxville, Kansas, and discovered during a renovation last summer. To complicate matters, the entire warehouse had been blown up by a saboteur last month.

"I can only process evidence so fast, Detective. And it's not like that's my only case. In fact, at the moment, I'm running tests for arsenic on the remains of the Crest View warehouse."

"Did you find any?" he asked.

"Not in this sample. It appears the arsenic-laced wood was used only for framing walls. The floor joists didn't contain arsenic, but their wood was sourced in North America. Only the batch of wood from China was contaminated."

"As we thought," he responded with a brisk nod.

She turned her attention back to the test tube in her hand, but he huffed audibly. She looked up once more, surprised that he was still hovering in her lab. He declared, "I *have* to find something to tie Dexter to the bodies in that warehouse."

"I thought your job was to be a dispassionate investigator and go where the facts lead you, and not go looking for facts to support your theories."

He huffed harder, turned on his heel and stomped out of her lab, his business-suit-clad physique entirely too tempting to be legal.

AN HOUR LATER, Reese was back. "Anything?" he asked without preamble.

"No. And I won't find any answers if you keep interrupting me," she snapped at him and his bedroom eyes. This time he'd lost the coat and tie and wore only slacks and a white dress shirt that showed off shoulders in no need of padding to make them appear athletic. He wasn't a bulky guy, but he definitely was in great shape. Moreover, his sleeves were rolled up to reveal leanly muscled forearms still holding over a bit of tan from last summer.

A flash of irritated blue was all she glimpsed of his expression as he turned and stomped out…again. She totally knew the feeling.

ANOTHER HOUR PASSED. This time he merely poked his head in through the hallway door and called out, "How about now?"

"Go away, Carpenter!" she called back. At the moment, she was bent over a spectrometer trying to recalibrate the stupid thing so she could run the last batch of wood slivers from the Crest View warehouse explosion.

She added for good measure, "And don't come back until I call you or you've got a darned good reason for interrupting my work!"

EXACTLY ONE HOUR LATER, her lab door opened again.

She didn't even bother to look up. "Reese, I could set my watch off your visits down here. Are you setting an alarm for every hour on the hour to remind yourself to come to my lab and bug me?"

"Yeah, actually. I am."

That made her glance sidelong in his direction. "You do know that pestering me incessantly isn't doing a blessed thing to speed up my work, right? I'm handling all this evidence as quickly as I can, and you poking at me isn't going to make the work go any faster. It's only ticking me off."

He shrugged and grinned without a shred of remorse.

Man, his smile was nearly as lethal as his eyes. It was all boyish charm and manly sex appeal. She looked down at her workstation hastily, not seeing a thing on her computer screen. "At least turn your alarm off," she muttered. "You're driving me crazy."

"I can work with crazy," he purred. "I would only be worried if you didn't have any opinion at all about me."

That made her head snap up. New tactic from him, perhaps? If badgering her didn't yield the proof he needed to convict Dexter, was Reese going to try to seduce it out of her? Gulp.

Right now, she was dissolving mortar scraped off bricks at the Crest View crime scene into a solution she would run through the spectrometer. She was hoping to find the chemical composition of the explosive used to demolish the building, and while she was at it, look for arsenic that might have seeped into the walls from the contaminated wood that was used to frame the structure.

"Go. Away. And quit bugging me. You're a pest."

"Aww, come on. I'm not that bad. Let me help with something."

She pointed a long glass pipette at him like a magic wand, waving the pencil-thick stirring stick at him and intoning, "Begonus pain-in-the-assikus."

He laughed, and darned if that mischievous sparkle in his eyes didn't get even more pronounced. "Admit it. I'm a cute pain the ass, though."

Her gaze narrowed. "Toddlers are cute. But that doesn't mean I want one running around my lab wrecking everything in sight."

"Did you just call me a child?" he asked darkly.

"I might've," she replied defiantly. Dang it. Her and her big mouth. It was forever getting her into trouble. And now an intimidating cop was abruptly staring at her in cool challenge, his eyes as hard and cold as chips of sea ice.

"We'll see about that," he murmured. "I'll bet I can change your mind fast enough."

"Oh, yeah? How?" she blurted. Dumb, dumb, dumb. The first rule of dealing with alpha males was never, ever to throw down a dare in front of one.

Reese moved swiftly around the front counter and he loomed over her, six feet tall to her five feet, five inches on a good day. In socks. Thick ones.

All that crackling sex appeal was suddenly back, pouring off him in tangible waves. Dude. How did he do that? One minute he was a total pro—just the facts, ma'am—and the next he was this smoking-hot chick magnet, all come-hither looks and irresistible, masculine charm.

It was those cursed bedroom eyes of his.

One thing she knew for sure, this man was strictly off-limits. No way was she sleeping with a guy who could kiss and tell to her big—protective—sis. And given that Reese and Jordana spent hours and hours together every single day at work, Reese would surely end up spilling the beans. Her sister was an excellent cop and talented interrogator. Jordana would pry every sordid detail out of her partner.

God, what she wouldn't give to be able to manage this infuriating man the way her sister did. As it was, he was a constant thorn in her side, continually commenting on her procedures, calling her out for every corner she dared to even think about cutting, watching her like a hawk, down to the most minute detail of her job.

It wasn't that she minded being held to a high standard or even to perfection. It was the insufferable way he did it that drove her around the bend. More than once in the past year, she'd seriously considered killing him. And she *did* know how to hide his body.

Honestly, she had no interest in dating any cop. Not only would it be it tricky at best to date someone she worked with, but cops were not her jam. They tended to be so confident. Assertive. Convinced of their rightness at all times.

Nope. Reese Carpenter could take his bedroom eyes and seductive smile and flash them both at some other poor soul who had no idea what an irritating man lurked behind them.

She took a step back and carefully released the deeply annoyed breath she realized she was holding. "Why are you here, Detective?"

"My name is Reese. Feel free to use it, dar—"

She interrupted his drawl. "Do *not* call me darling. Or honey, or anything pertaining to sugar. And if you call me little lady, I will have to shoot you."

He grinned. Lazy, sexy, *knowing*. What the heck did he think he knew about her that she didn't?

Nope, nope, nope. Not getting personal with this guy. She would not lob even a hint of encouragement in this supremely arrogant male's direction.

"How's the evidence processing coming from the bodies in the wall?" Reese asked in an abruptly impersonal, professional tone.

Whoa. Mental whiplash.

Something in her tummy fell in disappointment. Well, shoot. She wanted him to quit flirting, and now she was upset when he did? Yikes, she was a hot mess.

She cleared her throat, stood as tall as she could and

tried to sound marginally like the expert in her field that she was. "Umm, I just got back the analysis of the insect carcasses found in the wall with the bodies."

"Are they twenty-six years old, too?" he asked dryly. "We already know Olivia and Fenton were killed that long ago because of when the building wall they were hidden in was built. I can't understand why you wasted department money sending out some dead bugs to tell us that."

"Because I'm good at my job," she replied tartly. "And because I noticed right away that the types of bugs found in the walls with each body were different. But I'm not a forensic entomologist, so I spent some of your precious police budget on having an expert examine them."

"And?"

"And, the insects found with the woman were primarily mosquitoes, flies, and interestingly, earwigs."

"What's so interesting about earwigs?" he asked.

"They're predominantly spring insects."

"So?"

"The insects with the male remains included spiders, fleas, and notably, stink bugs."

"Stink bugs."

She nodded. "Stink bugs. They're predominantly a fall insect. We can conjecture from the different species of insect remains that our bodies in the walls were murdered some months apart. Something like six months. Ms. Harrison was closed into the wall in the springtime. Mr. Crane's corpse wasn't entombed in the wall until the fall."

She waxed enthusiastic, as she usually did when her job yielded fascinating results. "If we assume the killer or killers hid the bodies quickly after time of death, we can conclude that they were murdered *months* apart."

She finished in triumph, "We're looking at two distinct and separate homicides."

Reese groaned.

"What?" she blurted, startled. She'd expected him to be excited by her find.

"The department is stretched thin as it is investigating one murder. And now you want to double the workload?" he groused.

"I still think the two murders were committed by the same person. Both were struck in the back of the head by a person about six feet tall and right-handed, using similar force and similar blunt objects for each blow. You're still only hunting for a single killer. But two murder scenes. Two sets of motives."

"We'll never find the murder scenes. They were erased a quarter century ago. There won't even be trace evidence left by now."

A pang of grief stabbed her in the heart. Her best friend in middle school, Debbie Boyd, had been murdered almost fifteen years ago. Any evidence from her death was also likely degraded and long gone. Like her killer. Yvette's own frustration at having never solved Debbie's murder was the main reason she hadn't strangled Reese Carpenter already. She actually understood his burning drive to solve the Harrison-Crane murders.

"Speaking of murder scenes, how goes the processing of the materials we brought in from searching Markus Dexter's home?"

Dexter—one of the two main partners in Colton Construction, which built the Crest View warehouse—was the prime suspect in the cold case killings after he had mysteriously disappeared from Braxville shortly after the bodies were uncovered last summer.

She answered, "I'm digging through everything you

brought in as quickly as I can, but I'm a one-woman lab, and it's going to take me some time to get through it all."

The number of evidence bags brought in from the home numbered in the hundreds, and some of the contents would require scientific processing. She was still entering a description of the contents of each one into a database along with the date, time and place it had been collected. She had yet to even begin examining the evidence inside the bags.

"Have you found anything to link Dexter to the murders?" Reese asked. She detected an underlying note of desperation in his voice that actually provoked answering sympathy in her gut.

"Not yet."

"But you'll keep looking? You gotta help me out, here, Yvette. I *need* a positive link between Dexter and the murders."

Lord, that man was pushy. "It's not as if the guy left a candlestick in his desk drawer with a card taped to it saying, 'Murder weapon used in the library by Professor Plum,' if that's what you're asking."

"Are you always so prickly?" he demanded.

"When people interfere in my work and prevent me from doing my job, always."

He threw up his hands. "Okay, okay. I can take a hint. I'll get out of here."

"Did you actually have a specific reason for coming down here this time? I did make that a pre-condition for you coming back to bother me, as I recall."

Her lab was in the basement of the new Braxville Police Department building. It was as snazzy a facility as she'd ever worked in, and the new lab that came with it was first-class. She just wished there was funding for a second forensics technician to go with all the fancy, state-of-the art equipment.

Although, truth be told, Braxville wasn't normally a hub of violent crime, or much crime at all. The suburb of Wichita was usually a quiet, pleasant little place. She'd thought this would be a nice, quiet job when she'd come home to take the position after cutting her teeth in forensics at the big FBI lab in Quantico for a couple of years.

Reese was speaking. "…on my way out when these boxes of files were messengered over from the Colton Construction firm."

Boxes, plural? She mentally groaned.

He continued, "Fitz Colton's assistant sent them over. Apparently, you asked for these?"

He stepped out into the hall and dragged in a handcart with four, three-foot-long cardboard boxes stacked on it. He hefted each one onto the counter between them. From the weight of them, she gathered the things were stuffed from end to end with all of Markus Dexter's office files from nearly thirty years with the firm.

She groaned aloud this time. There went her evenings for the next month. No social life for her, no matter what Jordana and Bridgette said about her needing to get out more. She'd even made a New Year's Resolution at her sisters' urging to expand her life beyond the lab, maybe even date a little, this year.

Admittedly, it was a half-bottle-of-wine-induced resolution. But her sisters were not wrong. They'd both taken a chance and found love recently. In fact, they bordered on downright annoying to be around in their mutual, delirious bliss.

She supposed it wasn't a bad ambition to find for herself a tiny sliver of the happy glow that clung to both women these days. Not that the dating pool in Braxville was anything to write home about. Even though the town was growing and gentrifying fast, it was still a small town at its core. There were still plenty of country music, pickup trucks and dirt roads to be had here.

Funny, but it had taken going to the other side of the country to finally appreciate her hometown. As a restless teen, though, she hadn't been able to get out fast enough. Hence, Washington, DC.

It hadn't just been the offer of heading up her own lab that lured her back. Although, very few twenty-five-year olds got an opportunity like this. Her original plan was to stay here no more than three or four years and then head for another large city and a high-powered crime lab as a senior investigator. Maybe Denver, or even New York City, next time.

But now that she was back, she was finding that Braxville wasn't half as bad as she'd made it out to be when it was the only place she'd ever been.

She wasn't sure where the future would take her, now. Advancing her career would still take her to a big city. But reconnecting with her family might just convince her to put down roots here. She was torn…and she didn't like being uncertain about anything.

Meanwhile, she'd been back here almost exactly a year and had yet to go on a single date. It wasn't that she was horrible in the looks or personality department. Granted, she was a known workaholic. But she liked to think the right man could coax her out of her lab and into a better work-life balance.

Although, at this point, any work-life balance would be an improvement. Her social life was completely nonexistent. Her gaze refocused regretfully on the huge, dusty boxes of files sitting on the counter in front of her. And it was about to stay that way for a while.

Apparently, her New Year's Resolution to get out more, or at least date a little, would go the way of most resolutions, scrapped within a week of its making. Ahh well. It had been a nice dream while it lasted.

"You need some help going through these boxes?" Reese surprised her by asking.

"Umm, no. That's okay. I'm sure you're plenty busy chasing down leads of your own and doing detective stuff."

A slight frown gathered between his perfect angel-wing brows. "You sure?" he asked quietly. "That's a lot of files."

Cripes. He had a bedroom voice to go with those blasted bedroom eyes of his. Her heart pitter-pattered at the low, sexy rasp. But to be honest, it was the hint of gentleness, concern even, in his voice that did her in.

Nobody ever worried about her. She was smart, collected, organized. Had her life together. She didn't need anyone to help her out with anything. At least, that was what they all saw when they looked at her.

None of them saw the lonely young woman who often felt like an outsider in her own family. The Coltons had big personalities—big lives, big loves, big fights, big laughter. She was the quiet one of the bunch. An afterthought baby—an accident after the arrival of the triplets. An afterthought child, growing up in the background as the triplets took the lion's share of care and attention from everyone else in the family. A too-young afterthought when social outings were planned for her older siblings. Mostly, just an afterthought.

"If you change your mind and want some help with these files, let me know, okay?"

"Fine. Whatever," she mumbled.

Reese turned and left the lab, his frame lean and athletic in the way of a tennis player, or a martial artist. He was one of those naturally graceful people. And she was…not. She could find a way to trip over a crack in a sidewalk. Heck, the shadow of a crack in a sidewalk. Klutz was her middle name.

She sighed and reached for the nearest box of files. Yep. Almost too heavy for her to move down to the floor without dropping it. Sheesh. How did Reese make lifting this onto the counter look so easy? The guy might not be bulked up, but he was stronger than his frame suggested at a glance. The stupid boxes were crammed to the gills with what must be thousands of pages of documents. And it was her job to look at every last one. Ugh.

Depressed, she sat down at her computer to log the boxes of files as evidence and start a trail of custody so they couldn't be altered or tampered with. She was nothing if not a stickler for proper handling of evidence. Her private nightmare was the ever-present specter of mishandling or contaminating a piece of evidence and a killer going free because of her mistake.

She spent the remainder of the afternoon cataloguing the hundreds of fingerprints lifted from the Dexter home search. Not surprisingly, most of them came from Dex. Yvette had to give his wife, Mary, credit for being a heck of a housekeeper, though. The woman had left only two full sets of prints behind in the entire house. Given the size of the Dexter mansion, that was impressive. Talk about being a thorough cleaner. Her kind of woman.

Quitting time for the nine-to-five employees in the police department came and went, and she heard the police shift change over her head with a half hour or so of scraping chairs, clumping footsteps and vague sounds of laughter and talking. But, by six o'clock, silence fell over the building.

Wednesday was half-price beer night down at Dusty Rusty's Pub, and a lot of the cops liked to meet up there after work. Ever since she'd come back to Braxville she'd had a standing invitation to join the crew at Rusty's. Apparently, a bunch of the force was going there tonight to toast surviving New Year's Eve—the worst working day of the year for police.

She might've considered going—chasing after her New Year's Resolution—except she was wearing an old shirt and a pair of jeans that had gotten too loose in the past few months as she'd clocked too many hours on the Harrison-Crane murders and forgotten too often to eat. Not to mention, she wasn't wearing a lick of makeup, and this morning, she'd twisted her wet hair up into a bun that would still be damp if she let it down, which meant it would hang in sad chestnut strings around her face.

Goodbye New Year's Resolution, hello long night at the office digging through dusty, dull construction contracts.

Might as well get comfortable. She turned off the bright, institutional overhead lights and turned on the lamp at her desk, an antique she'd brought in to lend a tiny touch of femininity and personality to the antiseptic lab. It had a printed silk shade with pink cottage roses on it and pretty crystal bead fringe all around its scalloped bottom.

After kicking off her shoes, she slipped on a thick pair of fuzzy socks, pulled up a streaming classical-music channel on her laptop and brewed herself a cup of hot tea while Chopin piano nocturnes played soothingly in the background. "Well, Earl Grey, you get to be my date tonight," she murmured. "Here's to us, your lordship."

She'd been at it for a couple of hours, long enough to know that these boxes of files were going to be pure, unadulterated misery to slog through, when the lab door opened without warning.

She looked up, startled.

"You again! What do you want?" she complained as Reese Carpenter poked his head in.

He stepped all the way inside, carrying a large, flat cardboard box balanced in his left hand, and a six-pack of beer in his right hand. "Figured I'd find you here. I saw Jordana and Clint at Rusty's, and they guessed you'd still be here slaving away."

"Yeah, well, I've got an annoying detective riding my back day and night, demanding that I magically process weeks' worth of evidence with a wave of my magic wand." She gave the pen she'd been taking notes with a swish and flick in his general direction.

"Man, I hate it when cops throw their weight around like that," he commented wryly.

"Hah!" she responded. "What are you doing here at this hour?"

"What are you still doing here?" he demanded. "Aren't you a nine-to-fiver?"

She shrugged. "I'm working. I really am up to my eyeballs in evidence to dig through."

"Right. Enter *moi* to save the day. Or the night as it were."

"Seriously. What do you want, Reese?"

"You and me. We're having a date. Pizza and beers over a pile of Markus Dexter's files."

Her jaw sagged.

What. On. Earth?

Chapter Two

Sheesh. Did she have to look quite that shocked at the notion of him being a datable male of the human species? He wasn't a complete troll. Multiple women had told him over the years he had a bad-boy vibe. Apparently, that was a huge turn-on for many women. Never mind that he was a cop and committed to protecting truth, justice and the American way at all times.

Reese stepped fully into the lab, relieved as hell that it didn't have the same reek of chemicals and death that always pervaded the morgue.

"Mood lighting? Soft music? Were you expecting somebody, Yvette?"

She abruptly yanked her cute fuzz-clad feet off her desk and sat up straight in her chair. "No! I would never—"

"Hey, it's okay," he interrupted. "If you want to bring your dates down here, go for it. I mean, it's a little kinky. Crime lab and all. But it's still no skin off my nose."

"What dates?" she muttered under her breath.

His eyebrows shot up. Yvette wasn't dating? At all? Color him shocked.

"Really? You're not in a steamy relationship with some smoking-hot guy?" he asked as he set the pizza and beer down on the high counter across the front of the lab and walked around it.

She rolled her eyes at him. "I'm not about to start discussing my personal life with you."

He shrugged. "You could if you wanted to. Tell me about your personal life, that is. I can keep a secret. I know all of your sister's dirty little secrets, for example."

"Oh, yeah? Like what?"

He grinned. "Nice try, but my lips are sealed."

"Can't blame a girl for testing an assertion like that."

"What are you up to so late?" he asked, scanning the piles of papers filling the entire surface of her normally pristine desk. As he'd suspected. She was elbow deep in files from the ginormous boxes he'd brought her this afternoon.

She looked up at him with those huge, meltingly dark eyes of hers and he felt his knees go a little wobbly. "You didn't answer my question, Reese. Why are you here?"

Her skin was like literal velvet, pale and perfect, dewy looking. And he wasn't a guy who thought about skin being *dewy*, like ever. But hers was. She was so damned beautiful. He couldn't understand why every unmarried guy in the department wasn't down here sniffing around, but it was their loss if they didn't see her. He bloody well did.

He pulled over a chair from the conference table and sat down at a right angle to her at her desk before he answered her question. "I'm here because I thought you might need sustenance. And another pair of hands and eyes."

"But…why?" she asked blankly.

"Why not? Doesn't anyone ever help you just for the hell of it? Because you could use a little assistance?"

"No. Not really."

"Then, kid, your luck has changed."

A smile started slowly on that lush, kissable mouth of hers. Her chin ducked a little, and she glanced up at him sidelong, shy pleasure glinting in her gaze.

Good grief, how didn't every guy in town see how sexy she was? Not that he was complaining. Their loss. Less competition for him…

Whoa, whoa, whoa. He wasn't in the market for a relationship, and certainly not with his partner's baby sister. Down that path lay nothing but drama and misery. No way was he going to get himself trapped between two of the Colton sisters.

"What's your system?" he asked briskly.

"System?" Yvette looked up at him blankly.

"Surely you're not planning to study each and every piece of paper in this giant pile one by one, are you?" he asked incredulously.

She leaned back, looking mightily irritated. "How would you do my job? By all means. Enlighten me."

"Well," he said, scanning the folders on the table between them. "I assume most of the papers in there are construction related. Sales receipts. Contracts. Drawings. Permits. That kind of stuff."

"That has been the case so far," she said frostily.

"None of that is likely to have a damned thing to do with murder. I'd make one stack of files that have nothing but dull, boring construction junk in them. Then, the ones with correspondence, complaints, personal stuff— I'd make another pile of those. That one I'd take a closer look at, first. Then, if any clients jump out of that pile, I'd track down the construction files pertaining to them out of the bigger pile."

She looked annoyed, but shrugged in acquiescence. "That might be slightly faster," she allowed.

Slightly? It would shave days…weeks…off the process. But he was prepared to win gracefully. "How about you take a preliminary peek at the contents of each folder and then pass each mundane one to me? I'll alphabetize them by client name."

"Sort them by year first and then alphabetize within each year," she directed him.

He shrugged. "Fine. Let's rock and roll. We should be able to blast through these suckers in a few hours."

She squared her slender shoulders and reached for the nearest stack of files. "I've already looked at these. Nothing interesting in them. You can start organizing those while I get started on the next batch."

They fell into a rhythm, eating while they worked, her pulling fistfuls of folders out of the cardboard packing boxes, and then passing them to him one by one to put back in the boxes, sorted by date and name. They actually made a decent team. They were both focused and disciplined when it came to work.

After about an hour, though, he called a halt. "Break time. Do you need another piece of pizza or a beer?"

"Pizza," she said promptly.

He passed her a slice of Torrentino's finest with extra pepperoni.

"What does it say about me that I went to elementary school with Gus Torrentino?" she asked. "I'm feeling old all of a sudden."

"His older sister Mia was in a couple of my classes in high school. Nice girl."

"Her brother was a jerk. Used to pull my ponytail."

"Did you deck him?" he asked humorously. Gus had been a big kid and was a big man now. He rather relished the mental image of tiny Yvette standing up to the guy.

"As I recall, I kicked him in the shins. I didn't know yet to aim higher."

"Violent child, were you?" he asked dryly.

She scowled. "People had—still have—this annoying tendency to pat me on the head and treat me as if I'm some helpless little thing."

He twisted the top off a second beer and took an appreciative swig from it. "Duly noted. The lady is not helpless."

She made a face in his general direction. "Thanks for not trying to convince me that Gus liked me because he pulled my hair."

He frowned. "Bullying is bullying. Any boy worth getting to know would've treated you better than that. Been nice to you. Not tried to yank your hair out by the roots. My mama taught me to act like a gentleman around girls whether I liked them or not. My daddy taught me that the whole 'boys will be boys' excuse is just that. An excuse for bad behavior."

"I like your parents," Yvette declared.

"Have you ever met my parents?"

"No. But I already like them. They raised you right, or at least they tried. I'm now going to have to try to figure out where you went off the rails so badly."

He grinned at her, unfazed by her insults. Cops teased each other all the time, and his two younger brothers had made it their mission in life to try to get a rise out of him when they were kids. They'd rarely succeeded.

Shock of shocks, she smiled back. It was an intimate moment, made more so by the cozy lighting and pretty piano music playing softly. Glancing around the dim lab, he commented, "Who knew this place could actually be romantic?"

She shrugged. "It's the people in a space who create romance. Not the place itself."

"What's your idea of perfect romance?" he asked, his voice unaccountably rough. Weird. He didn't have a crush on this woman…right? "Let me guess. An expensive restaurant, a bottle of wine, candles and sparkly gifts."

She seemed startled that he'd pegged her. As if it was any challenge. Not. She'd hightailed it out of Braxville to the East Coast and a big urban center the day she'd graduated from high school.

"What about you?" she asked. "What's your idea of romance?"

"I like to be outdoors. I like mountains and beaches and campfires in any combination."

She laughed a little. "Then why on earth do you still live in Kansas? We have neither mountains nor beaches, here. Just mile after mile of pastures full of cows or fields full of crops."

"Eastern Kansas is a little hilly," he said defensively.

"Emphasis on little," she retorted, grinning.

"Yeah, but it's home. Family and friends are way more important than having a beach or a ski resort nearby. I can take a vacation to see those. But I like to be able to visit my loved ones easily and often."

He caught the frown that twitched across her brow. She didn't think family was the most important thing? Okay, that surprised him. She came from a big, loud, warm family. He'd have thought that, as a Colton, being close to family would have been something she identified strongly with.

"What's wrong with your family?" he asked curiously.

She looked startled at that abrupt question. "Nothing's wrong with them," she answered defensively. "They're fine."

What wasn't she saying about her family? He sensed a mystery. And it wasn't as if he'd *ever* walked away from one of those.

She reached for another stack of files at the same time he did, and their hands bumped. A jolt of…something… passed through him. Hyperawareness of her and of how close they were sitting, their shoulders practically rubbing, and their knees bumping into each other from time to time as one of them turned in their seat.

She spoke briskly, with what sounded like false energy. "We'd better get back to work."

Trying to distract him, perhaps? Or maybe hiding something. Which seemed out of character for her. She didn't strike him as the least bit secretive. Was she more shy than she let on? He had a hard time buying that explanation. She came across as supremely self-assured. But then, he'd only ever talked with her about forensics stuff before.

He leaned back, stretching his shoulders. "What do you like to do when you're not here and chained to your desk?"

She looked up, a startled expression on her face. "Umm, I like to garden."

Made sense. Her white cottage, with its wide porch and gabled roof, was neat as a pin and flanked by beautiful landscaping full of bright flowers. No matter what time of year he drove past her place, it looked like a postcard.

"What else do you like to do?" he demanded.

"Not much."

His radar for evasiveness fired off hard. "Nothing else?" Dammit, the interrogatory was out of his mouth before he could stop it.

Her gaze slid off to one side. "Well, I, uhh, play some computer games to wind down after a hard day at work."

"Get out! Which ones?"

She named a couple of the popular ones that millions of players congregated on, but not the overtly violent ones. No surprise. Like him, she saw the results of violence often enough in her work not to find it entertaining.

"We'll have to get online together sometime and adventure," he declared.

She blinked, looking downright stunned. "You play computer games?"

"They're good for my reflexes and the dopamine dump of defeating bad guys helps me deal with stress from the job. Next time I'm online, I'll text you."

"That would be fun," she responded doubtfully.

"I guess we have a second date lined up, then." Color him possibly more surprised than she looked. She was so not his type. He was a flannel-shirts-and-fishing kind of guy. She was a big-city woman all the way, sleek and polished…way out of his league.

He reached for the file folders she held out to him and glanced up at her in time to catch her staring at him. She looked away fast, and rosy pink climbed her cheeks. She was blushing? For him? Well, well, well. Not completely immune to his charms, after all, was she? Glad to know he hadn't completely lost his touch with the ladies. He'd been starting to wonder after her continuous cold-shoulder treatment.

After another hour or so of slogging through files, he called for another break, and this time didn't ask her what she wanted. He merely opened a bottle of beer and passed it to her. She sipped daintily at it, which made him grin.

"You're supposed to just tip it up and slug it down," he commented.

"If you're a sweaty from working outside on a hot day, maybe. I drink for the taste of it, not to get plastered, thank you very much."

"Let me guess. You're a wine-cooler type," he said dryly.

"Actually, I like a good single-malt scotch." She added, "To sip. And to savor."

"Okay then. Good to know. I gotta say, I'm surprised."

"I grew up in the Colton house. It was what the adults drank and what my older siblings snuck into when the adults weren't looking." She shrugged. "I used to ask to try it when I was a kid. Developed a taste for it over time."

"Your mother drinks whiskey neat?" he blurted. He'd met Lilly Colton, and she didn't strike him as a hard-liquor, hard-drinking woman. For one thing, she was a nurse. For another, she seemed the type to put kale in her smoothies and work out five days a week. For a woman with six grown children, she was fine looking and in great shape. Yvette reminded him a lot of Lilly, in fact. Yvette had her mother's auburn hair and porcelain skin. But where Yevette's dark brown eyes had come from was a good question. Both Fitz and Lilly Colton had blue eyes.

"When my mother drinks, which isn't often and takes something or someone literally driving her to drink, she has been known to toss back a shot of scotch."

"I'll be damned. You Colton women never fail to surprise me."

Their gazes met and that…something…passed between them again. A spark. Awareness.

Cripes. Who'd have thought he would find anything at all in common with this sophisticated, classy, intellectual woman, so unlike down-to-earth him?

That pretty pink color was climbing her cheeks again. He smiled a little at her and damned if she didn't smile back. Her gaze dropped to where their hands nearly touched on the file folders. Sonofagun. Yvette Colton not only knew how to flirt but was doing it with him. Well, go goose a moose.

She put aside her half-full beer and went back to work. "One last box," she announced. "With both of us working, we can kill it off tonight."

He had more paper cuts than he cared to count, and his eyes were crossing before she finally passed him the last folder, more like three hours later than two.

"Whew!" he exclaimed. "That was a bitch. How many folders did we pull out with personal information in them?"

"Only about thirty," she answered. "A far cry from the five hundred or so we started with."

He held out his closed fist and she stared at it in obvious confusion. "Fist bump?" he suggested.

"Oh." She shook herself a little. "Right." She reached out with her delicate, girly fist and touched her knuckles lightly to his big, callused ones.

"I hope you don't punch with a fist like that," he commented teasingly. "Didn't one of your brothers ever teach you not to stick your thumb inside your curled fingers?"

"They didn't teach me much of anything. The triplets were always more interested in each other, and my oldest brother, Tyler, was much older than me. I was mostly a nuisance to be tolerated by him."

He reached out and uncurled her fingers, guided her thumb to one side and recurled her fingers gently. "There. Now you're ready to properly punch someone."

"Good to know?"

He smiled lightly. "You never know when you'll need to haul off and defend your honor."

"This is Braxville. It's not exactly the wild, wild West."

"Take it from me. It has its dark underbelly. I would know."

She met his smirk with one of her own. "In case you forgot, I work for the same police department you do. I'm as aware as you are of the crimes that take place in this town."

So prickly, she was. Like a cute little kitten with its claws out.

"I didn't forget that you work for the department. It's just that you don't get out of this dungeon much. You don't roam the mean streets like I do."

She laughed, and the sound was rich and warm. It welcomed him to join in with her, in sharp contrast to her usual cool, distant demeanor. He tilted his head to one side, studying her as her humor faded.

"What?" she demanded.

"I'm curious about you."

"Nothing to be curious about," she retorted quickly.

"See? That right there. You don't want people getting to know you. When someone makes an overture, you push them away immediately. Why is that?"

"I do not!"

"Honey, I've been coming down here with evidence for the past year, and I don't know one, single personal thing about you. Not one."

"I told you not to call me honey," she mumbled.

"Fine. I don't know one damned thing about you, Miz Colton."

"My mother is Miz Colton. Not me."

"Can I call you Yvie, like your sister does?"

"No!"

She was working so hard to distract him—which was informative in its own right. She really didn't want anyone to get close to her. But he wasn't a detective for nothing. He wasn't an easy man to distract from his main objective, once he had one. And right now, he wanted to know more about her. "All right, Yvette. Tell me something no one in the department knows about you."

"This is work. It's not like I'm going spew every detail of my life to my colleagues. That would be wildly unprofessional."

"I get that. But we're not in the FBI, and this isn't Quantico. It's Braxville. Everyone knows everybody else. It's a tight community. And here in the department, we're family. But you hold yourself separate from the rest of us. Do you think we're not good enough for you?"

"Of course not. That's absurd!"

"Then what's the problem?" he persisted. Why he felt compelled to poke at this particular bear, he had no idea. But she'd bugged him ever since she'd come to work here. She was a mystery surrounded by a riddle wrapped in an enigma. Maybe it just went against his detective's soul not to understand what made her tick.

"I've got no problem. I think the problem may be yours, Reese. Perhaps you're just nosy."

He laughed easily. "Of course, I'm nosy. I'm a detective. It's in the job description."

"Well, I haven't committed any crimes and I'm not under investigation, so you can just take your nose and poke it somewhere else. In fact, you should go home. I didn't realize how late it was."

"We can look through the thirty files—"

"Go on. Get out of here. Scram."

Huh. This was a novel sensation. It wasn't often a woman kicked him out of anywhere. He stood up, collecting the remaining pizza. "You want the leftovers?" he asked gruffly, holding the box out to her.

"No, thank you."

"Cool. I'll have it for breakfast in the morning."

"Yuck," she muttered under her breath. "Bachelor food."

"I suppose you have eggs benedict, toast points and fresh-squeezed orange juice every morning?"

She snorted. "Hardly. I'm lucky to remember to drink a cup of coffee sometime before midafternoon most days. I'm so busy with these two cases that I barely have time to eat or sleep, let alone cook."

"I know the feeling," he responded fervently. The whole department had been working overtime to try to solve the baffling mystery of two dead bodies hidden in the walls of a building decades ago and to investigate the arsenic poisoning of a half-dozen Colton Construction employees.

He headed for the door and was almost through it before she called out softly, "Thanks for the help with the files. And thanks for the suggestion on how to sort them."

Wow. He didn't expect her to be civil after she gave him the toss like that. Strange creature, Yvette Colton. Cross between a fuzzy bunny and a prickly porcupine. Which he supposed made her a hedgehog. Good thing he liked hedgehogs.

Chapter Three

Yvette rolled out of bed Thursday morning feeling inordinately cheerful. What was up with that? It was a cold, gray day outside—that raw in-between of not quite cold enough to snow, but miserably cold and wet. Felt like a storm was coming. And the forecast on her phone bore that out. Temperatures were supposed to fall through the day and snow should roll in, tonight. But she still bounced out of bed full of energy and excited to get to the office.

Weird. Since when was she jonesing to dive back into the overwhelming workload piled up everywhere she looked? As she finished putting her hair up into a loose, attractive style, French braided in big chunks on the sides and ending in a messy bun at the nape of her neck, she reached for makeup and froze, staring at herself in the mirror. What was she doing? She never gooped up for work. Yet here she was, primping as if she was getting ready for a hot date.

Reese. This was all his fault. Him and his bedroom eyes.

What was wrong with her? Since when did one tiny scrap of attention from a man send her into orbit like this, crushing like a fourteen-year-old? He wasn't even a man she would have chosen, left to her own devices. More often than not, he was insufferable and infuriat-

ing, forever telling her how to do her job and not mind-
ing his own business. A wannabe cowboy, for crying out
loud. He was basically everything that drove her crazy
in males of the species.

Although, to be fair, he was also a walking advertisement for procreation. The kind of man who would give
a woman beautiful children…

Whoa. Full stop. She was only twenty-five years old.
She had *years* to go before her biological alarm clock
started jangling warnings to get busy making babies.
She didn't even want a serious relationship right now,
let alone a permanent one. Her New Year's Resolution
had been to get out. Go on a few dates. Not go looking
for true love and forever after.

But it would be nice to feel this sense of excited anticipation a little more often. To look forward to trying
new restaurants, checking out local hangouts, having the
occasional adventure. Her life since she'd gotten back to
Braxville had settled in a routine of pure drudgery. Work,
sleep and more work. When had she gotten so boring?

When she'd lived in Washington, DC, she'd done
something fun pretty much every weekend. She'd visited museums, gone to the theater, hiked, biked, hung out
with friends…and she'd had tons of friends in DC. Here,
she had her family. Her sisters. And both of them were
head over heels in love and too involved in their own relationships these days to spend more than the rare free
moment with her. Not that she blamed them or even be-
grudged them their delirious happiness. But she'd come
home and more or less turned into a hermit.

She opted to wear a simple white Oxford shirt and
a pair of khaki slacks today, lest she look like she was
trying entirely too hard. Stomping into a pair of fleece
boots, she grabbed her puffy down jacket. A certain chill

that her furnace couldn't quite knock out of the air in her house announced that the cold front was already here.

She'd spent so long fussing in the bathroom that she had no time to stop for even a cup of coffee this morning on her way to work. Ugh. She was going to be stuck drinking the acidic sludge the beat cops brewed up and euphemistically called coffee.

The morning briefing was just breaking up when she arrived at the police department, and officers milled around being social before they headed off to their various assignments.

"Yvie!" her sister called out from across the jumble of desks in the squad room.

She made her way over to Jordana's desk, which butted up against Reese's, so the two faced each other. Her affectionate and outgoing sister, so unlike her, gave her a hug. "You look fantastic, sis. Any reason for getting all shined up?"

She frowned. Count on Jordana to call way too much attention to her. "Can't I put on a little makeup without getting the third degree around here?"

"Okay, okay." Jordana threw up her hands. "Never mind."

Reese arrived at his desk and set down a steaming mug of coffee. "Hey, Yvette."

She started to smile at him but stopped herself in alarm when she remembered her nosy-as-heck sister was standing there observing the two of them.

On cue, Jordana looked back and forth between them shrewdly. "How'd your date go last night?"

Yvette stared. "How on earth do you know about that?"

"Oh, I'm the one Reese lost the bet to."

"What bet?" she asked ominously. She started around

the end of the desk to confront Reese. Surely, this bet thing had been his idea.

Jordana chirped behind her, "I bet Reese that I could beat him at darts. Loser had to come back here and help you dig through files last night."

She reached Reese and glared up at him. "You lost a bet? *That's* why you helped me last night?" Hurt and betrayal swirled in her gut. It had nothing to do with liking her? Or flirting with her? Or just being decent? It was some stupid bet?

And here she was, painted up like a clown for him because she'd thought he actually liked her. Might even be interested in her. But no. She was a freaking pity case! Humiliation roared through her.

He shrugged down at her. "What does it matter? We got a lot done."

Self-control had never been her strong suit in life. In fact, she was downright impulsive by nature. Maybe that was why she cocked back her fist, hauled off and punched him in the stomach as hard as she could. Which wasn't actually all that hard because she was puny, and his abs turned out to be made of tempered steel. Her fist basically bounced off his stomach.

But pain still exploded in her metacarpal bones all along the back of her hand, a sharp reality check in the face of having done something colossally stupid. She stared up at Reese in horror as he stared down at her in shock.

More furious at herself than at him, she ground out, "Thanks for teaching me how to make a proper fist. Jerk."

She spun and marched out of the squad room, her face on fire. Silence had fallen all around her, and her face heated up with every step as she crossed the broad space amid stares from everyone.

REESE STARED AFTER Yvette thoughtfully. Normally, he would not take the least bit kindly to anyone up and slugging him. But he'd seen something in her eyes just before she'd hauled off and hit him.

Hurt.

She'd thought he brought pizza and offered to help her because he liked her. And she was hurt to think he'd only done it because he lost a bet. And as she'd turned away, he'd seen something else. A glint of shame in her dark eyes as they'd brimmed with sudden moisture.

Aww, hell. Tears were his personal kryptonite when it came to women. Now he felt bad. She was right. He'd been a thoughtless jerk. The second his partner brought up the bet, he should have made it clear immediately that he'd enjoyed working with her last night. But he'd been so startled by the violence of her reaction and the quickness of it that it didn't occur to him to correct her impression until just now.

Dumb, dumb, dumb.

Truth was he *had* only helped her because of that bet. But he'd had a nice time with her. Enjoyed getting to know her a little. He'd definitely enjoyed slipping past that cool-and-distant exterior of hers.

A low, angry sound like a threatening cat might make in the back of its throat made him look up sharply. His partner had moved over to stand exactly where Yvette had just been. Damned if Jordana's hand wasn't curled into a fist, too. Cautiously, he kept his abs flexed. She snarled, "What did you do to my baby sister?"

"Whoa, there, Jordana. Slow down. Nothing happened between us. I didn't lay a finger on her. I only came over here and helped Yvette sort through Markus Dexter's work files. I swear. You can go down and look at the boxes we went through."

His partner's threatening stance eased slightly, but her fisted hands still didn't fall down to her sides.

Lord, these Colton women were firecrackers.

"Go ask her if you don't believe me," he added desperately, eyeing Jordana's clenched fists cautiously. "Nothing happened."

She stared at him a moment longer and then nodded once, tersely. He stepped back quickly and changed the subject. "So. Where are we with tracking Dexter? Any hits on his credit cards?"

She sighed, and praise the Lord, shifted into cop mode, as well. "No hits at all. He's gone completely off the grid."

"Which is suspicious as hell," he commented.

"Oh, yeah. I seriously want to sit down with him and have a long conversation."

He'd bet. The man's gun had been used to shoot her brother, and Jordana was nothing if not protective of her family. Dexter's wife claimed the weapon must have been stolen by the shooter, and no doubt Markus would corroborate that story.

Frustration rolled through his gut. The police were missing something. A link, a bit of evidence, to prove that Markus Dexter had killed the young woman found hidden in the wall, Olivia Harrison, and the older man beside her, Fenton Crane.

The police guessed the private investigator, Crane, had come to Braxville looking for the murdered woman, and that was what had gotten him killed. But they had yet to find a solid motive for her murder. Reese's working theory was that Dexter and the woman had been having an affair.

Jordana interrupted his train of thought with, "I talked with another one of Mary Dexter's friends from her church, yesterday."

"Did this one also know about the rumors that Dex fooled around on his wife a lot?"

"Sure did."

"Did she give up any names?"

"No," Jordana answered in exasperation that matched his. "Dexter was careful. It's purely rumors and hearsay that he was having affairs all over the place. Apparently, everyone but Mary suspected he was stepping out on her."

"How does a woman miss years' worth of cheating? She struck me as a reasonably intelligent and aware woman."

Jordana shrugged. "Maybe she stayed with him for the money. Or maybe she knew about the other women and was relieved she didn't have to sleep with him. Maybe Dexter's epically lousy in the sack."

"Possible." It was as valid a theory as anything else they had to go on, right now. "How do we prove he was sleeping with Olivia Harrison when she died?" he asked.

"No idea. Did Yvette have anything new for us any of the forty-two times you've gone down to the lab to ask her this week?"

She'd noticed that, had she? In light of last night's date and this morning's disastrous aftermath, he should probably lay off forensic lab visits for a while. Jordana was a formidable woman and not one whose bad side he cared to be on.

"Your sister got the insect results back from the burial sites. It appears the Harrison woman was killed in the spring and Crane in the fall."

Jordana nodded. "That tracks with our theory that Crane came looking for Olivia after she'd been missing for a while and that he found her killer."

"We just need that one piece of conclusive evidence to identify the killer," he declared.

"Or a confession. If we can find Dexter and bring him in, I'm sure we can get him to spill his guts. He's no hero."

"Not fond of your daddy's partner, are you?" he asked.

"Dex is the one who first thought it would be a good idea to use arsenic-laced wood from China. I think he's a cheat and coward who took off as soon as the consequences of his crimes caught up with him," she replied sharply.

"Your father gonna testify against Dexter in the arsenic case?" he asked. He already knew the answer to the question, but it was a secret that he'd been involved in the plea negotiations, so Reese pretended ignorance.

She nodded. "His lawyer has nearly finished up the paperwork on a plea deal."

"Is Fitz gonna get any jail time?"

"Not the way I hear it. He's going to testify against Markus, and the DA is going to agree to let him sell his company and turn over all the proceeds to the victims of the arsenic poisoning and their families by way of a fine."

"Ouch. That's a big hit."

She shrugged. "My parents have plenty of money without the company. They own a bunch of land and real estate. And with Braxville growing the way it is, the value of all that is skyrocketing." She added, "If we can't nail Dexter for murder, we can at least charge him with illegally using arsenic-laced construction materials."

"If Dexter knows what's good for him, he's halfway to Tahiti by now," he commented.

She shrugged. "Here's hoping Dex doesn't know what's good for him."

Reese sank into his desk chair thoughtfully. He also knew what wasn't good for him, and that was messing around with Jordana Colton's baby sister. His partner had flared up like a mama bear at the mere idea of him hooking up with Yvette.

Too bad. Yvette was one of the most fascinating women he'd met in a long time. He never could resist a good puzzle, and she was definitely more puzzling than most women.

Chapter Four

Yvette literally ran for her solitary lab in the basement of the police building to hide from the indignity of what she'd just done. Cripes. She'd just slugged a cop in a room full of cops. As soon as the police chief, Roger Hilton, heard about it, she had no doubt he would summon her for a well-deserved chewing out.

Dumb, dumb, dumb! She knew better than to let her emotions run away with her like that! She'd gotten away with stupid stunts like that as a kid, but she was an adult, now. Allegedly a professional.

Kicking herself mentally, she opened a random box of evidence seized from the Dexter home in a recent search of it. Peering inside, she spied a pile of datebooks, each with a year embossed on the cover.

She picked one up and opened it. The pages were starting to yellow with age and the handwriting was in Markus Dexter's messy scrawl, which she knew well, now, after having stared at thousands of pages of his personal documents last night. She turned the book over. In faded gold, the year was stamped on the cover. She glanced through it and noticed right away that all of Dexter's appointments and meetings were identified only with initials. Never a name. She thumbed through a few more of the annual planners, and the same thing was true of all of them. The man *never* used names in his datebook.

Odd. Secretive.

Out of curiosity, she pulled out a random file from the year group that Reese had so carefully organized last night. What a jerk…

Focus, Yvette. Don't let some jackass man distract you from catching a murderer.

This particular file was paperwork associated with an apartment complex Colton Construction had built. She riffled through it until she found Dex's notes from a meeting in April. The date and time were noted at the top of the paper. Perfect.

Noting the client's name, Randall Pardo, she opened Dexter's planner to April. Huh. On that particular date and time, the notation was for O.Q. Did Dexter actually use a *code* in his own planner?

Paranoid much?

She sat down at her desk and fooled around with how to get from R.P. to O.Q. It didn't take her long to figure out that if she reversed the initials to last name first and then first name, she got P.R. Then, she backed up one letter in the alphabet—*P* went to *O*, and *R* went to *Q*.

She checked a few more appointments in that year and the code held true. She poked around and found the datebook for the year they thought the murders had happened and tried the same code on a few construction appointments. But it didn't work. She tried all the other datebooks, and that particular replacement code only worked in a single year.

He changed his code every year? Holy cow. What was the man hiding, indeed? This was the sort of behavior indicative of someone living a double life. *What's your other life, Markus Dexter?*

She did note that, particularly in the oldest calendars, many of the "appointments" took place at night, some late at night. The year after the Harrison-Crane murders, however, even the times for appointments began to be coded also, and she couldn't tell anymore if he was setting up late-night assignations.

She picked up her phone and dialed her sister. "Hey, Jordana."

"Hey, Yvette. Are you okay? What on earth happened between you and—"

She cut her sister off sharply. "This is a work phone call. I found Markus Dexter's appointment calendars, and I thought you'd like to know he never used names, just initials. Furthermore, he used codes to record even the initials. And, he appeared to use a new code each year to refer to whomever he was supposed to meet and when. I'll try to work out the codes if I can."

"Wild. Give me a shout-out if you need help deciphering them."

"Will do. Also, were you on the team that searched the Dexter house?"

"No, but Reese was in charge of the search. Why?"

"I'm curious if any secret hiding places were discovered. Secret compartments, false bottoms in drawers, hollows under floorboards, that sort of thing."

"I have no idea. I'll ask Reese and have him get back to you."

"Or you can just relay his answer to me."

"What on God's green earth happened between you two last night?" Jordana demanded.

"Nothing. Absolutely nothing. He showed up with pizza and beer, and he alphabetized files while I separated them into useless files versus files of interest."

"He didn't come on to you? Make any advances?"

As mad as she was at Reese and at herself, she certainly wasn't going to throw him under the bus by claiming he'd been anything other than a perfect gentleman. "No, Jordana. Nothing like that. At all."

"Then why did you punch—"

"I'm up to my elbows in alligators down here. I really don't have time to gossip."

"Fine. Look. While I've got you on the phone, would you like to go to Dusty Rusty's tomorrow night with me and a bunch of the gang from the department? Lou Hovitz is having his retirement party."

"No way—"

"Before you say no," Jordana interrupted, "You kind of owe it to Reese to go. After that stunt you pulled this morning, you need to be seen in public making nice with him. And *not* punching him."

Making nice with Reese Carpenter was the *last* thing she wanted to do. But darned if Jordana wasn't right.

She huffed. "Fine. I'll go to your stupid party at Rusty's."

"Great! I'll tell Reese."

"Jor—"

Her sister disconnected the call before she could stop her from telling her partner. She honestly couldn't tell if Jordana was merely trying to patch things up in the police department or trying to throw her and Reese together to see for herself what kind of chemistry they had.

Good luck with that, sis. She and Reese weren't even oil and water. They were fire and dynamite.

At least Reese's harassment campaign of hourly visits ceased today. She was vastly relieved for the first few hours of undisturbed, tomb-like silence in her lab. But as the worst of her embarrassment wore off, she actually found herself glancing up every hour and waiting for the hallway door to open.

The day passed, hour by endless, agonizing hour, with no sign of Reese. Her shame morphed into disgust at herself for actually missing the supremely irritating detective. She missed insulting him and throwing him out of her lab, and she missed his teasing and constant suggestions on how to do her job. And darn it, she missed his bedroom eyes.

She spent the afternoon digging through Dexter's home evidence, looking for any notations by the search team of secret hiding places they'd found. Nothing of the like was indicated anywhere. Which led her to believe the search party had missed something. Any man who created a whole new code every year for writing down his appointments, many of which happened at night, well after work hours, had secrets and lots of them.

The interview with his wife, Mary, had indicated she knew nothing of his extracurricular activities with the ladies. Which meant Mary was lying or else he was hiding a major part of his life from her. At a minimum, he must have a hiding spot in his home where he left his wedding ring when he went out. Maybe cash or dedicated credit cards he used to finance his dating habits. A man as careful as Dexter surely wouldn't charge anything to a credit card whose bill his wife might see.

She was startled to realize it was nearly ten o'clock when she finally pushed back from her desk to call it a night. She'd broken the code on a few of the most recent appointment books—they'd been relatively simple substitution codes. But a quarter century ago, in the time frame of the murders, he'd been more cautious with his codes. More to hide, perhaps?

Was it ageist of her to expect that a man in his late thirties might fool around more than a man in his sixties? Either that, or Mary Dexter might have been more suspicious back then. If only she knew more about the couple's relationship.

In the meantime, her suspicion that the search of the Dexter home could have missed something important intensified. Of course, it wasn't as if Reese would listen to her if she told him he'd messed up. After all, he not only thought he knew how to do his own job, but also hers.

She would really love to put that man in his place for once. How awesome would it be to tell him how to do his job for a change? Even better, to show him up at being a detective.

In fact...

She grabbed her purse and coat eagerly. How cool would it be to shove his superiority in his face by finding a secret hidey-hole in the Dexter house that he'd missed? Excited at the prospect, she went up to the evidence locker to find out if Mary Dexter had given the police a key to her home so the police could check it while she was out of town. The police had apparently asked her not to return to the home until her husband was apprehended. Whether that was because they thought Marcus was a threat to his wife or they thought Mary might aid and abet him in fleeing the country, Yvette had no idea.

Indeed, the department did have a key to the Dexter house. She signed it out and hurried out to her car.

It was a frigid night and the wind was bitter as she crossed the parking lot. Snow scudded across the beams of light her car cast into the darkness, and the roads were treacherous with patches of black ice. The forecast storm had definitely arrived. The police were no doubt going to spend all night pulling cars out of ditches. She certainly didn't need to be one of them. Driving carefully, she guided her little car across town to the predictably ostentatious Dexter home and parked in the circular drive.

A surveillance detail had been set up to keep an eye on the house in case Markus Dexter came back, but no police SUV was parked out front. The unit assigned to the job must have been called out on some kind of emergency. No surprise with the roads as bad as they were. The Braxville PD was not a big outfit, and didn't always have the spare manpower to dedicate to this surveillance detail.

She hustled to the front porch, unlocked the door and slipped inside. Where to look for Markus's hidey-hole? The obvious place to start was a space he would consider his. An office or man cave.

His office was just to the right of the foyer behind a pair of French doors. The space was undeniably masculine, with dark paneling and heavy leather furniture. She took her time searching the furniture—desk, tables, cabinets—and then the room itself—bookshelves, walls, even the floor and ceiling. Nothing resembled a secret hiding place.

She walked through the rest of the ground floor and found no other room that stood out as a place Markus would consider his. She headed upstairs and found a billiard room, which she searched thoroughly. Nothing. She headed for the master bedroom. It was a shared space, but there would be dressers, maybe a closet, dedicated to his stuff. Still nothing.

Darn it. What if she was wrong? Relief took root in her belly that she'd gone on this wild goose chase alone, late at night, without telling anyone about it. She would hate to give Reese Carpenter even more fodder to tease her with.

She stopped in the middle of the master bathroom to think. What was she missing?

What about spaces in the house that weren't used often, like an attic or basement? The latter weren't common in this part of the world. The clay soil tended to heave and have terrible drainage, both of which made a slab foundation more practical than a full basement. Which she knew, compliments of growing up with a contractor father.

An attic, then. The house had a steep roof that surely had space under it for one. It took her a few minutes of searching to find a door tucked at the end of a hallway. She opened it and there was a narrow stairway leading up into blackness. Cold poured out of the unheated space.

Yes.

She felt around for a light switch on the wall but didn't find one. Fishing in her purse, she pulled out the fist-sized titanium flashlight she always carried. That was her. Little Miss Preparedness. More like Miss Afraid-of-Catastrophes. Ever since Debbie's murder, she'd always carried something hard and heavy that she could improvise with as a weapon. In some ways, she was still that kid, terrified that the boogeyman would come for her, too.

She pointed her light at the wooden treads beneath her boots, and spied a layer of dust on them. Several sets of footsteps had recently disturbed it. No doubt those came from the police who'd searched the place.

She pulled the door shut behind her and started up the stairs.

With each step it grew colder, and a couple of the stair treads squeaked noisily, just like in a bad horror movie. She emerged into the cavernous space under the eaves. It had a finished floor, but the eaves were exposed. Shelving was installed in the area in front of her, stacked with plastic bins neatly labeled: Christmas decorations, door wreaths, seasonal decor, summer clothing. One whole side of this area was filled with hanging-clothing racks full of garment bags.

The half of the attic behind the stairs was a jumbled mess of cardboard boxes, broken lamps, old furniture and general junk that looked straight off the set of a stalker movie. All the area lacked was a creepy doll staring back at her, or maybe a dude in a mask holding a chain saw.

A chill shuddered down her spine and she clutched her coat more tightly around her throat. The good news was this was exactly the kind of space she would expect Markus Dexter to hide something in.

The organized section of the attic smacked of Mary Dexter's highly structured home management. Which meant Markus would likely not have hidden anything in the bins.

Gingerly, she made her way into the pile of junk. The dust was thick back here. Thick enough that she doubted the search party had even gone through any of this stuff. Of course, maybe they'd taken one look at the thick layer of undisturbed dust on the floor and decided no one had been up here for so long that it wasn't worth their time to search it.

Not that she blamed them. It was painstaking work, going through the mess one object at a time, feeling each item, peering underneath it for something taped to the bottom, examining everything for secret spaces. She shoved her hands into the seams of chairs, lifted cushions, opened drawers and boxes and generally hunted for a needle in a haystack.

She'd been at it for long enough that her nose was numb and her fingers ached from cold when she thought she heard something downstairs. She paused, listening. If the furnace fan had been off, she would have put the hollow bump down to the heat turning on. But it had been running continuously since she came into the house. Maybe the police returning to their surveillance post? They'd probably seen her car and were coming in to say hello.

She opened her mouth to call out a greeting but a chill of foreboding across the back of her neck stopped her. Or maybe it was just the general creep factor up here that silenced her.

She made her way over to one of the dormer windows to peer out at the front of the house. That was weird. A sedan was parked at the curb, but no police cruiser was parked in the driveway behind her little car. Maybe they'd gone around back. Which made sense. It made the police less conspicuous in the upscale neighborhood and maybe they would catch Dexter unawares. She picked her way through the clutter to a window facing the back of the sprawling property. Only snow stretched away below her, pale and undisturbed in the darkness. No police cruiser.

Then who was downstairs?

A door closed somewhere below her feet.

Okay. There was definitely someone in the house. And it didn't appear to be the police.

Her heart exploded into panic mode, sending blood surging into her ears, roaring a warning at her to run. Now.

A door opened nearby. *Was that the attic door?*

A surge of adrenaline made her entire body feel light and fast, desperate to move.

She heard a creak. That was a stair tread! Someone was coming up here.

Oh God, oh God, oh God.

She looked left and right. There was only the one exit from the attic. No way to creep out of here stealthily, then.

A hiding place. She needed to hide.

Frantically, she hunted for a spot shrouded in darkness, large enough to hold her but small enough to avoid detection. Tiptoeing, she eased back into the corner of the eaves where the roof angled down close to the floor and wedged herself behind a rusty metal rack with outdated seventies and eighties clothing stuffed on it. She turned off her flashlight and crouched in the darkness.

Quickly, she pulled out her cell phone, shielding the glow with her body. She texted 9-1-1.

This is Yvette Colton. Am inside Dexter home with intruder. If cops, tell them to identify themselves. If not, send backup ASAP.

If it was police in the house, the emergency dispatcher would contact them and tell them to call out.

Another stair tread squeaked loudly, this one practically at the top of the staircase. She peered around the end of the clothes fearfully. *Please, God, be a uniformed police officer.* She was breathing so fast she was starting to feel lightheaded as a bulky figure cleared the stairwell.

That was a dark wool overcoat. Not a cop. The figure turned away from her and turned on a flashlight. She suppressed an urge to cringe away from the light. Human eyes were much better at catching movement than making out still shapes, so her only hope to remain undetected was to stay perfectly still and hope she'd picked an adequate hiding place.

The sounds of boxes shuffling and something heavy sliding across the floor interrupted the cold and dark.

She measured the distance from herself to the stairs. Nope, she couldn't make a run for it unseen. The flashlight was hard and warm in her fist, and she gripped it so tightly her fingers ached. The shadow across from her in the dark was large. Undoubtedly male. She had basic self-defense training, but she didn't relish a hand-to-hand fight against that much bigger an opponent. Especially alone, in the dark, with no one nearby to help.

Whatever the intruder was looking for was taking him a while to find. The occasional grunt and muttered curse were audible as the scraping and shuffling of junk continued. What on earth was he looking for? She hadn't searched that side of the attic yet, which was both good and bad news. The good news was her footprints and handprints weren't all over the stuff over there. The bad news was she hadn't found whatever this guy was searching for so diligently.

Her nose tickled. An urge to sneeze built in her sinuses. No, no, no! She eased her hand up to her face and pinched her nose tightly, praying for the sneeze to go away. She held her breath for interminable seconds of terror until finally, blessedly, the urge to sneeze faded.

Something fell over loudly across the attic, and she jumped at the abrupt crash.

"Dammit," the intruder bit out in a deep, gruff voice.

Was this Markus Dexter? In the flesh? Or maybe a friend he'd sent in to find something? Or was this a simple thief?

The sound of a vehicle's engine outside interrupted the deep silence of the night. She saw the bent-over shadow straighten sharply and freeze. No doubt listening as hard as she was. Was that a police car pulling up? Normally, they would come in with sirens screaming in a situation like this to scare off an intruder without harming the civilian caught inside the house.

The shadow threw open a trunk lid and tossed out the contents behind him with thuds and clangs. He scooped up something and turned, picking his way fast toward the stairs.

Drat! He appeared to have found what he was looking for and was now going to flee with it. Whatever that thing was, she desperately wanted to see what he'd come for. What if it was the exact hidden thing she'd been searching for? She couldn't let this guy just waltz out of here with it. And she had no idea who'd pulled up out front. It could as easily be this burglar's accomplice as a police officer.

The guy cleared the pile of junk and raced for the stairs. He was getting away! Panic and urgent need to stop him spurred her to her feet.

She stepped out of her hiding place and turned on her military-grade flashlight, yelling, "Halt! Police!"

The man lurched violently and threw one arm up, shading his eyes and casting a deep shadow over his face, which totally obscured his features.

"Hands up! Lock your fingers behind your neck!" she shouted, moving quickly through the junk pile. What she wouldn't give to be carrying a firearm right now. As it was, she scooped up a long candlestick in her off hand as she passed where it sat on top of a cardboard box.

But the intruder had other ideas. As she approached, still shining the light in his face and hopefully obscuring hers—so he wouldn't see how young and small she was—the figure backed away from her.

She moved to block his access to the staircase, but he charged forward holding something square and bulky in front of him. He slammed into her, knocking her down hard on her back. Her head hit the floor hard enough to daze her and she dropped both her flashlight and the candlestick.

As he kept on going, more or less charging right over her, she grabbed at his ankle, hooking her left arm around it. He stumbled, forced to stop. Kicking violently, he freed his leg but dropped the object he was holding.

A voice shouted from somewhere below. "Yvette! Where are you?"

The intruder, who'd started to turn around to grab whatever he'd dropped, jolted. For an instant, he hesitated. Then, he abandoned whatever he'd dropped and raced down the attic stairs, taking the steps three at a time. She pushed up to her hands and knees but her head swam with dizziness and nausea rolled through her gut. No way could she stand, let alone give chase.

"Up here!" she called weakly.

And then she did throw up. Blessedly, her stomach was empty due to her failure to eat pretty much anything all day, and only dry-heaved.

She heard running footsteps. Doors slamming. A car motor revving behind the house. And then silence fell once more. She lay with her cheek pressed to the cold floor, her head spinning, and failure roiling in her gut.

The intruder had gotten away from her. She should've been strong enough, fast enough, to stop him. But he'd run right over her. She *hated* being weak and small and vulnerable. It was all of her worst fears come true, save the part where she was murdered like Debbie. Panic still roared through her and realization that she'd just come very close to dying made her hyperventilate.

"Yvette! Where the hell are you?"

"Attic," she managed to call back.

Light spilled into the stairwell from below, and running footsteps approached her. She braced automatically for another attack.

"Yvette?"

Well, fudge. She recognized that voice. *Reese.*

She exhaled a wobbly breath, and all of a sudden, tears were leaking out of the corners of her eyes. She'd lived. For a few minutes, there, she'd been pretty sure she was going to die.

Big, gentle hands rolled her over. Sat her up. She surprised herself almost as much as she seemed to surprise Reese when she flung herself forward into his arms and let the tears flow. She clung tightly to his waist, absorbing his warmth and strength gratefully, inhaling the crisp scent of his aftershave as snowflakes on his coat melted against her cheek. It wasn't that she liked him for a second. It was just that…he was…well, safe.

"I've got you. The intruder's gone," Reese murmured into her hair. Then, "What the hell happened?"

"I… He… Ran… Fell…" she was gasping too hard to talk and her chest was being squeezed so tightly she couldn't breathe. And just like that, she was sobbing and shaking. No words at all came then. Just total relief that help, any help darn it, was here and that she hadn't died.

"Aftershock. Panic attack. Got it," Reese murmured. His arms tightened around her and he waited patiently for her to calm down.

He really was being half decent. But she still hated his guts.

Eventually, he tried again. "Tell me what happened up here. Did he hurt you? I need you to use your words."

Slowly, her terror receded in the shelter of his embrace. She shook her head.

"Can you talk, now?" he tried again.

She finally nodded against his chest.

Words. Right. She could do this.

She pushed back from his chest, and his arms fell away from her. The air was cold and unfriendly where his arms and chest had just been. She tried unsuccessfully to stand up, but Reese grabbed her shoulders lightly to hold her down.

"Let's take it slow. Where does it hurt?"

"My head."

Fingers passed over her scalp and neck carefully. "Jeez, short stuff. That's a nice bump you've got going, there. Did he hit you?"

She blinked, and it was her turn to stare into the blinding glare of a flashlight. "Could you get that light out of my face? My head already is killing me without having to look at it."

"Sorry." The beam tilted up toward the ceiling, and for the first time since he'd arrived, she made out his features. They were tight with concern. "Glad you're talking, again. Walk me through what happened, okay?"

"An intruder. Heard him downstairs. Then he came up here. I called for backup, but they—you—hadn't gotten here yet. He found something and started to leave with it. I had to stop him, but he slammed into me, and he—" She broke off, not only because she was babbling, but also because a terrible thought had just occurred to her.

"Did he take it with him?" she asked urgently. It hurt like heck to move her head, let alone focus her gaze to look around for whatever he'd been clutching to his chest when he'd charged her.

"Take what?"

"A box, or something big and hard about the size of a bread box."

"You mean this? It looks like a wooden jewelry box." Reese straightened from his crouch beside her and moved to an overturned box on the floor beside the top of the stairs.

"Yes. I'm pretty sure that's what the intruder was here to find."

"Who was the intruder? Did you get a good look at him?"

"No. I never saw his face. It was too dark and he hid it from me when I shone my light at him."

"What happened to you?"

"He charged me. Knocked me down. That's when I hit my head. I grabbed his leg, though. He dropped the box. Then he kicked free and bolted. Did you see him?"

"No. I came up the front staircase, but he must've taken the back staircase and run out through the kitchen. By the time I figured out he'd gone around me and I got back downstairs, I only saw taillights retreating in the distance. I didn't even get a model and make of vehicle, let alone a license plate," he said in disgust.

Another wave of nausea rolled over her, and she slapped her hand over her mouth. No way was she barfing in front of Reese Carpenter.

"You don't look so hot, Yvie."

"Don't feel so hot," she mumbled.

"Let's get you out of here. Can you walk?"

She honestly didn't know if she could stand. Reese reached down to her and lifted her by her armpits, then set her on her feet. She swayed as angry little men with jackhammers went to work trying to escape from her skull. She must have groaned, for Reese moved quickly to her side and looped his arm around her waist.

"Can you put your arm across my shoulder?" he murmured.

"You're hilarious. In case you hadn't noticed, I'm a wee bit height challenged."

He chuckled and shifted his arm to grip her shoulders, instead. "There. Now you can put your arm around my waist."

"What? Are you that desperate to have me put my hands on—" She broke off. *Do not initiate banter with the hot detective when you're in no shape to make it down these stairs yourself.*

His waist was hard and narrow beneath her forearm. She'd always been a sucker for a fit guy, darn it. She was a runner, herself. Although, the weather had been so bad the past few weeks and the workload at the lab so massive she hadn't even been out for a jog since Christmas.

"Easy does it," he murmured as he guided her down the steps. "Take your time. And let me know if you need to stop and rest."

She had to give him credit. For once, he wasn't being a total jerk. Gently, he all but carried her down to the second floor and guided her to a love seat in a reading nook. "Will you be okay here by yourself if I go get you a glass of water?"

She started to nod, but her head throbbed at even the slightest movement. "Yes," she sighed.

He moved away from her swiftly, and the panic from before surged forward again. She was alone. Vulnerable. And this big, empty house was creepy as heck. She was relieved when he approached her swiftly carrying a glass brimming with water.

"Here you go. Sip it slowly." She took the glass he held out of her and did as he ordered. While she worked on getting down the cold water, he pulled out his cell phone and asked for a patrol car to be dispatched to the Dexter home immediately. He told the dispatcher he would stay in the house until it arrived.

But given the weather and condition of the roads, "immediately" turned out to be more like a half hour. Long enough for her to start feeling a tiny bit more human and for her stomach to settle sufficiently for her to contemplate walking out of here under her own power. She listened as Reese ordered the uniforms to lock up the house, post no-entry tape and let nobody inside until he could get back here in the morning with a crime-scene kit.

And then he was back, standing in front of her, the jewelry box from before tucked under his left arm. She noticed for the first time that he was wearing jeans and a Kansas State University hoodie that made him look younger and infinitely less intimidating than the dark, severe suits he wore to work.

"Can you walk, or do you need me to carry you out of here?" he asked.

She looked up at him to see if he was making fun of her, but she saw nothing in his eyes to indicate that he was joking. Only worry shone in his baby blues. "I can make it on my own, thanks."

But, as soon as she stood up, a wave of dizziness washed over her and she swayed a little. On cue, he stepped close and wrapped his free arm around her waist.

"I said I can walk."

"I heard you. But I really don't want you falling down the stairs and hitting your head again."

"I can do it—"

He cut her off. "Yvette. I'm sure you can do it all by yourself. But let me help you, okay?"

"But—"

"Humor me. It'll make me feel better to steady you. I'm gonna feel like a complete jerk if you tumble down the stairs and break your neck when I could've lent you a hand."

How was a woman supposed to say no to that?

"Truce, okay? Just for tonight. You can go back to slugging me in the gut for no reason tomorrow."

She opened her mouth to declare that she had a reason for punching him, but then he would ask what it was, and she wasn't about to confess that she had a crush on him and was upset that he hadn't thought of their evening in the lab together as a date.

Seriously. How lame was that? When she thought the words through, she sounded like a total stalker.

She closed her mouth, kept her silence and let him guide her down the long hallway, down the stairs and out the front door. But when he guided her toward his pickup truck and not toward her car, she protested, "I can drive myself home!"

"I feel you trembling. You can barely walk. No way am I letting you drive. Besides, the roads are treacherous. My truck can handle the ice and snow worlds better than that shoebox on wheels you drive."

She opened her mouth to argue, but he pinned her with a look of concern that made the words die on her tongue, unspoken. Well okay, then. She let him open the passenger door of the truck, set the box inside, then put his hands around her waist and bodily lift her into the vehicle. The ease with which he hoisted her into the truck was a little shocking. He was *so* much stronger than he looked—and he looked pretty darned fit.

He went around to the driver's side, and the glow of the dashboard illuminated his profile. "How did *you* end up here at the Dexter house, tonight?" she finally got around to figuring out to ask.

"Dispatcher called me. I live about ten minutes away and all the other units were out on calls."

"Lucky for me."

"I'm sorry I didn't get there before the intruder hurt you."

"You got there in time to scare him off and make him drop whatever this is." She touched the wooden box sitting on the seat of the truck between them.

"Any idea what's inside it?" he asked.

"None. I'm eager to take a close look at it and its contents."

"First, I'm taking a close look at you."

Her gaze snapped up to his face, but he was staring out at the road and his expression gave away nothing. What on earth did he mean by that?

Chapter Five

Reese pulled into the attached garage beside his tidy little log cabin on the edge of town. He loved this place. Had bought the land raw and built this place with his own two hands. It took nearly three years to complete, and privately he was damned proud of it.

He came around to let Yvette out of the truck. She looked tiny and lost in that oversized fluffy coat, tucked inside his big heavy-duty truck. He'd about had a heart attack when he'd charged up those stairs to find her lying on the floor of the Dexter attic. She was lucky the intruder hadn't shoved her down the stairs or killed her outright.

He reached for her waist to help her down from the high truck seat, and she was slender even through her thick coat, but she recoiled.

"Truce, remember?" he murmured.

She nodded and let him lift her down from the high cab to the concrete floor.

"This way," he murmured, leading her around his truck and into the kitchen of his rustic home.

His sister-in-law called his taste *mountain-lodge-bachelor decor*. Whatever. It was comfortable and made him feel at home.

"Wow. This is nice," Yvette commented, looking

around the open living-dining-kitchen area. "Did it come like this or did you remodel?"

"I built the place," he mumbled. It had been a labor of love, and he was proud of the end result.

"From scratch? All by yourself? Impressive."

"I bought this piece of land when I joined the Braxville Police Department and worked on it bit by bit as I had the time and money."

"Wow. How did you get those giant ceiling beams up there?"

She was staring up at the vaulted ceiling and huge log rafters that supported the roof.

"Took a whole keg of beer to bribe enough guys from the department to come out one weekend and help me hoist all those big logs up there."

"I had no idea you were the DIY type."

He shrugged. "I like to make things, work with my hands. But I don't get much time for it in my current job."

"Especially not with a murderer running around on the loose," she murmured.

"Exactly." He reached for her shoulders. "Let me take your coat. Why don't you go sit by the fireplace and I'll make you something hot to drink. Tea, isn't it?"

She looked up at him in surprise. "That's right. How did you know?"

"You've been bringing a cup of hot tea to staff meetings for a year. I'd be a pretty terrible detective if I hadn't noticed that by now."

"Fair."

He filled a kettle and put it on the stove to heat while he rummaged in his cupboards for tea bags. He had a box buried somewhere in the back of one. Bingo. He pulled out the semicrushed cardboard box and prayed that tea didn't go stale fast. No telling how long this stuff had been in his kitchen. He thought his mom had brought it over sometime last summer.

"Mind if I build a fire?" Yvette asked from across the large living space.

"I'll do it. Gimme a sec to get your drink pulled together."

"I can do it, for crying out loud."

He rolled his eyes as he put two tall mugs, sugar and creamer on a tray. He poured the hot water, plunked in a couple of tea bags and carried the whole affair over to the coffee table in front of the fireplace. This was about as fancy as he got in his house.

Yvette sat on the raised stone hearth beside the big fireplace, leaning down and blowing on a small fire she was nursing to life.

"Why don't you use the bellows?" he asked, reaching for the tool and passing it to her from where it hung on a hook beside the mantel.

She rolled her eyes and commenced squeezing the bellows, sending puffs of air into her little fire.

He sat down on the sofa to watch her play pyromaniac. "Tell me something, Yvie. Why don't you want anyone to help you with anything?"

"I let people help me with stuff."

He snorted. "You were barely conscious and didn't want me to help you stand up, let alone walk out of that house. And just now. You wouldn't let me help with the fire."

She frowned in his general direction but didn't make eye contact.

"I have a theory on it," he announced.

"Do tell."

"You're the baby of the Colton family, right?"

"I hate that term."

"Exactly! I'll bet everyone in the clan treated you as if you weren't capable of doing anything by yourself."

She looked up at him, her eyes wide and startled. "How do know that?"

"Hello. Detective, here. Student of human behavior."

She shook her head. "Doesn't it get exhausting having to know everything about everyone and everything all the time?"

"What do you mean?"

"Do you ever sit and oh, read a book or watch a movie—or do anything—without analyzing it to death?"

"When I'm off duty."

"Oh." The syllable came out as a soft sigh of breath as she turned her back on him to stare into the fire, which was starting to lick up around the medium-size sticks nicely. It would be ready for a small log in another minute or two.

He frowned at the back of her head. What had he done wrong to make her disengage all of a sudden? For as surely as he was sitting here, he'd managed to hurt her feelings. Was it because she thought he'd gone off duty to bring her to his—

Oh.

She'd hoped him bringing her here was a sign of personal interest and concern.

God, he was an idiot when it came to women. He'd totally missed that one.

"So, here's the thing," he said. "I need to ask you a few questions about earlier and do the whole cop thing for about five minutes. Then, I'd love to hang up my badge for the night to just chill and hang with you. Is that okay?"

"Umm, sure." She gifted him with one of those sexy-as-all-get-out sidelong looks of hers that made her eyes look even more exotic than they already were.

Whew. *Nice recovery, my dude.* Close call, there, with being a total ass.

"Okay. How about you start at the beginning and tell me everything that happened tonight."

He listened with interest to her theory that Markus Dexter was secretive enough to have hidden things in his home. Made sense. He was less thrilled when she got to the part about deciding to go have a look for herself in Dexter's house to see if she could find something he and his search team had missed.

He bit back a sarcastic comment about her trying to do his job for him. *Truce, man. Remember? You declared it. Even if she is a bossy little thing.*

Well, hell. Is that how he came across to her whenever he tried to give her suggestions about how to run her lab? He was just trying to help. He knew this was her first gig running her own crime lab, and he had a master's degree in forensics, which meant he'd spent some time in crime labs while he was in school. He'd picked up a few things here and there that might be helpful—

He broke off his train of thought, yet again.

Was he actually the know-it-all she accused him of being? When had *that* happened? He'd always hated bossy bosses who got all up in his business.

"Are you okay?" Yvette asked, startling him.

"Yeah, sure. Why do you ask?"

"You tuned out on me, there, for a second."

He sighed. "I was having an epiphany that you might have been right all along."

"About what?"

"That I've turned into my old man."

"Meaning what?"

"He's a dyed-in-the-wool know-it-all. Always butting in with advice and suggestions."

"Ahh."

"What does that mean?" he demanded.

"Nothing. Just ahh."

He had to give her credit for winning benevolently. She could've rubbed his nose in what a giant idiot he was, but she seemed willing to let it go without any gloating or I told you so's. For which he was immensely grateful.

He mentally gave himself a shake. "Okay. So you went to the Dexter home and started searching it."

"Right. But I didn't find any false walls or hidden compartments anywhere on the first two floors. So, I headed up to the attic. I was poking around when I heard someone enter the house."

"Did you call out?"

"No. I checked outside through the attic windows and didn't see any police cars, so I concluded there might be an intruder."

"Is that when you called 9-1-1?" he asked.

"Technically, I texted 9-1-1. And yes, I asked for backup."

"Then what?" he prompted when she fell silent.

"The intruder came up into the attic," she paused, then confessed in a rush, "and I hid."

"Good call."

"Really?" she asked in a small voice.

"Absolutely. You had no way of knowing if the intruder was armed, violent or homicidal. I assume you weren't carrying a weapon of your own?"

"I may be an employee of the Braxville Police Department, but I'm a forensic scientist, not a gunslinger."

One corner of his mouth turned up. "Go on."

"While I waited for help to arrive, I watched him poke

around as if he was looking for something specific. When he found that box, he immediately headed for the stairs, and I panicked. I was worried he was going to get away with whatever I'd gone there to find."

"So, you thought it would be a good idea to confront this stranger…and do what? Demand that he hand over his prize?"

"I didn't get that far. I yelled for him to freeze and identified myself as police."

"You're not technically a police officer—" he started.

"I know that," she interrupted. "But he was about to leave. I had to stop him somehow."

"But instead of stopping, he rushed you, knocked you over and fled," Reese supplied. "How did you get him to drop the box, again?"

"I grabbed his leg as he ran past me. He stumbled and dropped it then. That was right when you yelled my name. He'd started to turn to pick up the box, but when he heard you calling out, he bolted."

"What are the odds the intruder was Markus Dexter?" he asked.

"I never saw his face. The man was about six feet tall and wore a long wool coat. It was bulky, as if he had layers of clothing under it. He had on a black knit hat, and gloves. He could be anyone. It's entirely possible Markus hired someone to come to the house and fetch that jewelry box. It would explain why the intruder took a while to find it."

"Dang it all," Reese muttered under his breath.

"I know you're jonesing to pin something on Dex, but I can't give you an ID I didn't make."

"Of course not," he agreed firmly. "We'll get him fair and square, eventually. Are you feeling up to looking with me at the box he dropped? I'm curious to see what all the fuss was about."

"We ought to take it back to my lab."

He glanced up at the windows. "Weather's getting worse. Roads are going to be nigh impassable soon. I say we have a look at it, here."

"Stubborn man," she mumbled under her breath.

"Practical man," he replied dryly.

"You weren't supposed to hear that."

"Sorry. Good hearing."

Her eyes narrowed. "Duly noted. Have you got a tool set with a small screwdriver, a magnifying glass and tweezers? Maybe a bright lamp? Oh, and a fingerprint kit?"

"Affirmative to all of the above. I'll assemble them at the kitchen table."

"I'll go get my cell phone," she replied.

"Why?"

"Pictures. Have to take them to enter the box properly into evidence. Assuming you plan to actually open it tonight," she added wryly.

"Oh, yeah. I definitely want to see what all the fuss is about. Bastard better not have hurt you over nothing."

"I'm not hurt."

"But you could've been. A few steps closer to the stairs and you could have taken a bad fall." The way his gut clenched at the idea of her lying broken and in pain—or even dead—at the bottom of that narrow staircase was shocking. He'd learned a long time ago how to distance his emotions from his work, but that skill seemed to have abruptly deserted him.

She seemed startled at the vehemence in his voice. Did she really have no idea that he thought of her as—

his train of thought crashed off the end of the rails and plunged into a mental abyss.

How did he think of her? She was certainly more than a colleague. A friend? A challenge? A potential love interest? Darned if he knew.

They reconvened at Reese's wood-plank kitchen table. It was a single slab out of what must have been a massive tree when it was alive. She ran her palm over the satin-smooth surface. "Seems a shame to kill a tree this magnificent just so you can have a kitchen table."

Reese smiled a little. "This table's been in my family over a hundred years. And my great-granddaddy planted some of the first trees in the Kansas prairie. Trust me. The Carpenter family has helped many more trees grow than we ever cut down. You can put away your environmental outrage."

She rolled her eyes at him while he clamped a bright work lamp with a telescoping arm to the edge of the table.

He turned on the light and Yvette's whole demeanor changed. He was fascinated to watch her focus her entire attention on the damaged wooden box. Did she do that with her lovers, too? Concentrate all of her attention like that? It was sexy as hell.

One corner of the inlaid mahogany box was crushed, no doubt where it had hit the floor, and she took several pictures of that.

She photographed it from every conceivable angle, including having him turn it upside down. When she was satisfied with the lighting and the shots she'd taken, she finally nodded to him. "You can open it, now."

Except the lid was locked tight. He tugged on it to no avail.

"Can you pick the lock?" she asked, "Or do you need me to?"

"I can, but I don't think this is a regular locking box. It looks like a puzzle box to me," he answered.

"How's that?" she asked quickly.

"See this piece in the lid? It slides slightly to one side in these tracks." She leaned in closer to stare at where he was pointing, and he smelled the sophisticated warmth of her perfume. Or maybe that was her hair. Either way, she smelled like old money. Class. Way out of his league, for darned sure.

"So, slide it," she said impatiently.

"The thing with puzzle boxes is you have to move the parts in the right order to get them to open."

"Will we hurt it if we move various parts and pieces while we try to figure it out?"

"Not unless there's some sort of booby trap built into it. In which case, a wrong move will usually break a small vial of acid or solvent that destroys or dissolves the treasure in the middle of the thing."

"What are the odds we can get this thing to open on the first try?" she asked in quick alarm.

"Zero." He studied the box for a moment more and added, "This looks like a tricky one. The first order of business is to get an idea of how many moving parts it has and where they are."

She nodded, leaning close to his shoulder to study the box as he tugged and poked at each side. They found various panels, springs, hinges and connection points, and over time got a feel for the thing.

"Check out that piece right there," she murmured. "Does it look like the flower would move independent of the surrounding inlay?"

"Looks like it. You have a discerning eye."

"Forensic scientist, here. You may be a detective and

answer why everything happens, but I make my living spotting subtle details that will tell me how it happened."

"Logical," he murmured. "Ready to give opening the box a try?"

"One sec." She photographed the box with various panels moved enough to one side to create a tiny crack in the exterior wood panels. "Okay. Go for it."

His gaze snapped to hers. Now there were words he'd been waiting to hear come out of her mouth for a very long time.

"What?" she asked quickly as she stared back at him.

His mouth quirked up in a half smile. "Never mind. If you don't get it, I don't plan to be the one to explain it to you."

"What? You mean the innuendo of me telling you to go for it? Exactly what 'it' are you referring to, Mister Carpenter?"

"Ugh. If you flatly refuse to call me Reese, I'll take Detective Carpenter over Mister. Mister Carpenter is my father."

"You're still on duty," she murmured. "That makes you Detective Carpenter."

"Stubborn woman," he muttered. He commenced fiddling with the box. And fiddling. And fiddling some more.

Nothing worked.

"Wanna give it a try?" he asked, passing it to Yvette. Might as well share the misery and have equal-opportunity frustration around here.

She worked on it for a while before passing it back to him. "I may need a drink stiffer than tea before we get to the end of this mystery," she declared ruefully.

He smiled at her, and she smiled back in camaraderie. It was nice. Really nice.

"We could always just take a hammer to it," he suggested.

"Perish the thought! It's evidence. We can't destroy it because we got impatient!"

He threw up his hands in surrender. "It was just a suggestion."

"Worst case, we can take it back to the lab and x-ray it. It sounds like there's metal rattling around inside it, somewhere. If we can get a good look at that, we should be able to figure it out."

"Cheater," he teased. "Giving up so easily, are you?"

She shrugged. "I'm pragmatic. I know when to cut my losses."

"And run?" he asked quietly.

She looked up at him, her eyes big and dark and serious. He could fall into those eyes and lose himself for a few decades if he wasn't careful. "Sounds like you're hanging up your badge and shifting to off-duty questioning, Detective."

"Guess I am. Let's take a break from that beast, shall we?" He lifted his chin at the box. "I've got a bag of marshmallows in the cupboard. Can I interest you in roasting a few of them over the fire? It's burned down to just about perfect embers."

Her whole face lit with joy, and he about fell over his own feet in shock. She was pretty all the time. But she'd just turned into a raving beauty right there in the middle of his kitchen. Holy moly. How did everyone miss how drop-dead magnificent this woman was when she smiled like that?

An overpowering need to make her do that again swept over him.

They carried the marshmallows and two long metal roasting sticks over to the hearth. They sat knee to knee and poked the sweets onto the sticks. He commenced carefully rotating his marshmallow, keeping it just the right distance from the glowing coals to gradually puff and turn a perfect golden brown. He watched on in horror as Yvette shoved hers close enough to the coals to catch on fire almost immediately.

She yanked it out and blew on it to put it out.

"Do you need a new one?" he asked.

She looked up, startled. "No. This is exactly how I like mine." To that end, she pulled the blackened, gooey mess off her stick, blew on it to cool it, and popped it into her mouth.

"Of course, that's how you like yours," he muttered, carefully withdrawing his evenly browned, perfectly puffed marshmallow from the fireplace and blowing on it to cool it.

"You mean because I'm not an anal-retentive over-roaster like you are?" she teased.

"No, because you're an impulsive, impatient sugar-burner," he replied.

"You live your way—I'll live mine," she retorted.

He shook his head and popped his marshmallow into his mouth. Mmm. Yummy.

Yvette had already put another marshmallow into the fire and incinerated the poor thing. She glanced up at him, catching him blatantly staring at her perfect profile. His cheeks heated. Hopefully, she would think it was the warmth from the fire doing that.

"Tell you what, Reese. Why don't you try one my way for a change? See if you like it."

"Only if you'll try one of mine."

"Deal," she replied, her eyes glinting in challenge.

She blew out the charred remains of her marshmallow and pulled it off the stick. "Open up," she ordered playfully.

He opened his mouth for her, and it was damned sensuous having her slip that glob of crispy-crusted goo into his mouth. He closed his mouth and captured her fingertips between his lips. She froze, her gaze lifting to his before she pulled her hand free. Slowly. Sexily.

"Like it?" she asked.

He liked the sweet softness of her fingers very much. He nodded, his mouth too glued together by melted sugar to speak.

"The burned part gives it a sharp undertone that nicely contrasts with the sweet, don't you think?" she said.

"I guess. But I still prefer my steaks with a char and my marshmallows without." He poked a new marshmallow on his stick. "Okay. My turn."

He carefully roasted the bit of sugar to puffed, golden perfection. "Try this."

He held it out and she leaned forward. She grasped his wrist with her light, slender hand, and took the marshmallow delicately from his fingers. *Did she mean to run her lips over the ends of his fingers like that?* She was certainly taking her sweet time sucking his fingertips.

His groin lurched to attention as her lush, rosy lips finally slid sensually off the ends of his fingers. She sat back, her head tilted to one side and her eyes closed as she savored the treat. *"Good Golly, Miss Molly."* Yvette Colton was a closet hedonist.

He could just imagine her eyes closed in ecstasy exactly the way they were now, her head thrown back, her entire body arched and relishing the pleasure he would give to her—

Dude. Don't be an idiot. Jordana would kill him if he laid a hand on her, let alone went to bed with her. This was his partner's baby sister, for crying out loud. His partner's very grown-up, very sexy, and if he wasn't misreading her, very flirty sister. They weren't exactly snowed in, but a storm was raging outside, and they were cozy and alone in front of a crackling fire in the dead of night. It didn't get too much more romantic than this. And she seemed to feel it, too.

She startled him out of his lascivious thoughts with, "You have a bit of marshmallow on the corner of your mouth. Right here." Using the pad of her thumb, she rubbed the corner of his mouth lightly.

"Did that get it?" he asked, his voice noticeably huskier than usual.

"No. Hmm." She leaned forward slowly, her gaze locking on his. "Guess I'll have to get it this way."

She closed the distance between them very slowly, giving him plenty of time to pull away. But he didn't. He sat perfectly still, unable to believe that this beautiful, fey creature was leaning in toward him, closer and closer.

Gently, so lightly he barely felt it, her mouth touched the corner of his. Her lips were soft and plump, and then—

Jesus, Mary and Joseph. That's her tongue.

She licked the corner of his mouth. It was a quick little flick with just the tip of her tongue against his skin, but there was no mistaking it. All of a sudden, there wasn't nearly enough oxygen in his living room. Either that or he was no kidding hyperventilating.

Cripes. He hadn't done that around a girl since he'd been about thirteen and first started noticing them as anything other than annoying not-boys.

"There," she whispered. "That's better."

Moving as slowly as she had, giving her fully as much time to withdraw as she had given him, he lifted his right hand to the back of her head. Threaded his fingers beneath that heavy, warm twist of hair gathered at the base of her neck, and gently, gently, urged her forward.

He brushed his lips across hers lightly, more an invitation than an actual kiss. She lifted her chin a bit and he tucked his a bit, and their lips met again, this time fitting together a little more firmly, a little more definitely a kiss.

Her mouth was softer than the marshmallows and tasted every bit as sweet. The fire was warm on the right side of his face, the room cool on the left side of it. Light and dark. Hot and cold. Yin and yang. As opposite as Yvette and him. And yet, they fit each other.

Not one to overdo on a first kiss, he lifted his mouth away from hers a few inches and whispered. "There. Now, *that's* better."

Danged if she didn't reach up, this time her fingers twining into his hair, to tug him forward once more, murmuring a little breathlessly, "Where do you think you're going? Come here, cowboy."

Chapter Six

Profound relief came over Yvette as Reese swept her into the circle of his arms and drew her all the way into his lap. He might be big and strong, but he was infinitely gentle with her. His jean-clad thighs were muscular under hers, and the bulky sweatshirt cushioned the hard physique beneath it just enough to make her new seat imminently comfortable. The overall effect was one of being surrounded in safety and warmth.

"You're so delicate," he murmured. "It feels like I'm holding a hand-blown crystal bird when you're in my arms."

Thank God. He didn't call her small, or heaven forbid, childlike. "I assure you, I won't break."

"Good to know," he sighed as his lips closed on hers. He didn't go in for the slobbery tonsillectomy, thank goodness. Rather, he kissed with finesse, his mouth alternately brushing across hers and moving more deeply against hers.

He kissed really well. Or maybe she was just really out of practice. Oh, God. Did a person forget how to kiss properly? Was she being a total geek?

He lifted his mouth a fraction of an inch away from hers. "What's on your mind?"

"Why do you ask?"

"You tensed."

He'd felt that? Dang. The man was tuned in to her big time. Oh, right. Observant detective in the house. Note to self: for once, the detective's intense observational skills were delightful. Fantastic, even.

"I was wondering where you learned to kiss like that," she murmured.

"Behind the gym in tenth grade, I suppose."

"First girlfriend?"

"Not exactly. Best friend's older sister. She wanted to practice kissing and only dragged me out behind the school to perfect her skills."

Yvette snorted. "That's what she said."

He grinned against her mouth, and it was the most delicious sensation having his lips curve against hers, warmth and humor permeating the kiss. She ran her fingertips over the short hairs at the back of his neck. They were as neat and orderly as the rest of him.

But then he tilted his head slightly and deepened the kiss. The humor drained from him, and something darker, hotter, sexier emerged from him. Her breathing accelerated, and excitement at the sudden danger of him made her tingle.

She'd always had a thing for bad boys, which was why she was single now. As maturity and common sense had invaded her dating choices, she had no interest in the drama and heartbreak that came with immature bad boys. Which left her knowing to choose sensible, boring men. Emphasis on boring. Single seemed like the better option for her.

But Reese apparently was both sensible and had this hidden other side. Who knew?

His arms tightened fractionally around her, and he made a faint noise in the back of his throat that sounded a whole lot like frustration. As in male, sexual desire being tightly reined in. Regarding her? Bless the man. No male had looked at her with anything other than the most passing of interest ever since she'd gotten back to Braxville.

His big hands moved, one sliding down to her waist, and the other up to cup the back of her head. Still, he was slow and careful in his movements, as if he cherished this moment and wanted it to be perfect.

She grew a little impatient and took the lead, kissing her way across his jaw until she reached his ear. She nipped his earlobe lightly and then swirled her tongue into the shell of his ear. He groaned aloud, then, and his arms tightened significantly around her. She shifted her weight, throwing her thigh across his hips until she straddled his lap. Better. Now she was at the right height to kiss him without having to tilt her head back.

Oh.

And to notice the hard ridge behind his zipper that she was now straddling in the most suggestive possible way.

She probably ought to climb off the poor man before she made him any more uncomfortable. She lifted herself to her knees, but Reese swiftly pulled her back down with effortless strength that stole her breath away altogether. He did turn to one side, though, shifting her far enough off his lap to remove the wildly intimate contact of their nether regions. Fair. But all the while, he never broke the kiss that had become blatantly sexual, now.

He ran his tongue along her lower lip, and then caught its plumpness lightly between his teeth. She gasped into his mouth and was shocked to realize she was arching her back, lifting her body up and into him eagerly. Thankfully, his forearm tightened across her shoulder blades and supported her because she was starting to feel more than a little boneless, here.

He slid his mouth down the column of her neck, and she threw her head back, giving him unfettered access to her throat. His mouth was fiery hot against her skin as he kissed the frantic pulse there. His lips slid lower, into the vee where the top of her shirt unbuttoned.

The hand at her waist came around front and fiddled at her neck for a moment and her shirt opened a little more. He took advantage of the exposed skin to kiss a little lower on her chest. He stopped at the upper reaches of her cleavage, though, and kissed his way back up to her throat and then across her collarbone as far as her shirt would allow. An urge to rip the garment off completely surged through her.

Her palms slid restlessly across his neck, under his chin, traced his jaw and cheeks. Flesh. She wanted flesh. To that end, she slipped her hands under his sweatshirt. Darn it. T-shirt. She tugged at the soft cotton impatiently.

Better. Warm, smooth, male skin.

Dang. The man had no body fat. At all. She felt only muscle and more muscle under her hands, hard and unyielding. Like the man himself. She might not always agree with him, but she could respect his certainty of who and what he was.

Reese slid off the hearth, taking her with him, and stretching out at full length on the thick, soft flokati rug in front of the fireplace. His body was a warm wall of man and muscle and she gloried in pressing into him. Their legs tangled together and his forearm was a living pillow beneath her ear as he leaned down to kiss her again.

She welcomed him with open arms, loving the way his sweatshirt rubbed lightly against her chest as he braced himself above her. He kissed her long and slow, taking his time, in no rush to advance his cause, for which she was incredibly grateful.

So many guys just fell on her. Kiss, tongue, grope, go for the bra hooks…as if it was a checklist to be hurried through en route to equally hurried sex. But Reese… Reese took his time, savoring every step along the way. She actually had no idea if sex was even his end goal here. She got the impression that possibly this was all he had in mind tonight.

Honestly, she loved how it took the pressure off her to put out, how she was able to just relax and enjoy the moment without having to mentally steel herself to say no and be blasted by accusations and recriminations about being a cock tease.

Eventually, Reese propped himself up on an elbow and smoothed her hair back from her face. He murmured, "I could look at you all day and all night and never get tired of doing it."

"I don't know. After a while your eyeballs might start bleeding."

"Why do you put yourself down like that?" he asked, tilting his head curiously.

"Saves other people the trouble of doing it, I guess."

He smiled a little. "Spoken like the baby of a family that engaged in a lot of teasing."

"Spoken like a man who knows my siblings."

"I know one of them quite well, and Jordana teases and makes jokes to lighten stressful situations." A look of concern flashed across his face. "This isn't a stressful situation for you, is it?" He sat up quickly.

She sat as well, but more slowly. "Not at all. In fact, I have been thinking about how nice it was not to feel pressured to end up in bed with you, tonight."

"For real?" he asked quietly.

"For real," she answered firmly. "You're a gentleman, and I really, really appreciate that."

He smiled a little sheepishly. "I've been called old-fashioned a time or two. Women looking for a hookup don't appreciate my desire to get to know them before I sleep with them." He shrugged. "First, I want—" He broke off.

"What?" she asked, dying to know what he wanted before having sex. Not that she was looking to—

Oh, who was she kidding? She was totally looking to have sex with him eventually.

"I want to get to know a woman. Have a personal connection. An actual relationship."

"Wow. That's enlightened of you."

He glanced up quickly as if checking to see if she was being sarcastic or not. She smiled and added, "I mean it."

She leaned forward, placing her hand on his cheek which was warm and smooth with just a hint of razor stubble starting to roughen it. She kissed him chastely, but found herself lingering over the kiss. Never in her life had she liked kissing a man the way she liked kissing this one.

He sighed and dropped a light kiss on the end of her nose. "It's getting late, and the roads have to be awful by now. I shouldn't have kept you this long. I'm sorry. It was selfish of me."

"Do you see me complaining?" she asked tartly.

He smiled and rose smoothly to his feet, then held a hand down to her. She laid her hand in his bigger, callused one, loving how his grip swallowed her whole hand. He tugged her to her feet. "Give me five minutes to warm up the truck and put the chains on my tires, okay?"

He went outside and she carried the mugs and marshmallows back to the kitchen. She studied the puzzle box sitting on his kitchen table. What secrets did it hold?

Reese came into the kitchen on a blast of cold air and commented, "I'll bring that box into your lab in the morning for you."

"Thanks."

"Bundle up. It's getting nippy out there."

Nippy hardly covered the way the cold hurt to breathe in and made her face feel stiff and numb. Frigid was more like it.

Reese followed her around to the passenger side of his truck and put his hands on her waist to steady her as she climbed in. She loved how his big hands spanned so much of her waist. Huh. Normally, she hated feeling small. But she liked it with him. Maybe because he seemed to like it so much.

He closed the door carefully behind her and then climbed in the driver's side. He backed out of his garage and turned out into the street, or rather the white sheet of snow roughly where she estimated a street to be.

Snow blew horizontally through the beams of his headlights, like crystalline diamond dust. She was silent, letting him concentrate on his driving. But after he made a left turn where he should have turned right, she piped up. "The Dexter house is in the other direction. That's where my car is parked."

"Do you have chains for your tires?"

"No."

"Exactly. I'm driving you to your house tonight. I'll pick you up in the morning and take you to your car, then. Assuming the storm has blown through by then and driving conditions have improved."

"That's way out of your way. It's too much trouble—"

He cut her off. "I didn't ask your permission. I told you what I'm doing."

"You're so high-handed!" she exclaimed. "And stubborn! And a know-it-all."

He shrugged, appearing unconcerned. "Do you have a safer idea?"

Safer? No. More convenient? Absolutely.

He must have taken her silence for consent to his plan because he said, "What time should I pick you up? Is eighty thirty too early? I have a meeting at nine."

"I—no. I mean yes. You can pick me up at eight thirty." She added with a huff, "That's fine." How did that man always seem to get the best of her? It was infuriating!

He pulled into the driveway of her Cape Cod cottage with its long porch and peaked roof covered in a thick blanket of white. He put the truck in Park but said, "Don't get out. I'll come around and help you."

"Reese. I can walk to my front door all by myself."

"And yet, I'm going to help you. My boots have cleats, and I see the sheet of ice on your sidewalk. Last thing I need is for the forensic scientist working on my big murder case to break her leg."

There he went again, being right. Darn him.

He lifted her out of the truck, set her on her feet and wrapped his arm around her waist. In his big, fleece-lined rancher's coat, he felt like a bear giving her a hug. She was chagrined when a big gust of wind hit, and her feet did slide out from under her about halfway to her front door. Reese caught her and steadied her until she regained her balance, and they made it up the steps and to the door without further incident.

She unlocked the door and, hand on the knob, turned to thank Reese.

He beat her to the punch, though, and said, "Thanks for tonight. Get some rest and call me if you develop any dizziness, nausea, vomiting or disorientation."

She recognized a list as warning signs of a concussion. "Will do."

"I'll see you in the morning." He leaned down, gave her one last lingering kiss and then gently pushed her inside.

In the morning, indeed.

She was shocked to realize she was practically floating through her house as she hung up her coat and got ready for bed. Man. She had it bad for him. She even set her alarm a half hour early so she'd have extra time to get up and get ready.

Her bed was icy cold when she climbed under the covers, and she missed the warmth of his embrace as she settled down to sleep and dream of marshmallow kisses.

THE STORM WAS still howling around her house when her alarm jangled, waking her from a delicious dream of a certain hot detective and his amazing kissing skills. Well, fudge. She'd been hoping to wear something cute to work today, but instead, she was going to have to go full Michelin Man.

She pulled on thin wool long johns, jeans, a white turtleneck and a thick sky-blue ski sweater with a ring of snowmen around the yoke. She pulled her dark hair back in a long clip at the back of her head and took extra care with her makeup this morning. She stomped into a pair of thick-soled after-ski boots and laid out her puffy down-filled coat, light blue hat with its jaunty white pompom, mittens and a long scarf.

Exactly at eighty thirty, Reese's big silver truck turned into her driveway. She could set a clock by that guy. Although, truth be told, it was reassuring to know he would always be exactly where he said he would be, when he said he'd be there. She'd dated enough flakes in her life to appreciate a punctual man.

She hurried into her cold weather gear as he walked up her sidewalk and opened the door for him just as he hit the front porch. "Hi there," she said brightly.

"Good morning. Are you always this chipper first thing?"

"Not usually before a cup of coffee," she answered, laughing. "I just happen to love a good blizzard. Always have."

"Were you the type to build a snowman and make a fleet of snow angels?" he asked as he opened the door for her.

"Absolutely. You?"

He climbed into the warm cab of the truck. "I was more the snow fort and piles of snowballs type."

"You have brothers, don't you?" she asked.

"Two younger ones. It was usually me in the fort with my brothers tag-teaming me from outside."

"In our house, snowball fights usually lined up girls against the boys."

"That doesn't sound fair," he protested.

She shrugged. "We girls usually lost, but we also usually got even by dumping snow down the collars of the boys' coats."

"Wow. Vicious."

"The motto of the Colton women is, Don't Get Mad. Get Even."

He grinned over at her. "Duly noted."

They drove a few minutes in silence, and it dawned on her that he wasn't heading toward the Dexter house and her car this morning, either.

"Where are we going?" she asked.

"My nine o'clock interview cancelled. Thought you might like a cup of coffee, or maybe some breakfast, before we go pick up your car."

"Why Mr. Carpenter," she teased in a thick southern belle accent, "are you asking me out on a date?"

He glanced over at her, his eyes unaccountably hot. "What if I am?"

"Well, I do declare." She fanned herself with an imaginary fan.

He grinned. "I'll take that as a yes."

They pulled in to the local diner, which was blessedly open and surprisingly busy. Apparently, a number of businesses had either closed or were opening late today, and given the number of children in the joint, schools were obviously closed, too.

A couple got up to leave just as they stepped inside, and the waitress waved her and Reese over to the table as she cleared it. They slid into the booth, and Yvette was abruptly aware of lots of stares, some surreptitious, some open, in their direction.

She murmured, "Why are people looking at us? Do I have mascara running down my face or something?"

"No. You're perfect. They're all staring because I'm with the prettiest girl in town."

She smiled shyly at the warmth in his voice. "Flatterer. Actually, I think it's because they're jealous of me being with the most eligible bachelor in Braxville."

He snorted. "I think one of your brothers probably holds that title."

"All my brothers are officially off the market these days. Or hadn't you heard?"

"That's what Jordana said. I'm happy for them."

"Or maybe it's just the dozens of women you've dated before, pitying me for being your next conquest."

Reese gave a wholly satisfying snort at that notion. "I don't date local women."

Really? Now, that surprised her. "Why not?" she asked.

"What if I have to investigate one or arrest one, someday? How awkward would that be?"

"So, you don't plan to date me, then?" she asked in a small voice.

"You're different. You're on the force."

"Hmm. You strike me as the type who wouldn't date someone you work with."

"Yes, but I don't really work with you. Our paths cross in our individual jobs from time to time, but you're not in my chain of command, and I'm not in yours."

"How do you know I won't commit a felony, someday?"

He tilted his head to study her for long enough that she had to suppress an urge to squirm. "Do you think of yourself as capable of committing a serious crime?" he asked.

She shrugged. "I suppose in the right circumstances. Like if someone I loved was in mortal danger, I might be capable of violence. Or if a child or helpless animal was being hurt, I might go after the abuser."

"Those would be classed as justifiable crimes. I doubt you'd be prosecuted in either scenario."

"What about you?" she asked curiously.

"Same. I've been known to be protective of my friends and family." He paused, then added, "Unfortunately, engaging in a certain amount of violence is a potential part of my job. My least favorite part of it, in fact."

"Have you ever…you know…shot anyone?" She asked the last part in a hush.

"Thankfully, no. But I have to be prepared mentally to do it."

"Does the idea bother you?" she asked.

"Of course, it does. I hate the idea of taking a life. I would consider it a complete failure on my part if I couldn't talk a person out of the thing that would force me to shoot them. My job is to prevent violence, not meet violence with violence. That's the last resort."

"That's a progressive view, Detective."

He shrugged. "It's the ethical and moral view. Has nothing to do with being progressive."

"That's you. Mr. Ethics-and-Morals."

Darned if his eyes didn't get that sexy glint in them again. "I'm not always an uptight good guy, you know."

"Do tell." She leaned forward with interest to hear this one. "When, exactly, do you set aside your white hat and superhero cape?"

"That's for me to know and you to find out."

"Challenge accepted," she declared immediately. Their stares met, and sexual lightning crackled back and forth between them. It was a wonder they weren't blowing this place apart with it.

Sudden awareness of being in a very public locale with half the town looking on burst over her. She broke the stare and looked away hastily.

"How's the back of your head feeling this morning?" Reese asked neutrally enough.

"Sore where I hit it, but I took a couple of aspirin when I woke up and the headache's mostly gone."

"Good. Means you probably didn't get a concussion. I was worried about you last night. You looked on the verge of puking, there, for a while."

"I was on the verge. But I was determined not to barf in front of you," she confessed.

He smiled. "In my line of work, I've seen most of the human bodily functions any number of times."

"Have you ever delivered a baby?" she asked.

"Two. Messy, but totally cool."

He leaned back and took a sip from his water glass before changing the subject. "How's your family doing? Y'all have been through a rough time recently, what with the arsenic thing and then the murdered bodies in a building the Colton Construction Firm built."

"If only that was all we were dealing with," she sighed.

"Oh, yeah? What's up?" He sounded genuinely interested, and not just like a nosy neighbor. Maybe that was why she gave him a baldly honest answer. That, and he would just ask Jordana what she was hinting at if she didn't go ahead and tell him herself.

"My parents aren't exactly doing great. They've had some sort of major falling out, but I'm not sure what it's about. It seems serious, though. They treat each other like polite strangers these days. Mom's totally giving Dad the cold shoulder."

He frowned a little. "Your mom is capable of giving anyone the cold shoulder? No way. She's one of the warmest, kindest people I know."

She shrugged. "At least my siblings seem to be happy for the most part. The whole gang seems to have found true love." She added wistfully, "Except for me, of course."

"Maybe you've already found it and you just don't know it, yet."

Her gaze snapped up to Reese's, and his eyes were shockingly serious. Was he talking about himself? They barely knew each other. They'd made out once over marshmallows. Holy moly.

A friendly looking older woman wearing an apron

approached the table. "Hey, Reese. Some weather we're having, isn't it? How are the roads?"

"Hey, Lola," he answered. "It's bad out there. Forecast calls for it to clear up around noon, though. I expect it'll take the snow plows a few hours to clear the major roads after that."

"Great. Maybe by quitting time I'll be able to get home without risking my neck. What can I get you kids to eat?"

"The special," Yvette and Reese said simultaneously.

"How do you want your eggs?" the waitress asked, pencil poised over a pad.

"Sunny-side up," Yvette answered.

"Over hard," Reese supplied.

"Bacon or sausage?" Lola asked.

"Bacon," Yvette answered promptly.

"Sausage," Reese chimed in.

It figured. The two of them never agreed on anything. Yvette mentally rolled her eyes.

"Toast or biscuit?"

"Wheat toast, buttered," Reese supplied.

"Can I substitute a bagel?" she asked.

"You bet."

Lola moved over to the pass-through window to the kitchen and shouted out their order.

Yvette smiled ruefully at Reese. "We're pretty much opposites in every way, aren't we?"

He shrugged. "We both wanted the special. That's agreement after a fashion. And, honestly, I like the fact that you're confident enough to do your own thing without feeling a need to imitate me."

"Keep that in mind the next time you're in the lab trying to tell me how to do my job," she retorted.

He grinned and poured her a cup of coffee from the steaming pot Lola set on their table. "Black?" he tried.

Yvette threw him a withering look. "Cream and sugar, of course. You can pretty much think about what you'd choose, do the opposite, and you'll get me right."

He rolled his eyes as he passed her the pitcher of cream and sugar dish. "I should've guessed you'd want your caffeine to taste like ice cream after the way you enjoyed those marshmallows last night."

She smirked knowingly. "The way I liked them best was on you."

Abruptly, his blue eyes were smoldering, the color of a flame burning super hot. "See? We agree again. I like marshmallows best on your lips, too. Or on the tip of your tongue. Or in the sweet, dark recesses of your mouth. Remind me next time to try out some marshmallow crème on other parts of your anatomy."

Suddenly it was her turn to be unaccountably out of breath. "Uhh, sure. That sounds—" she searched for a word. Sticky didn't convey the romantic vibe she was looking for. "—amazing."

"It's a date."

Wowsers. If she wasn't mistaken, she'd just agreed to have sex, or at least sexy foreplay with the hot detective.

Thankfully, their breakfast arrived before she burned to a cinder where she sat, charred to nothing by the heat in Reese's eyes. They ate quietly. Maybe he was as disconcerted by the direction of their conversation as she was.

She insisted on paying for the bill, both in thanks for last night's rescue and in gratitude for the rides he was giving her in his big, safe truck. The looks and side-eyes continued as they left the diner, and she was vividly aware of the light touch of Reese's hand on the small of her back as they reached the door. Was that just common courtesy, or was he sending a subtle signal to the single men in the room that she was taken? Either way, her heart pitter-pattered at the light, possessive touch.

"What's on your agenda today?" he asked as they pulled into the parking lot of the police department.

"Getting this rascal open." She patted last night's puzzle box resting on the seat between them.

"Shout out if you get stuck," Reese offered.

"Will do. What about you?" she asked as they walked carefully toward the building. "What are you going to do with yourself now that you don't have that interview this morning?"

"I'm going to go back and review the whole murder case one more time. See if anything jumps out at me in light of the recent information you provided about the murders happening at different times of year. That, and the fact that Markus Dexter has been paranoid and secretive for a long time."

"Shout out if *you* get stuck," she offered.

"Will do." He opened the building door and held it for her, saying as she slid past him, "Oh, and Yvette, would you mind dropping by my desk at some point to make a formal report about last night? I already filed a preliminary report, but I'll need a statement from you to make it official."

"Sure."

"I'll look forward to seeing you."

They traded quick smiles and parted ways in the lobby of the building. Reese headed for his desk in the squad room, and she headed downstairs to her lab. What a great way to start a day. She felt refreshed and energized after her meal—and conversation—with Reese. She counted it a victory that they seemed to have moved past their bickering to a more flirtatious brand of teasing. Marshmallows and making out would do that with a guy, apparently.

Chapter Seven

A quick X-ray of what she was starting to call That Blasted Box down at the morgue revealed one fascinating piece of information. Nestled in the exact center of the puzzle box was a metal key.

The rest of the box was made of wood, however, and the X-ray was not helpful in showing her how to open it. Which sent her to the internet and a deep dive into how Chinese puzzle boxes were built. She figured out quickly enough that this one had been handmade, which was not good news. It meant that the builder could have constructed it to open unlike any traditional puzzle box.

But she did learn enough about how the boxes were built in general to begin moving panels and pressing hidden buttons. Reese's suggestion to just smash the thing resonated through her mind ever more frequently as the day aged.

She was hunched over the stupid thing concentrating intently, her neck and shoulders cramping, and only sheer, cussed stubbornness keeping her poking and prodding at the box when a hand landed on her shoulder without warning. She jumped violently, leaped out of her seat and spun around, hands coming up defensively in front of her before she was even conscious of moving.

"Easy, Yvie," Reese said, stepping back and holding his hands up in the air.

"Sorry," she muttered, chagrined at her overreaction.

"That's some startle reflex you've got, there."

She winced. Unfortunately, she knew exactly where it came from. She'd had a coworker at Quantico who'd gotten excessively handsy with her until she'd taken an intensive, weekend-long self-defense class. The next time he'd snuck up on her and wrapped his arms around her waist, he'd gotten a nasty surprise in the form of a donkey kick to the groin and bloody scratches across his face.

He'd tried to press charges, but the senior lab supervisor had seen Yvette's attack as self-defense and promised to tell authorities about the guy's ongoing harassment of Yvette if the guy made a formal complaint. The handsy coworker had backed off. Soon after that incident, he'd transferred to another lab.

While she'd been grateful for the support, the jerk had gotten off with a stern warning to leave the female employees alone, and she was left with a hair-trigger startle reflex over being touched at work.

She sighed. "It's not you. I've had problems in the past with a male coworker grabbing me."

Reese's eyes widened, and then narrowed. He asked tightly, "Who is it?"

He thought she meant here in Braxville. "I had the problem in Virginia. Not here."

Reese relaxed fractionally, but the thunderous set of his brows didn't ease. "If anything like that ever happens to you here, you tell me about it. Okay?"

"It's all right. I can handle—"

"Stop being so cussedly independent, woman. If someone harasses you or does or says anything the least bit inappropriate to you here, promise you'll tell me."

"Umm—"

"Promise."

It was her turn to throw up her hands. "All right, already. I promise. But I've had a self-defense class. I can protect myself."

"I believe you. But I can kick someone's ass into last week. And if someone around here lays hands on you without your consent, it'll be needed."

Who knew Reese would go all caveman over protecting her right to consent? And who knew she would find it wildly attractive to have a man go all macho and protective on her behalf like this?

She gave herself a mental shake. "Change of subject— I found out what's inside the puzzle box."

"You opened it?" he exclaimed. "Show me how it works."

"No, I x-rayed it. There's a key inside. I haven't figured out the whole mechanism, yet. I think I've got it about half solved, though. Stupid thing is built in layers—puzzle boxes nesting inside puzzle boxes. Whoever built it was freaking diabolical. Maybe you can figure out the next layer?" she asked.

"I'd love to stick around and help you, but I've got that interview from this morning in about fifteen minutes. I thought I'd pop down to see if you'd eaten today."

Food? Oh, right. She glanced at the big clock on the wall over the door. It was going on three o'clock. She shrugged. "I'll grab something when I get hungry."

"No wonder you're no bigger than a hamster. You don't eat enough."

"A hamster?" she squawked. "I remind you of a rodent?"

He grinned. "A cute, cuddly rodent that you really want to pick up and hold and pet, except it'll bite the shit out of your hand if you try."

"I should punch you in the stomach again."

His grin widened. "You can try. But now that I know you're the impulsive type, I'll be on my guard."

"For the record, I don't generally run around attacking people."

"Good to know." He held out a paper sack. "I went to a deli for lunch, and I grabbed an extra sandwich. Just in case."

"If that's your afternoon snack, I'm not taking it."

"No, Yvie. I got it for you. Jordana said corned beef on rye is your favorite. I ordered it with extra mustard and light sauerkraut, exactly the opposite of how I would order it for myself."

"That's perfect!" she exclaimed. "Exactly how I like my corned beef sandwiches."

"Of course, it is," he replied wryly.

Whoa. He'd found out what her favorite sandwich was? In her experience, men didn't go to that kind of trouble unless they were seriously interested in a woman. "Umm, thanks." She took the brown paper bag and smiled up at him. "This was really sweet of you."

"I'd love to help you with that puzzle box, but I've got to run. Don't forget to come up and make a report about last night."

"I won't."

Except, after she ate the sandwich and went back to work on the box, time got away from her again. The next time she looked up it was nearly five o'clock. Rats. She locked the lab and hurried upstairs. Shift change was approaching, which meant not only were the day shift cops still at their desks, but the night shift guys were also milling around. She wound through the crowd to Reese's desk. He looked up from a file and his eyes lit with pleasure.

Warmth filled her belly as she smiled back at him.

"Here to make that report?" he murmured.

"Affirmative."

"Have a seat," he said formally.

She perched on the hard wooden chair beside his desk, and he pushed a yellow legal pad toward her along with a pen.

"I need you to write down what happened last night at the Dexter home in as much detail as you can remember."

"I can remember a lot of detail. I'm a forensic scientist after all."

"Then it'll be a long report."

"Okay," she said doubtfully, anticipating a bad case of writer's cramp. Biting her lower lip, she started to write. Out of the corner of her eye, she was vaguely aware of other cops checking out what she was doing at Reese's desk. Gradually, she became aware that Reese was starting to scowl. The longer she wrote, the grumpier his expression became. Finally, she looked up directly at him. "Am I doing something wrong?"

"Not at all. Continue."

"Then why do you look ready to rip the heads off bunnies with your bare hands?"

"Bunnies? I would never!"

"You know what I mean."

"Don't worry about it, Yvette. Finish your statement."

She put her head back down and wrote the last few lines, the part where Reese scared away the intruder and came upstairs to rescue her. As she laid down the pen, she heard a ripple of laughter behind her and turned to check it out. The laughter cut off abruptly, and a cluster of cops across the room looked away from her hastily, coughing conspicuously.

She looked back at Reese who did, indeed, look ready

to commit homicide. "What am I missing?" she asked him under her breath.

"You're missing some of the young guys being jack-asses behind your back. Ignore them."

"Jackasses how?"

He sighed. "They're making faces at me because you're sitting at my desk."

She frowned. "I don't understand."

"They think you're attractive and are harassing me about having a thing for you."

"Oh. Well, then. I can take care of that," she said breezily.

She stood up and moved around the corner of the desk as Reese watched her warily. Before she could lose her nerve, she took his face in both of her hands, leaned down and planted a smoking-hot kiss on him, complete with passion, heat and tongue.

Reese froze initially, but as his mouth opened against hers and she deepened the kiss, he abruptly kissed her back. His tongue sparred with hers and it was a duel to see who gave whom a tonsillectomy first. His hand came up and slid under her hair at the nape of her neck, urging her even deeper into the kiss. She melted into him, loving the way their mouths fit together, the deep, drug-ging suction, the carnal intensity of their lips and tongues clashing and blending.

Blood surged through her veins, her heart pounded, and honest to goodness, her knees went weak. Hot dang, that man could kiss the stripes off a zebra. She could fall into him and blissfully drown—

They were in the middle of the squad room, for cry-ing out loud!

She tore her mouth away from his and jerked upright,

panting. His hand slipped from her neck as she pulled away. For his part, Reese stared up at her, his blue eyes glazed, looking rather hectic, himself.

"Right then," she managed to choke out. She made eye contact with him for the briefest moment and then her courage failed her. She turned and fled. It was all she could do not to break into a run as she scurried across the squad room.

But as she passed by the group of now slack-jawed beat cops, she did gather herself enough to say cheerfully, "Pleasure doing business with you, gentlemen. Oh, and he kisses like a god."

She made it out into the hall before she sagged against a wall to catch her breath. When was she going to learn to control her wild impulses? Lord knew, they got her into trouble more often than not. She could not believe she'd just kissed Reese Carpenter in the middle of the squad room. *And he'd kissed her back.*

Thankfully, she made it all the way back to the basement without running into anyone in the hall. Her face felt as if it was on fire, and her hair was falling out of its bun where Reese hand plunged his fingers into it. She must look like a complete mess. A well-kissed, complete mess.

Oh, God. She'd just completely blown it with Reese. No way would he forgive her for embarrassing him like that. What had she been thinking? She liked him. Really liked him. He was the first man in a long time that she'd been seriously interested in, as in potential long-term relationship material. They were so different from each other, but also shockingly compatible. And she'd had to go and humiliate the man, in front of his coworkers, no less. She was the biggest idiot *ever*.

If possible, her cheeks burned even more.

The worst of it was she knew better. If she'd learned nothing from having three mischievous older brothers, it was not to rise to the bait when they dared her to do anything. But today, she'd taken one look at those leering cops, and it was as if they'd dared her to do something outrageous to wipe those smirks off their faces.

She ducked into a ladies' room to redo her hair, but there was nothing to be done about the razor burn around her mouth, the faint swelling and rosy color of her lips, nor about the rather dazed look in her eyes. *Enjoy it for the last time, girlfriend. Because as sure as you're standing here, you chased that man far, far away from you.*

Reese Carpenter might have a secret wild streak of his own, but not while he was at work. Never while he was on the job.

Depressed and disappointed in herself, she peered out into the hallway. All clear. Mortified, she ran for her lab, sighing in relief to make it inside without being seen by anyone.

But no sooner had the door closed behind her than her personal cell phone rang. Grimacing, she pulled it out of her pocket to see who was calling.

Jordana.

She would love to ignore the call, but her sister knew where to find her and wasn't the sort to let go of a bone once she had it firmly between her teeth.

"Hey, sis."

"What in the heck did you just do?"

Summoning her best innocent voice, Yvette responded, "What are you talking about?"

"You kissed Reese Carpenter? In the freaking squad room?" Her sister's voice rose in pitch with every syllable. It was not often that Jordana Colton actually screeched.

"Oh. That. Yeah." God, she hoped the words sounded easy-breezy. Truth was, her stomach was in a total knot, now.

"What were you *thinking*?"

"I was thinking that the guys making fun of him and me deserved to be put in their places and shut up."

"And you thought kissing my partner was the way to do that? Do you know nothing about cops? That kiss is already the talk of the whole department!"

Yvette closed her eyes in chagrin. Jordana was right. Police departments were as rife with gossip as any other workplace. Maybe more so. "Okay, fine. You're right. I should have realized it wouldn't shut anyone up."

"I thought you two hated each other's guts. Is there something going on between you two that I should know about?" Jordana asked suspiciously.

"God, no." As soon as the words came out of her mouth, she knew them for the lie they were. Well, partially a lie. Yes, there was something going on. A truce, apparently. The mother of all truces, in fact. But no, she had no interest in her sister knowing about it.

Reese was like a brother to Jordana. Which, by default, somehow made her and Reese siblings in Jordana's mind. At least, that was how she'd described it to Yvette some months ago when Reese and Yvette had gone through a particularly bad patch of sniping at each other, and Jordana had intervened to referee. She'd told them that she loved them both and wanted them to get along like her other siblings.

That seemed a lifetime ago. And yet, now that she thought about it, she'd thrown him out of her lab in no uncertain terms a mere two days ago. All of a sudden, there definitely was something going on between her and

the man who'd driven her crazy—not in a good way—
for the past year.

What *was* she thinking? Two days ago, she would have
laughed her head off at anyone who suggested that she
kiss Reese Carpenter, ever, let alone in the squad room.

"Could you dial back on kissing my partner, Yvie?
Your behavior reflects on me, too, you know."

"I'm sorry, J. I knew better. But I just got so mad when
they all laughed at him and me."

Jordana laughed a little. "It's not as if you've ever had
great control of your temper."

"Gee. Thanks. Love you, too, sis."

"Aww, c'mon, Yvie. I love you to death. But you and
I both know you can fly off the handle when properly
provoked."

She sighed. "Guilty as charged. I'll apologize to Reese
the next time I see him."

"That's between you two. I'll do what damage control
I can. I'll call it a joke. Make sure they all know there's
nothing going on between you two. That you two can't
stand each other."

"Umm, right. Sure. Thanks."

"You're still coming to Lou's retirement party, right?"

"I don't think so. Not after this—"

"Chicken."

Coltons were a lot of things, but chickens were not one
of those things. In fact, it was a long-held family tradi-
tion that no Colton ever backed away from a dare. It had
gotten her and all of her siblings in trouble from time to
time over the years. And apparently, it was about to get
her in trouble again, now.

"Fine. I'll go to your stupid party," Yvette declared.

Jordana hung up before she could call the words back.
Tonight, she had to correct her sister's mistaken im-

pression of whatever was going on between her and Reese. Convince Jordana they were…

They were what?

Friends?

Friends with benefits?

Two people who hated each other's guts but were wildly attracted to each other?

Heck if she knew what they were.

One thing she did know. She did hate not being completely honest with her big sister. But honestly, it was none of Jordana's business what went on between her and Reese off duty…except that it was. Reese and Jordana were partners. They needed total trust, complete honesty, and to trust their lives to each other.

She had no right to interfere in their working relationship. She sighed and started to call Jordana back. Except a text came through to her phone that made her fingers freeze on the numbers. A text from Reese.

I'll be down in ten minutes to get you. Be ready to go.

Gulp.

Chapter Eight

That man could be so bossy! So infuriating! Who did he think he was, ordering her around like that?

She interrupted her own tirade with a dose of cold reality. She owed him not only an apology, but a reckoning. If he wanted to come down here and chew her up one side and down the other, he had that right. She'd acted completely inappropriately and had embarrassed him. Time to face the music for her reckless behavior.

Glumly, she put away the puzzle box, powered down the lab equipment and locked the place up. Reese had barely opened the door before she turned off the lights, joined him in the hall and locked the door behind herself.

"Let's go," he said tersely.

At least the man had the good grace to get her out of the building before he ripped into her. That was classy of him.

Saying nothing to her, he strode out of the basement, leading her out the back way to a police-only parking lot behind the building. It was dark outside and his strides were so long and quick that she had to half jog to keep up with him.

He opened the passenger door of the truck for her and closed it behind her without comment. In fact, he drove out of the lot, turned down the street and made it all the way to the Dexter house, where her car was still parked, without breaking his stony silence. Was he that furious at her?

He pulled to a stop in the circular drive behind her little car and she blurted, "I'm sorry, Reese. I got mad that they were laughing at you—at us—and I didn't stop to think. I'm sorry I embarrassed you, and I shouldn't have done that in our mutual work environment. It was unprofessional and stupid. And given that I've been sexually harassed at work before, I should have known not to do the same to you—"

He leaned across the truck swiftly and kissed her hard as he swept his arms around her. He pulled her tight against his body and kissed her every bit as passionately as she'd kissed him earlier.

Shock stilled her in his arms. What did this mean? Was this some sort of revenge kiss? Or could it possibly mean he wasn't as mad at her as she'd thought? Was he punishing her? Saying goodbye? Showing her what she couldn't have in the future?

But then the kiss itself commanded so much of her attention that the little voices in her head faded into the background of his mouth moving against hers, his body moving against hers, his arms going around her and drawing her close.

His mouth was hot and wet and dark, and tasted of coffee. She threw herself into the kiss, gladly losing herself in him. In the moment.

Even now, he made her feel desired. Sexy. Beautiful. She reveled in the hardness of his chest, loved the strength of his arms. His breathing was fast and light, and she delighted in doing that to him as he kissed his way across her jaw and took the lobe of her ear lightly between his teeth. If this was a last kiss goodbye, she was going to miss this more than words could express.

"Next time you want to kiss me like that, do it in private, okay?" he murmured against her neck, just below her ear.

She froze. Had she heard him correctly? Next time? He was prepared to kiss her again, as in continue a relationship with her?

"Of course," she panted. She tilted her head back to give him better access to her throat, and he took immediate advantage of it to kiss the pulse fluttering wildly at the base of her throat.

His lips moved on the delicate skin there. "Because I don't want to have to stop kissing you again once we get started like that."

She leaned back far enough to look at his shadowed face as he lifted his head to stare down at her. His eyes were hard to see in the dim interior of his truck. "Does that mean you forgive me?" she asked in a small voice.

"Yup."

"Are you mad at me?"

"Nope."

"Are you sure?"

He continued to stare down at her in the electronic glow of the dashboard for a long moment. "Yes. I'm sure."

She smiled up at him tentatively. "I can't tell you how relieved I am. I was terrified I'd blown it with you."

He smiled crookedly. "Are you kidding? I'm a hero, department-wide."

"Why?" she blurted.

"You're generally considered to be the unattainable ice queen. The gang was pleased to discover you're human after all."

"Don't BS me. They're teasing you like crazy over it."

"Absolutely." A smile started with an upward curve of the corners of his mouth and spread slowly across his face. "But they're all jealous as hell of me."

"Why?"

"That was some kiss you laid on me."

"Mmm. It was, wasn't it?"

His mouth descended toward hers again. "Yes, ma'am. It was."

The windows of his truck were completely steamed up when Reese finally pulled away from her with a sigh. "I'm not making love with you in the cab of my truck. At least not the first time. But if we don't stop soon, that's exactly where we're headed."

She looked around, measuring the distance between the seat and the dashboard. "If you push your seat all the way back and I straddle—"

"Stop." There was enough pained discomfort in his voice that she took pity on him and didn't finish describing what she had in mind for christening his truck.

"You going to Lou's retirement party?" he asked casually.

Crud. She'd totally forgotten about that. "I think I'll skip—"

He cut her off. "I could really use you to show up, even if just for a few minutes."

"Why's that?"

"Your, umm, attention to me over the past couple of days is causing a lot of talk. It's interfering with me doing my job."

"I'm sorry," she said quickly.

"It's okay. I just need you to show up at the bar, be casual around me for a few minutes while I'm casual around you, and then you can split. But Chief Hilton's asking questions about whether or not you and I can work together professionally or not. I'd hate to have the, umm, recent incidents impact our performance reports."

Gulp. The last thing she wanted to do was hurt Reese's career or chances at promotion. And goodness knew, she didn't need any reprimands in her permanent file about harassing a coworker. Not if she wanted to get hired by a big, prestigious forensics lab in a year or two.

"I get it. Not to mention I owe you one for saving my neck at the Dexter house."

"You don't owe me for that. I was just doing my job," he protested.

"Nonetheless. I'm the one who's caused you problems with the boss. It's up to me to fix it."

She climbed in her car and followed him downtown to Dusty Rusty's. The parking lot was close to full with the muscular pickup trucks a lot of the cops favored, and she winced as she parked her little car among them.

She spotted Reese parking and waited for him to go inside ahead of her. Giving him enough of a head start that nobody would suspect they'd arrived together—she hoped—she took a deep breath, climbed out of her car and trudged toward the bar.

Casual. She could do this. They still hated each other's guts and were just enjoying a temporary truce. Reese was an uptight jerk. He made her crazy.

Yeah. Crazy to kiss him senseless and get inside his pants.

Drat. The I-hate-Reese pep talk was a total flop.

Plan B: go inside and ignore Reese. It was what she would have done a few days ago.

Okay. She could do that. She stepped inside and was bombarded by heat and noise and the overwhelming smell of beer. And man sweat. Ugh.

Did the fire marshal know this many cops were all

crammed into Rusty's tonight? She was half tempted to call the fire department and report a building capacity violation. Until she spotted the fire chief bellied up to the bar. Sigh.

"Hey, Yvie!" Her sister's voice rose above the din.

She turned toward the sound but couldn't see Jordana in the press of big bodies. Lord, she hated being short, sometimes. She stood on her tiptoes, craning to see around the crowd and finally spotted her sister's auburn hair between the shoulders of a couple of big guys hunched over the bar.

"Beer?" Jordana's boyfriend, Clint, shouted at her when she finally reached the bar.

"Hate beer," she shouted back. "I'll have a seltzer water with a twist of lemon." Not booze but it looked like a drink. Saved a whole lot of explanations about how she had so little body mass that she was a complete lightweight when it came to drinking. And besides, she made a practice of never drinking with her colleagues.

Eventually a glass was passed to her filled with clear, fizzy liquid, ice and a lemon section. Jordana and Clint had their heads pressed together and appeared to be having an intense conversation, so she picked up her drink to leave.

"Don't go," Jordana shouted. "We have something to tell you."

She turned back to the couple, who looked so in love they practically glowed. A frisson of jealousy shivered through her belly. Must be nice to find that great a guy and have him fall head over heels for you. She noted the way Jordana leaned into Clint's side and how he angled his body protectively beside her. Yeah. That. Having a little of that would be nice, someday.

"What's up?" She leaned in close to avoid having to shout at the top of her lungs to be heard.

"I've decided to move to Chicago to be with Clint. His vacation is over and he has to go back to work. I'm going with him."

She stared, shocked. Of all her siblings, Jordana seemed the most connected to Braxville. She was a cop, here, and everything. "What about your job? You love being a cop."

"Tyler has offered me a job in his company." Tyler was their oldest brother and a partner in a high-end security firm.

"It's based in Wichita, not Chicago," Yvette responded, confused.

"He's opening an office in Chicago and wants me to head it up."

Yvette looked back and forth between Jordana and Clint, who were still doing that glowing thing, darn it. "Well, of course, I'll miss the heck out of you, but I'm happy for you guys."

Jordana reached up to push her hair back and Yvette spied a sparkle on her sister's left ring finger. She squealed and grabbed Jordana's hand. "Lemme see! He proposed? When did this happen?"

"This afternoon. After I accepted Tyler's offer and it was official that I'm moving to Chicago."

The diamond was big and beautiful, surrounded by a ring of smaller baguettes and more diamonds across the band. "Dang, sis. That thing is a lethal weapon. Punch someone with that and they're going *down*."

"Hopefully, the security business will be slower paced than police work."

Yvette grunted. Not bloody likely.

Clint grinned ruefully at her. "I keep trying to tell her

to ease off the pedal a little, but I doubt that's going to happen any time soon."

Yvette laughed. "Good luck with that. We Coltons tend to live life at ninety miles an hour with our hair on fire."

"I'd noticed that," Clint replied dryly.

Yvette leaned forward and hugged her sister. "I'm so happy for you two. Now, if you'll excuse me, I have to go find your partner and act casual around him so Chief Hilton will stop asking if Reese and I can work together like adults or not."

She turned away fast to avoid being quizzed by her sister and plunged into the crowd. The trick at a party like this, where she knew a lot of people but none of them were close friends, was to keep moving and always appear to be headed across the room toward someone.

She kept an eye out for the police chief, Roger Hilton, and for Reese. If she could catch the two of them together, or at least in visual contact with each other, she could stroll up to Reese, act casual for a minute or two and then get out of here.

Rusty's opened up in the back to a big seating area with dartboards along one side and a dance floor taking up the back half of the party space. TV screens mounted along the ceiling opposite the dartboards played several different sporting events at the moment. Thankfully, they were muted and weren't competing to be heard over the noise of the whole police department, most of the fire department, most of the off-duty EMTs from the county hospital, and a host of other people from around town who knew Lou Hovitz.

Dang. Popular guy. If she retired tomorrow and threw a party, maybe a couple of her siblings might show up— if they weren't busy doing laundry or something equally important. She supposed her mom would come. Lilly was loyal that way.

Yvette continued to move back and forth through the crowd in search of her twin targets, to no avail. Funny how lonely it was possible to feel in the middle of a big crowd. She'd left behind all her friends of the past several years in Virginia when she'd moved back to Braxville, and she felt that loss keenly now.

"Why the long face?" a male voice shouted in her ear.

She jumped and spun around to face Reese. "Where did you come from?"

"I've been playing darts. Your sister just kicked my ass, again."

"We have a dartboard in my dad's billiard room. Jordana's been throwing darts her whole life. She's the Colton family champion."

"Are you kidding me?"

"God's honest truth," she shouted back.

He swore under his breath and then said to her, "Thanks for coming tonight."

"Do you know where Roger Hilton is? He's the one guy who needs to see us getting along tonight."

"He's dancing with his wife. Been out there a while."

She turned her gaze to the mass of people currently boot scooting their way around the dance floor. It was so crowded she couldn't spot the Hiltons at all. She leaned in close to ask Reese, "Should we wait for him to come off the floor and then go over together to say hello to him or something?"

"I have a better idea. Dance with me."

Reese grabbed her drink and set it down on the nearest table along with his half-empty beer. He grabbed her around the waist and spun her out onto the dance floor before she even had a chance to say no.

The music was just changing into a country song made for two-stepping, and Reese confidently began shuffling around the floor with her. She hadn't two-stepped in years, but she relaxed and let him guide her around the floor to the quick-quick-slow-slow rhythm. As it came back to her, she let her feet move on autopilot.

Reese wore a crisply starched white shirt with the sleeves rolled up to reveal fine dark hairs on his forearms. His jeans were probably pressed and starched within an inch of their life, but she didn't dare glance down to find out.

His hand was firm on her waist as he guided her smoothly around the crowded floor, his thigh occasionally rubbing against hers. She had to tilt her head back to look up at him which threw her more than a little off-balance. More than once, she had to catch herself by tightening her hand on his shoulder.

After two or three of those balance checks, each of which pulled her closer to him, she realized she was more or less plastered against him, her chest rubbing against his, her belly rubbing against the zipper of his jeans. Her breath came faster, and it had nothing to do with the dancing. Nope, her dance partner made her think about doing all kinds of hot, naughty things to his delicious body.

The song ended and the next one was slow and sexy with sultry vocals that melted her from the inside out. At least she hoped it was just the song. Otherwise, it was Reese having that dramatic effect on her.

He stared down at her, his normally blue eyes black in the dim light of the bar. Or maybe his pupils were so dilated that his eyes appeared black. Either way, his gaze smoldered with intense heat. Oh, dear. Was he feeling the incendiary attraction between them, too?

His hand pressed against her back, drawing her even closer against him until her thighs nestled on either side of one of his. They were in intimate contact from her knees to her shoulders, and everywhere she touched him, he was hard and burning hot.

Her right hand rested on his shoulder, and her left hand curled around his waist, where she noted there wasn't even a hint of an inner tube. Nope. This man was hard and lean, all muscle and restless energy.

And right now, that energy was aimed squarely at her. It vibrated through her, breaking the bonds between the molecules of her body until she felt like nothing more than a mass of tangled, separately tingling nerves. Taken all together, she was one giant hot mess.

Reese turned her in a slow, swaying circle, gradually spiraling her through the couples dotting the dance floor until the two of them were tucked in the back corner of the room, in the darkest, most heavily shadowed bit of the floor.

His head dipped down toward hers, and his mouth brushed against her temple. It was the lightest of kisses. It could even have been an accident. But then he murmured, "Is it just me, or is something definitely not casual happening between us?"

She pressed her eyes shut in chagrin. It was all she could do to stop herself from crawling all over his big, yummy body, right here, right now.

"We've got to dial this back," he muttered. "You know. For our careers."

"Right. Careers." Good grief. When did she get so breathless? All they were doing out here was swaying back and forth in slow motion. Nothing athletic that would steal all the air from her lungs like this.

She realized she was leaning in to him, craving the

heat of his body, reveling in the feel of it pressed tightly against hers. They fit together perfectly. He was taller than her, but not so much so that her small stature made her feel like a half-grown child next to him.

His arms surrounded her, holding her snugly against him. Given the quick rise and fall of his chest against her breasts she surmised he was relishing the contact between them as much as she was.

Casual. Careers. Truce. The boss.

Nope. Nothing was distracting her from her pool of liquid heat forming in the pit of her belly, yearning toward the hard, sexual promise of Reese's body to fill that hungry void.

He turned to put his back to the room, effectively hiding her from everyone else in the joint. One of his hands left her back and reached between them, tilting her chin up. He leaned down and kissed her carnally, his tongue plunging into her mouth in a rhythmic imitation of sex. She surged up into the kiss on her tiptoes, her own tongue swirling around his. The smooth glide of lips on lips, the wrestling tangle of their tongues, the mingling of breath, stole what little breath she had left.

Gasping, she dropped back to flat-footed on the floor, burying her face against his shirt. He smelled of man and something tangy and citrus and delicious. Even the scent of him sent waves of need rolling through her.

"Let's get out of here," he murmured against her temple.

"Right. Yes." Her mind skipped like a needle jumping to another track on an old vinyl album. "But, umm, casual. Boss. We have to be seen by Roger."

"Screw casual."

"I won't wreck your career." *Ta-da.* She *was* capable of forming a complete sentence!

"Screw that, too. Let's go." He surprised her by pushing her backward toward the wall behind her. She stumbled, shocked as it gave way and a blast of cold slammed into her shoulder blades.

A door. Rear exit, apparently.

Reese spun her outside and the door closed behind them.

"My coat—"

"I'll text your sister to pick it up," he muttered against her neck.

She threw her head back, loving the feel of his mouth on her bare skin. "Oh, that'll go over great with her." She stopped speaking while a head-to-toe shiver made her momentarily incapable of speech, then continued breathlessly, "No way will you be able to convince her there's nothing going on between us if we flee the scene of the crime without even grabbing our coats."

"I don't care what she thinks," he murmured as he caught her earlobe between his teeth and bit down gently.

"You say that now. Have you ever seen my sister get a bone between her teeth and refuse to let go?"

He laughed a little, a sexy rumble in his chest that she felt through her whole body. "Yeah, actually. I have." He straightened, throwing his arm over her shoulder and tucking her tightly against his side. "C'mon. It's freezing out here."

He hurried her over to his truck and piled her inside. From behind the bench seat, he pulled out a thick wool blanket that he threw over her and tucked in around her.

Moving around to the driver's side, he climbed in, started the engine and pointed at a rotating dial. "Give the truck three minutes and then crank that all the way to the right. It'll start throwing heat out at you."

He opened his door again.

"Where are you going?" she blurted.

"Inside to get our coats."

"Mine's cream wool with a belt—"

He interrupted gently. "I know. I work with you. I've seen you come and go from the office every day for the past year. I'm familiar with your various coats."

"You know my coats?" she asked incredulously.

"My favorite is the light blue ski jacket," he commented casually as he climbed out. She stared, open-mouthed as he shut the door and jogged off into the darkness. He paid attention to her *coats*? What did it mean? Was he merely observant, or did his attention to detail related to her mean…more?

No answers had come to her by the time Reese blew back into the truck cab on a gust of frigid air.

"Man. It's getting cold out there," Reese commented, pushing her coat across the now warm cab at her. "Feels like another storm may be blowing in."

"I should drive my car home," she said, reaching for the door handle.

"I'll drive you. Roads will already be getting icy."

"I have to get my car home, sometime," she replied dryly.

"It won't hurt anything spending the night here. I imagine a bunch of vehicles will end up being here overnight. Lots of cops inside are drinking and will know better than to drive afterward. Local rideshare guys are gonna get some good business out of Lou's party."

"You had a beer when I first saw you. Should you be driving?" she asked.

He ducked his chin a little. "I always buy one beer and dump half of it down a toilet. Then I carry it around the rest of the night."

"You don't drink?" she asked in surprise.

"Not often. And certainly not when I have to drive home. How about you? What was that in your glass?"

"Selzter water and a lemon," she confessed.

He laughed a little. "Who knew we were such a couple of stick-in-the-muds?"

"Speak for yourself, Detective," she replied tartly.

He grinned broadly at her. "I'll keep the secret if you will."

"Deal," she replied, smiling back.

Honestly, she was relieved not to chance the bad roads in her lightweight car without four-wheel drive or chains for her tires. Her father and brothers had been trying to talk her into trading her fuel-efficient little car in for something bigger and heavier, suited to the bad weather that was known to blow in at this time of year. But to date, she'd resisted. She'd forgotten how bad these sudden blizzards could be out here on the Great Plains.

Ruefully, she said, "I'm trying to repair my reputation in the department. Leaving my car here in a blatant advertisement that I've gone home with someone else isn't going to help matters one bit. As much as I appreciate your offer to drive me home, I need to get my car out of here."

He sighed. "Fine. I'll follow you to your place. If the roads are too bad for you or you get in trouble, I'll be there to help. And, be careful. There are black ice patches on the roads."

Black ice was the bane of Kansas roads at this time of year. The sun warmed snow and ice during the day into wet puddles. Then, at night, when temperatures fell below freezing, the puddles froze into sheets of clear ice that allowed the black pavement to be seen below. Hence, the name. The stuff was glass smooth and treacherous to drive on. Braking on a sheet of it was impossible. A car might as well be on an ice-skating rink.

"Will do." Reluctantly, she shrugged into her coat, climbed out of the truck and tromped through drifts of snow already a foot deep to her car. Reese helped her brush the snow off her windshield and windows while the interior of the car warmed up.

When she was ready to go, she flashed Reese a thumbs-up and he trudged back to his truck and climbed in. With him following a safe distance behind, she did, indeed, drive home exceptionally cautiously and arrived without incident in her driveway. She trotted out of her garage to Reese's truck, and he rolled down the window as she approached.

"Would you like to come inside? It's not late. Have you eaten? I can cook for us," she offered.

"Do you know how to cook?"

She snorted. "You don't have to sound so surprised. I've made it into my midtwenties, which means I've been eating for years all by my little self."

He rolled his eyes and turned off the ignition. "Yes, but is it edible?"

"Come in and find out. I dare you."

"You really have to stop daring me to do things. One day, you'll get in over your head."

"Never," she replied stoutly, opening the door from the garage into the house and kicking out of her boots in the mudroom.

"Big words, little girl," he teased as he followed her into her cozy kitchen.

"Who are you calling little?" she demanded as she turned on the lights and started pulling out food.

Grinning, he backed her up against the wall beside her refrigerator and kissed her long and leisurely. Goodness.

She could not get enough of kissing that man. Belatedly, she realized her hands were full of lettuce, carrots, tomatoes and celery. He stepped back, and she plunked the food onto the counter, then pulled out a cutting board and knife.

"Can I help?" he offered.

"Sit." She pointed the big knife at the kitchen table.

Grinning, he threw up his hands and sat. "Truce. It's still in effect, right?"

"As long as you don't make fun of my cooking, it is."

"Yes, ma'am." He grinned cheekily at her.

Those bedroom eyes of his were at it again, sparkling sexily and making her think about things she'd like to do with him on the kitchen table that had nothing to do with food. Dang, that man was lethal.

She forced her attention to the task at hand. Supper. She had a couple of nice steaks in her fridge, and she put a cast-iron skillet on the stove to heat up. When it was sizzling hot, she dropped in butter and seared the steaks quickly on both sides to seal in the juices. Then, she put the whole pan in the oven to finish off the sirloins. While they cooked, she boiled eggs, chopped romaine lettuce, ham, carrots, celery, onions and bacon, and put together a decent Cobb salad if she did say so, herself.

She put Reese to work snapping green beans and steamed those with garlic and butter after he was done. Just as she set the salad on the table the oven timer went off. She peeked at the beans, which were bright green, aromatic and tender. *Yes.* She whisked the steaks out of the oven to rest, plated them and the beans, and set the meal on the table with a flourish.

It was pure luck on her part that everything came together at once, but she was totally willing to take credit for it with Reese.

She sat down beside him and smiled. *"Bon appétit."*

"I have to admit, I'm impressed."

"You haven't tasted it yet."

He cut into his steak, and juice mingled with the butter. It was medium rare, succulent and tender. Again, sheer luck. But what Reese Carpenter didn't know about her hit-or-miss cooking skills wouldn't hurt him.

He groaned with pleasure. "Oh. That's a fine piece of meat."

His gaze snapped up to hers, startled. "Sorry. I didn't mean that the way it sounded."

She stabbed a piece of her steak daintily with her fork and waved it at him airily. "Never fear. I take no offense at the double entendre. I'm nobody's piece of meat."

"No kidding," he replied heartily.

"Meaning what?" she demanded. "Don't you think I'm attractive enough to be seen as meat?"

He put down his utensils and threw up his hands. "You are totally meat-worthy. But I in no way think of you like that—"

She burst into laughter. "I'm just messing with you."

He scowled momentarily but then dissolved into a grin. "So that's how it's gonna be, huh? Duly noted. Just remember, payback's a bitch."

"Bring it, buddy."

Clearly, he planned to delay his retaliatory teasing for he fell to his meal with enthusiasm and little talk ensued.

Near the end of supper, she finally worked up the courage to ask the question that had been bugging her ever since Reese forgave her in his truck. "How bad was the razzing after I left the squad room today?"

He looked up from his last bite of steak and grinned. "Actually, it went dead silent. Everyone was so shocked they didn't know what to say. First time I've ever seen that bunch speechless."

She winced. "I'm so sorry."

He leaned back with a sigh of pleasure. "That was a helluva good steak. Thank you."

"I don't have anything snazzy to offer you for dessert. I do have ice cream and some fresh strawberries I can slice over it."

"I'm stuffed. Nothing for me, thanks," he replied.

She leaned back, as well. "How did Jordana find out about our, umm, squad-room kiss so fast? She called me about thirty seconds after I got back to the lab."

"I expect somebody texted her." A frown crossed his brow. "Was she mad?"

"At me? Oh, yeah. She said it reflects on her and that she considers us both to be her siblings…which makes it weird, apparently."

"Hmm. Gonna have to have a chat with her about you, I guess."

He didn't sound thrilled at the prospect.

The elation she'd been feeling at his forgiveness evaporated. "I'm sorry—"

"Stop apologizing already," he interrupted. "You've done nothing wrong."

"Well, I did lay a big wet one on you in the middle of our mutual workplace."

"Which I willingly—correction, *eagerly*—participated in. That kiss took two people, in case you hadn't noticed."

She answered sarcastically, "I had noticed, thank you."

He snorted with laughter. "I do love a woman with a dry sense of humor."

"That's me. The Sahara Desert."

She started to get up to do the dishes, but Reese

reached out, grabbed her wrist and tugged her back down into her chair. "Oh no, you don't. You cooked. I'll do the dishes."

"If that's how you roll, I'll cook dinner for you every night."

This time it was her gaze that snapped to his, startled and chagrined.

Darn her mouth! When was she going to learn to think about what she said before the words just popped out?

"It's my pleasure to clean up," he responded blandly enough. But she caught the look of—something—in his eyes as he turned away. She couldn't tell if that was speculation or cold, hard terror in his eyes at her crack about doing this every night. Behind his back, she squeezed her eyes shut in chagrin. She was a total mess around him.

Sleeves rolled up and sponge in hand, which was possibly the sexiest look she'd ever seen on him, he said over his shoulder, "I forgot to ask if you've gotten into that puzzle box yet."

"No, but I'm close. I think there's only one layer of the puzzle left. Sucker has four layers to solve."

Reese murmured, "Which begs the question, what does that key open that's so important?"

"Dexter—assuming it was Dexter and not his wife—went to a whole lot of trouble to hide the key, that's for sure."

Reese replied, "Using the X-ray image of the key that you emailed me, I did a little preliminary research on it. My guess is that it's some sort of a safe-deposit box or locker key."

"Interesting."

"I showed the image of the key to the guys at all the local banks in Braxville, and they said it's not one of theirs."

"A bank in Wichita, maybe?" she suggested. "Or possibly Kansas City?"

He nodded and picked up a dish towel to start drying. "I had time to check with a few Wichita banks, today. I'll email the image to the rest of the Wichita banks tomorrow."

"If you don't get a hit, let me know. The FBI maintains an exhaustive key database that I have access to as a forensics investigator."

He looked over his shoulder at her and nodded. "Thanks. Will do." He put the last plate onto the dry towel he'd spread out beside the sink. She had a perfectly functional dishwasher, but she'd enjoyed sitting here watching the hot, macho man washing dishes. There was something unbelievably attractive about a man doing a domestic chore with ease and comfort.

She stood up and went over to the sink to wrap her arms around his hard, lean waist from behind. "Thanks for doing the dishes. And thanks again for forgiving me about the whole kiss thing."

He turned in her arms and wrapped his arms around her shoulders. Resting his chin on top of her head, he said quietly, "I'm not the giant ass you seem to think I am."

"I don't think you're a giant ass. Maybe just a little one. Sometimes."

His chest rumbled with silent laughter. "I love how you call me out. Keep me honest."

"I thought you were the one who always calls me out. You pick on how I do my job and how I run my lab all the time."

"I don't pick on you," he disagreed. "And I don't tell you what to do. I make helpful suggestions."

She laughed aloud at that. "Right. Forcefully."

"I'm sorry if I've been a jerk. I just really wanted to see you succeed."

Startled, she leaned back in his arms to look up at him. "Come again?"

"There was a lot of skepticism in the department about hiring a woman, and so young a woman, for your position. I was on the hiring review committee, though, and you were by far the most qualified candidate for the job. I've been in your corner since before you were hired."

"For real?"

He flashed that crooked smile of his again that was so endearing and irresistible.

She said softly, "And here I thought you were busting my chops and trying to chase me out of the department."

"Nope. Exactly the opposite."

She reached up and laid her palm lightly on his cheek. "Thank you, Reese."

"You don't have to thank me. You earned the job, and you've been knocking it out of the park ever since you got here. All the credit goes to you."

"Well, shoot. Now I'm embarrassed," she confessed.

"Don't be. Own the space you've earned."

"When did you become such a feminist?" she queried.

"Since my partner on the force showed me that women are every bit as good at police work as men, and since her sister showed me women make first-rate forensic scientists, too."

"Surely, your mother had something to do with this enlightened attitude."

He chuckled. "She would blister my butt if I was anything less than respectful to any woman. And I don't mess with my mama."

"I hear you. I wouldn't ever cross mine, either."

"Your mom is a sweetheart. She took care of my dad in

the hospital after his heart attack. She gave him just the right combination of kindness and tough love he needed to get back on his feet and change his eating and exercise habits."

Yvette smiled fondly. Her mother had often been a distant figure in her life, with a big family to care for, her husband's career to support and demanding career of her own. But she never for a moment doubted that Lilly loved her as fiercely as she loved all her children. Her mother had always called her *My special gift* and *My littlest angel.*

Reese commented casually, "Did anybody tell you your dad's coming to the police department tomorrow to turn himself in?"

"No." She'd temporarily forgotten about the arsenic case in the kerfuffle over the puzzle box, her mad crush on Reese and the whole kissing-in-the-squad-room fiasco. "Is it going to be bad for him?"

He shrugged. "There could be press. When is it ever good when reporters and cameras are around?"

Yikes. Not encouraging.

She led Reese into her sitting room, which she'd decorated like an English country cottage. The furniture was casual and cozy, a blend of old and new. The sofa and curtains were a buttery-yellow floral print, but their femininity was balanced by the masculine weight of the massive stone fireplace.

"Pretty room," Reese commented.

"It doesn't give you hives to be surrounded by all this girly stuff?" she asked doubtfully.

"I happen to like girls quite a lot. In my experience, they tend to come with girly stuff."

She smirked. "Sort of like men come with smelly socks, empty beer cans and butt-crack scratching?"

"You really don't like men much, do you?"

Her gaze fell away from his. "I like you."

"Why don't you like men in general?"

She sighed. "You'd have to be a single, reasonably attractive woman of dating age to understand."

"Try me."

"In high school and college, too many guys I knew were hopelessly immature and focused mainly on getting laid as often as possible. The word *no* wasn't always in their vocabulary. Some of them got angry and aggressive." She shrugged. "A girl learns to be cautious."

"Cautious how?"

She shrugged. "You don't take drinks or food from strange men in case they're drugged. You don't go to parties alone—always go with a couple of girlfriends—and for goodness' sake don't leave alone. Take a girlfriend to the bathroom with you. Don't engage with guys who smell like booze—I could go on, but you get the point."

"Didn't you meet *any* education-focused guys interested in pursuing serious careers and whose parents taught them how to treat a woman right?" he asked.

"I probably did, but I was so turned off by the other kind that I couldn't see the good ones hiding among the bad ones."

"We're out here. You just have to look for us."

"No offense, but you were the biggest jerk of all when I got to the department. Although, in your defense, you never came on to me."

"I'm sorry if I came off like a jerk. I just wanted you to make it, here. I should have trusted you to be able to handle being the first woman in your position."

"Is there still resistance to me in the department?"

"Not after today."

She rolled her eyes and sighed. "I'd prefer to be judged on my professional merits and not how I kiss."

He reached out and tucked a stray strand of her hair behind her ear. His fingertips traced the rim of her ear lightly. "Never fear. Everyone thinks you're scary smart and darned good at your job."

Thank goodness. "That's a relief, at least."

He smiled warmly at her.

"Why was it I hated you, again?" she asked.

"Because love and hate are only a hair's breadth apart?" he offered.

Love? Whoa. That was a big word. But he had a point. The sizzling friction between them this whole past year had morphed into something much more sexual and intimate in the blink of an eye. That wouldn't have happened if a lot of that simmering tension hadn't already been driven by attraction, unconscious or otherwise.

She cast about for a more neutral topic of conversation and ended up blurting, "What are you going to do for a partner once Jordana leaves the department?"

Reese froze, staring at her. "I beg your pardon?"

"Surely, she told you first. She's moving to Chicago to open up an office for my future brother-in-law's security firm."

"I...she...sonofabitch." He whirled away, shoving a hand through his dark hair, standing it up on end.

"Ohmigosh. She hasn't told you, yet. God. I'm so sorry." She stepped forward and touched Reese's arm tentatively.

He whirled, all but knocking her over with the violence of the movement, and ended up having to wrap his arms around her tightly to keep from knocking her right off her feet.

"Sorry," he muttered.

"No, I'm sorry. I just assumed. I'm so stupid—"

He kissed her ferociously, and she absorbed his anger, and what felt like something akin to grief, into herself in silence. But then his anger shifted. Intensified. Turned into something dark and sexy and dangerous.

He surged against her, kissing her with his whole body, and she flung herself at him in return. She couldn't get enough of this man. He backed her up against the front door and planted his thigh between hers, effectively pinning her in place. Not that she minded one bit. Her nether regions rubbed against the rough denim and her breath caught at the delicious sensation.

His hands plunged into her hair and his tongue plunged into her mouth, and she returned the favor, inhaling him even deeper into their kiss.

He must have realized he was crushing her for he turned suddenly, dragging her with him until his back was against the door and it was her turn to press into him, kissing him with all the pent-up intensity that had been building between them for months.

His mouth slashed across hers and she met him halfway. Their kiss was wet and hot, a sparring match between two aggressively attracted people who were rapidly spinning out of control. And it was glorious. The ridge behind his zipper was big and hard, and she pressed her belly hungrily against it. The peaks of her breasts rubbed against his chest, and her entire body felt light and energized, tingling and eager for more.

Gradually, Reese's mouth eased away from hers, and his hands stilled their roaming path across her back. She leaned back to look at him questioningly.

"I'm sorry," he sighed. "I shouldn't have fallen on you to take out my frustration."

She smiled a little. "Depends on what kind of frustration you're talking about."

He smiled reluctantly. "I just—losing another partner—it was a surprise—didn't see it coming."

"Another partner?" she echoed. "You've lost one before?"

She was still sprawled all over him, so she felt his entire body tense. His eyes shut down as if he'd just flipped an off switch in his brain. Whoa. She stepped back quickly, snagging his hand and pulling him away from the door and over to the sofa.

"Sit down. Talk to me, Reese. What giant nerve did I just hit?"

He shook his head and started to stand up, but she pushed on his shoulders, pressing him back down to the cushions. Not that she could brute force him into doing anything, of course, but he went along with her pressure.

"Talk."

He closed his eyes tightly for a moment, and when he opened them again, they were bleak. "I lost my first partner a few years back. She died. Shot in an arrest gone bad. I saw the gun. Too late. Tried to draw my own weapon. Wasn't fast enough. She went down." He stared over her shoulder at nothing, obviously seeing the whole thing again in his mind's eye. "So much blood. Bullet hit her aorta. She died in under two minutes. No time for an ambulance to get there. No backup. Just me holding her as her life slipped away…"

"Oh, Reese. I'm so sorry. I had no idea. I'm such an idiot."

"You had no way of knowing."

She said in a more upbeat tone, "Well, Jordana isn't dying. She's just moving away to be with her fiancé. Clint proposed today, by the way."

"Good for them. I hope they're happy."

She said dryly, "They're freaking delirious. It's disgusting."

Hah. That got a tiny smile out of him, at least.

She said, "She'll be back to visit all the time. Her whole family is here in Braxville. You're family to her, too."

"She's the irritating sister I never had," Reese said ruefully.

Thank goodness it was Jordana who'd been relegated to that role and not her. She channeled her mother for a moment and asked him, "Can I get you a cup of tea? Or a stiff shot of whiskey?"

He snorted. "You are a Colton, aren't you? When in doubt, offer food or drink."

"That's us. Always stuffing our faces."

"Then how do you stay so tiny?" he asked with a hint of humor in his voice.

Yep. He was doing better. The first shock of finding out his partner was leaving the force had passed, and he was going to be okay. She waved a casual hand at him. "I only dine on the souls of my enemies and drink the blood of small children. Keeps me trim."

That made him laugh reluctantly. "You don't fool me. You're not the evil ice queen folks in the department make you out to be."

"Don't tell them that!" she exclaimed in alarm. "I've worked hard to cultivate that image."

"Why's that?" Reese asked.

"Have you counted how many single, horny men there are in the Braxville PD? This is a small town, and eligible women are few and far between. The last thing I needed was for the whole police force to try to date me."

"Jeez. I'm sorry—" he started, moving to rise.

She grabbed his arm quickly. "You're fine. We have a truce, remember?"

"Right. Truce. You're sure you don't want to stop this—whatever this is—before it goes any further?"

"Positive," she answered immediately. More hesitantly, she asked, "How about you? Do you want to call things off?"

"Absolutely not."

They traded looks that were by turns warm and abashed. He cleared his throat. "Well okay, then. I'm glad that's settled. And now, I really do need to get out of here."

"But if we just decided to extend the truce—"

"If I stay any longer, we're going to pass way beyond a truce to a full-blown peace treaty," he interrupted.

"What's wrong with that?" she demanded.

He stood up, moving swiftly for the door. "I'm not a one-night-stand kind of guy. If we do this, we're going to do it right."

She frowned. "We're not doing anything right now."

"Patience, Yvie."

"Have you met me? I don't have a patient bone in my body!"

He laughed low and husky. "Ahh, this is going to be a fun ride."

She scowled darkly at him. "You'd better buckle up, buster."

"Roger that." Grinning, he reached for the doorknob.

"What am I going to do with you?" she asked rhetorically.

"You're going to come over here so I can kiss you good-night and thank you for that delicious dinner, and then you're going to show me out. Otherwise, the neighbors are going to wonder whose truck is in your drive-way in the morning."

"I barely know my neighbors' names. Stay."

"Don't tempt me. I make it a policy never to sleep with a woman on our first date."

"I thought sorting files in my lab was our first date."

He laughed a little, sounding pained. He drew her into a hard hug and dropped a kiss on top of her head. "Ahh, you are a firecracker. You're going to keep me on my toes, aren't you?"

"Baby, I'm no firecracker. I'm a tactical nuclear bomb-shell."

"Truer words were never spoken," he replied, grin-ning.

She did, indeed, walk him to her front door. A soft glow came from outside, peachy light from the streetlamps illuminating the blanket of fresh snow that had fallen in the past few hours.

Reese drew her into his arms, kissing her slowly and thoroughly. She kissed him back, throwing herself into the kiss with abandon. She loved everything about how he felt against her, his body hard and fit, his mouth warm and resilient, his tongue wet and sexy and impudent.

She sucked at his tongue, pulling it deeper into her mouth, and he groaned in reaction. Just when she thought she might have broken down his resolve to leave and convinced him to follow her back to her bedroom, he straightened all at once and took a hasty step back.

"Lord, woman. You're more temptation than I can stand up to."

And yet, he'd just backed away from her.

"Stay," she said softly.

"Not tonight. But soon. When we're more sure of each other."

What more was there to be sure of? She was totally sure she wanted to sleep with him.

"Dream about me, tonight," he said quietly, dropping a quick kiss on the tip of her nose. He opened the door and stepped out onto the porch.

"Maybe I won't dream about you," she tossed out.

"I'll bet you a dollar you do," he tossed back.

"You're such a know-it-all," she groused, smiling.

"It's not being a know-it-all if I actually do know what I'm talking about."

Laughing, she walked to the edge of the porch where the snow got deep and his footprints sank deep into the fluffy blanket of white on her sidewalk. "You keep telling yourself that, big guy."

"God, I love smart-mouthed women."

"Smart being the operative word."

He turned and strode back to her swiftly, kissing her hard and fast one more time. "Dream of me," he ordered her.

Darned if she didn't dream about him that night, too. Lovely dreams about dancing in the dark, smoking-hot kisses and laughter. Lots of laughter.

It was hard to be mad at him for being right, or for owing him a dollar, though, when she woke up the next morning with a smile on her lips.

Chapter Nine

Reese looked around the lobby of the police building, which had been set up for this morning's press conference. A raised dais held a podium and several light stands. In front of it, a dozen reporters already milled around, and more were coming into the building every minute. Broadcast vans lined the entire perimeter of the parking lot, their satellite-uplink dishes already pointed skyward.

He recognized several of the journalists from national news shows and winced. This was going to be a circus—a big three-ringed mess of one. He'd tried to warn Yvette obliquely last night, but he doubted she'd caught the hint as to how bad this was going to be.

Chief of Police Roger Hilton strolled up to him. "Everything ready to go? Colton knows what to do?"

Fitz Colton was turning himself in this morning to face charges in the arsenic-poisoning cases. The plan was to allow him to make a statement to the press first. Then, the police chief would speak. And then Reese would drop the bomb. A bomb he would've been fine lobbing a few days ago. But now that he'd gotten to know Yvette better, he was hating himself for having volunteered to be the bad cop in this scenario.

Fitz and his lawyer were in on the plan and had agreed

to participate in it as part of his plea deal, but none of Fitz's kids had any idea what was coming, today. It was important that the family's reactions be authentic and believable if this little charade was going to work.

The lobby continued to fill as the nine o'clock start time for the press conference approached. Two of Yvette's brothers, Brooks and Tyler Colton, walked in together and stood near the back, taking in the crowd with less than pleased expressions. Brooks's fiancée, a schoolteacher, wasn't here this morning. But Tyler's fiancée, Ashley Hart, walked in with Bridgette Colton—Yvette's other sister besides Jordana—and the two women made their way over to the Colton brothers. Neil Colton walked in with his girlfriend, Braxville mayor, Elise Willis, but they separated immediately as she headed for the press corps to say hello to some of the more famous journalists here this morning.

Jordana was at her desk right now, unaware of the circus forming out here. He would text her in a few minutes to come out if she didn't wander out on her own to check out the rising din of close to fifty journalists milling around chatting with one another and making last-minute adjustments to makeup, lighting and camera angles with their crews.

Yvette was the only other child of Fitz Colton not here yet. And she should walk in any minute expecting to go to work. He hated ambushing her like this, but the plan required her to walk in unprepared for this fiasco.

Honestly, he was surprised she wasn't here yet. Her workday technically started at nine in the morning, but she often could be found in the lab before seven o'clock. Perhaps his prediction had been true and she'd slept in late, dreaming of him. He smiled a little in anticipation of teasing her about it later.

A hand touched his elbow and he turned, startled. *Jordana.*

"What the hell is this?" she demanded under her breath.

"I guess word got out that your father was going to turn himself in, today."

"Jeez Louise. What a mess. Can we get all these people out of here? It's five degrees outside. They won't stick around for long if we can move them outdoors. I'll call my dad and tell him to delay coming in—"

"He's due in any second. You need to let this play out."

"The news cycle is as much about entertainment as facts. They'll nuke him!"

"It's too late to stop this thing," he responded. "If you send away national media outlets at this late moment, they'll make a story out of that and accuse the Braxville Police Department of a cover-up on behalf of your rich, powerful father. For your old man's sake, you have to let this press circus happen. His arrest has to appear fair and unbiased."

"I *know* that. But this sucks."

He couldn't resist giving his partner a tiny warning of what was coming. "Brace yourself. The worst thing you could do is intervene on his behalf with the press. Today—as long as the cameras are rolling—you have to be a police officer first and Fitz Colton's daughter second."

"God, I hate this," she said fervently.

At least she didn't argue with him about not intervening in the coming proceeding. It had been a calculated risk not to brief her on the plan, but Roger Hilton and the district attorney had agreed with Reese's assessment that Jordana wouldn't agree to play along with it.

He said quietly, "Call Clint. Ask him to come over and give you some moral support. And in the meantime, a bunch of your siblings have gathered in that back corner. Why don't you go hang out with them? I'll handle the questions from the press directed at us police that Roger can't answer. It would probably be best if a non-Colton detective fielded questions about the Fitz Colton investigation."

"Yeah. You're right. Thanks for taking the bullet."

He winced. A bullet indeed. He had no doubt she would want to empty a whole clip of ammunition into him by the time this press conference was over.

Whew. One Colton sister handled. Now, if only Yvette would get here so he could coax her to go down to her lab and avoid this whole show. Because a show was exactly what they had planned for today.

YVETTE TURNED IN to the police department's parking lot and stopped her car. The entire lot was crammed with vehicles, and the whole front of the thing was lined with television broadcast vans with network names sprawled over their sides. Many of them were major national news outlets.

Oh, God. This had to be about her father.

Panic erupted under her breastbone. Not good. So very not good.

She drove around to the auxiliary parking lot behind the building and found a spot in the very back of the lot, tucked in a corner next to a huge snowbank that butted practically right up against the side of her car. Good thing she was tiny and could squeeze out of the few inches she could get her door open.

She slipped and slid across the icy parking lot, skating her way into the police building. She was sorely tempted to bolt down the back stairs and hide in her lab, far from the cameras and noise. But her whole family would no doubt show up to support her father, and her absence would be glaring, not to mention disloyal.

Reluctantly, she headed toward the front of the building. Fitz had always been an intimidating figure in her life. She didn't know him very well—he worked long hours through her childhood building his beloved company, and he had a naturally gruff personality. He hadn't been a bad father. He just hadn't been a good one.

As she emerged into the main lobby, she gaped at the mob crammed into the large space. Good grief. She recognized every face in the entire front row of reporters crowding the podium. All the national news shows were here. Ugh.

Why couldn't a tsunami have hit or a volcano have erupted somewhere else in the world today to sweep the Colton Construction arsenic story out of the news cycle? Not that she wished a disaster on anyone else, of course, but she hated this with every cell in her being.

She spied Reese's familiar back in front of her and moved toward him. He turned as she approached, his worried eyes lighting with a brief, intimate smile for her.

"There you are," he murmured. "I was wondering if you were going to get here before the big show begins."

"This is awful. Isn't there anything we can do to get these people to go away?"

He shrugged. "It's a free press. They can cover whatever they deem newsworthy."

"And the fall of a rich, powerful man makes for a great headline," she said bitterly.

"I'm sorry about all of this, Yvette. I would shield you

from every bit of it if I could. In fact, why don't you just go on down to your lab? I'll text you when this is over—"

"I'm a Colton. We stick together."

He sighed. "Yeah, I figured you'd say that. It was worth a try, though. Your brothers and sisters are gathered in the back." He pointed toward the left back corner of the room. "That way." He added, grinning slyly, "Since you can't see them over the crowd."

"You're hilarious, Jolly Green Carpenter," she shot back, grinning.

She stepped away from him and her petite frame was swallowed by the mob. He was still trying to verify that she'd made it back to the cluster of Coltons when a ruckus erupted by the front door behind the crowd. Lights went on, cameramen turned their equipment to face the back of the room and journalists talked into their microphones.

He spied Lilly Colton's red hair first, as she was climbing out of a black Town Car. He did feel bad for her. She was a kind person, and this scandal had to have been hard on her. Her natural compassion couldn't have been at ease with the idea of her husband and his partner sickening and killing some of their employees.

Fitz climbed out of the car behind her. The vehicle pulled away from the curb. They must have hired someone to bring them down here. The blackout windows would have kept rotten vegetables from being lobbed at them as they drove through Braxville, at any rate.

Predictably, the press rushed Lilly and Fitz as they headed for the building, stopping them from even reaching the front doors of the police department. Reese sighed and spoke into the microphone clipped to the collar of his suit coat. "Can we get a few uniforms outside to usher Mr. and Mrs. Colton into the building?"

Quickly, several cops cleared the way, and the couple

stepped inside. Lilly peeled off to join her children—
thank God. At least she would be surrounded by loved
ones when the feces hit the fan. Of course, unlike her
children, she knew what was coming.

The district attorney hadn't wanted to tell her what
was going down today, but Fitz had rebelled at the idea
of keeping her in the dark. He'd complained that his marriage was already in the toilet and keeping this secret
from her might push Lilly over the edge. The DA had
caved, but only if Fitz made sure Lilly swore not to warn
her children about it in any way. This plan relied heavily
on genuine reactions out of the family.

Fitz made it to the dais and stepped up to the podium.
He pulled a folded piece of paper out of the pocket of his
suit coat and spread it out before him. The room went
expectantly silent as he cleared his voice.

"Thank you for coming today, ladies and gentlemen,
although I hardly think this moment warrants such attention. At any rate, as you all know, Colton Construction,
in which I'm co-owner, stands accused of using arsenic-
laced wood products, obtained from China some years
ago, in one of its construction projects. In the ensuing
years, several employees have become sick, and a few
have passed away from complications likely related to
exposure to this toxic wood.

"I am here today to turn myself in to the police to
face charges relating to these sad events. Furthermore,
as the majority partner in the firm with a fifty-one percent stake in the company, I would like to announce that
I have decided to sell Colton Construction. In accordance
with a plea deal I have struck with the Braxville District
Attorney's office…"

Reese tuned out as the statement droned on. He'd been
in the room when Fitz's statement was drafted and agreed

upon, and he knew that a detailed explanation followed of how the proceeds from the sale of the business would be disbursed through a neutral, third-party attorney agreed upon by Fitz and the DA.

While Fitz read on, Reese craned to see over the crowd, to find Yvette's face in the melee, to check in on her and make sure she was doing all right. Of course, this wasn't the part where things would get ugly.

There she was. She looked pale, her features drawn in stress. Did she feel bad for her part in proving the wood from the Colton project was the source of the arsenic that had poisoned the Colton workers? He sincerely hoped she didn't feel guilty for helping put her father in this uncomfortable situation. He'd done that to himself when he'd gone along with Markus's plan to cut financial corners and use the cheap Chinese wood that was known to be treated with toxic chemicals.

The arsenic acted as a pesticide to protect the wood from insect damage, but was outlawed for use in the United States for precisely the reason that it caused cancer in the people who handled it and worked with it.

He tuned back in to see where Fitz was in his statement.

"…and all remaining proceeds of the sale will be put into a trust fund administered by a neutral third party. Its funds will be available to pay for medical bills and expenses for the affected employees and their families, including the survivors of deceased employees.

"I will also personally be establishing a scholarship fund for the children of the affected employees to defray the costs of their higher education. I regret the decisions that led to this tragedy and accept responsibility for my part in it. I promise to do everything in my power to make it right for the affected Colton Construction employees and their families."

Fitz had balked at promising anything, but the DA had stood firm and insisted that the verbiage be in the statement. He wanted Fitz on the record with his word of honor.

Assuming that's worth anything. Reese wasn't so sure of that, anymore. At least Yvette didn't seem to have inherited her father's…flexible…sense of right and wrong. Besides, it wasn't like Fitz could ever make it right for the employees who'd died.

As soon as Fitz stopped speaking and looked up from the paper before him, the journalists shouted all at once, yelling questions about how much money would go to the employees, whether or not he was going to serve jail time, and whether or not the plea deal included any further admission of guilt.

To Reese, standing just to one side of the podium, the din was deafening. And it wasn't even directed at him. Dang. No wonder people talked about the press going into feeding frenzies.

The police chief stepped up to the podium and held up his hands for silence. It took a while for the reporters to settle down. He made a brief statement that the Braxville Police Department was committed to seeing the law enforced and investigating the charges fully and impartially. Then he said, "I'll pass any questions you have to the officer in charge of the investigation, Detective Reese Carpenter."

That was his cue. Reese stepped forward. Here went nothing.

He spoke into the microphone. "The arsenic investigation is an active case, and therefore, I'm not going to be able to answer any specific questions about evidence or the details of the case. I can tell you we have passed the case to the district attorney for review and that Mr. Colton has cooperated fully with the investigation so far. Before I take any questions, I would also like to speak for a moment about another major investigation the Braxville Police Department is involved in. As many of you are already aware, several months ago, the remains of two individuals, a man identified as Fenton Crane, and a woman, Olivia Harrison, were discovered hidden in the walls of another Colton Construction project. Today, not only will we be arresting Mr. Colton for the arsenic poisoning, but we will also be arresting him in connection with those murders—"

He was drowned out by a shout of surprise and a spate of questions that erupted from the crowd in front of him.

More important, many of the cameras swung around to capture the reaction of the Colton family to that shocking announcement. It was exactly why he hadn't told Yvette or Jordana what was coming today, and why only Lilly had any warning at all in advance of the announcement of Fitz's arrest for murder.

Predictably, the family looked equal parts shocked, alarmed and furious. Their expressions of dismay were everything he and the district attorney could have hoped for. Lord, he hoped those reactions were enough to convince Markus Dexter that Fitz Colton had really been arrested for the Harrison and Crane murders.

Otherwise, he'd just put that poor family through hell for nothing.

Eventually, the lights and cameras swung back to him.

He squinted into the blinding lights, trying desperately to see the Colton family's reactions, trying at least to find Yvette's petite silhouette in the cluster of siblings, to give her what silent moral support he could. But he couldn't pick her out at all. All he saw were black silhouettes before him. He couldn't make out any faces past the front row of reporters.

Someone called out, "Do you have proof that Fitz Colton killed that couple? What is it?"

Reese answered, "The Harrison-Crane case is also an active investigation, and I'm not at liberty to comment on any specific evidence we've collected regarding the case. Also, I'd like to remind everyone that, while we know the identities of the two victims, we know very little about their past lives or what circumstances brought them to their tragic ends. We cannot speculate on whether or not they were a couple or even if they knew each other. The Braxville Police would like to ask anyone in the public with information regarding the final days of Ms. Olivia Harrison or Mr. Fenton Crane to contact the Braxville Police Department." He recited the phone number for the tip line and gave out the general email address of the department.

He spent the next fifteen minutes repeating himself over and over that he couldn't share any details of the evidence on either investigation while reporters tried every way they could to trip him up and get him to reveal some new morsel of evidence.

Finally, the question he'd been waiting for was asked. A reporter called, "Where's Fitz Colton's partner, Markus Dexter? Is he going to be charged in the arsenic investigation and murder case, too?"

Reese leaned in to the mike. "Fitz Colton is the majority partner in Colton Construction, and with regard to the arsenic case, the responsible party for any actions taken by the company as a whole. As for the murder investigation, we're uncovering new evidence on a daily basis. Dexter is not the person we're looking into right now with regard to the Harrison-Crane murders."

"And that evidence implicates Fitz Colton?" the reporter followed up. "Hence his arrest?"

He smiled and shrugged. "I'm sorry. I can't comment on that. I can only repeat that Mr. Colton will be questioned after this press conference with regard to the Harrison-Crane case." He made darned sure to give the answer in a tone indicating that the evidence did, indeed, point to Fitz as the killer.

Time to wrap up. "Thanks for coming today, everyone. If you have any further questions, you can contact the public affairs officer for the City of Braxville." He turned off the microphone and stepped off the stage, craning to search over the crowd for Yvette.

He didn't need to see her face to know exactly how she would have responded to the surprise arrest of her father for the Harrison-Crane murders. She would be livid. She knew better than anyone that the evidence so far *didn't* point at her father, but pointed squarely at his business partner.

Fitz had agreed to play along with this charade in an attempt to coax Markus Dexter out of hiding. If Dexter believed he'd been cleared, the hope was that he might return to Braxville, or at least show his face to law enforcement wherever he was. A nationwide BOLO—be on the lookout—for Dexter had already been issued.

As it turned out, Fitz had been eager to help smoke out his old partner. He was pissed as hell at Dex for getting him and his beloved company into the arsenic mess by talking him into purchasing the tainted wood, and he wanted to see Dex hang if he'd actually committed the two murders and used a Colton building to hide the bodies.

Predictably, Reese was mobbed after the press conference by reporters trying to get a scoop and to trick or bully him into revealing something he hadn't during the press conference. He finally resorted to answering every question with a blunt "No comment," as he pushed through the crowd toward the back of the lobby.

He *had* to find Yvette.

Chapter Ten

Yvette's face was on fire. She couldn't breathe. Her chest had an iron band around it.

Holy cow. This was a panic attack. She had to get out of here, away from all these people. And at all costs, she had to avoid Reese. What in the heck was he doing, accusing her father of murder? She knew all the evidence in the murder cases—she'd personally logged in most of it in the stupid investigation. Even though she'd passed the most important testing off to other labs to avoid any appearance of conflict of interest and to avoid accusations of her tainting the evidence, she did know the results of all that testing.

And one thing she knew for sure: n o way was her father the killer.

It was a wild miscarriage of justice.

Her brothers and sisters murmured angrily among themselves, and she became aware that they weren't talking with her. Of course not. To them, she was the Judas. The forensic scientist who'd apparently—and secretly— set up their father for a crime he hadn't committed. She felt their emotional withdrawal as acutely as she felt their physical withdrawal from her.

It was subtle, but all of her siblings had moved away from her, circled around Lilly, turned their backs to her just enough to shut her out of their mutual circle of concern for their dad and of support for their mom.

Miserable, she turned and wriggled into the crowd, using her small stature to slip between reporters in the crush of bodies. She had no idea where she was headed. Just…away.

"You're Fitz Colton's daughter, aren't you?" a reporter asked, shoving a microphone under her nose. "Do you have a comment on your father's arrest?"

"Uhh, no," she stammered.

Another journalist closed in on her. "Hey, aren't you the forensics chick for the Braxville Police?" To the first reporter, the second one said, "She's Fitz Colton's kid, you say?"

Both journalists turned on her. "You investigated your own father? Proved he's a murderer? How does he feel about that?"

"No comment."

"Hey, guys! Colton's own daughter is the one who put him in jail for the double murders! This is her!"

And it was on. The press corps mobbed her, hemming her in so tightly she couldn't move and could barely breathe. Lights glared in her eyes, microphones were shoved in her face and a cacophony of voices shouted in her ears until she couldn't make out anything anyone said. Which was probably just as well.

She put her head down and did her puny best to push through the crowd, but to no avail. She might as well have been standing in a cage made of arms and elbows and microphone wires.

The panic from before magnified until she was breathing so fast and shallow she started to see black spots and feel lightheaded. The questions and accusations bombarded her mercilessly, and she felt as if she was drowning. An urge to shout for help nearly overcame her.

How could Reese have done this to her? Heck, to her family and her father? It was wrong on so many levels. Fitz didn't kill those two people. Of that, she was completely convinced. There was no evidence whatsoever to tie him to the murders. He wasn't the one who'd fled town when the bodies were uncovered. Nope, that had been his partner, Markus Dexter.

As for her, she totally wasn't so dumb as to process the evidence in a case against her own father like these reporters were accusing her of doing. She knew better than that. She'd mailed all the important evidence having to do with the Harrison-Crane murders to other labs to process. She only catalogued evidence as it came in and then figured out what tests to run and where to send it. It was Forensics 101. Never create even the appearance of a conflict of interest.

However, she also knew that, having been identified as a Colton, her only choice was to say nothing—nothing—to the press. Her professional reputation, her entire career really, rode on her keeping her mouth shut right now.

She looked around frantically for help in escaping the aggressive attention of the journalists, and saw Reese step down off the dais at the front of the room. He plunged into the crowd, and it looked for all the world like he was headed straight at her.

He might be able to help her get out of here, but he was the *last* person she wanted to see. She made a right turn and hooked her arm around the smallest journalist she could find, urgently pushing the woman aside. Must get away from Reese. But fleeing him in this mob was like swimming in peanut butter for all the progress she made.

Without warning, a hand gripped her elbow and she

turned sharply to give Reese Carpenter a piece of her mind over his ambush of her father, hack, her whole family. Except it wasn't Reese.

The man before her was older than Reese, a bit taller, with brown eyes and dark blonde hair. In great physical shape for a man in his fifties, this man held himself crisply upright.

"Oh! Uncle Shep," she blurted. "When did you get here? And why are you here?"

Quickly he led her toward the back of the building, away from the crowd of reporters. "I got here in time to catch the end of the press conference. And as for why I'm here, it's to lend moral support to my brother and my favorite niece. Are you okay, Yvie?"

"No, actually. I'm not."

The former navy officer and Fitz's younger brother wrapped her up in a big, warm hug that was exactly what she needed right now. His cashmere coat was soft against her cheek and warm from the heat of his body.

"It's all wrong," she mumbled against his chest. "He didn't do it."

"I know, kiddo. My brother may be a giant jerk at times, but he's no killer. Of course, you're in a position to help prove that. Is there anything I can do for you? Bring you food? Take you out for a coffee? Slip you out the back and get you away from this zoo?"

She looked up at her uncle gratefully. Over the years, he'd had a way of always being there for her when she needed him. Even though his navy career had taken him all over the world, he'd stayed in contact with her, calling her from ships to tell her stories of the exotic ports he'd seen. Now and then she randomly got a package in the mail from him with some pretty trinket from far away.

He'd been good to all his nieces and nephews, but the bond between the two of them had always been special.

When the triplets took up all the oxygen in the house, and quiet Yvie had been mostly ignored, he'd come home on leave and taken her to Kansas City on a special adventure, just the two of them. They'd gone to a baseball game, visited a museum and he'd even taken her to high tea in a fancy restaurant. He'd been the one who'd seen her when everyone else did not.

He'd made it home when she broke her leg falling off a horse when she was thirteen. He'd coaxed her back into the saddle by riding behind her and holding her in his arms until she wasn't afraid anymore. He'd taught her how to drive the car whose keys her father had carelessly tossed across the breakfast table and then left for work when she turned sixteen.

Uncle Shep had even been there for her senior prom. He'd walked her down the stairs from her room and sent her off with a kiss on the cheek and a whisper about how beautiful she was and how proud he was of her. Fitz had worked late that night.

She smiled up at her uncle in gratitude. "Thanks for always being here for me when I need you most. You're the best."

He responded as he always did, "Nope, that's you. You're the best."

They traded fond smiles.

"Where are you off to now, Yvie?"

"Down the rear stairwell."

"Not the parking lot to get away from the jackals?" he asked as he eyed the wall of bodies in the front lobby.

"I'm swamped with work in the lab. And a bunch of it pertains to the murder cases."

"Fair enough. Go prove Fitz's innocence. The whole

family's getting together for supper tonight, though. You'll be there, right?"

Gee. This was the first she'd heard of it. Talk about feeling left out.

"Yeah. Sure," she answered dejectedly.

Just what she needed. To be interrogated by the entire Colton clan about what evidence the police had on Fitz. Especially since she couldn't talk about it any more than Reese had been able to. Maybe Jordana would back her up if the whole gang came at her hard.

Shep gave her one last hug. "You head on down to your lab and I'll run interference up here so nobody follows you."

"I love you so much, Uncle Shep."

His eyes brimmed with warmth. "I love you, too, Yvette. I'm so proud of you. Now, scoot. I see a few reporters straggling this way."

"Bye." She turned and made a beeline for her lab.

She made it inside and leaned her back against the door while she caught her breath. Safe.

Well, not entirely safe.

As sure as she was standing here, Reese was going to try to barge in here and talk to her about her father's arrest. She had nothing to say to him, however.

Not only was it a gross miscarriage of justice, but he'd gone behind her back. As the department's forensic scientist, that offended her, and as the woman he was allegedly dating, it infuriated and hurt her in about equal measures.

As a deep sense of betrayal set in, so did certainty that she never wanted to see him again.

To that end, she locked the lab door from the inside and scrunched a towel along the bottom of the door so no light would shine out into the hallway. There. Now maybe everyone, especially Reese, would think she'd gone home for the day. Just maybe she could work in peace.

She turned around to face the tall shelves stuffed with evidence from the original Dexter house search, the boxes of files from the man's office, and that cursed puzzle box taunting her on her desk. Somewhere in that mountain of evidence, there had to be something to prove Dexter had killed Olivia Harrison and Fenton Crane.

Sheesh. Now she was doing exactly what she'd accused Reese of—deciding who the killer was and then looking for evidence to prove it.

She was a scientist. Dispassionate. Factual.

Let the evidence speak for itself.

Deep breath.

She strode over to her desk, determined to open the puzzle box today or just resort to smashing the thing.

It took about an hour, but at long last, a flat wood panel slid to the side, and a small black-velvet-lined compartment in the middle of the box was revealed. Nestled inside it was a metal key. After photographing it and donning latex gloves, she picked it up and turned it over, looking for any identifying marks. Nothing. It was just a key.

But to what?

Obviously, it was important, or at least secret, for one of the Dexters to have gone to all this trouble to hide it. She couldn't rule out the wife having hidden this key, but it was much more in keeping with Markus Dexter's character to carefully hide a secret key.

First things first. She dusted the key for fingerprints and lifted a partial of what looked like a thumbprint. It was a nice, clean print, though, and had enough arches, loops and whorls that she ought to be able to make a positive match with it.

She pulled out the sample prints of both Markus and Mary Dexter. It took her under a minute to verify that the partial print was Markus's. Yep. That was his key… to something.

She made a wax impression of it and then bagged and tagged the key as evidence. Meticulously, she wrote out the steps she'd used to open the puzzle box. That done, she reassembled, bagged and tagged the box. It was too big to fit in the safe she used for valuable evidence, but she did put the key in the safe.

Time to dig into the evidence collected from the Dexter house search. The first bag she opened contained a men's wooden hairbrush with black bristles. Gray hairs threaded through them. Given that Mary Dexter was blonde, it was a good bet the gray hairs were Markus's.

He hadn't given a DNA reference sample before he skipped town, so she was pleased at the prospect of getting one now. If any old DNA evidence was found on the bodies, they could compare it to Dexter's. Both corpses were currently being examined by a forensic archaeologist who specialized in old crime scenes.

She extracted several hairs from the brush that still had follicles attached to them and bagged them carefully. Although she was trained and qualified to process DNA, her lab in Braxville didn't have the proper DNA-sequencing equipment, let alone certification by the FBI. She boxed up the sample for shipping and quickly walked it down the hall to the mail chute. She hurried back to her lab and locked herself in once more.

It was cowardly to hide from Reese like this, but she was so mad at him right now she didn't trust herself not to punch him in the nose when she saw him. How dare he accuse her father of a crime there was *no* evidence to tie him to?

How could she have trusted him? She thought he was a good cop, an honorable man. Apparently, he was neither. Jerk. And to think, she'd been halfway to falling a little in love with the man. Last night, she'd even dreamed of them married and happy together. Gah!

She threw herself into her work with a vengeance, plowing through most of the remaining evidence from the Dexter house. The two seized laptops were both password protected, so she packed them up and mailed them off to a computer forensics lab in Chicago. Not that she expected Markus Dexter to have been dumb enough to leave behind a smoking gun on his computer. He didn't even put names in his address book. He surely wouldn't incriminate himself any other obvious way.

The five o'clock shift change started overhead with stomping boots, scraping chairs and faint voices talking and laughing. Reluctantly, she packed up for the day and headed out.

She cringed at having to face her family tonight. They would no doubt demand to know everything about the investigation of Fitz, and all she could say was that she had no idea what evidence the Braxville Police had. She prayed the clan believed her. She would hate to have them think she'd betrayed them and Fitz by trying to prove he was a killer behind his back.

She peeked out into the corridor. Clear. She literally ran for the back staircase, scurried up it and raced across the parking lot. She nearly spun out on a patch of ice in her haste to get out of the lot, but finally, she turned onto the street and breathed a sigh of relief. Lord, she hated sneaking around like this.

Debating whether or not to go home and change before heading over to her folks' place, she ultimately opted to procrastinate a little longer and change into more casual clothes. Once home, it became even harder to force herself to leave the security of her little house to go face the music. She dawdled over changing into jeans, letting down and brushing out her hair and redoing her makeup.

Eventually, the moment arrived when she could think of nothing else to do to get ready to go to her parents' house. With a sigh, she scooped up her keys and trudged out to her car.

As she approached her parents' massive estate, she caught herself slowing down more and more, well below the speed limit.

Ugh. When had she turned into such a chicken?

Since Reese Carpenter had put her in an impossible situation. That was when.

She decided that, if things got too nasty, she would claim to have an early meeting in the morning and flee the family gathering. It wasn't great as escape plans went, but it was a plan.

The entire circular drive and the concrete pad between the main house and the carriage house were crammed with cars. Oh, joy. The whole clan was here in force tonight. Her gut and her jaw both tightened.

If she was lucky, she would be able to slip into the kitchen and blend in with the crowd without anyone realizing she'd only just arrived. Goodness knew, she'd done it enough times over the years.

When she opened the back door, the smell of her mom's world-famous chili and a wall of noise assaulted her. It sounded like everyone was talking at once while crowding the huge kitchen and hanging around the massive island in the center of it.

"Hey! Look who the cat dragged in!" her brother Neil exclaimed.

Darn it. Busted. An assortment of her siblings and

their significant others stopped what they were doing to turn and stare at her. "Hey, everyone," she mumbled. "Carry on with what you were doing."

After a brief chorus of hellos, the whole gang went back to talking and laughing, and her moment in the spotlight blessedly passed. She was ridiculously relieved, but she was also perplexed. She'd fully expected to be jumped and interrogated within an inch of her life the second she showed her face. What was up with them not having anything to ask her about Fitz's arrest?

Also, everyone seemed surprisingly cheerful for a bunch who'd just found out their father had been arrested for murder.

Weird.

Her mother came over from the stove and gave her a hug. "How are you holding up, darling?" her mother asked sympathetically.

"Umm, fine. I'm just buried at work."

"I can imagine. It's not often Braxville has two big criminal investigations going at one time."

"How are you doing, Mom?"

Violet smudges under her mom's eyes gave away the strain that Lilly was operating under. Yvette also recognized in her mom's face a certain transparent quality to the porcelain skin she'd inherited from her mother. Her skin did the same thing when she was exhausted and stressed out.

"I'm fine, sweetheart."

"Are you sure? No offense, but you look tired."

"It's been a little rough. But all bad things pass eventually."

"How can you say that? Dad was just arrested for murder!"

"Fitz texted to say he'll be here any minute. He'll explain what's going on."

"Fitz is coming?"

"Yes, dear. He's out on bail."

The whole idea of her father having to be out on bail for anything set Yvette's teeth on edge.

"Talk to him when he gets here, honey. He has already spoken with the other children, but nobody could find you this afternoon and you weren't answering your phone."

"I had a lot of work to do," she mumbled.

"I'll let him explain."

Yvette frowned. That was an unusual undertone of steel in her gentle mother's voice. Great. What had her dad done now? Fitz and Lilly had been on precarious marriage footing more than once over the years, usually because Fitz was being an ass. Most of the time it had to do with him ignoring Lilly and/or the kids and choosing his company over his family.

The second-to-last person on earth she wanted to talk to right now was her father. Tonight's gathering was obviously going to be a casual affair as evidenced by the big pot of chili on the stove, a huge pan of baked potatoes on the counter and a buffet of stuffed-baked-potato fixings in bowls beside that. Because it was a work night, family members would undoubtedly come and go based on their work schedules.

But apparently, everyone would be expected to stick around at least until Fitz arrived. He was the patriarch of the whole clan, after all.

Yvette had just finished eating a stuffed spud and was rinsing her plate in the sink when the kitchen door opened on a gust of freezing-cold air. Two men burst inside and she turned around to greet her fath—

Reese. What on God's green earth was he doing here? He wasn't family! And he certainly wasn't welcome here the very same day he'd arrested the head of the family for a crime he didn't commit!

"Hey, shortcake," Fitz said casually, giving her and the wet plate a perfunctory hug before stepping around her to grab a plate of his own and load it up. He added, "Eat up, Reese. There's plenty of food."

Yvette moved over to Reese's side and muttered angrily, "You have some gall, showing your face around here."

Surprisingly, it was her father who responded. "Take your foot off the accelerator, there, 'Vette. Reese gave me a ride home from the police station. Least we can do is feed the boy by way of thanks."

Thanks? *Thanks?* Her father didn't owe Reese Carpenter thanks for anything!

Reese murmured to her father and she caught part of what he said. "…looks like she wants to kill me… should go…"

"Gimme a second to talk her down off the bridge and get a bite to eat. Then I'll take you up on that ride to the airport you offered."

What ride to the airport? And how was it her father managed to sound so condescending to her all the darned time? Sometimes, she got really tired of being treated like she was twelve years old around here. She turned away from both men with a huff and stomped out of the kitchen. Her father might have just told her in not so many words to cool her jets, but it didn't mean she had to stay in the same room with a Judas.

"Wait up, 'Vette."

God, she hated it when he called her that. She was neither a retired soldier nor a car. She stopped in the hallway without turning around to face her father.

He stepped into her field of vision and she looked up

at him reluctantly. He was a big man, and she was the only one of her siblings who'd inherited nearly none of his features. They all teased her about being made of the leftovers after the rest of them were created.

"Before you go off half-cocked, there's something you need to know," he declared.

"What's that?"

"As part of my plea deal, I agreed to participate in a sham arrest. The cops are hoping to draw out Dex. If he thinks I'm being charged with the murders, maybe he'll come out of hiding."

"You…they…what?"

"That whole business of me being arrested for the murders was an act. The press conference was a setup. I'm as eager as the next guy to see that bastard partner of mine's sorry ass behind bars, so I agreed to help. Your mom knew in advance, but the cops wanted to be sure the rest of the family reacted in genuine surprise this morning."

"Did Jordana know? She's a cop."

"Nope. Nobody but me, your mom, the district attorney and Reese. Oh, and my lawyer, of course."

"Of course," she echoed dryly.

But Reese had known. And he hadn't said a thing about it to her. He'd let her go into that press conference and get blindsided, and then get jumped by a pack of rabid reporters. Her family had turned on her, her police colleagues had turned on her and he'd abandoned her to face all of their silent blame alone.

As if his casual pronouncement explained everything and made it A-OK, Fitz turned away from her and headed toward the stairs. "I'll be down in a sec, Reese. I'm already packed."

Packed to go where? Why now, in the middle off all

these messes involving his precious company? What business could possibly be more important than being here in Braxville to support his family? All of her siblings were involved in the events of the past six months at Colton Construction in one way or another.

She looked over at Reese and asked tightly, "Where's he going?"

"The airport."

She huffed. "And flying to *where*?"

"I didn't ask."

"Are you lying to me?" she snapped.

"No!"

"Why should I believe you?"

"I've never lied to you, Yvie."

"Hah! You sure as heck didn't tell me about this morning's circus."

"That's not lying. That's omitting telling you something. And I did suggest there might be press present when he turned himself in."

"Same difference." She drew breath to lay into him more, but Fitz came downstairs just then carrying two big suitcases. As in *big*. The kind of bags a person could live out of for weeks or months.

Lilly rounded the corner form the kitchen and asked Fitz coldly, "Do you have everything you wanted from the house?"

"I left instructions with my assistant on where to ship the boxes in my closet."

"Fine." Lilly turned and left, her expression as icy as Yvette had ever seen it.

What on earth?

She stared back and forth between Fitz and Reese. "What am I missing? What's going on?"

Fitz answered lightly, "Oh. That. Your mother and I are getting a divorce."

"A…*what*?"

"Your mom will explain. I have to go. Don't want to miss my flight. Reese? You ready to roll?"

Reese took a step toward her. "Is there a time soon when you and I can talk?"

She looked up at him frigidly. "I have nothing to say to you."

He winced fractionally but replied evenly enough, "Fair. But I have things to say to you."

"Like what?" she snapped.

"Not here. Not now. Be with your family tonight. Tomorrow is soon enough for what I have to say."

Hah. As if.

Reese sighed and grabbed one of Fitz's big suitcases. He didn't make eye contact with her again. Fleeing the scene of the crime, was he? Along with her coward of a father? She was so speechless with shock she just stood there as the two men strode down the hall and out the back door.

The door closed, leaving behind only the distant din of her family talking and laughing as if nothing had happened. As if her family had not just imploded before her eyes.

Her feet felt like blocks of wood as she stumbled into the kitchen. Her mother and Jordana were standing side by side at the sink, rinsing dishes and loading them in the dishwasher.

"Mom?" Yvette asked in a small voice. "Dad just told me. Are you okay?"

Lilly turned around and dried her hands on a dish towel, leaning a tired hip on the counter. "I'll be fine, darling. Really."

"But—" she rushed forward and wrapped her arms around her mother's waist, hugging her tightly. Still slender and athletic, her mother felt strong. Stronger than she'd expected. In fact, it ended up being her mother hugging and comforting her and not the other way around.

When the shock abated enough for Yvette to think again, she leaned back to stare up at Lilly. "What happened? Was it the arsenic thing and the murder thing?"

"Oh, honey. It's been building for a lot longer than that. Years. Decades, really. Maybe since even before the triplets came along. Your father always loved work more than family. He has never been…emotionally available. I stayed in the marriage for you kids. And to be honest, because it was more convenient to stay than to go. But in the past six months, the situation has changed."

"So, it *was* the investigations and the bodies?" Yvette pressed.

"Not exactly." Lilly continued, her voice tightening, "I did agree to stand by your father through the arsenic investigation. His attorney felt strongly that a show of family unity would be important in gaining enough public sympathy for Fitz to avoid going to jail. But now that the whole fiasco is concluded, I'm free to move on. And that's exactly what I plan to do."

Yvette studied Lilly intently. Her mother looked almost transparent she was stretched so thin. She stepped forward once more to embrace her mother. "Oh, Mom. I'm so sorry."

Lilly accepted the hug but turned away soon enough, her eyes suspiciously moist, and left the kitchen.

"Way to go, Yvette," Jordana muttered, hurrying after Lilly.

She stood alone in the kitchen feeling like a heel for making her mom cry. She'd been trying to comfort Lilly.

But as usual, she'd zigged when she should have zagged with her family. She purely sucked at being a Colton.

"Hey, kiddo. Why the long face?"

Uncle Shep. On cue. There to look out for her when no one else saw her.

"Oh, Uncle Shep. Mom just told me about the divorce. You do know that just because your brother is divorcing my mom, you'll still always be family, right?"

He smiled crookedly at her. "You always did have a giant heart. Don't worry about me. I'll be fine. I'm just worried about your mother. She's been through so much…"

She reached out and gave Shep's hands a squeeze. "You'll be there for her, won't you?"

"If she'll let me."

"She loves you to death. Of course, she'll let you," Yvette assured him.

A strange look flashed through her uncle's dark brown eyes. She couldn't tell if it was hope or something else altogether, more akin to chagrin. "Go be with your mom and your brothers and sisters. I'm going to head back to the carriage house and not intrude tonight."

"But—"

He turned her by the shoulders and gave her a little push toward the living room. "Go."

Chapter Eleven

Saturday morning dawned gray and damp, the clouds low and pregnant with snow. The forecast was for more snow, and possibly lots of it, starting in late morning. Perfect. She could get to the lab, hunker down, and as the weather deteriorated, nobody would be dropping by to bother her. Nobody, as in Reese.

She finished going through the evidence collected from the Dexter house without finding a single thing of interest, let alone anything that pointed at Markus Dexter as a murderer. But it wasn't as if the guy was going to keep around the blunt object he'd killed two people with after all these years.

She continued working on cracking the codes he'd used for his address books and managed to decipher about half of them. It was clear the man had a thriving nightlife. An almost continuous string of initials dotted his evenings, many with late-night meeting times beside them. How could his wife have had no idea he was going out so much to meet other women?

She ate the lunch she'd packed for herself and finished up her final report on the arsenic investigation in the afternoon. Her final findings were moot now that the plea deal with her father was complete, and she could've just written up a few paragraphs and called it good. But she finished the job to the best of her ability anyway. She'd always believed any job worth doing was worth doing well.

Ugh. She was starting to act like Reese. His persnickety procedures were rubbing off on her. She corrected herself: she'd been careful and professional long before he'd come along and tried to tell her how to do her job, thank you very much.

At long last, the two big work tables in her lab were cleared off. All the Dexter evidence was sorted, labeled, cataloged and shelved. The samples from the arsenic investigation were analyzed and packed up, and she was even done with the massive collection of files from Dexter's office. Well satisfied that order had finally been restored in her lab and in her life, she closed up shop, turned off the computers and lights and headed home.

She was surprised to realize it was nearly eight at night and that close to a foot of snow had fallen since this morning. Man. Kansas was really getting clobbered this winter. More snow was falling lazily now, thick enough to be pretty but not a blizzard.

The parking lot was blanketed in a thick layer of white, and her little car looked like an overfrosted cupcake with mounds of snow on the hood and roof. She wasn't even going to be able to start it and defrost the windows until she cleared the snow away from her tailpipe.

She trudged around the back of her car and bent down to start pulling snow away from her car's exhaust with her mittened hands.

The shadow came at her fast, a flash of black out of the corner of her eye, barreling at her in snow-muffled silence. She started to turn. Started to fling up her hands. Started to shout. But the attacker was on her too fast, tackling her hard and driving her to the ground.

It turned out that the snow wasn't thick enough to

cushion her from slamming hard into the pavement beneath. Her shoulder hit hard and her head snapped to the side, slamming into the concrete with enough force to make her jaw ache from the impact.

She saw stars, dazed.

The weight on top of her was massive, and she tried to draw a breath, but nothing happened. Her diaphragm was paralyzed, the breath knocked out of her. Panic shot through her as she sucked ineffectively at the cold air. The stars turned into bright lights before her eyes and then narrowed down to a gray tunnel.

"Bitch," a male voice snarled.

She vaguely saw something dark and long—an arm maybe—lift up over her and then swing down fast toward her face. She managed to turn her face away from the blow, but the impact caught her over her ear on the left side of the head.

The explosion of pain inside her skull was absolutely excruciating. So that was what it felt like to have her head split open like a melon.

Blackness rushed toward her. Blessed oblivion, and she embraced it. Anything to escape the spearing agony roaring through her head.

And then there was only darkness and silence.

REESE STRAIGHTENED UP, leaning on the snow shovel for a second to catch his breath. The streetlights cast soft pink circles of light, and the heavy blanket of white lit the night with a soft glow that was beautiful and quiet. He loved the silence of a good snowfall.

He'd already finished shoveling his driveway and that of his neighbor across the road, an elderly widow. He'd just made a quick run across his driveway again with the shovel to push aside the inch of snow that had fallen while he was working on Mrs. Weintraub's drive. He went on call at midnight and needed to be able to get his truck out of his garage by then.

The vigorous exercise had helped work off some of his frustration at Yvie for being unreasonable last night. He reminded himself that she had good reason to be mad at him for not telling her about the sham press conference. He really wished he could have been the one to tell her it had all been an act. Fitz hadn't been exactly gentle or sensitive about breaking that news to her. But it was what it was. All he could do now was get her to listen to his sincere apology and do everything in his power to make it up to her until she forgave him.

It didn't help matters that her old man had sprung the news of his divorce from Lilly on her like that, either. He really wished he could've been there to comfort Yvette last night, but she wanted nothing to do with him at the moment.

It looked like the snow was letting up a little. He hoped Yvie was okay, that she'd remembered to go shopping and lay in groceries before this storm hit. The forecast was for as much as a couple of feet of snow, all told. The town was going to be completely snowed in soon—assuming it wasn't already.

He was tempted to run by her place to check on her, but she'd been so mad at him last night he figured he'd better give her a day or two to cool off before he tried to reason with her. A passionate woman, she was.

That, and he suspected some of her ire last night was directed at her father and not actually at him. He probably ought to let her sort that out on her own. One thing he knew, though. Unlike her old man, he was not about to abandon her.

He'd never liked Fitz Colton much—the guy had strutted around acting all self-important and as if he was the sole benefactor of the entire town for as long as Reese could remember. Granted, Colton Construction had provided a lot of jobs over the years. But that didn't make Fitz some kind of hero to Braxville.

This latest move of Fitz's, though—divorcing his wife and leaving his family to face the fallout of his screw-ups—that was massively selfish. A serious jerk move.

How was Yvette even his daughter? She was nothing at all like him—

His phone vibrated inside his coat. Crud. The department wasn't so overwhelmed that it was already having to call him in, was it? It was barely nine o'clock.

He pulled out his phone and stared at the caller ID in a combination of shock and profound relief. Yvette was calling. Thank goodness.

"Hey, Yvie. I'm so glad you called—"

"It's not Yvette. This is Lilly Colton. Is this Detective Carpenter?"

Alarm slammed into him. Why was Yvette's mother using Yvie's phone? Something bad had happened, as sure as he was standing here. Oh, God. Not Yvie.

"Yes. This is Detective Carpenter. What's wrong?" he asked sharply. "Why are you calling me on Yvette's phone? Where are you? *Where is she?*"

"I'm at the hospital. Yvette was brought in a little while ago. You might want to come down here."

He was already sprinting for his garage, slipping and sliding on the fine sheen of snow left over from shoveling the drive. "What happened? Is she okay? How bad is it?"

"We don't know much. She's unconscious. She appears to have suffered blows to her head."

Blows, plural? What the hell? His detective radar fired off hard. Had she been *attacked*? An image of Olivia

Harrison's desiccated body flashed into his head, the entire back of her skull bashed in. And that was when the panic hit him. He asked with faint hope, "Did she fall?"

Lilly's voice lowered, and it sounded as if she was cupping her hand around the phone. "The ER doc thinks someone hit her. That's why I'm asking you to come down here. I think maybe the police should get involved."

He leaped into his truck and it roared to life. "I'll be there in fifteen minutes. I'm already pulling out of my driveway."

"Then hang up and drive carefully. I'll meet you in the ER waiting room and take you back."

The strain in Lilly's voice was palpable. It was bad, indeed, if an experienced nurse like her was that freaked out.

It was all he could do not to floor the gas pedal as he made his way across town to the hospital. Only the deep snow and impaired visibility held him even close to the speed limit.

Yvie attacked? By whom? Where? How? How bad was it? Unlike in television, he knew that most people regained consciousness relatively quickly after being knocked out. But she'd been out long enough to be found and brought to the hospital. And she was still unconscious. That was not good. Not good at all.

Hang on, Yvie. Don't you die on me. And then he started praying.

He parked outside the hospital and ran, slipping and sliding, to the emergency room. When he burst through the doors, he immediately spotted Lilly waiting by the double doors leading to the examining rooms. Without a word, she turned and swiped her identification card to unlock the doors.

He followed her swiftly down a hallway to a small

room full of quietly beeping monitors. In a bed in the middle of all kinds of equipment lay Yvie, small and pale, covered in tubes and electrodes.

His heart literally skipped a beat. If there was any way he could trade places with her right now, he'd do it in an instant.

"What's her condition?" he asked low.

"Guarded. She's going down for an MRI in a few minutes to check for swelling or—" Lilly took a deep breath, "—or brain damage."

"What happened? What do you know?"

"Someone found her unconscious in the police parking lot, lying on the ground behind her car. It appeared she'd been digging out her tailpipe. There were, umm, tracks in the snow. I gather it looked there might have been a scuffle. An ambulance was called. She was dangerously chilled when she got here, and the officer who found her said there was snow accumulating on her coat. So, she might have been there for a while before someone found her."

His pulse was racing faster and faster as Lilly spoke and he had to talk around a lump in his throat when he asked, "Is she warmed up, now?"

"Yes. They put an electric blanket on her in the ambulance, and we've got one on her now." Lilly glanced at one of the monitors. "Her body temperature is almost back up to normal."

His impulse was to reach out and take Yvette's hand, which lay limply outside the covers with a clip over her index finger, but right now Yvette needed him to be a cop, first.

He squeezed his eyes shut for a second and then asked briskly, "You said she had been hit in the head?"

"Yes. There's a small bump on the right side of her

head, here. It's consistent with a fall." Lilly pointed out the bump visible under Yvette's still damp hair.

He nodded.

"And then there's this much larger bump on the left side of her head, over her ear. It's elongated and consistent with her having been struck by—" Lilly's voice cracked, and she paused for a moment before continuing in an admirably professional tone, "—consistent with a blunt object like a club or a pipe."

He swore under his breath. "Right. Do you mind if I take a few photographs of the wounds?"

"Not at all. It's why I called you down here, Reese. Somebody attacked my baby."

He paused in the act of taking out his phone to wrap his arms around Lilly in a brief, hard hug. "I'll find out who did this to her." She shuddered in his arms for a moment, then took a deep breath and stepped back, smiling bravely at him.

"Thank you," she murmured. "It has been a rough week."

"Yeah. You've been through it, haven't you? I'm sorry about everything that's happened, Mrs. Colton."

"Please. Call me Lilly."

"Lilly. Call me Reese."

They traded brief smiles, and then he turned to the business of documenting Yvette's injuries. He mentally girded himself and asked, "Are there any other injuries?"

"Minor scrapes on the right side of her face, but that's it. Nothing else."

He let out the breath he'd been holding. Thank God. She hadn't been sexually assaulted. "Was anything taken? Her purse? Her car?"

"I don't know. She didn't have her purse on her when they wheeled her in. I don't know if it was left behind in the parking lot. I found her cell phone in the pocket of her jeans."

He reached for his phone to make a call, but another nurse came into the room just then. "We're ready to take her down for the MRI. Do you want to come with her, Lilly?"

"Of course." Lilly looked up at him apologetically. "You won't be able to come with us. Do you mind waiting in the lobby?"

"How long will the MRI take?"

"About an hour, all told."

"I think I'll run over to the police station, but I'll try to be back by the time she gets out. Call me if there's any change in her status. *Any* change. And if she wakes up, I want to know immediately."

Lilly nodded, already unhooking monitors and helping the other nurse prepare Yvette to move. He stood back watching helplessly. He hated not being able to do anything to help, but he was completely out of his element here.

Lilly and the other nurse wheeled Yvie's bed out of the room and headed off down the hall quickly. He had a lot to do in the next hour, so he hurried out, determined to be back by the time Yvette's MRI was finished.

He headed for the police station and didn't have to ask where Yvette was found, because several cops were in the parking lot, using bright flashlights to examine the ground behind Yvette's car. The area was already taped off, and he noted with approval that the police were staying outside the taped area to conduct their search.

"Howdy, guys," he said tersely. "What have we got?"

Joe Brennan came over to join him. "Hey. Did you hear what happened to Yvette Colton?"

"Yeah. I just came from the hospital."

"How's she doing, man?"

"Still unconscious. They're doing an MRI now to check for swelling or bleeding in her brain."

The other cop swore. Police in general took it hard when one of their own went down.

"What happened? Who found her?" Reese asked.

"I did," Brennan answered. "I came out to my SUV because I forgot the sandwich my wife packed, and I saw a big pile in the snow behind Yvette Colton's car. It looked weird, so I went over to check it out. And it turned out to be her. She was covered in about an inch of snow and out cold. I called for an ambulance and then carried her inside."

"What was her condition then?" Reese asked tersely.

"She was a freaking popsicle and bleeding from a gash in the side of her head. Her pulse was thready. I yelled for some guys and they brought blankets and we lay down on either side of her. Made a human sandwich to try to warm her up."

"It looked like that gash was more than just a fall, so I went ahead and taped off the area behind her car as a potential crime scene, and then I dragged Eric's ass out here to help me take some pictures of the tracks and the blood and look for any evidence."

"Find anything?" Reese asked.

"No sign of a weapon. But I've got a good blood-splatter pattern on the rear fender of her car. Looks to me like some asshole hit her with a short object."

"Did you find her purse?"

"No. Does she usually carry one?"

Reese nodded. "It's pink. With little leather butterflies on the flappie thing and butterflies going up the shoulder strap." He held his hands about eight inches apart. "It's about that big."

"Haven't found it. Her car's still locked but we looked in the windows. Didn't see it there, either. Maybe she left it in the lab?"

"I'll run in and check. Thanks for being on top of all of this. And thanks for taking care of her, Joe."

"She's one of us," the cop intoned grimly.

Reese catalogued pleasure that the guy counted Yvette as a full-fledged member of the department, but his overriding emotion was panic. Yvette had been attacked and left to freeze out here. Had Joe not happened to stumble upon her, who knew how long she'd have lain out here. Would she have frozen to death before someone found her?

A cold, hard kernel of fury formed in his gut. He was going to find her attacker and by God make whoever it was pay for doing this to her.

He jogged down the stairs to the basement and spied the open door to the forensics lab as soon as he reached the long hallway. He swore under his breath and unsnapped the holster holding his pistol under his left armpit. Approaching the lab carefully, he stood to one side of the door and shoved it wide open.

No movement.

He spun inside low, reaching for the light switch and throwing the lights on.

Ho. Lee. Cow.

The entire crime lab was in shambles, ransacked from top to bottom. He scanned it quickly for any sign of movement. Nothing.

Moving as fast as he could among the wreckage, he made a circuit around the room, clearing it. Nobody was hiding in here. Without touching anything, he backed out of the room and pulled out his cell phone.

"Hey, Joe, it's Reese. Looks like Yvette's lab has been

broken into. I need you to come down here and tape it off as a second crime scene."

He examined the door carefully, paying close attention to the lock and card scanner outside the door. There were no signs of tampering or violence against the locks. Then how did the intruder get in—

Of course. Yvette's ID card. It would have been in her purse. Her missing purse. The assailant mugged her in the parking lot, knocked her out, stole her ID and came in here looking for something. But what?

They would have to do a complete inventory of the lab and figure out what, if anything was missing. But later. Now that he knew Joe Brennan had things well in hand here, he needed to get back to the hospital.

Joe arrived with a fat roll of yellow crime-scene tape and glanced in the lab. The guy whistled. "Wow. That's a right royal mess. I assume Ms. Colton didn't leave it that way?"

Reese laughed reluctantly. "She's as big a neat freak as I am."

"Damn. That bad, huh?"

"Tape it off. Don't let anyone in. The whole lab's gonna have to be inventoried to see if anything's missing."

"This what her attacker was up to, you think? Robbing her lab?"

"Looks that way."

"She keep anything in here like medications or controlled substances?" Brennan asked.

"Nope. Anything like that would be checked into the evidence locker." Which was upstairs and untouched.

"Want me to get started cataloguing the damage in there?" Brennan asked.

"If you don't mind. I'm going to head back to the hospital and wait for Yvie to wake up and give me a statement."

"Give her my best," Joe called after him as he spun away and hurried toward the stairs.

He only prayed she woke up to receive the well-wishes of her colleagues. Afraid like he couldn't ever remember being afraid, he headed back toward the hospital and Yvette.

Chapter Twelve

Yvette might have faded out in blackness, but she faded back into featureless, blindingly bright white light. Loud, pounding noises echoed all around her until her head literally felt like it was splitting in two. So excruciating was the pain that she willed herself to fade back out into blessed oblivion.

The next time she regained consciousness, it was quiet with only a faint, steady beeping noise to interrupt the deep silence. Her eyes fluttered open, and she was lying semiupright in a dim room. It looked like a hotel at first glance, but then the IV tower beside her with a tube leading to the back of her wrist registered.

Hospital.

Ahh.

She was cold. Was there another blanket? She told her hands to reach down to her thighs to check, but they only lifted weakly and fell back to her sides.

Something big and dark moved swiftly out of the shadows, startling her badly. She flinched away and her head exploded into the worst headache she'd ever had the bad fortune to experience. She heard a faint moan, presumably from her own throat. But she hovered in this strange place of detachment, her body present but seemingly far away from her. All except that pulsating, daggerlike pain stabbing the backs of her eyeballs. It was all too real and present. She squeezed her eyes shut and prayed for unconsciousness again. But this time, her body didn't cooperate. She was becoming more alert, more aware of the pain in her skull by the second.

"Easy, Yvie. It's just me. I won't hurt you."

Reese. Hurt her? Of course, he wouldn't hurt her. What was he talking about?

He approached her bed, his hands held out away from his sides in what she presumed was some sort of show of no intent to harm her.

She blinked in an effort to clear her vision—her right eye was a little fuzzy—to no avail. Two of him stood in front of her. She noted idly that if there had to be two of any man, he was a good one to duplicate.

"Hey, Yvie," the twin Reeses murmured gently. "How are you feeling?"

She felt like crap on a cracker, to be honest. Weird. Her thoughts weren't reaching her mouth. There was some sort of disconnect in her brain. Or maybe this was all some strange dream. What was he doing here? How did he get here? Confusion coursed through her fuzzy thoughts.

"Do you need me to call the nurse?"

Why would she need a nurse? What was wrong with her? How did she get here? Still, the questions didn't make it out of her head into verbal speech. What was wrong with her? Why couldn't she talk? Fear blossomed in her belly as she nodded, but the pain of moving her head was so excruciating that she stopped doing it right away.

Thankfully, Reese seemed to figure out that she needed some blanks filled in and obliged. "You're in the hospital, Yvette. You're going to be fine. You've had an MRI, and there's no bleeding in your brain. They're monitoring you here overnight as a precaution to make sure no more swelling develops in your brain."

Whew. This not being able to talk thing would be scary as heck, otherwise. As it was, it was annoying as heck. Was there some swelling already? Was that why she couldn't talk?

Reese continued, "As far as we can tell, somebody jumped you in the parking lot of the police department and hit you in the head. Joe Brennan found you lying behind your car covered in snow. Your mom is here. She was on shift when you came in and has been popping in to check on you all night."

All night? What time was it? How long had she been here? Had Reese been sitting here with her the whole time? That was actually really sweet of him.

"Do you feel up to answering a few questions for me? We're trying to piece together what happened to you. Figure out who did it."

Oh. Never mind. He was here on police business. He wasn't here as a man who cared about her. This was Detective Carpenter. Disappointment coursed through her, and she felt moisture fill her eyes. Was she actually crying over Reese? Cripes. She was a mess.

He reached out gently with the pad of his thumb and wiped away a tear that escaped to track down her cheek. "You're safe, Yvie. Nobody's going to hurt you again. I promise."

He seemed to think she was afraid, but honestly, she wasn't.

"Do you remember what happened to you?" he asked with gentle insistence.

She had to give him credit. He had a decent bedside

manner while interrogating a girl. But that was all this was. He needed information from her. He leaned down over her, his blue eyes sparkling like bright sapphires, his lashes dark and long. Lord, his eyes were beautiful.

"Do you remember leaving the lab?"

She closed her eyes, thinking back. Did she remember anything about whatever had happened to land her here? An image of clean work tables came to mind. Right. She'd finally gotten through the mountain of evidence from the Dexter investigation. She recalled feeling satisfied at the cleanliness of the tabletops. She would have shut down the computers and turned off the lab equipment, then turned out the light, locked the door behind her and headed out. Although she knew what her usual routine was, she had no memory of actually doing it last night.

"Were you carrying a purse when you left the lab?" Reese asked.

She opened her eyes to look up at him. A purse? She had no idea. *Think.* She hadn't packed her lunch yesterday morning. Which meant she'd have grabbed snacks out of the machine down the hall to nibble through the day. It also meant she probably would have grabbed her cute little purse with the butterflies. Not that she had any actual memory of doing so, darn it.

As for carrying it when she left the lab, of course, she would have taken it home with her. It would've had her wallet and keys in it along with her cell phone and various other bits and pieces.

But she didn't specifically remember anything about last night after that image of the work tables. Did they find her purse in the parking lot, or had it been stolen in a mugging? Was that what this was? A mugging?

Frustration at having been the victim of a crime coursed through her. She had all the training she needed to defend herself. But she'd been mad at Reese—more interested in sneaking out of the precinct and avoiding him than in being aware of her surroundings. This was her own stupid fault.

The one thing she hated most in the whole world was feeling small and helpless. Yet here she was, lying in some dumb hospital bed because she hadn't been paying attention and someone had taken advantage of her being a complete idiot.

She was so mad at herself that the tears in her eyes welled up even more out of sheer frustration.

"Hey. Don't cry. I'm here. I won't leave your side. I'll protect you."

What? Oh. He still thought she was afraid. He didn't realize she was angry at herself. She opened her mouth to try to force words out, to explain his mistake to him, but a spill of light from the hallway made her turn her head toward the door.

Mistake. Screaming pain ripped through her skull, and she groaned wordlessly.

Her mother moved over to the bed and picked up her hand. "Hi, sweetheart. Is your head hurting a lot?"

She nodded fractionally, but even that much movement sent the bad men with knives to work on the backs of her eyeballs again. She pressed her eyes shut against the pain.

"It has been long enough that you can have another ampule of morphine. Would you like to take it now?"

For the relief of a powerful painkiller, she was willing to nod one more time. Her mother fiddled with the IV tower out of Yvette's line of sight for a moment.

"There, darling. Give that a minute or two to hit your bloodstream, and you should feel better. It may make you sleepy, though."

Yvette got the impression that the comment about her

getting sleepy was aimed more at Reese than at her. And indeed, Reese commented, "I promise I won't bother her if she falls asleep."

"Good," Lily answered tartly. "My baby needs her rest."

Amusement coursed through Yvette. Gentle Lilly turned into a mama grizzly bear when one of her kids was upset or hurt.

Reese murmured, "She's not talking at all. Is that normal?"

Lilly glanced down at her, and Yvette knew her well enough to see the worry hidden at the back of her mother's gaze. "She did take a blow on the part of her skull just where the speech center lies. If there's even the slightest swelling in that part of her brain, it could impede brain function in that area. It would explain why she may not be able to talk just yet."

Her mom must have realized Yvette was hearing that with alarm, for Lilly looked down at her and added, "Don't worry, sweetie. It's a totally temporary thing. The MRI showed no brain damage or bleeding in your brain. As soon as the anti-inflammatories in your IV kick in, you'll be talking up a storm."

"Good. We need to know what she can tell us about who did this to her as soon as possible," Reese added.

"Cool your jets, Detective. The first priority is her health. And right now, she needs to rest."

He threw up his hands in surrender, and Yvette smiled faintly as the cool relief of the morphine flowed into her bloodstream and her eyelids drifted shut.

REESE WAITED UNTIL Yvette had been asleep long enough to be sure she wasn't going to wake up again soon and then stepped out of her room. He headed down the hall to an empty seating area and pulled out his phone.

"Hey, Jordana, it's Reese."

"What's up? What time is it?"

"Umm, it's about five thirty in the morning. Sorry to call so early, but I figured your mom hasn't had a free moment to call you what with pulling a shift here at the hospital and trying to stay on top of Yvette's condition."

"What condition?" Jordana sounded a whole lot more awake all of a sudden.

He filled her in quickly and finished with, "Look. I know it's none of my business, but Yvette is feeling a little…ostracized…by all of you, right now. My impression is that she thinks you're blaming her for not catching whoever murdered the bodies in the wall and for her dad having to get arrested to try to smoke out Markus Dexter. Hell, it's possible she's blaming herself for your folks' divorce."

"That's crazy."

"Just sayin'. She could use a little Colton love."

"Got it. Thanks. I'll call in the troops."

Alarmed, he added quickly, "But not right now, eh? She just got a morphine drip and passed out. Later today will be soon enough."

"But she's gonna be okay, right?"

"According to your mom, her loss of speech is temporary until the anti-inflammatories kick in. Other than that, she appears only to have a smashing headache."

"Any leads on the mugger?"

He lowered his voice instinctively, not wanting Yvette to hear him, even though she was a full hallway away from here. "Whoever mugged her appears to have swiped her Braxville PD identification card and broken into the forensics lab. The perp totally trashed the joint."

"Anything stolen?" Jordana asked quickly.

"Nobody can tell yet. It's a war zone. We're gonna have to go through and straighten out everything and then inventory every single piece of evidence in the whole lab."

"Ugh. What a nightmare that'll be."

He grimaced. "That's an understatement."

"Okay. Well, I guess I know what I'm doing after I round up the siblings and drag them all over to the hospital to shower Yvie in TLC. I'll head over to her lab after that and have a look around. See if I can figure out if anything was taken."

"I'm sticking around the hospital in case Yvie wakes up and can talk. I'm going to need a statement from her about what happened."

Jordana's silence was just a breath too long. She knew full well he didn't need to stick around the hospital for her sister to wake up. A nurse could call him just as easily if Yvie regained the ability to speak.

"Okay, then. Call me if her condition changes?" Jordana asked lightly.

"Will do." He debated for a moment and then added, "By the way, Yvie let it slip to me that you're moving to Chicago. She felt terrible about mentioning it when she realized I didn't know yet."

"Ohmigosh," Jordana said softly. "I'm so sorry. It should have come from me. It's just that I've loved working with you so much and I hate to leave the department behind."

"Tell you what. You have my blessing to go to Chicago and make lots of beautiful babies with Clint if I have your blessing to date Yvie."

"Hah! I knew there was something going on between you two!"

"Do we have a deal?" he pressed.

"Just so long as you know I'll have your head on a platter if you break my baby sister's heart."

"I'd expect no less of you," he replied dryly.

"Deal."

He disconnected the call and pocketed his phone, shaking his head. Jordana was not kidding. She would tear him up if he ever messed up with her baby sister. He hated to think what the Colton brothers would do to him if he broke Yvie's heart.

But it was worth the risk. She captivated him in a way no other woman ever had. He was thirty-one years old for crying out loud. He'd dated enough women to know how special she was, and furthermore, to know how perfect she was for him. He would like to think he was right for her, too. His steadiness and organization seemed like a good foil for her impulsiveness and creative chaos. If nothing else, she made him laugh and was endlessly interesting to be around.

Before the siblings got wind of it, he definitely owed her an apology for not telling her about the fake arrest plan for her father. Surely, she would forgive him for that. She was a smart woman and would understand that they needed all of the Colton kids' reactions to the announcement to be genuine and unrehearsed. Television cameras caught everything, after all.

He approached her door and was startled to hear voices coming from inside Yvie's room. He stopped outside, unsure of whether or not to barge in. If it was a doctor doing an examination or something, maybe he should wait out here—

"...swear she's going to be all right?" a male voice said from inside.

"I swear. I'll take care of our little girl."

That was Lilly Colton. Had Fitz flown back from wherever he'd jetted off to when he'd heard Yvette was hurt? But how was that possible? Reese's impression was that Fitz had headed outside the United States.

"She's all I have, Lilly. I can't lose her," the man said.

Lilly answered low, "We're not going to lose her. And you have me, too."

"Thank God."

Okay, then. Obviously, Lilly Colton had known for a while that Fitz was leaving and had already moved on to a new relationship. He hoped this guy treated her like gold. The way he heard it from Jordana, Fitz valued his business above all else in the world, including his family, and definitely more than his wife.

Reese heard rustling sounds as if Lilly and the man had moved together and were embracing. Definitely not a doctor, then. Who was this mystery man? And why was Lily calling Yvette their baby girl? Reese cleared his throat loudly and gave it a few seconds before he rounded the corner.

Surprise coursed through him, and just in the nick of time, he stopped his eyebrows from sailing up. Shepherd Colton? He and Lilly Colton were a thing? Since when? He sensed family skeletons lurking in the Colton closet. Ah, well. Every family had its own secrets and scandals.

"Any change?" he asked Lilly, lifting his chin toward the bed where Yvette slumbered in morphine-induced unconsciousness.

"No. If you want to go home and get some sleep, I can have the floor nurse call you when she wakes up."

"That's okay. I'll stick around. It's urgent that I speak with her the moment she's alert enough to answer a few questions. Even if all she does is nod or shake her head yes or no."

Lilly shrugged. "It's your neck and back in a bad chair."

Except no sooner had Yvette's uncle and mother left the room than an orderly wheeled in a pretty decent recliner chair for him, saying that Lilly had asked to have it brought in. He kicked off his shoes, covered himself with the blanket the orderly had left in the chair, leaned it back and closed his eyes.

But his brain didn't shut down right away. He replayed the conversation he'd overheard between Shep Colton and Lilly. The man had called Yvette all he had, and Lilly had referred to Yvie as *our little girl*.

Was it possible? Was the uncle actually Yvette's father? It would certainly cast a new light on the recent divorce announcement between Fitz and Lilly. Not that Reese cared one way or another who'd slept with whom in the Colton family. Given his own opinion that Fitz was more of a scumbag than not, he couldn't blame Lilly for stepping out on her business-obsessed spouse.

Did Yvette know?

She'd never once hinted at anything like that, nor had Jordana.

Nah. His money was on nobody knowing that. Assuming he was even interpreting what he'd heard correctly. Thankfully, it shouldn't impact the active investigation into the twin murders in the wall of the Colton-built warehouse. The case didn't require him to tell anyone that juicy little detail about Yvette's family.

Yep. That was one secret he would happily take to the grave. No way did he want to kick the foundation of her family out from under Yvette's feet. What she didn't know about her parentage wouldn't hurt her. He only prayed he was interpreting what he'd heard all wrong.

But in his gut he knew he wasn't wrong.

He tossed and turned for a long time in search of sleep.

THE NEXT TIME Yvette woke up, stripes of diffused light came through the vertical blinds covering the window and the clock on the wall across from her bed said it was nearly ten o'clock. Based on the sun, that would be ten in the morning.

Reese was stretched out in the recliner in the corner, asleep. A blanket was draped over him, and his shoes sat on the floor beside the chair. Relaxed in sleep, his face looked younger. Less intimidating. She would have liked to get to know this Reese, the one who set aside his cop persona to relax and just be a guy. A good-looking guy with enough kindness in his heart to sit in the hospital with her.

She knew the second he woke up, though, his eyes would harden, he would don his badge and he would start in with the questions about what had happened last night.

What *did* happen? She thought back, and still was able to retrieve nothing beyond that one image of her work tables being cleared off.

She did remember details from before that, though, including taking her cute pink butterfly purse to work. It was a sure bet she'd taken it out of the lab with her. She never left her purse at work. Which seemed to indicate that she had, indeed, been robbed.

She had to give it to the mugger. It took guts to target someone coming out of the police department.

Too warm, she kicked off one of the blankets and found the remote control for her bed and the television. The pictures on the controls were self-explanatory, and she pushed the button to sit the bed more upright. The whir of the motor woke Reese, and he sat up quickly, rubbing his face.

"Good morning, Yvette. How are you feeling? Can you talk yet?"

She opened her mouth to try. "Hi," she croaked.

"She speaks!" He kicked the footrest down and padded over to the side of her bed in his socks. "I never thought I'd be glad to have a silent Colton woman commence talking at me, but dang, I'm glad you're able."

"That is the most sexist thing I've ever heard," she snapped.

He grinned. "Like I said. Welcome back, Yvette."

She scowled. "Is there a glass of water around here? My throat is parched."

"Lemme get a nurse. I don't know if you're allowed to have anything like that. I wouldn't want to do anything to harm you when we're just getting you back."

He stepped out into the hall and was back in a second. He put on his shoes, folded the blanket he'd been using and shrugged into his suit jacket. She sighed. Detective Carpenter had shown up for duty.

She said, "I took my pink purse to work yesterday. It has little butterflies all over it and going up the shoulder strap. If it wasn't on me when you found me, then it was stolen in the mugging."

He nodded briskly and pulled out his cell phone. He stepped out into the hall, presumably to call the station, while a nurse helped her go to the bathroom and return to her bed, hauling her IV tower with her.

The headache was a constant, dull ache, emanating from a line of sharp pain above her left ear. She reached up and encountered a bandage on the side of her head. "Do I have stitches?" she asked the nurse.

"They weren't necessary. But you do have butterfly bandages holding your head wound shut. If you mess with those, the doctor might put a couple of sutures in."

"Got it. No messing with the bandages."

Reese stepped back into the room still on the phone.

"Is there anything else you can remember, Yvette? Anything you can tell us about your attacker?"

"I'm sorry. I don't remember anything about it. The last thing I remember is looking at the tables in my lab and being happy they're finally clean."

Reese snorted. Whether that was directed at her or something the person on the other end of the phone said, she couldn't tell.

He finished the call and came back into the room. He asked the nurse, "Any idea when Miss Colton can be released?"

"The neurologist wants to see her later today, and assuming she's doing well then, I should think he'd send her home." The woman turned to Yvette. "Do you have a roommate? Live with someone?" The nurse cast a suggestive glance in Reese's direction.

"No, ma'am," she answered.

"Well, you can't stay alone for a while. You've had a serious concussion. You'll need someone to keep an eye on you, watch out for dangerous symptoms to develop. While you rest today, you might want to think about who you'd like to arrange to stay with you."

"That's covered," Reese said briskly. "I'll be staying with her. Or rather, she'll be staying with me at my place."

Chapter Thirteen

Yvette whipped her head around to stare at Reese, which was an exceedingly bad choice. Blinding pain ripped through her head and she had no choice but to collapse back on the soft pillow and close her eyes, breathing in short, shallow gasps until the worst of the pain passed. By the time she opened her eyes, the nurse was gone.

"I'm not staying at your house," she declared.

"Who will you be staying with, then? As I recall, all of your siblings are in relatively new romantic relationships, and you don't strike me as the type to play third wheel comfortably. Your parents are in the middle of a divorce and are stressed out to the max. By your own admission, you haven't made friends in town since you've moved back. Except for me, of course. And besides, I want to do it. I can take care of you, and I can see to it you're safe."

"But—"

"But nothing. Don't tell me you can take care of yourself."

Her mouth closed. That had, indeed, been what she'd been about to say.

"You heard the lady. You can't be alone for a while. Discussion closed. You'll stay with me. I have plenty of room, and I figure you'll get in less trouble at my house than you would in your own home."

She frowned at him, but she had to admit he was probably right.

They were saved from any more debates by the arrival of her sister Bridgette, who looked as gorgeous as always. She was a golden person, golden skin, golden hair, golden, shining personality.

"Hey, Yvette. How are you feeling?"

"Like warmed-over mush," she confessed.

"I brought you a few little things—some mascara and gloss. A little blush. Oh, and a hairbrush and a toothbrush. A girl's gotta have a little confidence to face the whole Colton clan, eh?"

"The whole clan?" she echoed in dismay.

Bridgette leaned down and murmured, "Jordana has called out the troops and ordered all of us to stop by and visit you today. Which we're glad to do, of course. You should have called last night to let us know you were here. We'd have come by then."

"I was unconscious most of last night, I'm told."

Bridgette's blue eyes, so like their mother's, widened. "Just how badly were you hurt, Yvie?"

"It's nothing. I'll be fine." The last thing she needed was to have the whole family clucking over her like a bunch of worried chickens with their feathers all fluffed out. "Please, for the love of God, call off the reinforcements."

"Too late," Ashley Hart called from the doorway. She was Neil's fiancée and fully as gorgeous as Bridgette. A socialite and philanthropist, she'd have been stunning even without the best beauty care money could buy.

Yvette groaned under her breath.

"Tyler's parking the car. He'll be in shortly," Ashley commented, breezing into the room. "And I think I saw Brooks and Neil pulling into the parking lot."

This time, Yvette didn't bother to muffle her groan.

"How's the new house coming?" Ashley asked Bridgette.

"Luke thinks it'll be done before Easter, but I'm betting it'll be at least Memorial Day before we're into it."

Tyler, the oldest and most serious of the siblings, came into the room and dropped a fond kiss on Yvette's cheek before moving to stand beside Ashley and looping his arm around her slender waist. Neil, the criminal attorney came in right behind him.

Yvette grumbled at her lawyer sibling, "Don't you have to be at court or something, Neil?"

"Nope. No big cases pending at the moment."

"Drat," she grumbled.

Everyone laughed as Brooks, one of the triplets, rounded the corner and demanded, "What did I miss?"

Yvette rolled her eyes as he came over and yanked on her big toe through the blankets.

She looked over at Neil in chagrin. "No wonder you were so hot and bothered to get out of the hospital before. I get it now."

Tyler piped up with, "Hey. At least you weren't shot, Yvie." He was fully recovered from the gunshot wound he'd suffered a few months back, thankfully.

"Nah. I was just mugged. Garden-variety crime. Nothing fancy like you," she retorted.

The conversation ebbed and flowed around her with her siblings laughing and talking about their jobs and homes and general gossip. It turned out Ty and Ashley were planning to take a vacation soon, and a spirited debate over where they should go ensued with Venice and Maui emerging as the two front-runner choices.

When the conversation lagged, Yvette commented, "Gee, it's too bad Jordana's not here to enjoy this gathering of the troops that she arranged."

"Yeah. Where is she, anyway?" Neil demanded.

As if conjured by the question, Jordana turned the corner into the room no more than a minute later. "I see everyone's here," she commented. "That's great. I have an announcement to make. I've told Mom, and Yvie already knows, but I'm moving to Chicago to be with Clint, and I'm going to open up an office there for Ty's security firm."

Exclamations and congratulations were forthcoming, and Yvette was delighted not to be the center of attention as the others focused on Jordana. It was great of her family to show up like this, but frankly, the whole Colton clan at once could be a little exhausting.

Perhaps two minutes passed with nobody else coming into her now crowded room, but then one more body filled the doorway. Reese. The gang greeted him, and he joined in to the conversation easily.

Yvette noted that he and Jordana seemed to have come to an understanding, for the two of them were relaxed and joking with each other. Thank goodness. She would have hated to put a rift between them with her thoughtless revelation of Jordana's plan to leave the force and move away.

One by one, the siblings started to drift out, citing jobs and other obligations. Jordana was the last one left. She came over to Yvette's bed and leaned down, looking concerned. "Do you have any idea at all who could've jumped you in the parking lot, sis?"

"None."

"No enemies? Disgruntled exes?"

"You have to have exes for them to be disgruntled," she retorted.

Jordana smiled but the expression didn't reach her eyes. "I'm worried about your safety, Yvie. If last night's attack is related to a case you're working on, the attacker may not have gotten what he wanted."

"Meaning what?" she asked her older sister sharply.

Jordana sighed. "He might have meant you more serious harm than this."

"Are you tiptoeing around saying the attacker might have meant to kill me?" Yvette demanded.

"Well, yes," Jordana allowed reluctantly.

"I'd already thought of that," Yvette confessed.

Reese jumped into the conversation. "Don't worry, Jordana. I'm taking her back to my place and not letting her out of my sight. I'll see to it she's safe going forward."

Jordana nodded in relief. "Call me if you need help or you need me to spell you. Yvette can be a bit of a pill, especially when she's not feeling good."

"Hey!" Yvette exclaimed. "I'm an angelic patient."

Reese and Jordana both laughed at that.

A wave of fatigue washed over her and Yvette closed her eyes.

Reese murmured to Jordana, "Yvette's looking a bit droopy. Maybe we should let her rest a bit?"

Her sister took the hint, planted a quick kiss on her cheek and left.

"Thanks for kicking her out," she murmured to him.

"I knew it meant a lot to you to have your family rally around you, but you need your rest."

For the first time since she'd come back to Braxville, she felt like she was really home. She reached up to touch the bandages on the side of her head. "It's a heck of a way to finally reconnect with my family."

He smiled gently. "Maybe you can go a while without hitting your head again? It would help my blood pressure immensely."

Worried about her, was he? Okay, that made her insides feel even warmer and squishier. "I forgot what it's like to be part of a big family. Or at least, I forgot for a while what the best part of being a Colton is."

Reese did a strange thing. He frowned for a moment. His lips parted as if he was going to say something in response to that, but then he closed his mouth and turned away. What on earth?

Without looking back at her he mumbled over his shoulder, "I'm going to arrange for a police officer to stand outside your room. Once he gets here, I have some stuff to do. But, I'll come back in a little while to check on you. Get some rest, eh?"

"Umm, yeah. Sure." What was up with him? He kept blowing hot then cold with her, and it was confusing as heck.

The door closed behind him and silence fell around her. Alone at last. Her eyes drifted shut.

She dreamed of running after Reese as he strode away from her, calling for him to come back, and him never once turning around to even look at her.

She woke with a lurch, feeling lost and alone, abandoned by everyone she loved. Startled by how powerful her reaction to some stupid dream was, she reached up with both hands to dash tears off her cheeks. Sheesh. Since when had she become so sappy and sensitive?

From the doorway, a male voice boomed, "Yvette? Are you awake?"

Well, duh. She would be now if she hadn't already been. "Hi, Dr. Jones."

"I came to have a look at you and see how you're feeling."

"I'm feeling ready to get out of here."

The doctor smiled as he shone a blindingly bright little torture device of a light in her left eye. "All my patients say that."

She responded dryly. "You mean not everybody loves being poked and prodded awake every hour on the hour around the clock?"

His grin widened. "Well, I can see your ornery wasn't hurt in your mishap."

Not hardly. She was still ticked off at herself that she hadn't had more situational awareness when she went out to her car last night. She'd been so relieved not to run into Reese that she'd forgotten everything she knew about self-defense.

Another male voice spoke from the doorway. "What's the verdict, Doc? Can she go home today?"

She peered around the physician to see Reese leaning against the door frame looking long and lean and sexier than any one man had a right to.

"She can go home if and only if she's got someone with her around the clock for the next twenty-four hours. She's going to need to be woken up every couple of hours for at least one more day—"

Yvette groaned. "You're killing me with all this interrupted sleep. Is it really necessary?"

The doctor looked down at her sternly. "You have a serious concussion. Immediately after a serious head trama, there's a risk of you falling unconscious and slipping into a coma. You have to be woken up periodically to make sure that hasn't happened."

"Oh, please. I'm fine."

Reese spoke over her. "I'll see to it she's woken every two hours like clockwork. Any other care instructions?"

"I'll send her home with painkillers and antibiotics, and I need her to stay on anti-inflammatories for at least a week to prevent any swelling in or around the brain."

"Got it," Reese said briskly.

"Complete bed rest for the next day. She can only get up to go to the restroom. After that, limited activity for another three to four days. It goes without saying that she mustn't do anything that will shake her head or move it abruptly. No sports, no vigorous activity, no exercise."

"Party pooper," she mumbled.

Reese grinned at her and she gifted him with her blackest scowl.

The doctor left the room and Reese commented, "You're so cute when you're mad."

"Did you just call me *cute*? Now, I'm going to have to kill you. As soon as I can engage in vigorous activity, you're a dead man."

His grin widened. "I can think of a few vigorous activities I'd like to engage in with—" He broke off. "Sorry. That was out of line."

Her cheeks heated up until they felt on fire. He was thinking about sleeping with her, was he? "There's still the matter of you lying to me to deal with, mister."

"Me? I've never lied to you."

"What do you call not telling me about my father's fake arrest?"

"That's an omission, not a lie. I would never lie to you. We couldn't tell any of the Colton kids about it because the cameras were there to record your reactions. They had to be real."

She huffed. "I still don't like it."

"I didn't like doing it if that makes you feel better," he said soberly.

Actually, it did. But she wasn't about to admit that to him until he groveled a little more.

"I swear, Yvette. I will never lie to you—"

The doctor stepped back into the room and Reese broke off.

The neurologist boomed, "I've had a nurse send all your prescriptions over to the drugstore. They should be ready for pickup by the time you've finished the release paperwork and you're ready to get out of here."

For a man who worked around people with head pain a lot, the guy sure was loud.

"Thank you, Doctor," she said politely. She opened her mouth to forgive Reese for not telling her about the fake arrest of her father, but a nurse came in and shooed Reese out of the room.

The woman had a clipboard and shoved it under Yvette's nose. It took a half hour to wade through a mountain of documents with print too small for any reasonably sighted human being to read, but at long last, the woman held out a large plastic bag. "Here are your clothes and personal effects. Do you want me to help you get dressed?"

"No. That's okay. I can dress myself." Just how helpless did they all think she was?

She was dressed and seated on the edge of the bed, reluctantly admitting to herself that she had the beginnings of a monster headache coming on, when Reese came around the corner into her room.

"Let's spring you from this joint," he said jauntily.

"Thank goodness." She jumped off the edge of the tall bed and knives stabbed her brain from about fifty directions at once. Whoa. She paused until the pain subsided enough for her to actually see—

A hand gripped her elbow and Reese loomed beside her. Man, that guy was fast. That, and he could read her well. He must've seen the pain on her face and jumped over to support her.

"You okay?" he asked quietly enough not to send the knives back through her skull.

"Yeah. Sure," she mumbled.

"Liar."

"Just get me out of here. I hate hospitals."

He paced himself beside her as a nurse pushed her to the elevator in a wheelchair. When it opened on the ground floor, he jogged ahead and was waiting at the exit in his truck by the time she arrived. He helped her into the cab, shut the door gently and climbed in beside her. "I promise to drive like Grandma's soup and a couple dozen crates of fresh eggs are in the back of my truck."

"Thanks," she sighed.

He navigated out of the parking lot.

"I really do appreciate everything you've done for me. If you could just take me to my car, I'll go home and stay out of your hair for the next couple of decades."

Reese's frown was immediate and intense. "Did you not listen to the doctor? You can't be alone. The only reason he let you out of there was because I agreed to look out for you."

"Which I appreciate you doing. Deeply. But I'll be fine—"

"I swear to God, Yvette. If you tell me you can take care of yourself and don't need help one more time, I'm going to shout at the top of my lungs."

"Please, no," she blurted. Her head was already pounding.

"You're coming to my house. And that's that."

"You are so stubborn."

"Pot, meet kettle," he replied dryly.

She huffed and crossed her arms, sitting back in irritation as he drove past her house—literally past it—on his way across town to his place. Oh, he was just taunting her now.

However, by the time he pulled carefully into his garage and turned off the engine, she actually felt wilted and in need of painkillers and a nap, in that order. He opened her door and she moved to get out, but he stepped forward and shocked her by scooping her up into his arms.

"Reese! What are you doing?" She flung her arms around his neck to regain her equilibrium.

"I should think it's patently obvious what I'm doing," he said, using his hip to shut the truck door, and heading for the kitchen. He leaned down a little for her to turn the doorknob and entered the house with her. Another hip check to close the kitchen door and he strode through his house to—*ohmigosh*—his bedroom, where he deposited her on his bed and left to get her meds.

His room was neat and masculine. His bed looked handmade out of logs sanded smooth. She would bet he'd built it. There was something intensely intimate about lying in it, knowing he'd made it with his own two hands.

He came back, setting down several prescription bottles with her name on them and a tall glass of water. He'd picked up her medications for her? When? He must have raced out while she was filling out the discharge paperwork and gotten them.

He reached out again to pick her up so she could pull the blankets out from underneath herself. He set her back down on the soft mattress gently. Her arms still rested around his neck, and their faces were about a foot apart. Her heart fluttered at the sexy proximity of this man.

"I'm glad you're going to be all right," he murmured. "When I got that call from Lilly that you were hurt—" Reese's voice cracked.

"I'm tougher than I look."

"You don't have to be tough for me, Yvie. I'll take care of you and keep you safe."

"You can't always be there for me."

"I can try."

Their gazes melted together, hers in gratitude and his in concern. His eyes were so blue and beautiful she could lose herself in them forever.

"Kiss me, Reese."

His lips curved up. "Thought you'd never ask."

"You were waiting for me to ask?"

His hand slipped out from behind her knees and he ran his fingers across her forehead ever so gently. "You don't seem to have had much luck with men. I didn't want to scare you off."

"And here I was, worrying that I'd scared you off."

He frowned slightly. "Why would I be scared of you?"

"I think it's safe to say I've proven I'm a bit of an accident risk."

His frown dissolved into a wry smile. "Truth. But I'm generally pretty good at anticipating trouble and heading it off."

She smiled up at him. "You obviously haven't hung out around me for long."

His mouth lowered slowly toward hers. "No, but I'm looking forward to doing so."

His lips touched hers lightly, preventing her from responding. Which was just as well. She was totally speechless. Did he just admit to wanting a long-term relationship with her?

His lips pressed against hers a little bit more firmly, and she threaded her fingers into his hair to tug him closer. He resisted, and she finally mumbled against his lips, "I won't break."

"Still. Not gonna risk hurting you," he mumbled back, stubbornly refusing to increase the pressure of the kiss.

He did take his time, however, brushing her lips with his mouth, kissing his way lightly across her cheekbone to gently nibble her right earlobe. When she was panting a little and starting to feel more than a little hot and bothered, he lowered her shoulders to the stacked pillows and straightened. Took a step back from her.

"Lord, you're tempting," he murmured.

"Then don't stop."

"Doc said no vigorous activity for a week. If I don't stop now, there are definitely going to be vigorous things going on in my bed."

"Well…hell."

He laughed down at her. "Can I get you something to eat? Maybe a drink?"

"How about a stiff shot of vodka?"

"Can't mix your pain meds with alcohol."

"You're such a buzzkill."

"That's me. The old stick-in-the-mud."

She looked up at him quickly. "You're not a stick-in-the-mud. Far from it."

"That's not what you've spent the past year telling me."

"I didn't know you for the past year."

"And you think you know me now?" he asked, sitting down on the edge of the bed.

"I'd like to think so."

"Then how can you blame me for not telling you about your father's staged arrest? Not only was I doing my job, but I'm trying to catch Markus Dexter and solve a murder. You know Gwen Harrison. It's agony for her not to know who killed her mother and if that killer is still alive. I would never do something like stage your dad's arrest just to harass your family. The Coltons have been through plenty in the past year."

She sighed. "I believe you. I was just so shocked and angry at the unfairness of the accusation I didn't stop at the time to think about why you'd have done it."

He reached out to tuck a strand of hair behind her ear. "Thank you for giving me the benefit of the doubt when you did stop to think about it."

"Don't thank me. I was trying to avoid running into you when I raced out into the parking lot last night and didn't pay attention to my surroundings."

"I'm sorry."

"You don't owe me any apology for that. I'm the one who didn't trust you. I'm sorry."

"If I accept your apology, will you agree to accept mine?"

"I guess so."

"Grudge holder, are you? Good to know," he teased.

She answered seriously, "Actually, I'm the least grudge-y of all my siblings and me."

He smiled warmly at her. "I'm glad the air is cleared between us. Now, I'm getting out of here so you can take a nap. You look exhausted."

She actually was, but she said stoutly, "I'm fine."

"Yvie." His voice was reproachful. "We've been over this before. You don't always have to be fine for me. You can show weakness or fear or sadness—or anything, really—and I won't think any less of you. I'm not your brothers. More importantly, I'm not your father."

And on that note, he turned and left the room, leaving her to stew in her own thoughts. He wasn't her father? That was an astute observation. How did he know that Fitz only seemed to value strength in his children?

Although, she supposed to meet Fitz was to recognize that about him.

She did wish her father had paid more attention to her when she was a kid. Maybe told her, or at least shown her now and then, that he loved her. She wished he'd been at least a little proud of her. Heck, Uncle Shep had told her more often that he loved her and was proud of her than Fitz ever had. Sigh.

She dumped a pain pill out of the bottle on the bed stand and swallowed it with several gulps of water from the glass. As the sweet relief washed over her, she closed her eyes and let the deep silence of Reese's cabin in the woods envelop her.

Chapter Fourteen

Reese cracked open his bedroom door to check on Yvette, but she was out cold. Good. She needed the rest. From watching her in the hospital, he knew she would likely sleep for several hours after taking one of her pain pills. He set an alarm for her next wake-up check and backed out of the doorway.

He went to his kitchen at the far end of the house and called the precinct. "Hey, Jordana. How goes the clean-up of your sister's lab?"

"Slow. The intruder really trashed the place." She added, "Oh, and speaking of which, we checked the logs, and it turns out Yvette's ID badge was used to gain access to the forensics lab."

"So the mugger knocked her out, stole her ID out of her purse and got into the lab?"

"Looks that way."

"Anything missing?" he asked.

"Yeah. That big puzzle box Yvie's been sweating over."

His partner might as well have punched him in the gut. That box again? What was so danged important about it? Or rather that key hidden inside it. "And the key?"

"It is logged into Yvie's database as being locked in

her wall safe. Which, I'm pleased to report, the robber did not break into. So, the key should still be safe in there."

That was great news. "Any luck figuring out what that key unlocks?" he asked his partner.

"Nope. I've got emails out to every bank within a three-hundred-mile radius of Wichita. If it's a safe-deposit box, someone will respond."

"Hopefully sooner rather than later."

"Nobody except Yvette or Chief Hilton knows the combination to the safe. He's at his hunting cabin this weekend, and Yvette has been unconscious, so nobody has opened the safe to verify that the key's inside."

"If her paperwork says it's there, it's there," he replied confidently.

"How's Yvie?" Jordana asked.

"Tired. In pain. Trying to be tough."

"That sounds like her. Thanks for taking care of her. I'd have volunteered to take her to my place, but it's in chaos right now."

"Why's that?"

"Packing for the move," Jordana admitted.

He frowned. "I didn't realize you were going so soon."

"If you'd found the love of your life, would you mess around for long getting to her side?"

He envisioned Yvie, pale and beautiful against his pillow when he'd left his bedroom. "Nope. I'd get her as close to me as possible and keep her right there."

"There you have it."

"Holler if you need help packing," he offered.

"You're doing plenty looking out for Yvette. That's an enormous weight off my shoulders."

He disliked the idea of Yvie being perceived as a weight of any kind to her family. She was a lovely person and independent as all get-out. She hated being a burden to anyone. But it wasn't his job to fix the Colton clan's family dynamics.

Thoughtfully, he pulled out vegetables and a pot roast and got to work making a big pot of beef stew.

Surely, Markus Dexter was the intruder who'd bowled over Yvette in the attic of the Dexter home. There'd been no sign of forced entry to the house, which indicated someone with a key had been the intruder. Of course, Yvie might have left the door unlocked when she'd entered. He would have to ask her when she woke up.

If Dexter had been the intruder who'd gone looking for the puzzle box in his own attic, it stood to reason he was also the mugger in the parking lot and thief of the box from Yvie's lab.

And, if that logic was correct, the attack in the parking lot also indicated that Dexter was not averse to violence against others. Now that he thought about it, the mugger had hit Yvette in the head…which was the same way both Olivia Harrison and Fenton Crane had died. Blunt trauma to their skulls. Was her recent attack further proof that Dexter was the killer of Harrison and Crane?

He woke Yvette at the two-hour mark after she'd gone down for her nap, disturbing her just long enough for her to mumble at him to go away.

Smiling a little, he backed out of the room to let her sleep. About supper time and almost time for another two-hour check on Yvette, headlights coming up his driveway flashed through his front windows.

Who'd driven all the way out here after dark? He wasn't expecting anyone. He shrugged into his holster and unsnapped the flap over his service weapon as the car parked in his driveway.

Standing to one side of his front window, he was startled when Lilly Colton got out of her car and headed up his sidewalk. He opened the door for her and she thrust a big deep casserole dish at him.

"What's this?" he asked. "And please come in."

"It's my world-famous banana pudding. Yvette's favorite."

"It's kind of you to think of her."

"She is my baby," Lilly said a bit tartly, sounding just like her daughter when Yvette was irritated. He grinned at the resemblance between mother and daughter.

"I'm glad someone remembers that," he retorted.

"You don't like us Coltons very much, do you?"

"I like most of you just fine. But to be brutally honest, I'm not a huge fan of your husband."

"Neither am I. That's why I'm divorcing him."

Interesting. She was divorcing him and not the other way around? "I'm sorry about that—"

She waved a brisk hand. "No condolences necessary. I should have done it years ago. I waited until all the kids were grown and settling down into their own lives. But now I wonder if I should've done it long ago and saved them having to put up with an absent father—" She broke off. "I'm sorry. You didn't ask to hear about my marital problems."

"I don't mind. You were my dad's nurse a few years back when he had a heart attack, and my family credits you with whipping him into shape and convincing him to finally take better care of his health."

She laughed a little. "Oh, dear. I hope I wasn't too hard on him."

"Not at all. You gave him exactly the kick in the pants he needed."

"Mom? I thought I heard your voice."

He whipped around to see Yvie standing in the doorway, her hair tousled, squinting at the bright light in his kitchen. "What are you doing out of bed?" he demanded.

"I'm not dead for crying out loud, and my legs aren't injured. I can walk."

Lilly threw him a commiserating look and said gently, "Sweetheart, you have a serious concussion. I'm sure Dr. Jones told you to stay in bed for several days and rest."

"I can't sleep twenty-four hours a day, Mom."

"No, but you can rest twenty-four hours a day."

"Thank you," he chimed in. "You heard your mother. Back to bed with you, Yvie. I'll bring you a bowl of *my* mother's world-famous beef stew, and if you eat all of that, you can have a bowl of *your* mom's world-famous banana pudding."

"Banana pudding?" she exclaimed, and then immediately winced. Her voice much lower, she continued, "Thank you, Mommy."

Lilly moved over to kiss her on the cheek and give her a gentle hug. "You're welcome, darling. If you need anything, you call me, okay? And, Reese, if you need a break from her, I'm happy to come over and sit with her while you escape for a bit."

"I'm not *that* awful a patient," Yvette complained.

"Then what are you doing out of bed?" he asked wryly.

"Fine. I give up. I can't fight both of you. I'll go back to bed, if just to get some peace and quiet." She called back over her shoulder as she disappeared down the hall, "And a bowl of my mom's pudding."

He took the opportunity to turn to Lilly and ask quietly, "How are you doing? I know it's none of my business, but you've really been through the ringer these past few months."

"It's kind of you to ask, and I'm surprisingly good.

I have more support than I ever knew I had, and I'm at peace with my decision to leave Fitz."

Was Shepherd Colton part of that surprise support network? He was sorely tempted to ask Lilly why she and Shep hadn't told Yvette that he was her actual father, but it was emphatically none of his business.

Lilly left quickly after that and Yvette called out that she was starving, so he put the matter of her parentage from his mind.

YVETTE HAD A SECRET. She loved sleeping in Reese's bed. Not only was it huge and comfortable, but it smelled like him. She could snuggle down under the thick comforter and feel completely surrounded by him even when he wasn't there.

He'd wanted to send a patrol car out to watch the house when he had to go in to work, but she'd argued nobody except her family knew she was out here, and she was perfectly safe by herself for a few hours. Reese hadn't liked it, but he'd eventually given in.

He made quick trips in to work after her first twenty-four hours of constant wake-ups ended, but he refused to talk about anything that was going on at the department with her. Which she took as a bad sign. He was avoiding stressing her out.

Gradually, her headache eased, and by day four it had mostly disappeared. She felt pretty good and was starting to get bored and housebound. When Reese went to the office on day five, she declared herself sick of being sick and got out of bed and dressed as soon as he left the house.

She picked the place up, raided the kitchen and discovered that he had all the ingredients for homemade spaghetti from scratch. She set to work pulling together a big pot of sauce and setting it over very low heat to simmer all day. Then, she built herself a fire in the fireplace. It was impossible not to remember the kisses they'd shared in front of it before. And yes. She wanted more.

To that end, she hunted around in his pantry and found some candles. She set the table for two and made a centerpiece of pinecones and some bright holly berries she brought inside. She stood back to observe her work. Considering that she was working within the limits of a bachelor pad to create a romantic atmosphere, she declared her efforts not bad.

She heard his truck pull into the garage, and she checked her makeup and hair in the bathroom mirror quickly. Thankfully, her mother had brought over a bag with some of her clothes and toiletries the day after she brought over the pudding.

She swept out into the living room just in time to see Reese step into the kitchen and stop cold. "What have you done? You're supposed to be resting!"

"This was restful. I'm bored to death, and cooking a nice dinner was relaxing. Think of it as therapy for me."

He hung up his coat and came over to kiss her leisurely. He confessed, "I like coming home to you like this every day. I look forward to seeing you the whole time I'm at work. Is that weird?"

"Not weird. No weirdness at all." In fact, it made her insides jump with pleasure and little warm fuzzies skitter across her skin.

He held her chair for her at the table. "You sit. I'll serve us."

She smiled when he set a plate heaped with a giant pile of spaghetti and sauce in front of her. "Fattening me up so no other guys will look at me?" she murmured.

He slipped into his seat, grinning. "What if I am?"

"Then I'd say we're getting serious with each other."
Whoops. All of a sudden, the light humor of the moment
evaporated, leaving the two of them staring awkwardly
at their plates.

"Forget I said that," she mumbled. "I'm an idiot and
my mouth frequently gets ahead of my brain."

He smiled a little. "In my experience, your brain
moves at light speed most of the time."

They dug into the meal and didn't talk much for a few
minutes. But then Reese said, "If you're bored, maybe
I could bring home something from your lab for you to
work on a little? Nothing strenuous. If you promise not
to overdo—"

"That would be amazing!" she exclaimed. "My laptop,
maybe? That way I could get emails and keep up with
correspondence on various pieces of evidence I've sent
out for analysis."

"I'll bring it home with me tomorrow." He added carefully, "Seeing how you're feeling better, maybe now
would be a good time to tell you that whoever mugged
you in the parking lot also stole your ID badge and broke
into your lab."

She gasped. "Was anything stolen?"

"The puzzle box was taken. And, umm, your lab was,
well, trashed."

"What? How bad?"

"Jordana and a couple of the other guys have spent
this week putting it back together as best they can. The
department's insurance is paying for replacing the lab
equipment that was damaged."

"What equipment? How damaged?"

"It's a few machines. You're safe. That's what matters."

She sat back, staring at him. The wreckage must have

been bad, given the way he was avoiding her questions. "Was any other evidence taken?"

"Unknown. Jordana has been going through your database of logged evidence and trying to match it to stuff in the lab. But she's no forensics expert. I've been helping out where I can, but some of what you do is beyond my training."

"Gee. I'm glad you finally admit that maybe I know more about my job than you do."

He rolled his eyes.

"When can I go to the lab to check it out? Will you drive me in tomorrow?"

"The doctor said to rest."

"The doctor said three days after a day of bedrest. It has been five days since the incident. I'm fine."

Reese raised a sardonic eyebrow at her. "If I could erase the word *fine* from your vocabulary forever, I would do it in a minute."

She rolled her eyes back at him. "All right, then. I'm fully recovered, have no headache and am sick of being marooned out here in the middle of nowhere. I want to get back to my work. My important work that will help nail a murderer."

"You don't like it out here? I thought you'd find my cabin restful and quiet."

Darn it. He sounded hurt.

She sighed, her indignation broken. "I love it out here. I love the quiet and the trees, and your place is incredibly comfortable and pleasant. But I have a job to do, people depending on me. I need to get back to it. How would you feel if you were in the middle of a murder investigation and had to stop working on it for a week?"

"Which is pretty much what has happened this week," he said with a sigh. "I ought to be putting in sixteen-hour days on the Harrison-Crane case, and instead, I'm going into work a few hours a day in and around making sure you don't overdo it. Which I wouldn't have any other way, mind you."

She stared at him in dismay. "I don't want to keep you from your job. What you do is important."

He looked up quickly, meeting her gaze with surprising intensity. "You're more important. Hands down."

She stared back, stunned. More important to him than his precious career? Wow.

"And you're not mad about me taking you away from your work?"

He frowned. "Of course not. Family always comes before work no matter how important the work might be. It's not even an issue for me."

Oh. Huh. Maybe it was an issue for her because her dad had always put his work above his wife and kids. "You're sure about that?" she asked in a small voice.

He leaned forward and took her hand in his. "When I saw you in that hospital bed unconscious, my world... ended. And it didn't begin again until you woke up and spoke to me."

"I... You... We..." It wasn't often she was at a complete loss for words, but she was now. She reached out and laid her hand over his on the table. He flipped his hand over beneath hers and twined their fingers together.

"Yeah. That," he muttered in response to her stammering.

"We haven't even...we hardly know each other...it's too soon..." she tried.

"I know." He finally lifted his gaze to hers. "But there you have it. I fell for you like a ton of bricks."

Panic at how fast he'd fallen for her and she for him

roared through her. "I have all kinds of quirks and flaws you don't know about. I'm a basically terrible person."

"Perhaps I should be the judge of that?" he suggested wryly.

"Easy for you to say. You're perfect," she snapped.

He laughed at that. "Oh, my dear Yvette. I'll never be half good enough for you. I'm just a hick cop from a small town in Kansas. You…you're royalty around here."

"God, I hate being a Colton, sometimes."

His gaze shuttered and slid away from hers. The same thing had happened once at the hospital. What had they been talking about then? Something to do with her father—

Reese stood up abruptly, carrying their empty plates over to the sink.

"I made a pie," she said tentatively.

"You bake?"

"I do. It's apple pie. It was the only kind I know how to make that you had the ingredients for. I didn't know if you'd like that or not."

"Apple pie is my favorite," he said in a muffled voice. "Of course, it is."

"I guess that means you hate apple pie?" he asked.

"Nope. Love it. Warm with ice cream melting all over it."

"Glory be. We agree on something for once."

She looked over at him sharply. "How can you declare that you've fallen for me and then be snarky over how we don't agree on anything?"

"Haven't you ever heard that opposites attract?" He turned around, sleeves rolled up, wielding a towel as he dried the big pot she'd cooked the pasta in.

"I've also heard that opposites combust when combined, ultimately consuming and destroying each other."

He shrugged. "That may be true in a science experiment, but I think people whose weaknesses and strengths compensate for each other can be the strongest couples of all if they can learn to accept each other's differences."

"It didn't work out for my parents," she said sadly.

Reese replied tartly, "When the difference between two people is that one's an asshole and one isn't, that's not a great foundation for a relationship."

"You really don't like my dad, do you?"

"Nope. Not one bit. He let his partner talk him into doing something that would get people killed, and he knew it. He had a great family and chose to ignore it, and now he has bailed out on all of you and left you guys holding the bag for his crimes. The rest of you Coltons have to walk around this town bearing his name and his blame, while he's taken off."

"Do you know where he went?" she asked.

"I have an idea."

"Well? Where?"

"I'm not at liberty to say. One of his conditions for signing the plea deal was he didn't want anyone in his family to know where he's going to settle down next."

She sat back, shocked to her core. She realized her jaw was sagging open but didn't have the wherewithal to shut it.

Reese turned to look at her. He must have seen how that bombshell had hit her for he moved over to her side swiftly and pulled her out of her chair and into a big, tight hug.

Dishes forgotten, he bent down, scooped her off her feet and carried her into the living room, which was lit only by the light of a sluggish fire burning hot and slow. He sat down on the overstuffed sofa in front of the fireplace with her still in his lap.

"I'm sorry you had to find that out from me," Reese murmured against her temple. "I'm a jerk for just springing it on you."

"I recall springing Jordana's move to Chicago on you, so I'd say that makes us even. Do my siblings know? Oh, God. Does my mom know?"

Reese winced and she put her palms on each side of his face and forced him to look at her. "Does my mom know?" she repeated.

He sighed. "I believe it was your mother who asked for it. She wanted a clean and complete break from your father."

She stared up at Reese in dismay. "What did he do to her? She's not a vindictive person. She doesn't cut anybody out of her life like that."

He closed his eyes tightly for a moment. When he opened them, their blue depths swam with pain. "You'd have to ask her."

"You know more than you're saying," she accused.

To his credit, he replied candidly, "I do have an idea why she did it. But that information is not mine to share. You'll have to ask her."

"I will! Right now!"

"Maybe right now you should rest and relax a little after overdoing way too much today."

"I made a pot of spaghetti," she said scornfully.

"And the rest of a nice meal, and you baked, and cleaned if I'm not mistaken."

"Well, maybe I did dust and straighten up a little." She paused, and added, "And do a couple loads of laundry."

Her gave her a withering look.

"I swear. I feel fi—" She broke off. "I feel great."

"Good. Let's keep it that way," Reese replied.

"Does that mean you'd kiss me in front of the fire again if I asked you to?"

Reese laughed against her lips. "I thought you'd never ask."

"You can ask me, too, you know."

"Cool. Wanna make out?"

She swatted his arm as she laughed at him. "You can do better than that."

"Hmm. Let's see. How about this? It feels like I've been waiting for you my whole life. Now that I've finally found you, I can't get enough of you. I love the feel of you in my arms, the softness of your mouth, your passion, your intelligence, your humor. Would you do me the great honor of consenting to make passionate love with me?"

Making love? Well, then. "Wow. That's, umm, much better."

"Are you swept off your feet?" he asked hopefully.

She laughed up at his ridiculous expression. "Blown away."

"And?"

"And what?"

"Do you accept my offer?"

"Oh. That." She pretended to think about it for a few seconds. Then she said all in a rush, "Yes, you romantic man. Of course, I accept."

He wasted no time lowering his mouth to hers, capturing her lips for a lingering, cinnamon-and-apple-flavored kiss.

"You taste good," she murmured against his mouth.

"So do you."

"Remind me to keep an apple pie in the house at all times," she replied.

He kissed his way down the column of her neck and back up. "I could go for chocolate cake, or maybe brown-

ies, too. You'd taste good flavored chocolate. The creami-
ness of your skin and the tartness of your tongue would
pair perfectly with that."

She gazed up at him as she reclined in his arms, more
relaxed and at ease that she could ever remember being
with any guy. "Oatmeal cookies," she announced.

"I beg your pardon?"

"You'd taste great with oatmeal cookies. Not a bland
one. A really good one with lots of spices and flavor. It
would have to be a cookie because you're practically a
walking milk commercial, and you remind me of whiskey or maybe rum. The raisins and spices in an oatmeal
cookie would go perfectly with that."

"And here I was, thinking I was pure vanilla."

Her lips curved wickedly, "I certainly hope not. Personally, I prefer a little spice in my life."

His eyes smoldered with interest. "Do tell."

"I'm a show, don't tell, kind of woman."

"My kind of woman." He stood up, setting her on her
feet in the flickering light of the fire. He ran his hands
across her shoulders and down her arms to her hands,
which he grasped lightly and brought up to his mouth
for a kiss.

When he released them, she laid her palms on his
chest, measuring the width of his shoulders and the bulk
of his pectorals as her hands slid down his ribs to his
waist.

"You're so beautiful," he breathed. "All woman." He
trailed his fingers through her hair, pulling long strands
forward over her shoulders. "Your hair feels like silk."

She touched his jaw with her fingertips. "Yours feels
like sandpaper."

"Do you want me to go shave?"

"No. I like you this way. A little scruffy, very masculine. I like you best when you're not all buttoned down, polished and starched. Relaxed, off-duty you is the man I fell for first."

"Are you admitting you've fallen for my cop self, too?" he asked with a little smile.

"Maybe."

He tilted his head to one side, studying her quizzically, and she relented, saying, "Okay. Fine. I've fallen for that side of you, too. I like everything about you."

He let out a long, slow breath as her words sank into him, becoming part of him. His gaze went dark and serious. "I like everything about you, too."

"Everything you know, maybe. There's still a lot about me you don't know."

"I'd like to learn, Yvie."

Very slowly, she rose on her tiptoes, never breaking eye contact with him. She paused when her mouth was only a few inches from his and whispered, "I'd like that, too."

He closed the gap between them, kissing her slowly at first, reverently, even. It was so easy to sink into him, so natural. She loved losing herself in a kiss like this, with him. She felt absolutely safe with him, but she loved the edge of danger that clung to him, a promise of more passion than met the eye, of an alpha male to be unleashed.

She deepened the kiss, opening her mouth, doing everything in her power to draw out the dark and dangerous side of this man. She rubbed her chest lightly against his, relishing the way her nipples had tightened and become so sensitized that she gasped a little at the brushing contact.

The only light in the cabin was the flickering glow of the fire, and the darkness was sultry and mysterious around them. Reese reached for the hem of her sweater and paused in the act of starting to lift it over her head.

"Ground rules for tonight," he said quietly. "If you get a headache at any time, you'll tell me immediately. Yes?"

"But if I do that, you'll stop. And maybe I won't want you to stop, umm, whatever you're doing."

"Which brings us to the second ground rule. The doctor said no vigorous activity. You are to sit back and enjoy and not exert yourself. At all."

"Well, that sounds like no fun."

"Have a little faith. I believe you can have fun without overdoing."

"Challenge accepted," she said jauntily.

He shook his head. "You have to learn to turn down a dare now and then."

"I'm a Colton. We don't know how."

His eyes glinted. "Fair enough." He gently lifted the sweater over her head carefully avoiding her bandages. The laceration on the side of her head was healing nicely but she appreciated his caution with the wound.

She ran her fingers across the fine cotton of his dress shirt, reveling in the hard muscles beneath it as she reached for the small buttons and one by one pushed them through the starched fabric. The fabric peeled back to expose the base of his neck, a few dark chest hairs poking up, hinting at more below. She continued to unbutton the shirt, shoving it aside as she went, loving the feel of his smooth skin and crisp chest hair beneath the pads of her fingers. His heat and hardness drew her in and excited her deep in her core in a feminine place that responded powerfully to him.

She unbuckled his belt and slowly pulled it from around his lean waist. When it came free, she dropped it to the floor.

He lifted her cotton turtleneck over her head next, and her face popped free all at once,

"Is your head okay?" he asked in quick concern.

"I would tell you it's fine, but you would get mad. It doesn't hurt, and as far as I can tell, I'm not bleeding."

"Promise you'll tell me if anything hurts your head at all," he murmured.

"Will do."

"And tell me if you don't like anything we do."

"All right already. Any other rules of engagement, Officer?"

"My badge is in the kitchen. I'm not a cop in here."

"Just the way I like it best. No work between us and you fully in the moment with me."

"I'm right here. All yours."

She reached up to cup his face in her hands. "Same. I'm here, and yours."

He started at her right ear, kissing his way slowly down her neck, across her shoulder and down into the warm valley between her breasts. He reached the lace of her bra and dropped to his knees, then resumed kissing a path down her stomach to the top of her jeans.

He paused there, unbuttoning her waistband and unzipping the denim pants. He tucked his fingers into each side of her jeans and slowly shoved them down, skimming his hands over her hips and down her thighs.

She planted a hand on his shoulder for balance as he guided her feet clear of her pants legs. And then he kissed his way back up the outside of her right thigh to her hipbone, and then back up her stomach.

He stood and unzipped his own trousers, stepping out of the pooled wool at his feet. As she'd suspected, he was lean and hard all over his body. His abs were ridged with muscle, his thighs more powerful than they appeared at a first glance, wrapped in long slabs of muscle.

His skin retained a faint golden cast left over from what must have been a dark summer tan. Unlike her. She'd inherited Lilly's porcelain skin that burned at even the slightest exposure to sun, and hence she lived in hats and sunscreen nearly year round.

"You look like a statue of a Greek goddess," he murmured.

"Yep. That's me. Stone cold and hard as rocks."

His mouth curved up into a smile against her shoulder. "I meant your skin is alabaster and perfectly smooth. Also, I meant that you're an image of female perfection."

"Me? Not hardly."

He sighed, a gust of warm breath against the base of her neck. "When will you stop putting yourself down? Do you realize that every time you insult yourself, you're also insulting my taste in women? I chose you. Out of all the women I could have fallen for, I fell for you. If you can't honor yourself, at least honor that."

It was her turn to sigh. "I'm sorry. I make jokes when I'm uncomfortable."

His head jerked up and he stared down at her. "Why are you uncomfortable? Are we moving too fast for you?"

"Goodness, no. If anything, we're moving too slow! I'm impatient as heck to get naked and horizontal with you. I'm uncomfortable because I'm self-conscious about…how I look," she finished lamely.

He smiled a little. "Every woman I've ever known is self-conscious about how they look. But here's the thing. You're going to have to take it on faith that I find you beautiful. Beautiful and sexy and desirable above all other women."

Wow. That was nice to hear.

He continued to skim his hands across her skin lightly as he spoke. "If I wanted to be with another woman, I would have pursued this hypothetical other woman and not you. But the fact is, I've been waiting for you my whole life. And now that you're here, I have no interest in any other woman. None."

"You make it all sound so easy."

He laughed aloud. "Honey, you've been anything but easy. You've thrown up every roadblock in the book at me, and I've had to find a way around every last one. You've been a challenge like no other." He added, leaning in to drop a light kiss on the end of her nose, "Totally worth it."

She didn't bother arguing the point. He was right. "And you still want me?" she asked in a small voice. "You're sure?"

"Positive."

He took her face gently in both of his big callused hands, cupping her cheeks as if they were the most delicate crystal. He kissed her sweetly to prove the point, ever so slowly deepening the kiss until her head slanted to one side, his to the other, and their tongues swirled together in a sexy tangle of wet, hot need.

Without breaking the contact of their mouths, he bent down slightly, reached one arm behind her thighs and scooped her up into his arms. It was one of the best advantages of being petite. Big strong men like him could pick her up and literally sweep her off her feet.

"Protection?" he murmured.

She answered briskly, appreciating his concern for their health and safety, "I'm on the pill and haven't had sex with anyone since I came back to Braxville. I am so STD-free it's depressing."

"Ditto. I haven't been in a relationship in…longer than

I care to stop and count, now. I'm happy to use a condom if you want, though."

"Fair. And thank you."

"I'm a safety guy."

"We'll see about that before I'm done with you. I plan to shake up all that caution and rule following of yours."

He laughed. "I look forward to it."

He strode swiftly down the hall to his bedroom and lowered her carefully onto the mattress. Unwilling to break the yummy contact with him, she kept her arms looped around his neck and urged him down with her. He stretched out beside her, supporting his weight on an elbow as he leaned over her to continue kissing her.

She loved the feeling of him pressing her down deep into the thick comforter and plush mattress, and she wanted more of it. She twined her legs with his and rolled more fully onto her back, dragging him with her.

He laughed a little against her mouth. "Impatient much?"

"Extremely."

"Good thing I like to take my time and savor the journey, or else this would already be over if you had your way."

She growled a little in the back of her throat.

"Oho, so the kitten has claws, does she?"

She pushed him onto his back and pressed up onto her elbows on his chest to mock glare down at him. "I'm no kitten, mister. I'm a wildcat, thank you very much."

"A very tiny, ferocious one," he teased, rolling her over and reversing their positions. She was aware that he'd made a cage of his arms around her when he'd very carefully rolled her over, protecting her the whole time from taking any of his weight.

"I appreciate your concern for my health, Reese, but

I promise, I really am fine. My cut has a nice scab and has fully closed, and my brain is no longer scrambled. At least no more than it was before I got jumped."

He smiled against her collarbone, his mouth warm and firm. As his kissed his way across it, he ended up in the hollow of her throat, licking and then nipping at the sensitive skin there.

"Come up here and kiss me, you tasty cookie of a man."

The heat of his mouth left a trail of devastation in its wake as he kissed his way up to her mouth. Tingles raced down her spine, ending in the vicinity of her toes, which curled in tight delight.

She turned into him and buried her nose in his neck. She couldn't get enough of his scent, mingled with a clean, citrus aftershave. It was the same delicious, masculine scent that rose off his pillowcases and had comforted her through her worst pain this past week. He smelled like safety to her. Warmth. Sun-drenched beaches and lazy waves rolling ashore and hissing back out to sea.

Her bra straps fell loose as he unhooked it in the back and pushed the narrow straps off her shoulders. She shrugged out of it and tossed it aside, sighing with pleasure as his warm hand cupped her breast, his thumb rubbing lightly across the pebbled nipple.

"Cold?" he murmured.

"Turned on."

"Yes," he said under his breath in satisfaction. Then, louder, "You're perfect."

"Keep telling me that. Maybe someday I'll believe you," she replied a little breathlessly, arching her back into the drugging pleasure of his thumb rolling back and forth across that sensitized peak.

He leaned down and his mouth replaced his thumb,

making her gasp aloud as electric shocks radiated through her whole body. She reached for him, sliding his briefs off his hips. He kicked them the rest of the way off. The flat plane of his stomach was irresistible, and she ran her palms across it. She followed the well-defined V of muscles lower to the hard shaft of his erection. It filled her fist as she grasped its burning heat. He was rock hard—no need to ask him if he was turned on or not.

His flesh bucked in her hand as she ran her hand up its length to smooth her thumb over the satin tip. Hah. She'd get him to hurry things along, yet.

"Still determined to take all night getting around to making love to me?" she asked archly.

"Tease," he muttered against her breast. His free hand slid lower, following the inward curve of her waist and the upward curve of her hip, then plunging down to cup her core.

She felt her pulse pounding through the swollen, hungry flesh there as his fingertips stroked her once, twice.

"You're not the only one in a hurry," he murmured.

"Ahh, but I make no secret of wanting you right now."

"Your wish is my command."

He pushed lightly against her shoulder and she rolled onto her back, her thighs opening to welcome his explorations. His finger stroked her folds, finding the swollen bud within, so sensitive and slick she nearly came up off the bed when his fingertip rubbed across it.

"Please, Reese. Can we get this show rolling? I'm dying, here."

He laughed, burying his face against her neck for a moment. "We really are yin and yang."

"Well, if your yang doesn't get busy soon, my yin is going to throw you on your back and have its wicked way with you."

"As fun as that sounds, I want you to take it easy tonight."

"Easy? I don't want easy! I want it hot and wild and hard, and that's just the beginning." She tightened her hand around his cock, tugging it toward her in open demand.

He groaned in the back of his throat, and rolled away from her. She opened her mouth to protest until she realized he was fishing a condom out of his bed stand.

Finally, blessedly, he rolled over her, lowering his weight carefully between her legs. Impatient, she wrapped her legs around his hips and pulled him down to her. He resisted for a moment, reaching between them to position himself, and then he was pressing forward, a slow, careful glide of slick, hungry flesh coming together.

"You okay?" he asked.

"Better than okay. Amazing."

He filled her deliciously. He started to withdraw, and her legs tightened convulsively around his hips. He chuckled a little. "I'm not going anywhere." As promised, he surged forward a little more forcefully this time.

"Oh, that's nice," she sighed.

"Honey, you're a lot of things, but merely nice is not one of them. You're spectacular."

She smiled up at his shadowed face and he smiled down at her. "How did I get so lucky to find you?" she asked.

"Maybe I found you. Lord knows, I've been looking for you for a long time."

"Really?"

"Swear to God. I was beginning to despair of ever finding the kind of woman I want. But I just couldn't bring myself to lower my standards."

She brushed her fingertips along his jaw lightly. "Exactly. And then…you."

Their smiles mingled in a kiss of wonder and shared

joy at the minor miracle of having arrived at this moment with each other. It wasn't one to be rushed through, but rather savored, treasured and remembered for always.

He began to move within her, and she rose to meet him, catching his rhythm quickly. He kept the pace maddeningly slow, but she had to admit it felt great. Beyond great. Her body had time to build layer upon layer of pleasure toward a towering climax unlike anything she'd ever experienced.

And still he moved within her, stroking her even higher. Huh. Had all of this always been possible and her previous lovers simply been too hasty and too selfish to take her here?

On and on their lovemaking rolled through the night, by turns leisurely and tense, but always tender and intimate. He never looked away from her, never hid the pleasure transforming his features into pure joy. And she smiled back at him, hoping he could see at least a little of the brilliance of her joy.

When she'd had at least three orgasms and was building toward number four, he finally sped up the pace a little. Her breath came in sharp, shallow gasps as pleasure clawed its way through her entire body in search of release.

"Harder," she gasped.

"Don't want…to hurt you…"

"My head is fi—in no pain." She added in desperation, "Please. I want you."

She gripped him tightly with her legs, urging his hips forward, and wrapped her arms around his neck, hanging on for all she was worth. She tugged his head down for a kiss and sucked his tongue, urging him to plunge it into the dark recesses of her mouth in a matching rhythm to their lovemaking.

He groaned and she felt his entire body tensing. She arched up against him as well, straining with him toward ecstasy.

All at once, her orgasm exploded throughout her being, scattering her in a million directions. She cried out in pleasure and Reese's entire body shuddered against hers. They rode the wave together, crashing toward a far shore, flinging themselves onto it together, exhausted and sated.

He collapsed against her, but even then, he sagged on his propped up elbows, careful not to crush her.

"Head check?" he panted.

"Whatever's better than fine."

He rolled to one side, gently gathering her onto her right side against him.

"You've killed me," he sighed.

"I gather that means we've passed the compatibility-in-bed test?"

"There was a test?"

"Well, it was possible that we would have no chemistry at all in this way."

He laughed a little. "We've had chemistry from the first moment we met. It was just extremely flammable chemistry."

"Explosive," she agreed.

They lay together in silence, their hearts beating in unison as the wind whispered through the pines outside and rattled together the branches of the deciduous trees. The peace of the moment was complete. She'd never in her life felt so right with another person. This was exactly where she was meant to be. She grew drowsy and limp against Reese's equally relaxed body.

He murmured sleepily, "How long until I can reasonably ask you to marry me without creeping you out?"

That jolted her wide awake. "Uhh, I don't know. Certainly not yet."

Reese didn't respond. She waited a moment and then gave him a light poke in the side. He let out a light snore. Had he even been awake when he'd asked the question? She fell back to the pillow, blown away. He was thinking about proposing, was he? Even if only at a semiconscious level?

Wow. Double wow.

She was equal parts thrilled and terrified at the prospect. She'd avoided long-term commitments literally her entire life. Was she ready to commit the rest of her life to one man—to this man?

Did he propose to all the ladies in his sleep immediately after great sex? Or was she special? Worse, did he actually mean it? Or was it merely the random ramble of a dreaming mind?

An urge to slide out from under his arm, creep out of the room and flee the scene roared through her.

Chapter Fifteen

Reese woke up lazily, more relaxed than he'd felt in months. It took a second for his brain to kick in and remember why he felt so freaking great this morning. Yvie. Sweet, sexy Yvie. He'd guessed she would be a generous, enthusiastic lover, and she hadn't disappointed him. In fact, he suspected she'd held back pretty hard last night on account of her head wound. She had an adventurous streak that was sheer self-confidence and enthusiastic enjoyment of sex. He couldn't wait to make love with her when she was fully healed.

He reached out for her and encountered cold sheets. An empty pillow. He sat upright quickly, alarmed. He swung his feet out of bed and grabbed a pair of jeans, slinging them on fast. Padding through the cold cabin barefoot, he headed for the kitchen and his truck keys. She hadn't pulled a runner, had she?

He rounded the corner into the kitchen and screeched to a halt. Yvette stood at the stove, turning over strips of bacon frying merrily in a pan. She wore his dress shirt from last night, and her slender, gorgeous legs were bare in all their sexy glory. His man parts stirred with interest.

"Hey, beautiful," he murmured, stepping up behind her to wrap his arms around her waist. "You should have stayed in bed and let me cook breakfast for you."

"I thought you had a big meeting this morning."

"Ugh. Work. Yeah, I do. Jordana and I are going to make one more run at Mary Dexter. Surely, she knows something about her husband that she's not telling us."

"Past something like knowing he was sleeping around, or current something like where Markus is hiding out?"

"Either. Both." He snitched a piece of already-fried bacon from the paper covered plate, and Yvette swatted at his hand.

"You like your eggs over hard, right?" she asked as he turned away to pull orange juice out of the refrigerator and get a pot of coffee brewing.

"Good memory."

"You're not the only person around here who pays attention to details," she replied. "Although, I have to admit I was impressed that you knew what my missing purse looked like. It's not a guy thing to register cute purses."

He shrugged modestly and set the table efficiently.

"I assume my purse hasn't been found?" she asked.

"Nope."

She sighed. "I had to cancel all my credit cards and order new ones. What a pain."

"It's better than the alternative. If that was Dexter who attacked you, he's fully capable of murder."

"Who else would it be?" she asked, carrying the frying pan over to the table. She lifted his eggs out onto his plate and two sunny-side-up eggs onto hers.

He held her chair for her, seating her with a quick kiss to the side of her neck. "I approve of your attire, Ms. Colton."

She looked over her shoulder at him, her eyes glinting appreciatively. "And I approve of yours. You can come to breakfast with no shirt on any time you like."

He sat down and reached out. Their fingers touched

in sweet reassurance and affection. How was he going to last for hours without touching her again?

Unfortunately, he couldn't linger over the meal or make love to her before he had to take off for work. He took a quick shower and rolled his eyes when he discovered that Yvette had already showered before him and managed to get every towel in the bathroom soaking wet.

He grabbed a dry towel from the linen closet, totally willing to put up with wet towels if it meant having Yvette Colton in his life. He dressed and stepped out into the living room—and stopped in shock. Yvette was fully dressed and even wearing a coat. She stood expectantly by the back door of the kitchen and had a determined look on her face.

"I'm going to lose my mind if I have to stay home another day. I promise not to work too long, and my car is still at the department. I can drive myself home."

His stomach dropped like a lead brick, thudding to the vicinity of his feet. "But I want to keep an eye on you until your attacker is caught. I like having you here with me."

"I like being here, too. But you must be sick of me by now—"

"I want to spend the rest of my life with you. Of course, I'm not sick of you. If you want to stay at your place, that's fine. I'll grab a few things and meet you there tonight." He added, "If you want me there. I get it if you'd like some time to yourself—"

She interrupted, rushing forward to throw her arms around him. "Of course, I want you with me. I just wasn't sure you'd want to be seen at my place."

He threw her a withering look. "We're in a relationship, now." He added for emphasis, kissing her between each word, "You. Are. My. Woman."

"Which makes you my Neanderthal," she quipped. "I'm nobody's property."

He rolled his eyes. "That's not what I meant, and you know it."

She laughed up at him. "I know. But you'd hate it if I didn't keep you on your toes."

"Truth." He followed her out to his garage, shaking his head and smiling privately to himself. That woman was surely going to lead him on a merry chase over the next seventy years or so. He made a mental note to ask Jordana what kind of jewelry Yvette liked. Would she be a traditional diamond engagement ring kind of woman, or would she prefer some other stone? A nice sapphire, perhaps, or maybe an emerald.

They arrived at the police department and parted ways after he gave her a quick warning not to freak out when she saw the shape her lab was in. She promised not to have a fit, they snuck a quick kiss in the stairwell and he hustled off to his interview with Mary Dexter.

The woman was punctual to the second, which didn't surprise him given how neat a house she kept. Bit of a control freak. Which worked to his and Jordana's advantage. They'd agreed in advance to play softball with the woman and try to trick her into revealing something rather than coming at her hard. To date, Mary had been exceedingly stubborn when confronted directly for information about her missing spouse.

He poured her a cup of tea with a splash of cream and two lumps of sugar, the same way she'd taken it the last time she'd been here. Instead of taking her into an interrogation room like before, Jordana showed her to his desk and then pulled up a second chair to make a cozy little circle of the three of them. His job was to talk. Jordana would sit back and observe body language. Or more accurately, look for tells of lying.

"Thanks for coming in this morning, Mrs. Dexter," he said warmly. "I really appreciate it. We wanted to let you know there was a break-in at your house a few nights ago."

"Was anything stolen?" she asked rather too calmly for a woman who seemed obsessed with the tidiness of said home.

"We were hoping you could help us with that. Maybe you can go home, take a look around. Check for any missing valuables. The robber did drop one item on his way out." He pushed a picture of the puzzle box across his desk to show her.

"That old thing?" she said scornfully.

"What is it, if you don't mind my asking?" he murmured innocently.

"It's one of those Chinese puzzle boxes with hidden panels. Markus kept it on his desk. Called it his golden parachute."

"Is there gold on it or in it?" Reese asked, trying to sound as dim-witted as possible.

"I have no idea. I doubt he even knew how to open the thing. It was bulky. Ugly. I kept trying to get him to throw it out and put something tasteful on his desk, but he always laughed at me and refused."

"Huh. Did it have some sort of special sentimental value to him?" he followed up.

"Not that I know of." Mary's voice took on a note of caution.

Dang, she was sharp. Time to shift subjects.

He leaned back casually. "At any rate, I've got permission for you to return to your house. We don't believe your husband is planning to return to it any time soon."

"My, my. That's so generous of you," she snapped.

"I'm sorry for the inconvenience," he murmured.

His contrite tone seemed to disarm her indignation a bit.

"Also, I wanted to let you know that your husband is now being classed as a missing person." Missing and wanted for murder, but he conveniently omitted the last bit. "To that end, we'll be turning our resources in the future to helping you find him. We're concerned at his continued absence and hope that no foul play has befallen him."

Myriad emotions flitted across Mary's face, foremost among them confusion. Interesting. She didn't know what to make of the downgrade from murder suspect to possible victim.

He leaned forward and lowered his voice. "If I could speak off the record for a moment?"

She nodded her haughty assent.

"I'm worried about the quality of the security system in your home, ma'am. If you're going to be staying there alone, I would personally recommend an upgrade. Motion detectors, sensors that will let you know when a window or door opens, that sort of thing. If anything should happen to you, I'd never forgive myself."

A normal human being who'd just found out that their home, their personal sanctum and refuge, had been violated, would show at least a modicum of nerves about being home alone.

But Mary literally snorted down her nose at him before declaring scornfully, "My current security system is perfectly fine."

She wasn't the least bit worried about the intruder, huh? Interesting. That lent credence to his theory that it had been Markus himself who broke into the Dexter house to search for that puzzle box. And furthermore, Mary knew it had been her husband.

"At a minimum, ma'am, you should change the security code. We believe the intruder obtained the code, somehow, and disabled your home alarm."

"Fine. Whatever."

"If you would like patrols to continue coming by your home for a few weeks, please let us know."

She waved a dismissive hand at that suggestion.

Oh, yeah. Markus had totally been the intruder who'd run over Yvette.

"If you'll wait here a moment, I'll go fetch your house keys from the evidence locker. Can I get you another cup of tea? It'll take a few minutes to do the paperwork to get your keys."

He stood up, leaving Jordana to take over chitchatting with Mary. His partner had known the woman most of her life. If anyone could coax information out of Mary Dexter, it was Jordana.

He signed out the house keys quickly and then loitered by the evidence locker until Jordana texted him an okay.

Mary left the building quickly, and he turned with interest to his partner. "Well?"

"She's been in Kansas City the past few weeks. Claims to have been visiting a friend but couldn't produce the friend's name."

"You think she was visiting Markus?"

"Possible. Mary gave me the name of the hotel she stayed at. I'll make a call to confirm her alibi and find out if she had male company."

He nodded and looked up quickly as a familiar form caught his attention across the room. Yvette's trim silhouette.

"What're you grinning like a fool for?" Jordana snapped.

"Yvette's here," he murmured.

"Dang, you've got it bad for her, don't you?"

"I'm going to marry that girl."

"What?"

"She doesn't know it, yet, so don't say anything." He looked up, saw the stunned look on Jordana's face and blurted, "Don't you punch me, too." That was all he had time to say before Yvette reached their desks.

"Hey, guys. I've got something you need to see. Do you want the old news or the recent news first?"

"Old," he and Jordana said simultaneously.

"Right. So, I got the DNA results back from a strand of hair I collected off Markus Dexter's hairbrush. I'll have to get a sample from him to confirm that it was actually his hair, and I'd like you guys to get a warrant for that when we find him."

Jordana frowned. "I don't understand. Why does it matter if it was his hair or not?"

Reese knew that look in Yvette's eyes. She was bursting with excitement over something. "Because the owner of that hair is Gwen Harrison's father."

All of a sudden, a bunch of pieces fell into place. He blurted, "Markus Dexter is Gwen Harrison's father?"

"If that hair is Markus's, yes."

Jordana jumped in excitedly. "That's our motive! Olivia Harrison was having an affair with Markus Dexter and it went sour. He killed her over it."

Yvette beat him to the punch, correcting, "We know he had sex with Olivia at least once to have fathered her daughter. That doesn't necessarily mean they were having an affair. And Gwen was several years old when her mother died, so he didn't kill her right away. My guess is she had the baby and started pressing him to leave his wife. That would be why he killed Olivia. Either way, it's a heck of a motive."

Reese spoke up. "What's the new news?"

"I got a hit on the key from the puzzle box."

He lurched upright in his desk chair. "Do tell."

"It's from the Kansas City Freeport."

His jaw sagged. "The freeport?"

Jordana chimed in with "What's a freeport?"

Reese explained. "They're bonded warehouses that accept cargo and shipments from other countries. A freeport can hold cargo indefinitely without ever sending it through customs. The stuff basically sits in lockers, in limbo between countries, as long as it's inside the freeport building."

Jordana frowned. "Why on earth would Markus Dexter have a locker inside a freeport?"

Yvette answered soberly, "He's hiding something. It's valuable, and he doesn't want any US authority knowing it exists. He's either avoiding paying taxes on it or it's illegal."

"How do we get a warrant to search it?" Jordana asked.

Reese winced. "That could be difficult. The contents of the freeport are in transit between countries. It would have to be a federal warrant."

Jordana groaned. "Great. I guess I'm spending the rest of the day doing paperwork, aren't I?"

"Sorry, sis," Yvette murmured.

Reese commented, "I wonder if Mary Dexter knows her husband has a daughter."

Jordana met his gaze sharply. "Could be interesting to find out. But you're going to have to tread lightly around her. Disarm her."

Yvette snorted. "That woman always scared me."

Jordana snorted back. "I don't know why. You were always the only one of us kids she could stand."

"Really?" Reese asked quickly.

"Oh, yeah. Yvette was a quiet, mousy little thing who dressed in girly clothes and was always neat and clean. Mary thought she was the perfect child."

He'd seen Yvette tussled and hectic after they made love, and frankly, it was his favorite way to see her. "Come with me to drop the bomb on Mary?" he asked her.

"Umm, sure. What do you need me to do?"

"Go get Markus's hairbrush, and I'll meet you out front," he answered.

When Yvette slid into his truck a few minutes later, she lifted the center console and slid all the way across the bench seat to plaster herself against his side. "I've missed being with you," she murmured.

"It has only been a few hours," he replied humorously.

"I know. A lifetime."

He laughed under his breath. "God, I love you."

She froze against him.

Oh, crap. Should he retract the statement, or would that make it even more weird? Should he let it stand as nothing more than a casual remark? Pretend he'd never said it? Paralyzed with uncertainty, he ended up doing nothing. The moment passed. Yvette eventually relaxed against his side, and she didn't make any grand or awkward statement in response.

Mary Dexter answered the front door of her mansion and promptly gave him an earful about cops tromping around her house in muddy boots and ruining her rugs. He finally got a word in edgewise to apologize humbly and ask to speak with her.

In a huff, Mary led him and Yvette into the living

room. It was as stuffy a space as its owner and he perched on the edge of a deeply uncomfortable Victorian sofa. Mary and Yvette sat on the matching one across a coffee table.

Yvette opened her purse and pulled out a sealed, plastic evidence bag. She said softly, "Miss Mary, I'm hoping you can help me with something. Do you recognize this hairbrush?"

"Turn it over," Mary demanded.

Yvette turned the bag, and the elaborate monogram on the back became visible, a large *D* with an *M* and a *J* on each side of it.

"Where did you get that? I gave that to my Markus for his birthday years ago."

"You're sure it's his?"

"I can't imagine there's anyone else in Braxville with an imported boar's-hair brush with the initials MJD engraved on it."

Yvette nodded. "If you look closely, you can see some hairs in the bristles. Do those look like Uncle Markus's?"

"Why, yes, dear. You can see the gray roots and that stupid hair dye he uses to cover the gray in his hair."

Nice touch, calling him Uncle Markus. Yvette was putting Mary more at ease than he'd ever seen the woman.

"Why are you asking me all of this?" Mary asked, pinning him with a suspicious look.

He answered gently, "Ahh. That. Well, we ran a DNA analysis of several of the hairs from this brush. Turns out the hairs come from Gwen Harrison's genetic father."

"Markus? He's the Harrison girl's father? He and Olivia—" She broke off, visibly pale and stunned.

Yvette reached forward and took Mary's hand, patting it sympathetically. "Is it possible anyone else used that brush? Any male guests to your home who might've gone upstairs and borrowed it?"

"Guests—no—I don't like other people in my home… I think I feel faint…"

Yvette stood quickly and help her lie back. He grabbed a few pillows and passed them to Yvette to put behind Mary, while he pulled a crocheted blanket off the back of the sofa and laid it over her. "Rest, ma'am."

"Thank you, young man."

She wasn't that old. But if she wanted to play the frail old lady, he would go along to gain her trust.

"Oh, Aunt Mary, I'm so sorry," Yvette murmured. "You've been so brave over the years, looking the other way all that time. It's not fair that he did this to you."

"All those women," she moaned. "And I never said a word. Never confronted him. I kept the peace. I was a dutiful wife."

"And to have him betray you like this," Yvette tsked. "It's disgraceful."

"How could he?" Mary wailed.

Reese mentally grinned. Here it came. The righteous fury.

"I could kill him," she declared. "And to think, he wanted me to protect his sorry neck."

Yvette glanced at him over Mary's head and he nodded fractionally.

Yvette said sympathetically, "He doesn't deserve you. You've always been too good for him."

"I'm the one who came from the good family, you know. I had money. He used my trust fund to buy into your father's company. And then this! Why, I'll take all the money out of the bank accounts. It should all be mine, anyway. He wouldn't have a dime if it weren't for me agreeing to marry him and finance his business ventures.

I'm the one who told him to invest in Colton Construction in the first place. Your daddy always had a good eye for real estate. I told Markus to take advantage of that."

"And then to run away like this and leave you holding the bag," Yvette made an indignant noise. "I can't imagine how you'll face his daughter. Ohmigosh, and all your friends when they find out…"

Mary groaned, and her diamond-clad fingers fluttered to her forehead. "I'll have to leave, too."

"You won't join him, will you?" Yvette asked in horror.

"Goodness, no. Kansas City won't be nearly far enough away to hide from the shame. But I have no interest in leaving the country, either. Oh, dear. What shall I do? I have people on the West Coast. My sister. We never got along, but maybe I could spend some time with her."

"I'm sure she'll understand," Yvette soothed.

Reese pulled out his cell phone and texted Jordana quickly. Dexter is in Kansas City. Planning to leave the country. Send alerts to customs and TSA to detain him on sight.

"How soon is Uncle Markus planning to leave the country? Maybe if he goes quickly enough you won't have to leave Braxville and all your friends."

"Oh, in just a few days."

"Do you know the details of his trip?" Yvette asked casually.

"No, no. He was going to go alone. He wanted to send for me later, but I hadn't made up my mind if I was going or not. I'm plenty sick of his shenanigans after all these years and all those women."

Yvette sat down on the edge of the sofa beside the older woman. She lowered her voice and asked conspiratorially, "Did you know the Harrison woman? Olivia, I think her name was?"

"Beautiful girl. I'm not surprised she caught his eye. She had a friend in town who she used to come visit. They came to church together. That's where we met her—" Mary's voice became a hiss of fury. "He picked her up at *church*."

Yvette made an appropriate sound of shock.

"I hope he burns in hell," Mary spat.

"Aunt Mary, I found something strange in a piece of evidence that came into the lab a few days ago. It was a puzzle box with a key inside it. Do you know anything about that key?"

Mary frowned. "What was it a key to?"

"I was hoping you might know."

"He always was secretive." Mary's voice lowered to a hushed murmur. "Once, I found a whole bunch of money in the back of his desk drawer and a fake driver's license. It was his picture but it had a different name on it."

"What ever would he need something like that for?" Yvette responded on cue.

"He said it was a joke. But I never believed him. I figured he used it to get hotel rooms for him and his sluts."

"Do you remember the name on it?" Yvette asked, sounding suitably shocked.

"James McDowell. As if anyone couldn't see right through that to realize it was his initials scrambled. And his middle name is James for goodness' sake. It's not even a good fake name."

Yvette laughed a little. "You're so much more clever than he ever realized."

Mary responded archly, "All men think they're so smart. But we women…we always know what they're up to."

Reese suppressed a smile. He was happy to be the stupid detective who'd brought along the one person on earth Mary would spill her guts to. Yep. He was quite the moron.

He made a hand signal over Mary's head to Yvette to wrap things up, and she asked Mary if she could call a friend to come sit with her. Someone agreed to come over, and he and Yvette made their excuses and left.

They drove away from the Dexter house, and a few blocks away, he pulled over to the curb. "Come here, you amazing woman." He pulled her into his arms and gave her a resounding kiss. "You were magnificent. She sang like a bird."

Yvette threw her leg over his leg and straddled his hips, grinning down at him. "I like interrogating people."

"If you'd like more training in how to do it, I'd be glad to arrange it."

"It's so…bloodthirsty. No wonder you love your job."

He laughed at her enthusiasm and kissed her again, loving her excitement.

"Can I convince you to christen this truck?" she asked hopefully.

"Soon, darlin'. Right now, I want to drive you home and put you to bed."

"Oooh, sounds fun. You'll join me?"

"You need your rest," he tried.

"What I need is you."

He sighed. "You are possibly the worst patient I've ever been around."

"I know. Isn't it great?"

He smiled up at her ruefully and set her off his lap. And it was, indeed, great stripping her naked, laying her down in his bed and making slow, sweet love to her.

But eventually, real life called. Or rather, texted. Jordana had verbal approval on the warrant for Markus Dexter's locker in the freeport. They needed only to drive to Kansas City to pick up the signed warrant and then they could find out what Markus was hiding.

Chapter Sixteen

Yvette woke up with the setting sun pouring in through the window in crimson glory. "Reese!" she called. "Are you home?"

No answer. He'd undoubtedly gone back to work and left her to sleep the afternoon away. Which she, in fact, had. She showered and dressed, and noticed her phone had several text messages when she picked it up in the kitchen.

The first message was from Reese. Gone to Kansas City. Will call you when we arrest Markus.

Perfect. She still had a bunch of emails and paperwork to go through from being out of the office for several days. She'd just settled down in front of a fledgling fire with her laptop when she heard the sound of a vehicle coming up the drive.

Odd. She didn't see its headlights. Nor did she recognize the sound of its engine. That definitely wasn't Reese's truck. One of her siblings, maybe. It would be like Lilly to send one of them out to check on her.

A firm knock at the front door drew her out of her seat to open it, a greeting on her lips.

"Hi—" she started. She stopped. Stared. Blurted, "What are *you* doing here?"

"Come with me. Right now," Markus Dexter snarled.

"What? No. I'm not going anywhere."

His hand lifted away from his side. "Wanna bet?"

She stared in shock at the handgun pointed at her belly. "Are you kidding me?"

"I assure you, I'm not. Let's go. Now."

"I'm going to need shoes and my coat, Uncle Markus." She threw in the title to remind him of her lifelong relationship to him. He was sporting a scruffy beard and looked rather more unkempt than she was used to. He had a hard edge about him now, which was new.

"Make it fast."

She turned, thinking frantically. How to let someone know she was being kidnapped? He followed her into the bedroom where she made a production of fishing her boots out of the closet, strewing all of her shoes around the floor of the closet. She dumped several pairs of socks on the floor as she opened the drawer, too. She threw a huge log onto the fire as she passed by it, confident the thing would burn most of the night. She didn't close the steel mesh curtains in front of the fire and prayed she didn't burn Reese's house down. But he would know something was terribly wrong if she'd made a mess and hadn't made the fire safe before leaving.

She grabbed her coat off the rack by the door and surreptitiously dropped one of her mittens on her way out. It was the best she could do on short notice.

Markus herded her into the back seat of what looked like a rental sedan, where he zip-tied her hands together in front of her. Sheesh. He didn't think much of her survival skills if that was all he did to her. But she wasn't about to complain.

He drove away from the house, and she sat quietly in the backseat, trying to figure out where he was headed. Cell phone coverage out here could be spotty. They went around the city center of Braxville on country roads and appeared to head generally east. She dared not wait any longer to call for help. She reached into her front jeans pocket surreptitiously and pulled out her phone.

It was hard to type while covering its lighted face with one zip-tied hand and trying to press letter keys with the other. It was painstaking work, but she finally typed out a message to Reese.

Kidnapped by Markus. Heading eastish in gray sedan. Not hurt.

REESE LOOKED AWAY from the window impatiently as his cell phone vibrated. "Take over watching the entrance," he told the Kansas City detective at the other window in the cramped office. They'd set up a surveillance hide on the freeport across the street from this warehouse's front offices. He didn't love the sharp angle to the front door from here, but this building had a second floor that lifted them above street traffic and parked cars.

Darkness was falling and streetlights threw dull pools of light on the slushy pavement. The lights were off in the office, of course, so he stepped back from his window perch to pull out his cell phone.

Shielding it with his hand, he opened the text from Yvette, smiling already.

And then he read her message.

Had he not had so many years of experience on the force, he'd have dropped the phone in his panic. As it was, he yelled, "Come here, Pat! Oh, my God. Call the SWAT task force commander. And the FBI while you're at it."

"What the hell?" the other cop said.

It was easier to shove the cell phone at the guy than try to explain.

"Oh, shit," the other cop responded. "I'll call the hostage-negotiation guys, too."

Ohgod ohgod ohgod. Reese paced the office they'd commandeered for this operation as frantically as a caged tiger.

Belatedly, it dawned on him that he should text her back. Let her know he'd received her message. But what if an incoming text made noise? Got her in trouble? Worse, what if Markus turned off her phone?

Pat poked his head into the room. "Come with me. We're shifting this operation to the SWAT command center, now that we know where Dexter is. What's the woman's phone number so we can get a GPS location on it and track it?"

He rattled off Yvette's phone number quickly as he all but ran from the building. He jumped into the unmarked car with the Kansas City cop, who blessedly drove like Yvette's life depended on it across town to police headquarters.

Thankfully, it took about two minutes to bring the SWAT operators on call up to full speed. This was not their first rodeo. They called in a full SWAT team and began preparing a briefing for them.

In about two more minutes, a red blip popped up on a large wall monitor. Someone superimposed a road map of Kansas on the screen, and it became clear quickly that Markus and Yvette were headed this way.

Unable to wait any longer for the process to unfold, he asked the SWAT team commander, "Now that we've got positive ID on the vehicle, can I text her back? Let her know we're on our way?"

He waited through a brief, agonizing conference among the tactical experts.

One of them turned to Reese. "She's a cop, is she?"

"Forensic scientist for a police department."

"Close enough. She the type to panic?"

"Not at all," he answered firmly.

"Okay. Tell her we're tracking her and then ask her to delete the text conversation."

"Got it."

He texted quickly, We're tracking you and need you to delete all my texts after you read them. He hesitated for a moment and then typed quickly, I love you. I promise you'll be safe. ALL the law enforcement types are here. Hang tough and keep him as calm as possible.

He waited three minutes or so for a response but got none. He hoped she'd gotten his message and merely wasn't in a position to respond right now. And then he prayed. He'd found her so recently. He couldn't lose her, now. In what universe would that be fair or right?

When he was sure Yvette wasn't going to respond immediately, he placed a quick phone call to Jordana.

"Hey, Reese. What's up?"

"We've got a situation. Markus has surfaced. He apparently went to my cabin and kidnapped Yvette. She's texting me from a car he's driving toward Kansas City, as we speak."

Jordana swore colorfully, which was wildly unlike her. "What can I do?" she demanded urgently.

"Pray. If they're headed for the freeport they'll arrive in about an hour and a half. I'll update you as I can. SWAT's gearing up, and the FBI's on scene. She'll be okay. I promise."

Jordana said soberly, "You can't promise that, and you know it. But if anyone can make sure she comes through this safely, it'll be you. Take care of my baby sister, Reese."

"You know I'd give my life for her."

"Yeah. I do. How are you holding up?"

"I'm on the ragged edge," he confessed. "This is way too much like the last time."

"You mean when Christine was taken hostage?"

"Yes." He shuddered at the memory of his partner's lifeless, bullet-riddled body lying in a pool of blood beside the corpse of the man who'd killed her. An image of Yvette dead the same way flashed through his head and he nearly lost it. His breathing sped up until he felt lightheaded and nauseated.

"I can hear you hyperventilating, Reese. Breathe, buddy. Yvette's smart, levelheaded and resourceful. She won't do anything stupid and heroic like Christine tried to do."

Jordana knew the details of his first partner's death at the hands of a deranged criminal with a bag full of weapons and ammo. The man had been trying to achieve suicide by cop, and had taken Christine Crocker hostage to draw as many police as possible to his home. When he'd tried to shoot at the police outside the home he'd holed up in with her, she'd leaped at him to stop him. He'd panicked and shot her. By the time police dropped the shooter, entered the home and found Christine, she'd bled out.

Reese snorted. "You know as well as I do that Yvette would do something stupid and heroic."

"All right. Fine. She can be impulsive. But she has you to live for now."

"Is that enough?" he asked desperately.

"It has to be. Believe in her, Reese. This time will be different. This will end well."

"From your mouth to God's ear," he said fervently.

Jordana said lightly, "By the way, you two are doing a terrible job of keeping your relationship secret. It's all over your faces any time you're in the same room together. You two look freaking radiant, for crying out loud."

"Uhh, I don't know what to say."

"You'll need to go public sooner rather than later that you two are in love."

"I'm totally in love with her. But I don't know how she feels about me. I mean I know she likes me. But does she love me?"

"Oh, she's a goner. I've never seen her look at another man the way she looks at you. She's head over heels, my dude."

How was it possible to be so elated and so panicked in the same breath? She had to be okay. She *had* to.

YVETTE'S COMPOSURE THREATENED to crack when the text from Reese finally came in. She read it quickly and then deleted it like he'd asked. The car was currently traveling a dark stretch of highway, and she was afraid the glow of her cell phone screen would be visible to Markus from the front seat, so she didn't dare try to respond to Reese, right now.

She wasn't surprised that Reese had called out every law enforcement agency in this part of the country the moment he got that text. She took his advice and decided to attempt to strike up a conversation with Markus. Although frankly, she was more interested in throwing him mentally off-balance than in keeping him calm. The calm ship seemed to have sailed a while ago where her father's ex-partner was concerned.

"So, Uncle Markus. I found out today that Gwen Harrison is your biological daughter."

The car swerved sharply and then righted itself. "What the hell are you talking about?"

"I ran a DNA test on some of your hair. You and Olivia Harrison are Gwen's biological parents. Did you know Olivia had your baby?" She was tempted to add, *When you killed her*, but there was no need to antagonize him *that* much.

"I didn't even know the Harrison woman, let alone have a child with her."

Riiight. Because DNA lied all the time. Not.

"Aunt Mary's plenty pissed off about it."

That made him squawk, *"What?"*

"She threatened to empty out all of your bank accounts. In fact, she might have already done it this afternoon, she was so mad."

Markus snorted. "That bitch always thought she had me by the short hairs because of her family's money. But she never knew I put back money for myself. Squirreled it away in accounts she didn't even know existed. Bit by bit, I've wiped out that old hag."

Hag, huh? "So, Aunt Mary isn't the quiet, docile wife she acts like in public?"

That got Markus going but good. He ranted about his wife for most of the next hour. Long enough for her to start seeing signs for the suburbs of Kansas City.

Under the cover of his tirade about how Mary Dexter had everybody fooled, she sent another text to Reese. Approaching Kansas City. And I love you, too.

HE TEXTED HER back immediately with the question that had been agreed upon would be asked the next time she contacted him. Are you in imminent danger?

Her response was fast. No.

Thank God. His legs actually felt weak with relief. He replied with, Police following you in unmarked cars.

SWAT and FBI mobilized here in KC. Sit tight and don't provoke him. Don't be a hero.

She didn't respond right away. A sinking feeling that she wasn't willing to agree to that settled heavily in his gut. He tried again. Keep your head down, stay quiet, don't do anything unpredictable. Let the professionals take care of you.

She responded right away with a single word that made him smile reluctantly. Fine.

If she was cracking jokes right now, she must not feel as if her life was in danger at the moment. That was reassuring. But still. She was the prisoner of an armed and angry man who'd killed before and could kill again.

"DID YOU KNOW they arrested Fitz for the whole arsenic scandal?" she said conversationally. "And they're questioning him about the Harrison and Crane murders. Do you think he killed those two?"

"Definitely."

"Why, I wonder?" she asked.

"He was the one having an affair with the Harrison girl. Hell, I'll bet he's that Gwen girl's father. You should test his DNA."

Denial, much? She already had her father's DNA profile in her database, and it hadn't been the one that popped up as a perfect parental match to Gwen Harrison's. But she was happy to play along with the lie if it kept Markus talking.

"Where are we headed, Uncle Markus?"

"To the Kansas City Freeport. You're going to get my golden parachute out of storage for me, little girl. And then, I'm out of here."

"What is this freeport place?" she asked innocently.

"Don't play dumb with me, Yvette. You're a cop. You know darned good and well what a freeport is."

"I'm not a police officer—"

"Cut the crap. You swiped my puzzle box."

"I did not! You're the one who fished it out of your attic and then dropped it on the way out the door."

"So," he commented. "That was you in the attic. I thought I recognized you."

"I knew I recognized you," she retorted.

"You found the key, didn't you?" he accused. "I figure it took you cops about two minutes to figure out it belongs to a safe-deposit box. But I fooled you all. It's a freeport and not even technically US territory. You can't touch my stuff in there."

Far be it from her to explain to him that federal laws still applied to any facility located on US soil.

"How am I going to help you get into this freeport place?" she asked.

"Shut up. I'll tell you what to do when we get there."

"Sure. No problem," she replied evenly.

As they approached the outskirts of Kansas City, she risked texting, Going to freeport. She expected Reese and company would already have anticipated that, but it didn't hurt for them to have confirmation of Markus's destination.

It wasn't too much longer until they pulled up in front of a long, low building that stretched away into the darkness in both directions.

"You're going to go inside in front of me," he directed, "and show them the warrant I have."

"What warrant?"

"I know a guy. He forged one for me."

"What guy?"

"Quit interrupting. You're gonna show the warrant and your police ID."

"I don't have my police ID—"

"I have it." He held up her cute pink purse with the butterflies from the night of the mugging.

"You knocked me down in the parking lot and took my purse?" she exclaimed.

"Shut up. And don't make me tell you to be quiet, again." He shoved her purse at her. "Show your ID to the guy at the front desk along with the warrant. Make him unlock my storage unit for you. I couldn't find my key in your cursed police department. Turned the place upside down, but there was no sign of it. Where'd you put it, anyway?" he asked truculently.

"It's locked in a safe where all valuable evidence is stored."

He swore in frustration.

He resumed giving her orders. "When the guard leaves, you'll put everything on the table into this bag." He lifted a large duffel bag from the front seat of the car.

The bag was clearly empty. Thank goodness. She'd been worried when she glimpsed it as she'd climbed into the car that it might have weapons inside it.

"When I have my stash, you and I will walk out of the freeport. Nice and quiet. Got it?"

"Yes. I like the nice-and-quiet part."

"If you do anything, try anything, I'll kill you. Understood?"

"Uncle Markus. I would never do anything to hurt you, and I can't believe you'd do anything to hurt me," she said in as innocent a voice as she could muster.

She climbed out of the car and waited patiently while he draped her coat over her zip-tied wrists. He grabbed her elbow and yanked her along beside him, growling,

"Don't mess this up. I'll shoot you, and I'll shoot the guard. His life is in your hands, Yvette."

She refrained from looking around the parking lot. It wasn't necessary, anyway. She could feel Reese nearby, his gaze upon her. She figured there was probably a whole SWAT team out here somewhere, too, if she knew Reese. Which meant there would be snipers covering every angle. They wouldn't shoot until Markus did something to threaten her or the security guard inside the lobby of the freeport, or until the commander on scene gave an order to take the shot.

Her guess was they would let this play out as long as she wasn't in immediate danger. It would help the prosecution if he took personal possession of whatever he'd stashed in the freeport. He wouldn't be able to claim it had been planted or that it wasn't his. Not to mention, he would need to remove whatever was in his storage unit for it technically to be on US soil.

The security guard looked up from behind a high front counter. His eyes were hard and even. She would lay odds he was an FBI agent.

Markus nudged her with his elbow. Right. She was up. An attack of nerves startled her as she opened her mouth to speak. Until now, she'd been mostly calm, feeling relatively confident that Reese would take care of her and everything would be fine.

But now, with the hard bore of Markus's pistol jammed against her side and the security guard looking up at her intently, the reality of her danger slammed into her full force.

"May I help you?" the guard asked.

"Umm, yes. I'm, umm, from the Braxville Police Department, and I've got a warrant to search one of your lockers."

Markus took her ID card from her purse and passed it over to the guard, along with the forged search warrant.

The guard looked at it for a while and passed it back to her. She started to reach for it with her tied hands, but Markus snatched it off the counter quickly.

"Do you have the key?" the guard asked.

"No, we don't," Markus responded for her.

"I'll send a guy with you, then, to unlock it." A second guard, big and fit looking and also reeking of being a federal agent, stepped out of a door behind the first guard.

"Come with me," the second guard said.

Frantically, she tried to figure out how to signal this guard, who looked plenty big enough to take down Markus, that her captor had a gun hidden under his coat. But, with Markus's pistol literally pressed against her side, her options were limited. Maybe when they got to the storage unit she would get an opening.

The guard walked in front of them down a wide hallway lined with doors spaced at even intervals. Other than the concrete floor and walls and dim sconce lighting, this could be a regular office building.

"Here we are," the guard said. "Do you want to go in alone, or shall I accompany you?"

"Alone," Markus said quickly. "You first, Yvette."

The guard threw open the door, and complete darkness was all she saw. Markus jabbed her side with the pistol and gestured with his head for her to reach for, presumably, a light switch.

Everything happened all at once.

She reached with both hands for the wall, Markus shoved her inside and then the guard jumped for Markus. She stumbled and fell as the door slammed shut behind her, landing on her knees and then pitching forward. She rolled and hit the floor with her right shoulder, disoriented.

Markus swore violently in the complete darkness, and she rolled away from the sound of his voice hastily. The light switched on, and she was in a small room, perhaps six feet wide and maybe ten feet long. A single table stood in the center of the room and she lay curled up next to one of its legs. Markus was pointing his pistol at the door with both hands.

She grabbed the table leg in both hands and hoisted herself to her feet. She stared at the contents of the table. It was covered in tall stacks of cash, bundled into rubber-banded packets of twenties and hundreds. She guessed at a glance that at least a couple of million dollars was stacked there. One corner of the table held two passports with New Zealand covers, and an assortment of jewelry—a couple of diamond rings, a gaudy gold watch, a necklace with an impressive emerald in it and a tangle of other pieces.

Markus tossed the duffel bag at her. "Put everything in that."

She commenced awkwardly shoveling the cash off the table into the big bag as Markus pressed his ear to the door. He swore aloud at whatever he heard.

"Okay. Here's how this is going to go down. You and I are walking out to the parking lot together and getting in my car. You're driving me to the airport, where I'm going to get on a charter plane that's waiting for me. If you don't mess this up, maybe you get to live. Otherwise, I'll blow your head off."

Not while she was driving the car, he wouldn't. If she was incapacitated, she would crash the car, he wouldn't get to the airport and he might get hurt. Once they reached the airport, though, that was another story.

Shoving her in front of him, he forced her to crack

open the unit's door a few millimeters. "I'm coming out!" he shouted. "Any funny business, and the girl is dead!"

"Understood," a familiar voice called out.

Reese? He was out there? A wash of warmth went through her trembling body.

"Open the door wider," Markus ordered, pressing his pistol to the back of her head. The barrel was hard and cold against her skull.

Nervously, she did so, praying there wasn't a hair trigger on his weapon. One slip of his finger, and she would be dead. Of course, it was also possible the snipers outside would accidentally take her out in the course of trying to stop Markus from leaving.

"I'm coming out first," she called. Her ad-lib ticked off Markus, who jabbed her neck painfully with the weapon.

"Let's go," he snapped, shoving her forward.

The hallway was lined with men in full tactical gear. Kansas City SWAT, if she had to guess. All of their weapons were trained in her and Markus's direction, and it was the scariest sight she'd ever seen. All those hard, emotionless faces pressed against eye sights, staring back at her. As she'd suspected, Reese had called in *all* the law enforcement in this part of the country.

"All of you, stay in front of me," Markus ordered.

It was a slow procession, waiting for the various tactical officers to move ahead of them toward the exit in an ever-increasing crowd of black uniforms and weapons. The parade spilled outside, and Markus's car had been repositioned at the side door.

She slid across the passenger seat with Markus's pistol pressed to her neck, just below her right ear. She crawled awkwardly over the center console, and lowered herself carefully into the driver's seat of Markus's car while he climbed in after her, never taking the pistol's aim off her.

He seemed to know that the second he gave all those cops outside even the slightest opening, one of them would take him down. He slouched down below the level of the windows as she started the car, his shoulder against her side and his pistol still maddeningly aimed at her head, now pointing up at her jaw from underneath. She knew all too well that would be a lethal angle from which to take a bullet.

An escort of police patrol cars led her out of the parking lot slowly and drove toward an airport. Their lights flashed, but blessedly, their sirens were silenced. She counted four police cruisers in front of her and a dozen or more trailing behind in a slow-motion parade of flashing lights. She didn't see the big SWAT vans, but she suspected they'd gone another route to the airport, racing to get there and get set up before she arrived. The cop cars in front of her drove well under the speed limit, lending credence to the idea of giving the tactical folks time to get into place.

Markus was agitated beside her, and the more nervous he got, the more nervous she got.

They were escorted directly out onto the tarmac and up to a low, sleek business jet. This was it. If Markus was going to kill her, now was the time. He could just as easily use the pilots as his hostages. Her usefulness to him would be done the moment he set foot on that airplane.

"YOU GOOD, DETECTIVE CARPENTER?" the SWAT officer asked him after tugging Reece's shirt collar up a little higher.

"Yep. Let's do this."

He jumped out of the tactical van and stepped around it. The Learjet Markus had chartered was parked on the tarmac with its front hatch open and steps folded down. A pair of FBI agents sat in the cockpit, dressed as pilots.

The gray sedan pulled to a stop in front of the jet, and he spied the petite form seated at the wheel. Surely, Markus would use her as a human shield and not shoot her until he got inside that plane. The guy was smart enough to know the cops would take him out the moment he killed Yvette.

Yvette's door opened. From his vantage point, Reese saw Markus practically lying on her lap. Very slowly, she climbed out of the car, her hands clasped behind her neck.

Reese stepped forward and she spotted him.

Their gazes locked, and for a moment, everything around them fell away. There was no crisis, no madman with a gun pointed at her, no SWAT team. Just the two of them. Here and now. In love.

And apparently in sync, for she shook her head slightly in the negative, as if to tell him not to do what he was about to.

He'd had to argue and ultimately beg to be the guy to make the close approach to Yvette and Markus. Through sheer cussed stubbornness, though, he'd prevailed and convinced the crisis team leader to let him do this.

He walked forward slowly, his hands held well away from his sides.

"Stop right there!" Markus shouted at him. "Don't come any closer. I'll shoot!"

"Hey, Mr. Dexter. How are you doing, sir? I'm sure you remember me—I'm Reese Carpenter of the Braxville Police Department."

"What are you doing here?" Dexter demanded.

"Well, you're from my town. I thought you might be more comfortable talking to somebody you've met before than to a total stranger."

"What do you want?"

This was a good sign. The man was rational enough to follow the conversation and ask logical questions.

"Well, I'd like to make a trade with you, Mr. Dexter. Myself for Miss Colton."

"No!" she cried.

He smiled ruefully at her and continued, speaking over her protests. "I'll be your hostage in her place. Let her go and you can have me. She's a civilian and has no part in all of this."

"Like hell she doesn't," Dexter sneered. "She's the one who kept turning up evidence that closed the net around me. First that damned arsenic thing, and then those bodies. Nobody was ever supposed to find those. But Fitz. He wouldn't listen, would he? Had to renovate. Couldn't be satisfied with the building he had. Always wanted things to be bigger and better. The man's ambition knows no limits."

Reese made a sympathetic sound. "I have to admit, it was really satisfying to arrest Fitz Colton and take him down a peg. Did you happen to see that on TV?"

Dexter devolved into a rant about how overdue the arrest had been, and Reese let him vent to his heart's content. And while Markus monologued, Reese eased closer and closer until he was practically within arm's length of Yvette.

He saw the pistol against the back of her neck, jerking and sliding around as Markus raged. Terror tore through him that Markus's finger would slip and pull that trigger, ending the life of the woman he loved.

No more time to wait.

No, she mouthed.

Trust me, he mouthed back. Dammit, her life depended

on her letting him help her in this moment. She had to let go. Just once in her life. Let him take care of her.

"Yvette, step to your right so I can take your place," he said easily.

"No!" Markus yelled.

Reese made eye contact with her, silently begging her not to question him. To trust him. To do exactly what he asked of her.

She nodded very faintly.

He said merely, "Drop."

YVETTE RELAXED ALL her leg muscles at once and let gravity take over. She plunged toward the ground, falling without warning. Time slowed as the tarmac rushed up at her, and all she could think was that with her body out of the way, Markus would have a clear shot at Reese.

A scream started in the back of her throat, and by the time her body slammed into the ground, it burst out of her in a piercing shriek.

A gunshot exploded above her head at extremely close range deafening her and vibrating through her almost as if it had hit her. Reese grunted in front of her, staggering back. A blackened hole in his white shirt, directly in the center of his chest told the tale. Markus Dexter had shot him at point-blank range.

"Nooo!" She screamed. Rolling to her hands and knees, she launched herself forward at Markus's knees as hard as she could spring.

She slammed into his legs, knocking him backward just as the pistol fired again. Markus fell backward hard, slamming down to the tarmac with her sprawled across his legs. She scrambled to push up, but something big flashed past her, moving fast.

Reese. He landed on top of Markus, both of his hands

gripping Markus's wrist just below the butt of the pistol. The two men wrestled for control of the gun, and she rolled to one side to get out of Reese's way. On her knees, she looked for an opening to help, and when Markus rolled away from her with Reese still plastered to his front, she slammed her fist forward as hard as she could at the spot just over Markus's kidney.

He groaned, and she punched him again. He jerked his hands down and the pistol disappeared between Markus's and Reese's torsos. It exploded once more, this time the report of the gunshot muffled.

Both men collapsed with Markus on top of Reese.

"Nononononono…" She moaned as she lunged forward, grabbing at Markus's shoulder and yanking at him with all her strength. Reese couldn't be dead.

She'd just found him. He couldn't be dead.

They hadn't had enough time together. He couldn't be dead.

She wanted so much more with him. He couldn't be dead.

She would die without him. She was already dead…

Chapter Seventeen

Pain.

As if someone was splitting his chest open.

Unable to breathe. Unable to speak. Unable to move.

And then there were hands. So many hands, lifting away the massive weight from his chest. Picking him up. Standing him on his feet. Tearing open his shirt.

A SWAT guy saying jovially, "Good thing you had a vest on, man. That bullet would have gone right through your heart. Reese looked down, and a flattened disk of lead was half embedded in his Kevlar vest.

"That must hurt like hell," the SWAT guy continued casually. "Close-range shot like that. You're lucky it wasn't any bigger caliber of pistol or a shot like that could've busted a few ribs. As it is, I'll bet you get a wicked bruise on your chest."

"Yeah. No doubt," he managed to gasp past the pain.

And then something new barreled into him, warm and soft and fierce.

Yvette.

"Hey, babe," he managed before she half choked him to death with her arms wrapped around his neck too tightly for him to breathe.

"A little air," he gasped.

Her arms loosened. But not much.

There was a flurry of activity as the SWAT guys climbed off Markus, handcuffed him and hauled him away, escorted by a bunch of armed police.

"Don't you ever scare me again like that," Yvette declared against the side of his neck.

He turned his head and captured her mouth with his. Ignoring the pain in his chest, he wrapped his arms around her and held her so tight he actually lifted her off the ground.

"I died when you told me to drop," she confessed. "You were going to sacrifice yourself for me."

"Yes, but I knew I was wearing a vest and you weren't."

"But what if he'd shot you in the head?"

"Yvie, Markus Dexter is a lot of things, but a good shot is not one of them. During one of his interviews with the district attorney, Fitz griped at length about what a crappy hunter Markus was and how he scared away all the wildlife because he was such a lousy shot."

"Still—"

He cut her off gently. "I'm fine."

"You are *not* fine! You just got shot and are going to be seriously bruised!"

He grinned down at her as he let her slide down his torso until her feet touched the ground. "Now you know how I feel when you tell me you're fine."

"All right. We're agreed that neither of us will ever be fine again, then?"

"Deal," he replied, laughing.

THE NEXT FEW days were a whirlwind of activity for Yvie. She had to give a statement to the police, a statement to the FBI and more statements than she could count to the press.

Markus was arrested and being held by federal authorities. After Mary testified that it was her husband's intent to flee the country, a judge declined to set bail for him, so he was cooling his heels in a prison cell in Kansas City.

He was forced to give a new DNA sample, and when confronted with the confirmed DNA evidence that Gwen Harrison was, in fact, his daughter, he finally confessed to having had an affair with Olivia Harrison.

Yvie was able to use Markus's own datebooks to show assignations with Olivia over the span of three years. He claimed that Olivia insisted on getting married, but that Mary wouldn't grant him a divorce.

Mary, no longer interested in protecting her husband, confirmed that Markus had, indeed, asked for a divorce right around the time Olivia Harrison was murdered.

As for Olivia's and Crane's bodies ending up hidden in walls, Yvette and Reese went through Dexter's files again and found orders for fake construction delays in Markus's own handwriting. Those delays would have emptied the job site and allowed him to sneak the bodies into the building and hide them in the walls.

When confronted all the evidence, Markus finally broke down and confessed to killing Olivia Harrison and hiding her body in the wall of the Colton warehouse.

Given that Fenton Crane's cause of death was identical to Olivia Harrison's, it wasn't difficult to get Markus to admit to killing the private investigator, too.

On top of all of that, Markus was formally charged with attempted murder in the shooting of Tyler Colton. Seemingly broken by the earlier confessions, he admitted to shooting Ty immediately when asked about it.

Practically the first chance Yvette had to be alone with Reese was when he picked her up in his truck two weeks after the kidnapping to drive to Kansas City, where they attended a touching memorial service for Olivia Harrison. Yvette's brother Brooks made a moving eulogy about Olivia and the wonderful daughter she'd given the world.

After the service, Yvette noticed Brooks having an earnest conversation with Gwen's grandmother, Rita. At the end of it, the two exchanged a warm hug. Yvette murmured to Reese, whose arm she hadn't let go of since they got out of his truck, "I'll bet Brooks just got approval to propose to Gwen from her grandmother."

"Good for him," Reese replied warmly. "I was annoyed with him when he kept butting into the murder investigation of Gwen's mother, but I get it now. The man was drowning in love and so dumb with it he couldn't help himself."

"Is that why you decided to take a bullet for me?" she asked tartly. "You were dumb in love?"

He grinned unrepentantly. "Guilty as charged."

No surprise, at the conclusion of the gathering, Brooks got down on one knee and proposed to Gwen—who tearfully and joyfully accepted. Everyone applauded, and it was a happy note to end a somber event on. Yvette was delighted for the two of them. After everything Gwen had been through, she'd surely earned a happy-ever-after. And Brooks couldn't quit beaming. She'd never seen her brother happier.

The congratulations and socializing wound down, and while Gwen and Brooks elected to spend the night at her grandmother's house to start the more joyful project of planning their wedding, the rest of the Colton clan headed back to Braxville for a family supper.

It would be their last time together for a while, since Jordana and Clint were about to head out for Chicago. Yvette sat back and enjoyed the noisy meal, letting the conversation flow around her full of laughter and warmth. This was the sound of family. And she loved it.

Reese reached under the table for her hand, and she smiled at him as their fingers twined together. He knew how much it meant to her to be part of all of this. He squeezed her hand, and the brand-new engagement ring on her left finger bit into her flesh. She was still getting used to it being there, but it wasn't coming off again for the rest of her life. They hadn't set a wedding date yet, but she was thinking about something small, maybe next summer.

Luke and Bridgette spent much of the meal picking Tyler's and Ashley's brains about the best places to eat and shop in Wichita, but near the end of supper, Bridgette called for everyone's attention. Yvette frowned slightly. Was her sister actually blushing?

Bridgette continued, "Luke and I have an announcement to make. You know when he had to go on that buying trip to Las Vegas a few weeks back? I, umm, went with him, and well, we got married while we were in Vegas."

Yvette squealed along with the other women at the table, and everyone congratulated them warmly.

Luke grinned, abashed, and said, "Now that your family knows we eloped, does this mean I can wear my wedding ring, now?"

Bridgette laughed. "Why? Are you getting tired of sweet old ladies throwing themselves at you?"

"Yes. Yes I am," he replied fervently.

"While we're making announcements," Neil piped up, "Elise and I have a little news. We found out yesterday that we're expecting twins."

Yvette's face hurt from smiling so much, and she and Reese congratulated them warmly. Of course, being Coltons, the clan did razz Neil and Elise thoroughly over who was going to change the most diapers in their household.

Brooks asked from the other end of the table, "Any more announcements while we're at it?"

Lilly spoke up from the head of the table. "Umm, yes, actually."

Everyone fell silent and stared at her, startled that she, of all people, apparently had news.

Yvette was even more surprised when Uncle Shep got out of his seat at the foot of the table and walked down its length to stand beside her. But Yvette about fell out of her chair when Lilly reached up and took Shep's hand in hers and laid her cheek fondly on the back of his hand.

Lily said simply, "Shepherd and I are getting married."

Dead silence fell over the table.

Yvette stared in slowly dawning joy.

Reese was the first to break the shocked silence. "That's fantastic. Congratulations to both of you. Here's to many happy years. You both deserve it." He raised his beer glass in their direction.

There seemed to be a collective blink and deep breath around the table, and then everyone was talking at once, congratulating Shep and Lilly, and laughing in surprise... and not surprise.

There always had been a certain something between the two of them. Now that Yvette thought back over the years, Lilly had leaned on Shep many times when Fitz had let her down. The same way Yvette, herself, had.

Shep said quietly, "We have one more announcement to make. By rights, we should do this in private first. But as I've come to learn, not much of anything stays private in this family for long. You all seem to operate on the theory of one for all and all for one. With that in mind, I'd like to ask all of you to give Yvette your un-qualified support."

Yvette froze. Everyone was looking at her, glancing back and forth between her and Shep. Reese's hand tightened reassuringly around her fingers, and she was grateful for his silent comfort.

"What's up?" she croaked.

Lilly said quietly, "Honey, Shepherd and I have something to show you." She passed a folded piece of paper to Jordana on her left, who passed it to Clint, who passed it to her. Frowning, Yvette unfolded it.

It was a DNA test. A paternity match. She saw the heading on the sheet of paper. Paternity results for Yvette Elizabeth Colton.

What on earth?

She glanced farther down the sheet and stared. Her jaw fell open. She read the sheet again.

Tears filled her eyes as she shoved the sheet of paper blindly at Reese. She stumbled to her feet and headed toward her mother—

—and her father.

She flung her arms around Uncle Shep's waist and squeezed for all she was worth. "Is it true?" she asked against his chest. "Are you really my father?"

She vaguely heard a collective gasp behind her.

"Yes, sweetie, it is. I've suspected for years. But when you were in the hospital after the mugging, I asked your mother for permission to run a DNA test to prove it. Are you okay with this?"

"I'm more than okay with it!" she exclaimed. "I've always secretly wished you were my real daddy." In quick remorse, she looked down at her mother, whose face was streaked with tears. "I mean, Fitz wasn't an awful parent. It's just that whenever I really needed a father, Uncle Shep was always there for me."

"I know, darling," Lilly said through her tears. "He

was always there for me when I needed him most, too. And now he's going to be part of the family, officially."

Lilly looked down the table at the other children. "I hope all of you can forgive me. But Shepherd and I felt that Yvette was owed the truth. Your father and I had a complicated marriage, and I was far from perfect, too. I hope you can be happy for Shepherd and me and that you won't hold this against Yvette. If you want to be angry, be angry at me."

Jordana was the closest to Lilly and leaped to her feet to wrap Lilly in a tight hug. "I love you, Mom. As long as you're happy, I'm happy for you."

The other children rushed forward, and before long, Yvette was smothered in a massive group hug that included a great deal of tears and laughing.

Eventually, she started to feel claustrophobic, and using her small stature to her advantage, wiggled free of the whole gang. Reese was standing right in front of her when she popped clear and he opened his arms in invitation.

Relieved, she stepped into the circle of safety and trust and let him wrap her up in his love.

"Are you okay?" he whispered against her temple.

"More than okay. I might even be that F-word."

"Just this once, I'm okay if you use it," he replied humorously.

She gazed up at him in adoration. Her life was truly complete, now, all the voids filled. She had the father she'd always dreamed of, and she had the man she'd always dreamed of. Her family was whole and happy. The Coltons had weathered the storm of the past year and come out stronger and happier than ever. Love had seen them all through crisis and disaster, fear and loss.

"Oh, Reese, I'm fine. Perfectly, wonderfully fine."

* * * * *

LET'S TALK

Romance

For exclusive extracts, competitions
and special offers, find us online:

MILLS & BOON

THE HEART OF ROMANCE

A ROMANCE FOR EVERY KIND OF READER

MODERN

Prepare to be swept off your feet by sophisticated, sexy and seductive heroes, in some of the world's most glamourous and romantic locations, where power and passion collide.
8 stories per month.

HISTORICAL

Escape with historical heroes from time gone by. Whether your passion is for wicked Regency Rakes, muscled Vikings or rugged Highlanders, awaken the romance of the past.
6 stories per month.

MEDICAL

Set your pulse racing with dedicated, delectable doctors in the high-pressure world of medicine, where emotions run high and passion, comfort and love are the best medicine.
6 stories per month.

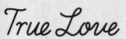

Celebrate true love with tender stories of heartfelt romance, from the rush of falling in love to the joy a new baby can bring, and a focus on the emotional heart of a relationship.
8 stories per month.

Indulge in secrets and scandal, intense drama and plenty of sizzling hot action with powerful and passionate heroes who have it all: wealth, status, good looks…everything but the right woman.
6 stories per month.

HEROES

Experience all the excitement of a gripping thriller, with an intense romance at its heart. Resourceful, true-to-life women and strong, fearless men face danger and desire - a killer combination!
8 stories per month.

DARE

Sensual love stories featuring smart, sassy heroines you'd want as a best friend, and compelling intense heroes who are worthy of them.
4 stories per month.

To see which titles are coming soon, please visit

millsandboon.co.uk/nextmonth

JOIN US ON SOCIAL MEDIA!

Stay up to date with our latest releases, author news and gossip, special offers and discounts, and all the behind-the-scenes action from Mills & Boon...

 millsandboon

 millsandboonuk

 millsandboon

It might just be true love...

MILLS & BOON

HISTORICAL

Awaken the romance of the past

Escape with historical heroes from time gone by. Whether your passion is for wicked Regency Rakes, muscled Viking warriors or rugged Highlanders, indulge your fantasies and awaken the romance of the past.